Praise for
STEPHEN R. LAWHEAD's
THE PENDRAGON CYCLE

"EVOCATIVE... INTRIGUING...
ENTHRALLING."
Locus

"THE FAMILIAR TALE [IS] SINGULARLY
REWORKED... LAWHEAD'S INTERPRETATION
IS DIFFERENT AND DISTINCTIVE."
Kirkus Reviews

"LAWHEAD MANAGES TO GIVE THE OLD TALE
NEW MEANING AND FASCINATION.
A FINE STORYTELLER, HE BRINGS THE
ARTHURIAN CHARACTERS TO LIFE
WITHOUT SACRIFICING ANY OF THE
HAUNTING PLEASURE OF THE LEGENDS."
Omaha World Herald

"HIGHLY RECOMMENDED."
Library Journal

"LAWHEAD EVOKES THE BEST
OF BRITISH FANTASY."
Encounters

Other Books by
Stephen R. Lawhead

BYZANTIUM

THE PENDRAGON CYCLE

TALIESIN
MERLIN
ARTHUR
PENDRAGON

THE DRAGON KING TRILOGY

IN THE HALL OF THE DRAGON KING
THE WARLORDS OF NIN
THE SWORD AND THE FLAME

THE SONG OF ALBION TRILOGY

THE PARADISE WAR
THE SILVER HAND
THE ENDLESS KNOT

GRAIL

Book Five of
THE PENDRAGON CYCLE

STEPHEN R. LAWHEAD

AVON · EOS

This is a work of fiction. Names, characters, places, and incidents either are the product of the author's imagination or are used fictitiously. Any resemblance to actual events, locales, organizations, or persons, living or dead, is entirely coincidental and beyond the intent of either the author or the publisher.

AVON BOOKS, INC.
1350 Avenue of the Americas
New York, New York 10019

Copyright © 1997 by Stephen R. Lawhead
Published by arrangement with the author
Visit our website at **http://www.AvonBooks.com/Eos**
Library of Congress Catalog Card Number: 96-6605
ISBN: 0-380-78104-2

First Avon Eos Paperback Printing: June 1998
First Avon Books Hardcover Printing: July 1997

AVON EOS TRADEMARK REG. U.S. PAT. OFF. AND IN OTHER COUNTRIES, MARCA REGISTRADA, HECHO EN U.S.A.

Printed in the U.S.A.

WCD   10 9 8 7 6 5 4 3 2 1

For Bob and Lois

Pronunciation Guide

While many of the old British names may look odd to modern readers, they are not as difficult to pronounce as they seem at first glance. A little effort, and the following guide, will help you enjoy the sound of these ancient words.

Consonants—as in English, but with a few exceptions:
c: hard, as in cat (never soft as in cent)
ch: hard, as in Scottish Loch, or Bach (never soft, as in church)
dd: th, as in then (never as in thistle)
f: v, as in of
ff: f, as in off
g: hard, as in girl (never gem)
ll: a Welsh distinctive, sounded as "tl" or "hl" on the sides of the tongue
r: trilled, lightly
rh: as if hr, heavy on the "h" sound
s: always as in sir (never his)
th: as in thistle (never then)

Vowels—as in English, but with the general lightness of short vowel sounds:
a: as in father
e: as in met (when long, as in late)
i: as in pin (long, as in eat)
o: as in not
u: as in pin (long, as in eat)

w: as "double-u," as in vac*uu*m or t*oo*l; but becomes a consonant before vowels, as in the name G*w*en

y: as in p*i*n; or sometimes as "u" in b*u*t (long, as in *e*at)

(As you can see, there is not much difference in i, u, and y—they are virtually identical to the beginner.)

Accent—normally is on the next-to-last syllable, as in Gwalc-*hav*-ad

Diphthongs—each vowel is pronounced individually, so Taliesin=Tally-essin

Ten rings there are, and nine gold torcs
on the battlechiefs of old;
Eight princely virtues, and seven sins
for which a soul is sold;
Six is the sum of earth and sky,
of all things meek and bold;
Five is the number of ships that sailed
from Atlantis lost and cold;
Four kings of the Westerlands were saved,
three kingdoms now behold;
Two came together in love and fear,
in Llyonesse stronghold;
One world there is, one God, and one birth
the Druid stars foretold.

S.R.L.
Oxford, 1987

Prologue

Men are such pathetic, lumpen things—so predictable in their appetites, such slaves to their tedious desires and pleasures. Creatures of dull habit and savage compulsion, they waver between one and the other, never perceiving anything of the world beyond their animal passions. Why, the cattle of the field know more of life.

Ah, but it is all too easy. I have long since tired of their trivial ambitions and endeavors. Ignorant brutes, they deserve every misfortune their beast of a god can rain down upon them.

Where is real strength? Where is true courage? Where is genuine discipline harnessed to uncompromising volition, and both allied in total harmony, each subject to the other? Where are such treasures to be found?

On the battlefield, in the heat of the fight? Ha! That is what men think, and as in all else they are vastly mistaken. War is children with dirty faces squabbling over the dungheap. In war, life—that single most precious substance in the universe—is bartered cheap, thrown away, wasted, traded for a prize which will not last beyond the changing of the seasons. Fools, all of them! Blind, ignorant fools—it is pure joy tormenting them.

Only that which endures beyond time is worth having.

Well I know it. I, who have given all for the mastery of time and the elements, know the value of life. Truly, truly, I have spent my life on the things that endure. Not for nothing am I called the Queen of Air and Darkness.

Chapter One

I, Gwalchavad, Lord of Orcady, write this. And no gentle labor it is. Nor less rough the reading, I fear. Unlike Myrddin, or the brown-cloaked clerics, I am no master of the scribbler's craft. God's truth, the sword hilt better fits my hand than this close-pared reed. Even so, I am assured my crabbed script will live long after the hand that framed it is dust. This Brother Aneirin assures me, and he is wise in such things. So be it.

I was born in sight of Ynys Prydain, with my brother and twin, Gwalcmai—both sons of noble Lot, himself a king of the Orcades. My birth, in itself, is of small consequence. But for Arthur, I would have lived all my days in that wild place and never traveled beyond the boundary stones of my father's island realm; but for Arthur, my life might have passed in hunting, fishing, and settling the squabbles of petty chieftains. I would never have heard of the Kingdom of Summer—much less the Grail—and truly, I would not be writing this at all.

Still, I will persist in my endeavor so you may know the way of it. Anyone with ears has heard of Arthur and his trials and triumphs; tales and more tales flood the land from Lloegres to Celyddon. Many bards tell them now, and a few of the monkish kind have written them, too. A sorry scribe I may be, though perhaps not least among these gall-stained ink-spillers.

They speak of wars and battles, and that is right. They tell of brave men defending the Island of the Mighty with their lives. These tales are good, and some are even true; I take nothing away from them. But my task is ordered differently.

See, now, it is the Grail I tell: that strange stirrer of marvels, that most uncanny vessel of desire. Dangerous, yes, and more beautiful than words alone can tell, it is the holiest treasure in all this worlds-realm. But for Arthur, that precious cup would surely have been forgotten, and its healing virtues lost through ignorance and neglect. Yet, truth be told, but for Arthur, none of the terrors and tribulations I describe would have befallen us. But for Arthur, the Grail was almost lost, and a flame of Heaven's pure fire extinguished on the earth.

That is a tale few have heard, and it is worth more than all the others. Ah, but I race before myself. Know you, the Battlehost of the Ancient Enemy is large, and falters before nothing save the True Word. And the sound of the clash when those two combatants met will echo through the ages, I do believe it. Blessed among men, I was favored to ride at my king's right hand in the foreranks of the fight. Tremble and turn pale; sain yourself with runes and strong prayers, call upon the company of angels, and harken well to my warning: where great good endures, great evil gathers close about. This I know.

Hear me! Speak of the Grail and you speak a mystery with a secret at its heart, and I, Gwalchavad, Prince of Orcady, know the secret as none other. If the telling gives you pleasure, well and good . . . but I should not like cold eyes to read it in this book.

Therefore, look to your heart; look long and hard. If you are friend to all that is true and right, then welcome and read on. But if you would savor the sauce of slander and shadow tricks, feast on lies, betrayals, and seductions, you will find little to your liking here. Blessed Jesu, I mean to tell the truth of what I know.

Thus, I begin:

For seven long years we warred against the ravaging Saecsens—seven years of hardship and privation, misery, torment, and death. Under Arthur's command, and with the aid of the Swift Sure Hand, we prevailed in the end.

This is well known—indeed, even small children know how the warhost of Britain raised the wall on Baedun Hill and destroyed the bold invader—so I will not say more, except to point out that we had scarcely drawn breath from our hard-fought victory at Baedun when we were beset by the wandering Vandal horde. Fighting first in Ierna, then in Britain, we chased Amilcar, that greedy boar of battle, over most of Lloegres before he was subdued.

A strange war, that; it lasted little more than a season, yet brought more waste and destruction to our land than all the Saecsen battles put together. Why is it that trouble always seems to come in threes? For with the havoc of the Vandali came plague and drought as well. Those who grumble and complain would do well to remember that the Pendragon had three enemies to fight, not just one. If there is another king who could have done better against such odds, then show me that man, I say, or shut your mouth. There is no pleasing some people. Though many raise their voices in accusation and make loud lament over lost lands and such, I still think Arthur chose the better course.

The thing is over now, in any event, so it does no good to piss and moan. If they knew the Bear of Britain at all, they would realize their miserable whining only hardens his conviction the more.

Better a trustworthy foe than a treacherous friend, and we have seen enough of scheming friends. The Island of the Mighty is better off without the likes of Ceredig, Morcant, Brastias, Gerontius, Urien, and their rebellious ilk always making trouble. The Devil take them all, I say. They will not be missed.

Where were they—those who make such loud complaint—when Arthur stood against the Vandal lord? Urien and Brastias thought to usurp the High King's portion, but did I hear them offer to take the High King's place on the blood-soaked battleground? Gerontius was ever quick to goad the others in their petty rebellion, but did I see bold Gerontius in the forefront of the fight?

No, I did not.

We had amassed the greatest warhost seen in Britain

since Great Constantine—twenty thousand men and fifteen thousand horses! Yet, on that fearful day Arthur faced his foe alone, and the treasonous lords were nowhere to be seen. Well, they made their choice. So be it. But instead of insulting Heaven with their lament, they would do better to offer heartfelt praise that they possess both breath and tongue to complain.

Arthur paid dearly for the peace we now enjoy. When they carried him from the field of battle, so, too, were our hearts borne away—and the sun and stars as well, for we walked in darkness without Arthur.

"They have taken him to Ynys Avallach," Rhys said, his face gray with fatigue and worry. "If you know any prayers, say them now." For if Arthur would be healed, it must be in that holy place and none other. The Wise Emrys knew best what to do. Rhys then delivered Arthur's last command. "You are to conduct the Vandali to the north, where they will take possession of lands surrendered by the rebel lords. Any Britons living in these realms will be cast out and their settlements made forfeit by their lords' treason."

Thus they departed, leaving us to establish the peace Arthur had won. We divided the warhost; Bedwyr, Cai, and I conducted the new Vandal chieftain, Mercia, and his tribes to the lands Arthur had granted them in the north. Cador and the rest of the Cymbrogi—the name is Arthur's choice, it means companions of the heart— turned their attention to overseeing the departure from these shores of the traitors and their followers whose lands had fallen forfeit.

Burdened by weight of numbers, and fatigued with all the fighting we had endured, we made our way north very slowly, leading the Vandal host, searching out water along the way. Far easier said than done, I fear; with each passing day the drought deepened, causing hardship from one end of the land to the other. It broke my heart to see holding after holding deserted—many had fled to Armorica—but worse still were the burned-out strongholds, those which plague had ravaged and destroyed.

If the sight of so much suffering made us heart-heavy,

the thought of displacing honest British folk from their homelands brought us to despair. Oh, it is a hard, hard thing to tell a man his home must be surrendered and all his life's labor has come to naught because his rogue of a lord has broken faith with the High King. Stab that man in the heart; it is kinder in the end, I swear it.

I loathed the task set before me, and prayed for a way to evade what must be done. Day after day, as we moved the Vandal host northward, I prayed to God for a miracle.

Behold! My prayer was answered, not with a miracle, but with a resolution almost as good. One night, the sixth or seventh since leaving our encampment near the battle-field at Caer Gloiu, Mercia and his priest approached Bed-wyr's tent. Bedwyr had brought Arthur's camp chair and tent as the sole, scant consolation of a miserable journey. We were enjoying a moment's rest after another arduous day.

"What do they want now?" growled Bedwyr.

Like Bedwyr, I desired nothing more than to end this day of heat and dust in good company. "I will deal with them," I said, thinking to send them away; I stood to call out.

"Stay, brother." Bedwyr sighed, changing his mind. "As we have not had more than a dusty glimpse of them for a day or two, we had better allow him his say."

Swarthy Mercia, dark hair and eyes—darker still in the fading twilight—hailed us with his customary salute, striking his heart with his fist. The once-captive priest, Hergest, spoke when Mercia spoke, saying, "Greetings, friends."

"Greetings," Bedwyr replied bleakly. After days of herding Vandali, he was finding it hard to muster any enthusiasm for their concerns.

"Sit down if you will," I said, making a gesture towards courtesy. "We would offer you a cup to wet your throats on such a sultry day, but we have nothing to put in it." I said this last to discourage the appeal I knew was coming. Every day since the beginning of this journey, one or another of the barbarian chieftains had come before us to demand a greater water ration—sometimes two or

three on the same day. What little water we had was
shared out to all in equal measure, as I told them—each
and every day.

"It is hot, yes," said Mercia. His speech, though broken, was rapidly improving. No doubt Hergest was a good
teacher.

"Yes," Bedwyr answered, leaning back in his chair.
"We need rain—the land needs rain."

"My people thirst," Mercia said bluntly.

Bedwyr reacted irritably. "Am I a fountain? I just said
we need rain. It is a drought, you know. Everyone is
thirsty."

Mercia gazed mildly back, undisturbed by this outburst.
He glanced at Hergest, who uttered a few harsh-sounding
words in his own tongue. The Vandal merely nodded and
loosed a lengthy torrent of barbarian jabber.

When he finished, he nodded again, this time to the
priest, who said, "Lord Mercia wants you both to know
that he would be less than noble if he did not ask for
water when his people are thirsty. He intended no disrespect."

"Very well," Bedwyr muttered, somewhat chastened
by his reply.

"Mercia also says that he is unhappy," continued
Hergest. Before Bedwyr or I could frame a reply, the
priest said, "The source of his unhappiness is this: rooting
Britons from their homes sits ill with him. To be the cause
of such hardship does make him seem small in his own
eyes."

"I understand," Bedwyr told him, "but there is nothing to be done. The hardship to the Britons has come
about by the willful action of their lords who broke faith
with Arthur. The punishment is shared by all. That is the
High King's command."

When the stalwart priest had conveyed my meaning,
Mercia answered. "I quarrel not with Arthur's judgment.
But I would offer a—ah, an understanding," he said,
speaking through Hergest.

"Yes?" asked Bedwyr warily. "What is this understanding?"

"Allow us to settle unclaimed lands," suggested Mercia through his priest. "Let stay who will, but tell them we will not possess inhabited British holdings."

This was unforeseen. "And let Britons and Vandali live together in the same realm?" I asked.

"If any care to stay," Hergest answered. "The Vandal would share the land with any willing to share the land with them."

"Is he earnest?" Bedwyr inquired, pulling on his chin.

"Indeed." Hergest assured us adamantly. "He has spoken to the other chieftains, and they all agree. They would rather settle the wilderness than displace the innocent." He paused. "May I explain?"

"If you can."

"It is this way," said Hergest. "Arthur's generosity is more than they expected and it has shamed them. The people of Vandalia are a proud race, and resourceful. Because need is great, they will accept the land Arthur has decreed for them, but their pride recoils from causing hardship to the kinsmen of those who have befriended them."

I shook my head in amazement. "Hardship? Blessed Jesu, only a few days ago these bloodlusting barbarians were plundering and burning these same British settlements!"

"That," Mercia spat, "was Amilcar's doing." Obviously, there was little love between the defeated Vandal king and his minions.

"And is Mercia so very different?" Bedwyr asked harshly, pressing the matter, I think, to see what sort of man the new king might be.

Without hesitation, the priest replied. "Mercia regrets the plundering and burning that Amilcar inflicted on this land. It was war. Such things happen. But now that Mercia is lord of the Vandali, Hussae, and Rögatti, he has pledged friendship with Arthur. This friendship he values greatly, and would increase its worth by extending it to the Britons holding the lands wherein the Vandal tribes must settle."

I was amazed. The suggestion showed both benevolence and shrewdness. The cunning I might have ex-

pected, but the compassion in the barbarian's suggestion
took me by surprise. I looked at Bedwyr, who looked at
me, rubbing the back of his neck.

Hergest saw our hesitation. "Mercia does not ask that
you trust him—only that you try him."

"It is not a matter of trust," Bedwyr said slowly. "The
summer is far advanced; there is no time to raise crops
before winter comes. You will require dwellings, and cattle pens, and . . . everything else. Where will you get
them, if not from the Britons?"

When the priest had explained Bedwyr's words to him,
the young chieftain smiled. "We are not without skill in
such matters," he replied through Hergest. "Besides, the
wise ones among us say that this winter shall be like those
of our homeland in the southern sea. It will do us no
harm."

"Winter in the north is harsh and long," Bedwyr told
him, "as I know only too well."

"Your concern does you honor, Lord Bedwyr," Hergest answered. "But would not homeless Britons suffer the
winter as readily as homeless Vandali?" He lifted a hand
to Mercia. "My lord says that if we are to live under
Arthur's rule, let it be among Arthur's people."

The young chieftain's eyes shifted from Bedwyr to me,
and back again—willing us to believe.

I regarded him carefully, uncertain what to do. Truly,
they offered us a way out of the hateful task of forcing
people from their homes—countrymen whose only sin
was having unfaithful noblemen for lords. What would
Arthur do?

I was on the point of sending them away to allow us
to think the thing through when Mercia said, "Lord Bed-
vyr . . . Lord Galahad"—that was as much as he could
make of our names—"please, I beg you, let us prove the
trust that has been granted us."

"Very well," Bedwyr said, making up his mind at
once. "Let it be as you say. We will conduct you to unclaimed lands and there you shall make your home. I
leave it to you how to divide the realms between your
tribes. Make your settlements as you will. But there is to

be no trouble between your people and the Britons who choose to remain.''

He said this sternly, every word an implied threat. Mercia rushed forward, knelt before him, seized his hand, and kissed it. No doubt this was a common thing among the Vandal kind, but we are not so accustomed. Bedwyr snatched his hand away, saying, ''Rise, Mercia. You have the thing you seek. Go and tell your people.''

Mercia rose and stood a little apart, smiling his good pleasure. ''A wise decision, Prince Bedwyr,'' Hergest assured us; he touched a hand to his throat and I noticed he no longer wore the iron slave ring.

''Make certain I do not live to regret it.''

''The Vandali are barbarians, it is true. They give their word rarely, but when they do, the vow endures to the fifth generation,'' the priest affirmed. ''I trust Mercia.''

''May God be good to you,'' Bedwyr told him. ''I am content.''

''I am heartily glad you are content,'' I told Bedwyr when they had gone. ''I only wonder what Arthur will say when he hears what we have done.''

''I care nothing for that,'' replied Bedwyr. He turned away quickly, adding, ''I pray instead he lives to hear it.''

Chapter Two

Bedwyr retreated to the tent, but I remained outside, thinking, and listening to the sounds of the camp settling in for the night. Twilight deepened around me. I watched the dusky slope of the distant hillside begin to glow as campfires wakened in the darkness; soon the aroma of roasting meat stirred me.

What has become of Rhys? I wondered, thinking that he should have returned long ago.

He and a small company of warriors had gone in search of water as soon as we halted our day's march. We were camped in a shallow valley, and there were streams in the surrounding hills. Finding water had become the chief task of each and every day; we did not neglect any possible means of filling the waterskins and jars. As we moved farther up the vale, the streams narrowed and thinned, and the search became more difficult. We had not located any drinking water this day, so Rhys had undertaken to continue looking.

The rest of the Cymbrogi were nearby, having established camp at a second place on the hillside. We did this by way of guarding the Vandal host, yet allowing ourselves a ready retreat. For though they were no longer armed—their spears alone filled three wagons!—there were so many of them that we could easily be overrun. Thus, we always made two camps a short distance apart and kept watch through the night.

"He will soon return," Bedwyr assured me when I

pointed out that it was well past dark and still no sign of
Rhys and his company. "Why uneasy, brother?"

"How much water remains?" The Cymbrogi also stood
guard over the water wagons, lest anyone try to steal another share.

"One day at full rations," he replied; he had already
reckoned the amount. "We could go on half rations, but
I would rather wait until Rhys returns to make that decision."

I left him to his rest, and returned to the campfire feeling uneasy and troubled—though I could not think why.
Perhaps I was merely tired. It seemed like years since I
had slept more than two nights in the same place . . . years
since I had slept without a weapon in my hand. Once
Mercia and his folk were settled, I thought, we will begin
to enjoy the peace we have all fought so long to achieve.

A pale phantom moon rose and soared like a silent
specter over the narrow valley. I supped on something
tough and tasteless—stewed saddle, perhaps—and finished the last of my day's ration of water. I retreated to
the tent and lay down, but found the closeness inside sti-
fling; so I took up the oxhide and stretched out on the
ground a short distance away—whereupon I found I could
not sleep for the barking of the camp dogs. I lay on my
back with my arms folded over my chest, gazing up at
the heavens, marking the slow progression of the moon,
and wondering if the mutts were always so loud.

I lay a long time before realizing that I was listening
for Rhys' return. I identified all the night sounds of the
camp—horses whickering and jittery at their pickets,
the tight voices of the sentries as they moved along the
boundary, the far-off call of a night bird in a distant tree—
all familiar, yet made peculiar by my listening. Or perhaps
it was something else—something in the air making them
seem that way.

I must have dozed without knowing it, for when I
looked again, the moon was well down. I heard the short,
sharp challenge of a sentry, and the expected reply. I rose
at once and made my way to the picket line to see Rhys

and his band dismounting. Some of the men swayed on their feet, exhausted by their long search.

"Good hunting?" I called, hurrying to join them.

Rhys turned when he heard me. The look on his face halted me in my steps. "Rhys?"

He tossed a quick command over his shoulder and then stepped near. "We found a spring," he said, his voice husky and strange. Perhaps it was merely fatigue, but I have seen terror often enough to recognize its many guises, and I thought Rhys wore it now.

"A spring, yes," I said, searching the steward's face for a sign. "Good. Well done. Is it far?"

He took my arm, wheeled me around, and started walking me away. When we were out of hearing of the men, he said, "No, not far. The spring is not large, but it supplies a pool. We can get water there." He paused, hesitating, uncertain how to proceed.

"Rhys?"

"There is something queer . . ."

"About the spring?"

"Yes."

"You said it was not far—"

"Indeed, it is just beyond the hill." He lifted a hand, but the gesture died and he lapsed again into a hesitant silence.

"Well?" I demanded, growing impatient with his reticence. "Speak, man."

His reply was swift and harsh. "I do not like it! Something queer is out there." He glowered at me.

"Calm yourself," I said soothingly. "Come to the tent. Sit down. You have not eaten anything all day. You must be starving. Come, Rhys."

I led him to the tent and sat him in Arthur's chair, then roused one of the younger men who served the Dragon Flight. "Wake you, Baram," I said. "Rhys has returned. Fetch food and water."

Rhys sat slumped in the camp chair, his head bent forward, resting in his hands. I had never seen him so. "Food is coming," I said, dragging up a stool. Thinking to distract him from his thoughts, I began telling him about our talk with Mercia and Hergest. In a little while, Baram appeared with the food; I dismissed him to his rest once more, and served Rhys myself.

When he finished eating, he seemed in better spirits, so I said, "Now, then, tell me about this strange pool you have found."

Rhys nodded, took a long draught of water, swallowed slowly, and then began. "We came upon it before sundown. It is no great distance from here, and we discovered it soon after we began. There is a rocky outcrop on the hillside, and a beech grove below. The leaves on the trees looked fresh—not wilted like all the rest—so we rode to the place for a closer look. The grove hides a cleft in the rocks—pass through it and you come to the pool."

Rhys' voice trailed off, as if he were revisiting a painful memory of long ago. His dark eyes were downcast and he clutched the empty water jar tightly.

"A cool place to escape the sun," I observed, encouraging him to continue. "It must have been a welcome find."

He glanced at me and then away again quickly. "We entered the grove and rode to the pool," he said after a moment. "I dismounted and heard a sound . . . singing— it sounded like someone singing, but though the grove and pool are small, I could not see anyone." He fell silent again.

"Hiding in the rocks, perhaps," I remarked.

He paid me no heed, but sat hunched forward, his jaw bulging as he clenched his teeth.

"Rhys," I said softly. "Fear for nothing, man. It is Gwalchavad beside you now."

After a time, he said, "I knelt to drink. I remember stretching forth my hand to touch the water. . . ."

"Yes? And then?"

He raised his eyes and the fear leapt out in his glance. "I do not know!" He stood abruptly. "I reached toward the water and I—when I looked again, it was night and the moon was shining in the pool."

"Night comes quickly to these glens," I offered half-heartedly. "It must have been later than you knew."

"Am I a babe in arms to know nothing of day or night?" he shouted.

"Calm yourself, brother. I only meant—"

"I remember nothing of what happened in the grove. One moment it was bright day, and the next I knew, it was night—and that far gone."

I gazed at his anguished expression and tried to soothe him. "Perhaps you fell asleep. It was hot and you had ridden long. You were tired, and it was cool in the shade. Overcome by your fatigue, you fell asleep, and why not? A little nap is no bad thing. The men with you, did any of them remember falling asleep?"

"No—they remember no more than I," he said, his voice tense with the effort of holding it steady. "All I know is that the sun shone as I knelt, and when I stood again, the sky was bright with stars and night was far advanced. We returned at once."

"It is disturbing, perhaps," I granted, "but nothing to worry over. No doubt you make more of it than there is."

Rhys glared defiantly. "It is sorcery!" he growled. "Mark me, something evil lurks there."

I slept ill, rising at dawn to ride with Rhys to the enchanted pool. As he had said, it was no great distance away, lying in a narrow valley just a hill or two away from camp. A grove of beech trees stood at one end of the glen, dark in the shadow of the hillside. There were six men with us, leading the wagons, for I was determined to have that water, enchantment or no.

We dismounted at the edge of the grove and stood for a moment gazing into its dark-shadowed heart, as into a cave or tomb. It was quiet, but not unnaturally so.

"Do you hear?" Rhys whispered.

"It seems peaceful enough."

"Aye, too peaceful." He arched an eyebrow knowingly. "There are no birds."

"Well, it may be they have gone—" I began.

"And this the only water nearby?" he challenged. "The dell should be alive with birds."

"Stop whispering!" I told him sharply. "If there is anyone here, they will have seen us long ago. Come." I started into the grove. "Let us examine the pond."

Night's chill hung in the shaded depths of the grove—as if the sun's warming rays had no power to penetrate beyond the outer branches of the trees. We passed between the leaning boles and ducked under low-hanging limbs, and after a few steps came to the water. My eyes gradually adjusted to the dim light, and I saw that though the pool was not large, it was set in a deep, rock-rimmed bowl. I made my way to the water's edge and looked in, but could not see the bottom.

A gray rock rose from the far end of the basin like a great squatting toad. I heard the slow rhythmic drip, drip, drip of water splashing from the rock into the dark water.

"You see?" whispered Rhys. "It is just as I told you."

"It is an unlovely place, to be sure," I replied. "But I find nothing amiss here."

"No," he answered after a moment's silence. "Nor do I. Whatever was here is gone now." He turned pleading eyes to me. "There was something."

"I believe you, brother."

He turned away, stricken afresh. "I remember now—it was . . . it was—" His jaw worked as he struggled for words. "I was suffocating—as if a hand clenched my throat. I could not breathe. My lungs felt as if they would burst. I remember thinking I must breathe or I will die. And then . . . nothing—until I saw the moon's reflection there." He pointed to the center of the rock bowl and looked up through the branches of the trees as if he thought he might see the moon once more.

I also raised my eyes and scanned the leafy bower above us. The branches of the close-grown trees wove a dense roof over the pool; not a scrap of blue sky showed through anywhere.

Rhys shifted uneasily beside me. "On my life, Gwalchavad," he said softly, "I thought it was the moon." He paused. "I saw something glowing in the water, I swear it!"

"Did you say that you had tasted the water?" I asked and, kneeling, cupped my hand and dipped out some water. I raised it to my nose and sniffed, but could smell nothing unusual. I put my hand to my lips and wet my tongue. The water was warm and tasted slightly muddy, but not at all bad for that.

"What say you?" Rhys watched me closely.

"I have tasted worse," I replied.

Rhys squatted beside me and reached out to cup some water. As he did so, I observed a strange mark on the fleshy part of his upper arm. "What is this?" I wondered. "A wound?"

The skin was broken and discolored—pierced by what appeared to be small pricks at regular intervals.

"It looks like a bite," I remarked. "An animal of some kind. A dog, perhaps?"

Rhys looked stricken. "I remember no bite."

"Well," I said, "it is not so bad. No doubt you have forgotten."

"Gwalchavad," Rhys said, his voice thick, "I would know if I were bitten by a dog." He craned his neck and held his arm to look at the wound. "I would remember."

Once, when I was but a lad, my brother, Gwalcmai, and I had found a cave and entered to find a sleeping bear. I still remember the awful sick dread that overwhelmed me as I heard the slow, snuffling breath, saw the black, shapeless mass of fur, and realized that we had stumbled into a death trap unawares.

I felt the same feeling now: as if we had intruded on something better left undisturbed.

Glancing around quickly, I stood. "Let us fill the water casks and leave this place."

As soon as the wagons were loaded, we left the grove and hurried back to find that the Cymbrogi had struck camp and were ready to leave on another day's march. Seeing no good reason to tarry, Bedwyr called the order, and Rhys raised the hunting horn and blew a lengthy, rising blast to signal our departure. The long, disorderly ranks of Vandali began moving once more. I watched for a moment; then, steeling myself for another endless, scorching day in the saddle, I lifted the reins and rode on.

Chapter Three

The only person I ever loved did not love me. I was young then and foolish, I know. I wielded not a fraction of the power I now possess, or things might have gone differently. The arrow was meant for my sister.

Does that surprise you, my sweet? How so? Charis never spared a thought for me. She was already grown when I was born, and though we shared the same father, Avallach the Invalid never spoke two words to me in all the time I lived under his roof.

The beloved Briseis was dead and cold in her grave long, long before my mother shared the great king's bed. He needed Lile; and it is true he would have died but for her healing skill. Avallach used her, depended on her, but he never loved her. Even in death Queen Briseis commanded Avallach's affections, and Lile the nursemaid was merely tolerated. Poor Lile, she wanted so to be his wife, and though he married her in the end, she was never more than his mistress.

Even I, a barefoot grubby child with dirty hands and snotty nose, could see that my mother was insignificant, and in my infant heart I vowed never to allow myself to descend to insignificance.

Oh, but I would look at Charis, so beautiful and strong. The sun in its glory was not more radiant and bright. I wanted nothing more in all the world than to be like her, to be her. When I saw the way my father looked at her, the way his eyes filled with love and admiration for his

18

*golden-haired daughter, I wanted it all the more. I would
have given the world and everything in it just to have
Avallach smile at me the way he smiled at her.*

He never did.

At first, we harbored some small hope that the drought
would slacken its hold the farther north we rode. That was
not to be, however, for the hills beyond the Hafren Vale
were just as dusty as those we had left behind, and the
streambeds were just as dry. Nor did a single cloud ever
darken the sky. From dawn to dusk the heavens remained
empty, the sun rising and setting in a firmament of fiery
white, like a ball of flame simmering in a lake of molten
iron.

I have heard of desert lands where rain falls but once
a year, though I had never known Britain to suffer so for
lack of rain. Searching for water to keep ourselves and
the Vandal horde supplied became our sole occupation.
Fortunately, there are springs in the central hills where we
could refill our casks. If not for these founts deep in the
earth, we might have died of thirst.

Thus, with God's help, we were able to keep moving
until reaching Afon Treont. Though the bracken on the
hills was brown and tinder-dry, and the Treont was showing a wide band of cracked mud and lumpy stone along
either bank, there was at least good water to be had in the
long lake just to the north.

There, we paused to rest for a few days. The animals
could drink their fill from the shallows, but the better
drinking water was farther out, beyond the green, stagnant
pools; we had to use boats to get it—a labor which exhausted most of the day—and the warriors were far from
pleased about the tedious occupation.

"Ferrying water casks in coracles is like herding geese
on the back of a pig," declared Cai. He and Bedwyr stood
on the bare rock shore watching the small round boats
struggling with their loads.

"I see it keeps your tongue wet," observed Bedwyr
sourly.

"Only just," replied Cai. He watched the tipsy boats

for a moment, then said, "I suppose we must be moving on again soon."

"Nay," Bedwyr replied. "I am thinking we will stay here."

"But Arthur said—"

"I know what Arthur said," declared Bedwyr edgily. "But he could not know how hard it is to keep these people fed and watered."

"Rheged is still some way to the north," Cai pointed out, rubbing his whiskered chin.

"And I am thinking this is far enough!" Bedwyr growled. "God love you, Cai, but you do know how to fret a man."

The flame-haired Cai shouldered the affront with placid acceptance. "I merely suggest—"

"With this damnable drought, there will be no harvest in Rheged or anywhere else," Bedwyr explained sharply. "Why go all the way to Rheged when they can just as easily starve here?" Indicating the dark-wooded hills beyond the lake, he said, "At least here they can get water and whatever can be had from the forest."

"I see your point," replied Cai.

"You do?" asked Bedwyr suspiciously.

"It is a good plan—as good as any other."

"Also, the settlements hereabouts are not so many that the folk will be hard pressed by the Vandali," said Bedwyr, continuing his argument.

"Enough! I said it was a good plan. The sooner we settle these ... these people, the sooner we can head south. I am anxious for word of Arthur."

"And I am not?" demanded Bedwyr. "You are the only one eager for word of Arthur, I suppose?"

"If it is a fight you are wanting," Cai answered gruffly, "go argue with Rhys—no doubt he will oblige. Two of a kind, the both of you."

Bedwyr flared, but held his tongue. He gave Cai a dark, smoldering look and stormed away, grumbling to himself. Cai watched him stumping along the lakeshore. "And take your temper with you!" he called at Bedwyr's retreating back.

I saw what had happened. "Do not be angry with him," I said, moving to Cai's side.

"Am I angry?" he shouted. "Am I the one biting the head off anyone who happens by? Anyway, he started it—him and his foul mood."

"The heat," I suggested, "is making everyone surly."

"Och," agreed Cai, clucking his tongue. "By the Holy Three, I wish it would rain." He turned a clear blue eye towards a sky just as clear and blue. "Just look at that, would you? Not a cloud anywhere—not a single cloud all summer. It is uncanny, I tell you." He drew a damp sleeve across his face. "It is too hot to stand out here any longer. I am going back."

He stalked off, leaving me to watch the laborers on the lake. The round stones all along the shore were black where the moss had been blasted by the sun—like skulls whose flesh had been burned to a dry crust. The drought was, I reflected, exposing and killing much that was green and tender. Only the tough and deep-rooted would survive. As with plants, so with people.

Upon returning to camp, I discovered several more riders preparing to leave. Bedwyr was sending word to the surrounding settlements. "Never fear, I have saved Urien's settlement for last, brother," he informed me. "That one will require a man of wisdom and judgment. That is why I am sending you, Gwalchavad."

"You are too kind."

"As we are staying here," Bedwyr said, "we will let the chieftains and headmen come to us. Why not? It saves us chasing all over Britain bringing the bad news."

"It saves some of us, perhaps."

"Well," said Bedwyr with a wry smile, "a borrowed horse never tires."

"What am I to tell them?"

"Ah, that is where your wisdom and judgment will be invaluable."

First light the next morning, I called two of the younger warriors to accompany me on my errand; they were raw, fresh-featured youths, one named Tallaght, the other named Peredur. They were glad for a chance to quit the coracles for a day or two, and we left as soon as the horses were saddled, striking north and west, searching for the trail Bedwyr maintained we would find, and which would lead us to Urien's fortress in the south Rheged hills. As Bedwyr knew the land, I did not doubt him in the least, but it seemed to me that we rode a long way before finding anything that resembled the track he had described.

"Is this the trail, do you think?" wondered Tallaght doubtfully.

"We have seen no others," I replied, looking at the narrow, overgrown track—little more than a beaten path through thick bracken. "It will serve until we find another. Who knows? It may become more serviceable farther on."

With that we rode on, eventually coming to a stand of birch trees—the outriders, as it were, of the thickly forested hills farther on. As there was a bit of grass showing green in the shade of these trees, I decided to stop and let the horses graze a little before continuing on our way.

The wood was cool and it felt good to get out of the sun for a while. We dismounted, refreshed ourselves from the waterskins, and then lay back in the long grass to doze—an indulgence denied those enduring the swelter and confusion of the lakeside.

It seemed as if I had just closed my eyes when Peredur nudged me. I came awake with a start. "Shh!" he warned, his face close to mine. "Listen."

There came a light, buoyant sound—such as the breeze might make of a summer's evening, or a rill as it slips and splashes through the glen—but the sound was made by a human voice, and I found it enchanting. Tallaght and Peredur were sitting all hunch-shouldered, their faces tight and swords half drawn.

"Have you never heard singing?" I said, climbing to my feet.

"Never like that," Peredur murmured, regarding me strangely. Tallaght, too, appeared unnerved by the sound.

"Put up your blades," I said, "and let us find the creature making this delightful sound."

The two obeyed reluctantly, and I wondered at their

odd behavior. Likely they had fallen asleep and the singing had wakened them out of a dream. However it was, I put the matter behind me and proceeded into the wood. The singing seemed to drift to us in fits and starts, which made locating the source more difficult than it might have been; just when we thought we had found the singer, the sound would stop, only to begin again slightly farther away.

"She is leading us into the forest," I whispered to Tallaght after we had chased a while. "You and Peredur go around"—I made a circling motion with my finger—"I will drive her towards you, and we will catch her between us."

"She?" wondered Peredur.

"A maid, most certainly," I asserted. "I have never heard a man who could sing like that. Now, then, let us see if we can catch this elusive songbird. Ready?"

The two nodded, and I started ahead once more; they waited until I had taken a few paces and then darted off the trail on the run. I proceeded at a slow but steady pace, taking care to make more noise than necessary in order to maintain the illusion that there were still three hunters in the chase. Walking along, listening to the lilting song drifting back to me, and watching the flickering patterns of sunlight on the path, I fell into a reverie. It seemed as if I walked not in dappled forest light in the heat of another dry day, but in the cool dawn of a fine misty morning. I fancied that I could even smell the sweet fragrance of spring flowers as I passed, though these were long since gone.

And then, all at once—so swiftly that it startled me—I stepped into a glade. There, on the grass before me, sat a beautiful young woman, flaxen-haired with tawny skin. She seemed to have fallen on the path, for she lay on one elbow and the mushrooms she had been gathering were scattered about her. Her mantle had risen, revealing a shapely leg. She was bare of foot and head; her golden hair was uncombed, but long and tightly curled, giving her the look of a wild thing.

My sudden appearance seemed to have surprised her,

for she glanced up, catching her breath as her eyes met mine. Jesu save me, those eyes!—deep green and ever so slightly slanted, giving her a most beguiling aspect. She was dressed poorly; her mantle was smirched, the hem ragged; there were holes where it had been torn. Clearly, she had been digging with her hands, for the fingers of both were filthy.

She sat in surprise for a moment, her lips half parted, as if uncertain whether to scream. Seeing her agitation, I raised my hands to show I held no weapons and said, "Peace, sister. I mean you no harm."

She looked at me curiously, but made no move to stand or speak. I moved a step closer, and we looked at one another for a long moment. I had never seen eyes so clear and so green.

"Are you hurt?" I asked, bending low on one knee. "Do you need help?"

Still she made no answer.

I was about to repeat the question when Peredur and Tallaght burst into the clearing. They were sweating and breathing hard from their run. They looked first to the young woman and then to me; Tallaght's bewilderment melted at once to relief, but Peredur stared, his expression growing strange.

"We have found our singer," I said, and motioned the two of them closer. To the young woman, I said, "You need have no fear. These men appear more fierce than they are."

Glancing at the warriors, the girl hastily pulled her tattered clothing over her legs and began struggling to her feet.

"Allow me to help you," I said, leaning forward and offering my hand. She looked at my hand but did not take it. I said to the warriors, "I think your rough looks have stolen her voice."

Peredur's odd expression altered; his eyes showed white all around. He appeared distressed and confused, as if in terror for his life.

"Calm yourself, brother," I said. "There is no harm. See, we have upset the lady. To disturb one so beautiful

is surely a sin.'' Addressing the young woman, I offered
my hand once more. With a quick glance to the others,
she took it and allowed me to raise her to her feet.

"I am Gwalchavad," I told her, and asked, "What are
you called?" She declined to reply, so I said, "We are
making for Urien Rheged's stronghold. Perhaps you
would kindly show us the way?"

She regarded me closely, watching my mouth, then
pointed through the trees to the west.

"And is it far?" I asked again. Without a word, she
knelt and began gathering the mushrooms she had spilled
onto the path. "Here, men, help her. Perhaps she will lead
us to the fortress."

Tallaght stooped and commenced retrieving the mushrooms; Peredur, still staring, made no move. "Well? Will
you stand there gaping all day? Lend a hand," I commanded. "We must be getting on our way."

He bent to the task with, it seemed to me, extreme
reluctance. I could make no sense of the lad's strange
behavior. Had he never met a beautiful girl before? What
manner of man allowed himself to be so unnerved by a
pretty face and a comely foot?

We made short work of gathering the scattered mushrooms, which she received without a word and secured in
a fold of her mantle. "Now, then," I told her, "if you
would not mind leading us to the fortress? We have business with your chieftain."

She turned and started walking in the direction she had
pointed. I started after her, advancing only a few paces,
however, when Peredur called out, "Wait! We should not
leave the horses behind."

I suppose that in the distraction of the chase, I had
forgotten about them entirely. "You and Tallaght fetch
the horses and join us on the trail. I do not think the
settlement can be far away."

With that I turned and continued on. The young woman
walked ahead of me, quickly, but pausing every now and
then to glance over her shoulder to see if I was still behind. She moved so swiftly, I found it a chore to keep
pace with her.

Gradually, the wood began to thin and the land to rise. And then we stepped from the trees into the full, bright sun. Cleared land lay before us planted in fields; the crops were withered, however, leaves and stalks dry and rattling listlessly in the sun. Beyond the fields, squatting atop the broad crest of the hill, stood the timber wall of the stronghold. A well-used track emerged from the wood not fifty paces from where I walked, and made its way to the fortress gate. I wondered how we had missed such a well-traveled road in our search.

The young woman halted just ahead of me, gazing at the stronghold. I moved to stand beside her, and she pointed to the place.

"I thank you for leading me," I told her. We started across the field together, and had just reached the trail when I heard a shout behind us and turned; the young woman continued on without looking back.

Peredur and Tallaght emerged from the wood, leading my horse. They rode to where I stood waiting. "The trail led from the glade," explained Tallaght. "I cannot understand how we missed it before."

"Nor can I," added Peredur.

"Well," I replied, "at least we will not have to search for it on our return." Taking the reins from Tallaght, I said, "You can go ahead, if you like. I will walk with our guide." At this, both warriors exchanged uneasy glances, but I ignored their odd behavior and quickly joined the young woman on the trail.

We walked towards the gate—a steady climb as the hill rose steeply at its summit—and the young woman kept her eyes on the stronghold and said nothing. Approaching the gate, we were hailed by a man brandishing a spear. "Greetings!" he called, hastening forward to meet us. "I give you good day!"

I gave the gateman my greeting, whereupon he looked at the girl beside me and stopped in his tracks, losing control of his spear, which fell to the ground. He bent to retrieve it and stood staring at us, his mouth agape like a beached fish.

"We come looking for the caer of Urien Rheged," I told the man. "Have we found it?"

"That you have, lord," he replied slowly; he seemed to have difficulty taking his eyes from the girl. For her part, she regarded the man without expression; indeed, she seemed to look through him to the settlement beyond. "But if it is himself you are wanting, I must tell you he is not here," the man said. His attention shifted to the two warriors coming up behind me. "Is it far you have ridden today?"

"We have come from the Pendragon," I answered. "Our camp is no farther than a short day's ride."

"The Pendragon!—here?" cried the man. "But our lord is gone to join him in the south." His eyes, fearful now, shifted quickly to me. "Has Urien been killed? I must tell Hwyl—I must tell him at once."

He made to dash away then and there, but I held him. "Stay, friend. Calm yourself. All will be explained in good time." I smiled to assure him we meant no harm. "Ah, but it is too hot to be standing here in the sun. Perhaps there is a shady spot within." I gestured towards the fortress. "My men and I could use a drink—and the horses as well."

"Forgive me, lord," spluttered the man. "I am a hound for yapping on so. Come with me, and I will lead you to Hwyl—he holds the throne while Lord Urien is gone."

The man turned on his heel and rushed off. I took a step or two, and noticed that the young woman was not following. Indeed, she paid not the least heed to the conversation that had just taken place, but was still gazing at the fortress as if entranced by the sight.

Stepping once more beside her, I touched her arm and said, "We are going up now. Perhaps you could lead us."

She gave a shudder, as with cold, and came to herself once more. She looked at me, nodded, and proceeded to follow the gateman. I fell into step behind her, and the two warriors came after. We passed through the gates and into the foreyard of the caer. It was a large fortification, well provided with numerous storehouses and dwellings. People occupied with their daily chores paused in their work to observe us; a few called greetings. Most, if not all, regarded the young woman beside me with looks of unguarded curiosity.

The gateman ran before us into the hall, reappearing a moment later with another man, tall and slender and, despite the gray in his thinning hair, alert and ready-handed.

"Greetings in the name of the Pendragon," I said. I told him who it was that addressed him and presented the two warriors with me. "We have come to speak to the chieftain here, and secure his aid."

"I am Hwyl." The man stepped before me. "Urien's chieftain I am, and I give you good greeting, Lord Gwalchavad." He held out his arms to me by way of welcome. It is an old Celtic custom that when two friends or kinsmen meet, they grip one another by the arms and look into each other's eyes to exchange their greeting. We do this in the north and in the islands, too, although I did not expect to receive such a welcome here. But then, I thought, they did not yet know of Urien's banishment; our reception might sour when they heard what I had to tell them.

Turning his eyes to the young woman, he gave her an appraising look and said, "I would greet your friend, but you have not told me her name."

"I had hoped you could tell me," I replied. "As we found her within shout of the stronghold, I assumed she was one of your people."

"My people?" wondered the chieftain, much surprised. "But you are mistaken. I am certain we have never seen her before."

Chapter Four

Hwyl appeared unsettled by the simple suggestion that the young woman might belong to his tribe. "Know you, I would remember her," he stated firmly, "if I had ever seen her before—and I have not." He shook his head emphatically. "She is not of our folk."

"Well," I said, "perhaps some of your people know her. No doubt she comes from a holding nearby."

"Perhaps," allowed Hwyl reluctantly. Addressing the girl, he asked, "Do you have kinsfolk hereabouts?"

Although she turned her eyes towards him as he spoke, she gave no other sign that she had heard the question. He asked again and received again the same uncomprehending stare.

"See, now," said Hwyl, beginning to lose patience, "this reluctance is unseemly. We have asked kindly, and expect an answer. We mean you no harm."

"Please," I said to Hwyl, "I believe she is mute. She has not said a single word since we found her." Seeking merely to reassure her, I reached out and touched her gently on the arm. "May God have mercy on her soul, it is a pity."

However light, my touch produced an astonishing result. The young woman pulled her arm away as if my fingertips had burned her flesh. She held the arm stiff and close to her, staring wild-eyed as she backed away from me, rubbing the place my hand had touched. She took three steps and began trembling and shaking all over. Her eyes then rolled up into her head, showing nothing but white. Meanwhile, her mouth framed a scream, but no sound emerged. She then collapsed, falling to the ground, where she began thrashing and rolling, as if in unbearable agony.

I was beside her in two steps. "Bring water!" I shouted, kneeling over her. "Hurry!"

Hwyl sent the gateman scrambling away for water. I called to Peredur and Tallaght, "It is the heat. We must get her out of the sun."

"Bring her into the hall," suggested Hwyl, going before me.

By the time the two warriors had dismounted, I was already striding for the entrance. It took all my strength to hold her, for the tremors threatened to throw us down at every step. I could feel the muscles of her back and arms, stiff and tight as iron bands. Somehow, I reached the doorway and stumbled in.

Owing to the high roof and lack of windholes, the hall was dimly dark and much cooler. Along one side of the great room was a series of wicker partitions separating a number of sleeping places. I carried the stricken young woman to the first of these and lay her down on the straw pallet, and then stood helplessly watching the convulsions coursing through her body.

Two women from the settlement entered and rushed to the young woman's side. One of the women carried a water jar, and the other some rags. Kneeling down in the straw, the first cradled the young woman's head in her lap while the other wet the cloth and began applying it gently to her forehead. This produced a soothing effect and, in a moment, it appeared the more violent of her spasms had passed; the girl closed her eyes and lay back, still trembling and shaking somewhat, but quieter.

"Go about your affairs," said the woman with the water jar. "We will look after her and bring word of any change."

I thanked her kindly and, leaving the young woman to the elder women's care, summoned Tallaght and charged him to tend the horses. But Hwyl interposed, saying,

"Please, have no care for the beasts. Cet will see your mounts watered and rested. Join me at table. We will share a cup instead."

Thus we settled with Hwyl at the far end of the hall where a table stood beside a long hearth next to a large chair made of oak and covered with the hides of three or four red stags. A young boy appeared as soon as we sat down; he carried a bowl of ale, which he placed on the table. He looked to the chieftain for approval and, receiving it in the nod of his elder, turned and ran away.

"That is Ffinn, my young nephew; I am teaching him to serve in the hall," explained Hwyl. "All those of an age have gone with Urien to fight the war in the south, but as you are here, no doubt they will be returning soon." Lifting the bowl, he took a drink and passed it to me, saying, "Welcome, my friends. The comfort of this hearth is yours for as long as you care to stay."

I drank—the brew was cool, dark, and sweet—and with great reluctance passed the bowl to Tallaght. "Your welcome cheers me," I told the chieftain. "It is too long since I have tasted ale so good. Already I am regretting that we cannot stay longer."

He offered the cup around once more, and said, "Be it short or long, your stay is more than agreeable. We have had no word from the south at all."

A quick, sharp thrust is best, I thought, drawing a deep breath. "Word is not good," I told him. "The war is over, but the price has been high."

"I feared as much," remarked Hwyl grimly. "Is Urien dead?"

"No," I answered, grateful for the opportunity to set the matter in a different light. "No, he is not dead—though perhaps he might prefer it."

Suspicion clouded Hwyl's features. "Death is more than enough for most men, I find."

"Hwyl," I said, "your lord has been banished from Britain." I let that sink in a moment before explaining. "Urien broke faith with the High King and joined a faction that rebelled against Arthur. The rebellion was crushed, and the leaders exiled to Armorica along with any who would go with them. Urien will not be returning to Rheged."

Hwyl, staring at the empty board before him, was shaking his head and muttering to himself. I might have let him find out later at the council, but I know if I were in his place, I would wish to learn the worst as soon as possible so that I could warn the settlement and begin making plans.

"I am sorry to bear such bad tidings," I continued, and then drove the blade home: "The lands of all who joined in the rebellion are forfeit to the High King, and he has given them to another."

The chieftain raised his eyes at this. His face was ashen with shock and dismay. But his reply surprised me. "Bad tidings, you say," he mused, shaking his head ruefully, "and that is only the half of it." He looked at me as if staring hopelessness in the face. Then, turning once more to the contemplation of his barren table, he said, "God's truth, I always feared the worst."

"Did you, now?"

"Alas, Urien is no steady man; as a boy he was a flighty lad—so unlike his father. I always hoped he would come to a better nature, but no—he has grown reckless, headstrong, and inconstant. Unhealthy in any man, such character is perilous in a ruler. Even so, I hoped . . ." He looked at me with sad, haunted eyes, his mouth quivering, his voice thick. "That we took him for our lord I do most deeply regret."

"I am sorry it has come to this," I told him.

Hwyl, struggling to hold himself, simply nodded; he was too overcome to speak. Peredur extended the bowl to me, indicating that I should give it to the chieftain, which I did. Hwyl accepted the ale and braced himself with a last, long drink.

"It is bad for you, I will not deny it," I said when he had finished, "yet it need not be the ruin you fear."

"No?" His interest pricked. "If there is some way to avert the judgment, lord, I beg you to tell me."

"There is," I assured him, "if you will abide it." I then extended the small hope I had brought with me.

''The man who has been given these lands is not willing that any should be cast out. He has said that any who wish to stay in their settlements may do so, and has vowed that the protection he affords his own people will be extended to all who remain in his realm.''

Thinking he saw the answer to his troubles, Hwyl seized the proposition at once. ''Then we will stay! By God, we will stay.''

''Wait until you have heard all,'' I cautioned. ''You may have different thoughts when I tell the rest.''

Hwyl, unwilling to throw aside the promise so quickly embraced, said, ''Tell me, then. It can be no worse than I have heard already.''

''It is this: the man of whom I speak is not a Briton.''

''No?'' A frown of concern creased his brow. He imagined the worst, and confronted it head-on. ''Is he Irish, then?''

''He is not Irish, either,'' I said. Peredur and Tallaght knew what was coming and tensed as if to meet a blow. There was no way to say otherwise, so I told him the blunt truth. ''This man is the lord and leader of the enemy we have been fighting in the south.''

''Blessed God in Heaven,'' breathed Hwyl, aghast at such harsh justice.

I allowed him to grapple with this, wishing we had another cup or two to help digest this meal of stones. ''His name is Mercia, and he is lord of the Vandali, who have been conquered. The enemy king who made war on Britain has been vanquished, and in exchange for peace, his lords have sworn fealty to Arthur Pendragon. It is Mercia's desire to occupy unsettled lands; he purposes that his people should raise their own settlements and strongholds. What is more, this Mercia has vowed that he will take nothing that is not given freely, and will strive for peace between his people and the Britons who remain under his care.''

Hwyl was silent for a time, coming to terms with what I had said. ''We can stay—that is certain?'' he asked finally.

''Mercia has made this promise—I cannot honestly

vouch for its certainty. But you need not answer me now. Hold council with your people," I advised. "Summon the other chieftains and talk to them."

"If we left our lands, where would we go?"

"There is no provision for you elsewhere."

"So that is the way of it," concluded Hwyl bitterly. "It is either remain and be ruled by an enemy, or become like the Picti and wander the hills knowing neither hearth nor home."

I did not allow his budding anger a chance to flower. "Yes, that is the way of it. In the Pendragon's name, you and your chieftains are summoned to a council of all whose lands are forfeit," I informed him. "You are to deliver your decision then." I signaled to Peredur and Tallaght that it was time to go. The two rose at once, and I instructed them to ready the horses.

"Will you not stay the night?" asked Hwyl, but the warmth of hospitality had grown cool. His shoulders were slumped now, as if under the weight of his grief and the hard judgment he must endure.

"We have disturbed the peace of this place more than enough," I answered. "I think we should leave you to your deliberations."

Hwyl did not disagree, but merely nodded and said, "That might be best."

I told him when and where the council would be held, and then took my leave of him. He walked with me out of the hall, passing by the place where the young woman lay. The two looking after her rose as we approached. "She is sleeping soundly now," the elder woman reported.

"Was it the sun?" I asked.

"Aye, it was," the woman replied. "Nor, I surmise, has she had a bite to eat for a good few days."

"She was gathering mushrooms when we found her."

The woman regarded me suspiciously. "Those? Even one of those would kill a horse," she explained as if I should have known better.

Hwyl asked, "What would you have us do with her?"

"Might she stay here?"

"She does not belong here," said Hwyl firmly. "That much I know."

"Her people may be searching for her," the woman offered. "But she is in no wise fit to travel."

"Perhaps," I suggested, "you could take care of her for a few days and bring her with you when you come to the council. There will be people from other settlements in the region; someone may know her."

"That we will do," Hwyl replied. "Now I bid you farewell."

"I wish our meeting had been otherwise," I told him. "I am sorry."

The chieftain shook his head. "Urien has brought this calamity upon us, not you. I must speak to the people and decide what is to be done. We will come to the council and give our answer."

We left the settlement then, all thoughts of ale vats far behind us, and rode as far as we could before daylight left us. We made rough camp along the way, and slept under the stars. I was long awake, however, thinking about the young woman we had found, and the strangeness of that finding. But stranger things were to come.

Chapter Five

Rejoining the Cymbrogi next day, we found the entire lakeside camp in an uproar. We rode into the midst of a throng, shouting and clamoring outside the tent. Everyone was so excited that it took some moments before I could make myself heard. Finally, leaning down from the saddle, I seized the shoulder of the nearest warrior. "Why this turmoil?" I demanded. "What trouble?"

"Trouble!" he cried, twisting around to see me. "There is no trouble, Lord Gwalchavad," he replied, grinning, "unless you think the happy return of our Pendragon a quarrelsome thing."

"Arthur returned?" I wondered. "So soon?" Handing the warrior the reins of my horse, I left him to care for the animal as a reward for his impudence, and pushed my way nearer the tent. I caught sight of Cai, attempting to subdue the enthusiasm of the crowd with an inadequate supply of gestures and grimaces.

Pressing my way to him, I said, "Where is he?"

"Ah, Gwalchavad! Thank God you are here. I could use another hand."

"They say Arthur has returned—"

"Aye," he confirmed. "He lies within"—Cai indicated the tent behind—"and might welcome a mote of peace and quiet." Turning once more to the crowd, he frowned. "Listen to them now!"

He made to renew his efforts at silencing the clamorous Cymbrogi, but I restrained him. Putting my hand flat on

Cai's chest, I demanded, "But is he well, brother? Just tell me that."

"See for yourself," he replied, brushing off my hand. "For if you will not help, at least get out of the way."

Cai's reply gave me little direction for my expectation. I stepped quickly to the tent and reached to withdraw the flap, not knowing whether I should find a king more dead than alive. The mood of the warriors was high, but as downcast as they had been since the High King was taken away, they might have easily mistaken Arthur's return— holding it a thing more hopeful than was otherwise warranted. Crowds, I know, have a way of believing only what they want to believe.

Oh, but I had seen the wound. Men who sustain such injury, even if they survive, rarely recover their full vigor—as many a battle-scarred veteran will attest. Though I am no healer, I know whereof I speak, for ever since I was old enough to throw a spear without falling off my horse, I have followed my king into the fight and have seen the crippled and dying afterwards. May God have mercy, I have myself sent to the Judgment Seat more men than I can remember.

Yes, I had seen Arthur's wound: deep it was, and brutal. The blood ran dark in hot, pulsing rushets. When they carried him from the field, his skin was pale as that of a corpse, his hair lank, and his eyes sunk back in his skull. As I say, I was no stranger to that appearance. Still, I never thought to see Arthur wear it.

Plucking up my courage, I grasped the tent flap, pulled it aside, and stepped quickly in. Scarcely less crowded inside than out, I shouldered my way farther into the tent's interior, straining for a glimpse of Arthur, and saw the back of Bedwyr's head, and beside him Rhys; Cador and Llenlleawg pressed near also. I shoved closer, almost trembling with uncertainty.

I pushed in between Bedwyr and Cador. Bedwyr, glancing back, saw that it was me, and shifted a half step aside. And there was Arthur, sitting in his camp chair, impatient with Myrddin, who was bending over him. Gwenhwyvar stood behind, resting her hands on his broad shoulders, a satisfied smile curving her lips.

Arthur looked up at my appearing, and cried, "Gwal-chavad! Welcome, brother; I hoped you would soon join us." He made to rise in greeting, but the Emrys tugged him back down into the chair.

"Let me finish," Myrddin muttered.

"I cannot sit here all day!" Arthur complained. "The men are waiting. I must speak to them."

"We *will* be at this *all day* if you do not sit still long enough for me to put this on you!" snapped Myrddin.

"Ah, look at you now," said Arthur, glancing around and grinning at what he saw. "It is Earth and sky to see you, brothers." He reached out to seize Bedwyr by the arm.

"Stop squirming," Myrddin insisted. "A moment more." Arthur raised his eyes heavenward as the Emrys bent over his work. "There!" said Myrddin finally, stepping back. "We are finished."

Arthur glanced down, holding up his arm, bent at the elbow. I saw the dull gleam of red-gold encircling the High King's upper arm. It was an armband, but unlike any I had seen before: a dragon, its serpentlike body encoiled, glaring fearlessly upon the world with red-flecked ruby eyes. A handsome ornament, to be sure; God alone knows where Myrddin got it.

It came to me that the trinket's form was not unlike the image on the standard which Uther had made and carried into battle. Having revived Uther's old title to such magnificent acclaim, Myrddin thought to adorn the occasion with a worthy reminder of Arthur's lineage; tradition, they say, is a powerful and influential friend to those who honor it.

"At last!" said Arthur as he jumped up, making for the tent flap. There was not the least hesitation or difficulty in his movements. If I had not seen him sprawled at death's gate, life ebbing with every beat of his heart, I would have thought myself deceived. Could this be the selfsame man? How was it possible a wound of such dire consequence could be healed so quickly?

He pushed through the crush of onlookers, patting their

backs and calling their names, but moving on, eager to
get outside. "We will drink together, friends," he called,
lifting the oxhide flap and stepping through. That was Arthur, truly, forgetting that we had only tepid lake water—
and were fortunate to get that, much less any ale!—with
which to hail his safe return.

Snagging hold of Llenlleawg as he followed Arthur out,
I asked, "How is it possible?"

The lanky Irishman merely looked at me and grinned,
but passed along with no reply. Turning to Myrddin, I
said, "Will no one tell me anything?"

"Greetings, Gwalchavad." The Emrys spoke soothingly. "You had a successful journey, I hope?"

"Never mind about me," I answered. "How is it that
Arthur is healed? What is the meaning of the armband?
And why is it that—"

"Peace!" said Myrddin, raising his hands against my
onslaught. "I can answer but one question at a time. We
have been to Ynys Avallach," he said, "as you know—
to obtain for Arthur the healing we could not effect ourselves."

"You have succeeded marvelously well," I remarked.
The others had quickly cleared the tent, leaving Myrddin
and me alone for a moment. Outside, the cheering grew
loud and then died away as Arthur began to address the
Cymbrogi.

"I had little to do with it," Myrddin assured me. His
voice grew solemn. "Arthur lived, but only that much and
no more." He held up a finger pressed against his thumb
to show how narrow was Arthur's claim on mortal life.
"I do not know how he clung to a cord so slender, but
he did."

"Yes? And then?"

"Heaven was with us, and he was healed," Myrddin
answered, regarding me mildly. "He is as you see."

"Yes, yes," I said, impatience getting the better of me.
"I can clearly see, but how?"

"It was a miracle," he explained, "but a miracle of
such provenance that it allowed no witnesses. I cannot tell

you how, nor will Arthur speak of it. Perhaps one day he will tell us, but not yet.''

Despite Myrddin's words, I sensed there was still much that he would not say. ''But Cai said—''

''Cai refuses to believe his eyes,'' Myrddin declared flatly. ''As for the golden armband,'' he continued, ''it belonged to Uther. Ygerna had it made for him after they were married; it gave him the idea for the dragon standard. When Uther died, Ygerna kept it for her son, always believing he would one day become High King like his father.''

''Why did you wait until now to give it to him?''

''Whenever did I have a better chance?'' Myrddin demanded. ''We have scarcely had space enough to draw breath from one battle to the next.''

''No doubt that will change,'' I mused. ''Now that we have rid ourselves of invaders and rebellious Britons, we can enjoy a season of peace.''

''That is what I have been saying all my life,'' Myrddin replied tartly.

Chapter Six

I *remember lost Atlantis. Though I was but a babe in arms when the calamity came upon us, I can still see the Isle of Apples as it was then, before the destruction. The Great Palace was much reduced from its former glory; owing to Avallach's long, wasting illness, everything was falling into neglect. Even so, to my childish recollection all was leaf-green and golden sunlight, endless gardens and mysterious rooms no one entered anymore.*

My mother turned the gardens to her use. Lile was wise in the ways of root and stem; she knew the lore of herbs, and her medicines were most potent. We would spend entire days in those gardens, my mother and I—she working among her herbs, and I playing at her feet. She believed me too young to understand, yet she told me everything she knew about the plants. "This is Three Hearts," she would say. "It is useful for stanching the flow of blood, and for purging the bowel."

In this way Lile awakened in me the thirst to master the plants of healing and death. But there was much, much more than she knew. The Magi of Atlantis had amassed the lore of every age and realm, and though it took what would have been a lifetime for a mortal, this lore I also acquired. In Broceliande's deep wood I found what I sought. A remnant of our race had taken root there—Kian's people, Avallach's son and Charis' brother. There among the tall trees and deep shadows, they had built a city. I found it, and found, too, the knowledge I craved.

There was a book—from Briseis' library it came. The queen loved her books. I do not think she ever read it, but it was saved. I think Annubi, the royal family's faithful sage and counselor, may have had something to do with that. If Lile kindled the flame of love for secret lore, Annubi fanned that flame into an all-consuming fire. At first it gave him pleasure to tell me things; he was lonely, after all. Later, however, he had no choice. I made certain of that. He served me, and lived at my command.

Annubi was the first man I bent to my will, and I learned much about the power of the female sex. When I had wrung him dry, I let him go. Indeed, I hastened him on his way. He was the first, but not the last. Far from it! There have been so many. Each has had his purpose— wealth, power, position, blood—I choose them well, and take what they have to give. Whatever is required, I become: queen, wife, lover, whore. It is all the same to me.

Myrddin was right, of course; there had been little time for anything other than fighting. Sometimes it seemed to me that we spent all our days ordering our weapons; if we were not sharpening them, we were repairing them, and if not repairing them, we were sharpening them again. Whenever we had a spare moment, we looked to our horses and tended our wounds, always anticipating the next battle, the next war.

Though the Vandali had been defeated, we remained wary—unwilling, perhaps, to think that peace had finally come to the Island of the Mighty. We had been cruelly disappointed before.

But, as the Wise Emrys had suggested, over the next few days Arthur began to tell how he had come by his miraculous healing—an intriguing tale, made more so by the simple fact that, apart from Avallach, Arthur was its only observer and as he had been lying at death's gate at the time, he was not best placed to say what had happened. And though he spoke with great enthusiasm, and greater reverence, the details remained hazy.

I gleaned there was something about a cup, and a heavenly visitation, and a prayer in a strange language by Lord Avallach. Of the holy men at the abbey, there was never a mention; thus, I supposed they had little to do with the matter. Indeed, the chief agent of the miracle seemed to be the cup, or bowl, which Arthur had seen, or thought he had seen, in Avallach's possession.

"You drank something from the cup?" wondered Bedwyr. We were sitting at table, Arthur and the queen together with Myrddin and a dozen of the Dragon Flight—the elite of the Pendragon's warhost—in the tent which served as a hall for us when we were on the battle trail. It was late, but we were exulting in our king's return and reluctant to leave the tent. "A potion, or elixir? One of Paulus' concoctions?"

Arthur pursed his lips. "That may be so," he allowed. "I cannot remember. Avallach held it like this." He cupped his hands as if cradling a bowl. "No, wait," he said, shaking his head, "it was the other one—Avallach never touched it."

"The other one?" Cai demanded with growing frustration. "You mean to say there were two bowls now?"

"No, not two bowls," Arthur retorted, "two people: Avallach and some other."

"The angel," suggested Gwenhwyvar helpfully, and everyone around the board turned his head to stare at her. "We all saw her," she insisted. Appealing to Myrddin, she said, "Tell them, Myrddin; you must have seen it."

But Myrddin, scowling now, refused to speak.

"There was an angel," she maintained defiantly. "We saw her."

Cai instantly resumed his inquiry. "Did the angel speak to you, Bear? What did she look like?"

"If you say it was an angel, so be it," replied Arthur equably. "I thought her one of Avallach's servants."

This drew a snort from Myrddin, who folded his arms and turned his face away.

"But what did they do?" demanded Bedwyr. "Did they touch you? Did you touch the bowl?"

No, said Arthur, he did not think he was touched, or

touched the bowl—other than to drink, if indeed he had drunk from the cup. There was speaking—a prayer, he thought, from the way Avallach prostrated himself—but in a language unknown to Arthur. There was light, yes, a blaze of candlelight that whelmed the room in shimmering radiance most wonderful to see. And there seemed to be music. Arthur definitely thought he heard music, but neither singing, nor harps, nor pipes, nor anything else he had ever heard before; but since neither Avallach nor the heavenly servant had produced this music, he could not be certain precisely how it might have come about. He was more certain about the delicious fragrance that accompanied the appearance of the bowl. It was, he said, as if all the flowers of summer were tumbled together, each lending sweetness to the other and blending into an odor at once divine and indescribable.

These assertions brought more questions from Cai, Bedwyr, Cador, and the others who, despite Arthur's hazy recollections, seemed determined to solve the mystery. Those who were there, however, appeared reluctant to speak. Gwenhwyvar made but simple comments of correction, while Llenlleawg and Myrddin spoke not at all. They were, I suspect, unwilling to scrutinize the miracle too closely, and were content to allow the mystery to remain.

In the end, however, the continued assault on the mystery grew too much for Myrddin. Drawing himself up, he strode to the table and struck the board with the flat of his hand. "Enough!" he shouted, his voice a command even the deaf would obey.

Glaring down along the board at those huddled on the benches, he said, "Listen to your mindless nattering! You stand in the presence of a holy miracle, and you yammer away like foolish children without a thought in your heads."

"We only want to understand," complained Bedwyr sourly.

"Silence!" roared Myrddin. The terrible scowl on his face challenged anyone to speak, and no one deigned to brave the challenge. "Since you desire to know," he continued stiffly, "I will tell what can be told. The bowl, as you have it, is called the Grail—know you that it is none other than the welcome cup used by our Lord Christ himself at his last meal when he sat and supped with his friends. On that same night he was betrayed, and the next day was scourged and crucified.

"One of the Christ's many followers was a wealthy merchant known to us as Joseph of Arimathea, the same who provided the meal that night, and the tomb as well. Joseph kept the cup, which the Lord had blessed, and when the first believers were driven from Jerusalem, he brought the holy vessel to Britain. Joseph and his friends established the first church in the west, and it was here on Ynys Prydain that they raised the first altar to the Risen Christ.

"Alas, that first church passed from this worlds-realm, for the people were not yet ready to hear and receive the True Word. Joseph and those with him died in their time and were buried beside the lake beneath the Tor, where Avallach and Charis now reside, and where the monks have raised their abbey, but the Grail abides. Through means unknown to any save Avallach, who alone guards it, the Cup of Christ is preserved.

"In truth, it is the holiest object that abides on earth. Its marvels are beyond telling, and I know whereof I speak, for once, when I was stricken and dying, this self-same Grail preserved and healed me, and behold! now it has healed Arthur." Raising an admonitory hand, he said, "But I warn you, do not think to discover the how or why of it: no man can tell you how it effects its healing, nor why some are healed even while others perish. Truly, it is enough to know that it endures as a special sign of God's good pleasure; accept it, revere it, and let it be. Instead of worrying heaven and the angels with your ignorant chatter, you should rather throw yourselves to the ground and repent of your folly."

So saying, Myrddin turned abruptly and departed. The company sat for some moments in silence, pondering Myrddin's curious warning. Then, slowly, talk resumed, somewhat more respectful this time, but no less excited.

After a time, Arthur, visibly moved by what the Emrys had said, spoke his mind. "Myrddin is right; this is a thing too holy for idle speculation. We would do well to guard our tongues."

"Better still," suggested Cai, "we should pay homage to the cup—for healing our king."

To Cai's manifest amazement, everyone agreed wholeheartedly. Arthur commended the plan and lauded Cai's suggestion, embellishing it with the small addition of a special contingent of monks to offer prayers and psalms on behalf of the holy object and the realm. Thus would the Pendragon establish his reign, and the Kingdom of Summer commence.

Dazzled by glory, we all retired to our sleep that night in a mood of high expectation. Surely now, after the Saecsen wars and the battles fought to subdue the invading Vandali, we could lay aside our weapons and embrace the practice of peace so long abandoned in our homeland. We dreamed that night of returning to peaceful pursuits, growing contented and prosperous, and enjoying the fruits won by our swords' harsh labors. Having dreamed the glorious dream, we rose the next morning to greet the sun rising on a new and splendid epoch, the beginning of the Summer Kingdom, Taliesin's oft-told vision when peace, love, and honor would govern Britain's island brood.

Arthur regretted that he could not ride south at once. "Be at ease, Bear," steady Bedwyr reassured him; "the council is soon finished—a day or two more, and we are done here."

As we might have expected, Myrddin thought little of the notion. "Has it not occurred to any of you," he inquired tartly, "that there is good reason why the Grail has remained hidden all these years? I have every confidence Avallach knows best what to do. Hear me, Arthur: do not think to meddle. Leave it alone."

But Arthur would not listen. Thanking the Emrys for his advice, he proceeded to do the opposite, and the plan quickly grew to include not merely a simple service of homage, but a perpetual choir, too, and a church in which to house them all. "A seemly structure," Arthur said, "where any who are weary and oppressed can come and see the cup blessed of the Savior King himself." He was convinced that just beholding the sacred vessel would work wonders for those who made pilgrimage to view it.

This, he said, would be the first of many marvelous undertakings with which he would commence his reign. More and greater ventures would follow as bright dawn follows storm-torn night.

Nevertheless, Bedwyr had summoned the lords and petty kings of the region in the king's name, and much as Arthur desired to hasten south to Ynys Avallach, he must abide until the council finished and the Vandal problem was laid to rest for once and all. The necessity rubbed him raw, but he endured, filling the time with schemes and dreams which he elaborated at great length to any who happened near. Oh, it was a wonderful sight to see, and one which I thought had passed forever: Arthur, in the blazing vigor of untempered youth, inflamed by his vision of a Holy Britain even now entering the harmony and prosperity of the Summer Kingdom.

Myrddin held himself apart, viewing this turn of circumstance with a sour expression. Although he appeared ill-disposed towards Arthur's schemes, he yet seemed loath to quench the fire that kindled them. Like everyone else, I suppose, he was only too happy to have Arthur hale and whole once more, and could not bring himself to steal even the smallest mote of the king's joy, or dampen the Pendragon's ardor—not that anything could.

When I asked him what he thought of Arthur's plans, the Wise Emrys merely shrugged. "It matters not a whit what I think," he intoned somberly. "The High King will have his way in this, come what may."

I thought this strange, or at least unusual. Myrddin's behavior was often inexplicable, but rarely proud, and never mean-spirited. No one else seemed to notice Myrddin's gloomy indifference, and this concerned me, too. I began to meditate on what Myrddin had said about the Grail, and weighed his words against Arthur's zeal, but arrived at no firm conclusion.

Still, as I looked around me, I saw that at least one

other held some portion of Myrddin's reserve. Gwenhwyvar, who had at first matched Arthur's fervor with her own, now appeared to be waning in her enthusiasm. As the others were all too caught up in the golden glow of important doings, I decided to discover Gwenhwyvar's heart in the matter.

"It is not lack of faith that has brought me to this pass, but lack of strength," she confided. "That man wears me out. He has ten new plans before sunrise, and those ten have each spawned ten more before dusk. He hardly sleeps, and all the scheming makes him amorous. I get no rest, Gwalchavad. Truly, it is like sleeping with a whirlwind." When Gwenhwyvar realized what she had said, the color rose to her slender throat. "Do not tell him I said that."

"Never, my lady," I assured her. "But do you think he is right?"

"I want to believe him," she insisted, adding, "And certainly he speaks like no other man. If the Summer Realm can be brought into existence by dint of zeal alone, Arthur will succeed handsomely. And if we are able to accomplish even so much as a tenth part of all he has planned, I have no doubt our deeds will live forever."

Her words were noble, to be sure, but I could not help noticing an edge to her voice, whether of doubt or of uncertainty, I could not say. Perhaps it was merely the fatigue she had mentioned. Still, I marked it and remembered, thinking to myself that the two people closest to Arthur—Myrddin and Gwenhwyvar—were not wholly with him.

The next day, the first of the region's lords began arriving for the council. As I think of it now, that was when the trouble started.

Chapter Seven

Hwyl of Rheged was among the first of the noblemen to appear; he arrived at the lake camp with chieftains from the three holdings he protected. He also brought the young woman we had found in the forest and left in his care. Truth to tell, what with Arthur's unexpected return, I had not spared a single thought for the stranger until the moment I set eyes on her once again.

If she remembered me, she gave no sign, for as she passed, her face remained impassive and her gaze moved over me without the slightest recognition as she regarded the Pendragon's camp. She appeared slightly the better for her sojourn among Hwyl and his people—her long hair was neatly braided, and her clothes were clean—and since she appeared well treated and content, I turned away and thought no more about her.

Others arrived from surrounding lands: Arawn, Gryffyd, and Euan, who held settlements east of the Treont; Rhun, Hasner, Ensyth, and Gwrgan Ffrych, from the hill country to the west. Each came in the company of such chieftains and headmen as were deemed appropriate to attend the council in the absence of their respective kings. We welcomed them and bade them assemble before the Pendragon's tent, where the High King waited. Arthur's camp chair, which he used as a throne when on the move, had been set up outside the tent, on a red oxhide on the ground. Four spears—two upright and two crossed—were established behind the chair, and the Pendragon's shield hung from the crossed spears. The High King received the homage of his noblemen with good grace and an easy manner, speaking warmly to each one as he came before Arthur.

In all, I believe there were upwards of fifty noblemen who answered the summons, along with many warriors and women. Of those, two of them—Cyllin ap Caradoc and Cynfarch—had ridden with Arthur during the Saecsen War, and were happy to see him once more. Had they known barbarians were soon to be thrust into their midst, they might not have embraced their Pendragon so warmly.

So far as I knew, only Hwyl—the chieftain I had personally alerted—came prepared to deal with the matter at hand. I dreaded thinking what would happen when the others learned of Arthur's judgment.

Strife was the last thing on Arthur's mind, however, and though he had not forgotten his decree and its inevitable upheaval, I believe he misjudged the intensity of the feelings so provoked. In his present humor, he could not conceive of the difficulty others would have swallowing the bitter cup he offered. So full of peace and goodwill himself, I think he really imagined all men readily and eagerly sharing his joy. Certainly his radiant and extravagant manner smoothed the way. Even so, it was a rough ride over rugged ground.

As anyone save Arthur might have expected, the sudden announcement that their lands had fallen forfeit to barbarians did not sit well with the noblemen of the region. Stunned by the High King's declaration, they sat glaring in icy silence while Arthur explained the nature of the rebellion against him and its unfortunate consequences. Then, much as I had done with Hwyl, he held out their only hope.

"This is what I have decreed, and this is how it will be," he said solemnly. "Treachery has reaped its reward; however, it has pleased God to temper justice with mercy so that the innocent do not suffer unduly for their ignoble lords' disloyalty. Before me this day, Mercia, Lord of the Vandali, has vowed to uphold and protect those who remain on their lands within the realm he has been granted.

You may keep your settlements and holding, your fields, flocks, and cattle. He has undertaken the oath of Christ and forsworn all other gods. Added to this, he has given me his solemn pledge that he will take nothing from you that is not freely given."

Intended to soothe, these words kindled instead. Indeed, it was as if Arthur had thrown oil onto a sputtering flame. The anger of the noblemen's responses singed the very air.

"Swear faith to a barbarian!" roared Lord Ensyth. "I never will! I am a Briton, and abide none but a trueborn Briton over me! Neither will I see my lands given over to foreigners."

"Nor I!" shouted Arawn, his neighbor to the north.

As if this were the signal they had all been waiting for, the whole assembly leapt up as one. Shouting, thrusting fists of defiance in the air, each striving to be heard above the others, the council quickly lost all semblance of order. The Cymbrogi instinctively closed ranks around the Pendragon, put their hands to their sword hilts, and looked to return force with force. Llenlleawg, Cai, Bedwyr, Rhys, and I took up our places and stood to face the uproar.

Arthur, having caused the commotion, yet appeared surprised at the vehemence with which the noblemen expressed their views. He sat gazing in mild amazement as the council collapsed around him. Myrddin, frowning, hovered at Arthur's right shoulder, bent, and spoke a word into the king's ear. Arthur merely raised his hand and dismissed the suggestion, allowing the tumult to continue.

I suppose he thought such an overheated blaze would quickly burn itself out and he could more easily persuade the dissenters once their tempers had cooled. This, I fear, was too generous a reading of the situation. For the more they clamored, the hotter and more angry they grew.

Truly, I believe it would have ended in blows and bloodshed if not for the abrupt appearance of the mute young woman. Because of the confusion, I do not know how she came to be there; it seemed to me that she simply emerged in the midst of the chaos to stand among the angry lords.

For my own part, I had been looking at Arthur, should any command be forthcoming, and when I glanced back, there she was—standing as placidly as a maid in a meadow, hands folded in front of her, cool and chaste, dressed in a simple white mantle tied at her slender waist with a bit of blue, her fair hair glowing in the sun: a vision, as I thought, could not appear more lovely in my eyes.

Her unexpected presence unsettled the council. The shouting continued for a moment and then ceased as, one by one, the irate lords fell silent and an uneasy hush passed over the assembly. The girl herself seemed not to know or mind the effect of her arrival; indeed, she seemed oblivious to all save the Cymbrogi ranged before her; these she regarded with the innocent interest of a child beholding a new and fascinating game.

She took a hesitant step forward, and then another, pausing demurely, her green eyes wide and glowing with delight. The rapt look on her face was enchantment itself.

As I say, a moment or two passed before the council recovered its voice, and when it did, the fury that had formerly threatened Arthur now demanded to know who was this woman, and what she meant by invading the proceedings and interrupting their deliberations.

Well, Arthur was at a loss; he looked around him for anyone who might offer an explanation. I hastened to his side, saying, "I know this woman, lord—rather, she is known to me."

"Who is she?" he asked, glancing at her once more. Bedwyr leaned close to hear what I had to say.

"I cannot say, but—"

"Why is she here?"

"Again, I cannot say," I replied.

Turning to me, Arthur grinned. "If this passes for acquaintance with you, Gwalchavad, I wonder that you ever meet a stranger."

"Arthur, please," I begged. "I only meant that I have seen her but once before—when I rode to Urien's stronghold to summon Hwyl to the council."

"She is Hwyl's kinswoman, then?" wondered Arthur, stealing another glance at her.

"No, lord," I answered, and quickly explained how I had come upon her in the forest. "She seemed in distress from the sun and hunger," I said, "so I left her in Hwyl's care. At my suggestion, he has brought her to the council to see if anyone knows who she might be."

"Why?" asked Bedwyr. "Can she not speak for herself?"

"That is the problem," I told them. "She is mute. She cannot speak a word."

Arthur nodded, and then stood, raising his hands to quiet the complaint that was threatening to overtake us once more. "Friends!" he called. "Calm yourselves. There is no cause for concern here. I have it that this young woman is a mute who has lost her way. I ask you now if anyone among you knows who she may be, or where her people might be found."

There followed a short interval wherein the noblemen and chieftains discussed the matter among themselves, and when they had done so, it emerged that no one knew her, nor did anyone know whether any clan might be missing one of its members.

Not satisfied with this reply, Arthur appealed to them once more, asking them to search their memories. The council resented the suggestion and reacted swiftly and angrily. It was quickly established that no one, save Hwyl and his folk, had so much as set eyes on her before this day. On this, at least, they all agreed—almost as vehement in their agreement as they had been in their contention with Arthur.

Curious, I thought, that the mere presence of the young woman should arouse such passionate denial. The assembled noblemen were fervent in their protests of ignorance. Shouts of "She's not of our kin!" and "Never seen the like of her!" formed the general opinion, and I was put in mind of Hwyl's brusque rejection when he had first set eyes to her.

Looking on the maid, fair as she was and not at all displeasing in any aspect, I wondered what could provoke such ardent animosity. This, and she had not so much as breathed a word. What was it that men saw in her that frightened them so?

Turning to Myrddin, Arthur shrugged. ''I think she is not known in these lands. What should be done with her?''

Upon hearing the question, I glanced at the Wise Emrys, expecting his answer, and was startled by what I saw. Myrddin's countenance, formerly flintlike in the heat of the opposition against Arthur, was now transformed. Eyes wide, he stared openly, with an expression of such melancholy tenderness that I was embarrassed to see it. What is more, he seemed not to have heard Arthur speak, but continued gazing in this foolish, love-struck fashion until the Pendragon nudged him and asked again for his advice. Only then did the Emrys come to himself.

''Do with her?'' he asked, regarding Arthur with mild distaste—as if the king had blurted a stupidity. ''Let her remain with us until we find her kinsfolk, of course.''

Arthur ordered Rhys to take the girl and deliver her into the care of some of the women. Rhys, unaccountably, grew discomfited by this simple command; he blushed crimson to the tops of his ears, and stuttered a hasty reply under his breath, begging to be spared this duty. Though he fumbled for words, his eyes pleaded most eloquently, and he even began to sweat as he stammered out his excuse. So distracted was he that Gwenhwyvar stepped in for him and said that perhaps it would be best for all if she made provision for the young woman instead.

The Pendragon, anxious to get on with the council, readily agreed with his queen, and Gwenhwyvar stepped forth to take the girl aside. But the young woman had other ideas, for even as the queen moved from the throne, the girl started forward; she took three steps towards us. Gwenhwyvar hesitated, allowing her to approach.

The fair stranger came nearer, but it became apparent that she was not looking at Arthur, nor the queen, nor any one of us. Her bright green eyes were firmly fastened on another. I looked around me to see who it might be:

Myrddin? Bedwyr? No, neither of these. Rhys? Cai? Cador? No.

The young woman moved nearer, and I saw that she stopped before Llenlleawg, who stood at rigid attention, spear at his shoulder, gazing into the distance above her head, as if trying mightily to ignore her. But she would not be ignored, for she put out her hand and took him boldly by the arm, as if claiming him for her own. Only then did he lower his gaze to regard her with an expression devoid of any warmth or welcome.

"It appears she has chosen her champion," Arthur observed dryly, "and I cannot fault the choice." He then called to the Irishman to lead the young woman away. Gwenhwyvar went with them, and as soon as they had gone, the council began to grind ahead once more, but more slowly this time and with less roaring and breast-beating—as if all their anger had been expended and their passions leeched away by the curious interruption.

In the end, the noblemen were persuaded to the virtue of accepting Arthur's terms. Any lingering resistance melted away at Mercia's arrival. The Vandal prince strode at once to where Arthur sat on his camp chair, and prostrated himself at the High King's feet, stretching himself full length upon the ground, his face in the dust. The barbarian then took hold of the Pendragon's foot and placed it on his neck and lay as dead before his sovereign lord.

Arthur then raised the barbarian to his feet and allowed him to embrace the High King like a brother. This unabashed display of submission and acceptance went some distance towards convincing the yet reluctant nobles that the Vandali were earnest in their regard for Arthur. Unwilling to be bested by barbarians in displaying loyalty to the High King, the Britons made a point of renewing their vows of allegiance, placing themselves likewise beneath the Pendragon's sovereignty.

Arthur acclaimed them one and all. "Rejoice, mighty chieftains," he told them, bestowing the favor of his winning smile, "for a great good has been born in Britain today. You have put battle and bloodshed behind you and welcomed the stranger in your midst in order that peace should obtain throughout the land. For this I commend you, and I make bold to prophesy that from this day, as the Realm of Mercia prospers, so Britain will prosper.''

He then declared a feast in honor of the new accord, and even made a joke at his own expense, saying that any king who feasted his lords on bread and water, instead of meat and ale, was a king who risked his life in a lion's den.

A small jest, but the noblemen laughed heartily, for by this they understood that the drought was just as hard, if not harder, on the High King as it was for them, and that he had allowed himself no greater luxury and largesse than the least of them possessed. Truly, I believe this endeared Arthur to them and bound them to him far more tightly than anything else he could have said or done. They loved him for it, and the mistrust and hurt feelings of the day dwindled to insignificance.

Thus, the council ended, and the noblemen departed, hailing one another loudly, and talking together as they made their way to the place of feasting. ''That was well done, Bear,'' Bedwyr said, watching them go. ''You have carried the battle.''

''Let us pray the peace endures,'' Arthur replied. Rhys then called him away to attend another matter, and the others departed also, leaving me and Myrddin alone beside the empty throne.

''A strange day,'' I said, watching the others leave.

''Yes,'' Myrddin agreed absently, ''very strange indeed.''

''I feared the council would end in bitter bloodshed; instead it ends in a feast of friends.''

''Oh, that, yes,'' muttered Myrddin, only half listening to me. ''Who would have thought it?''

Then, without taking his leave, he simply turned and walked away. I stared after him, and as he moved slowly off, I thought I heard him speaking to himself.

''She chose Llenlleawg,'' he said, his voice hushed and oddly strained. ''A curious choice—or is it? Great Light, what does it mean?''

Chapter Eight

We did not linger in the north a moment longer than necessary. The great warband was assembled for the last time so that the Pendragon could pay tribute to their stalwart devotion and reward their sacrifice with high words—and good gold, which he shared out from the wealth of his war chest. He then dismissed them and, having seen Mercia placed on a solid footing with his neighbors, struck camp and headed south. The warriors departed in knots and clumps, so that the journey became one long leave-taking as we said farewell to our swordbrothers, sending them back to hearth and kin. I do believe Arthur embraced each one and sped him homeward with a word of gratitude and praise.

Accordingly, we reached the southlands far fewer in number than when we rode out; only the Dragon Flight and a scant handful of the younger Cymbrogi remained to serve the High King as we came within sight of our destination, Ynys Avallach, the Isle of Avallach, a place of peace and a haven of rest.

The great Tor rises from the surrounding marshland like a mountain rising above the clouds. Atop this mountain sits the Fisher King's palace, a huge, wall-bounded, many-chambered edifice made of honey-colored stone; it boasts a high-vaulted great hall, large stables, and two high towers either side of its wide timber gate. A causeway connects the Tor with the nearby hill on which the abbey is built; the fields of the monks lie to the east, and to the north is the first of a multitude of low, shapely hills.

In the evening light, the palace glows like sunstruck gold and its image is reflected in the fine lake at the foot of the Tor. Owing to his fondness for plying the waters of that lake in his small boat, Avallach is known as the Fisher King. A king he is, to be sure, but unlike any I have ever known: he is the last monarch of the Fair Folk, the last of that graceful, elegant race. He is also Myrddin's grandfather, and his daughter Charis is Myrddin's mother. To see them is to know where the Wise Emrys received his stature and regal bearing.

Not so many days had passed since we last saw the soft southern hills, and yet the region seemed vastly changed, for what the dry, hot wind did not steal, the plague destroyed. Indeed, as we drew nearer our destination we more often passed abandoned holdings—several of which had been occupied when we first rode north. Each day of the drought drove more people off the land: some fled into the forests, where they might hunt and forage; others abandoned Britain for foreign shores.

Even Arthur, despite his hopeful vision, looked upon the forsaken settlements with a mournful eye. He spoke little, but the gloomy expression on his face declared his mind well enough. The king held it a calamity. Bedwyr, his closest friend, tried to comfort him. "They will come back, Bear," he said. "When the drought ends and the plague has run its course, they will all come back."

But Arthur only nodded glumly, and said, "I pray you are right."

Even the sight of Ynys Avallach with the splendid Tor soaring above the placid lake failed to lift the Pendragon's spirits. Where always before it had been a pleasant, if not joyful, sight, this time it appeared to us a lonely place, steeped in dolorous airs and failing light. Though Myrddin said he was behaving like a child to take on so, Arthur paused, leaned in the saddle, and looked long upon the solitary Tor and its crowning palace.

Finally, Myrddin grew disgusted and rode alone to alert the monks and Fair Folk of our arrival. The welcome, when we received it, more than made up for the sorrowful end to a journey begun in high spirits. Mind, I have seen the Fair Folk before, and more than most, but I am always astounded by them: it is as if the mind cannot long hold to such splendor and gradually lets the memory slip away. I know no other way to account for it. Even so, to say that each time I renew my friendship with Avallach and his folk I fall afresh under a spell of charm and grace, is to speak but half a truth. Because of Avallach and Charis, a spirit of peace abides in that place the like of which is rare in our war-rent world, God well knows.

Then again, perhaps it is myself who, possessing a cold and wayward heart, cannot easily conceive that places such as Ynys Avallach exist. Alas, I fear I have seen too much of blood and strife, and it has corroded my soul. And yet, bright hope! In coming to the Tor, I am welcomed as a brother, and reminded of the beauty I have forgotten, and I am recalled to the pursuit of higher things.

There is Avallach, most worthy lord, he of dark and imposing mien, a man whose nobility is proclaimed not in word and deed alone, but in every limb and sinew. He is a king whose realm, as they say, is not of this world. Arthur is a big and handsome man, but next to Avallach, even our beloved Pendragon seems but a lanky stripling of a youth, green and ungainly. The Fisher King is tall and his voice is like soft thunder falling on the ear from a friendlier clime; when he smiles it is as if the sun itself has come from behind a cloud to light the drear shadow-crowded way with dazzling warmth. Myrddin has said that Lord Avallach is the last of his kind, and I believe him; but while he endures, our wave-encompassed isle is a better place by far.

And then . . . Charis: to speak of her is to demean with words what is best expressed in song; a wordless melody of the kind oft stroked on the harp in Myrddin's hand is the best description, I do believe, for when the harp strings sing and the heart sheds its weariness and rises to the eternal dance, that is what it is like to behold the Lady of the Lake. The name was Taliesin's bestowal, and it speaks to the shimmering mystery of her. She is womanly grace and all things female made rounded flesh and blessed of the fairest form. Elegance finds its meaning in her movements, and to hear her speak is to know how heaven's bright citizens address their immortal kind.

A man of crude weapons and rough ways, I know my praise shames the object it would exalt, so I will say no more, save this: imagine the thing which holds for you a blessing of gentleness and comfort, that incites to virtue without reproof even while it soothes with beauty, and you begin to glimpse the wonder that is Charis. I am not alone in this appraisal, mind. I have it on solid authority that the first of our race to behold Charis went down on their knees in worshipful reverence to the vision they believed heaven-sent. I am not convinced they were entirely wrong.

There are other Fair Folk, too, and I will speak of them as opportunity allows, but I would establish here how I felt upon seeing their beguiling race once again. As I say, mere moments in their welcoming presence and melancholy fell away, sorrow vanished, and the nagging anxiety that dogged our steps fled back to its dank abode.

Our meal in the Fisher King's hall that night, though simple fare, was a feast. We went to our rest with hearts healed and whole once more. The next days were bliss to one and all, the trials and travails of the Vandal invasion were swept away, and our spirits restored in that peaceful, gentle place.

See, now: I have said nothing in all this of Llenlleawg and the strange young woman. The omission was apurpose to set the piece in its proper place, so to speak. Rest assured, the mute young woman was with us every step of the way, though quiet, as might be expected. Curiously, her unnatural silence contrived to draw even the slightest of attentions. I observed her effect on others whenever she was near: the eye forever stole in her direction; untethered thoughts drifted her way. Though making no demand of any kind, she yet exerted an uncanny influence and her presence loomed in our midst like a great standing stone on a silent moor.

For her part, she seemed happy to journey with us, eating, sleeping, riding, acquiescing to her lot with grace and forbearance, as it seemed. Nor did anyone suspect Llenlleawg might be anything but happy with this arrangement. The tall Irishman was never given to complaining, true; he once fought an entire battle with a broken spearpoint in his thigh and no one knew of it until two days later, when he fainted while trying to remove the shard himself.

He is like that—a true son of Ériu through and through, and no one who knows him at all can ever claim to know what he will do or say next. In battle, a whirlwind is more temperate and a storm-gale more serene than is our Llenlleawg. Moody and restive as the ever-shifting waves that surround his soggy homeland he may be, but I will thump the man who speaks an ill word of Llenlleawg.

I tell this so you may know how it came about that no one spared a thought for the Irishman or his flaxen-haired companion all that long way south; Llenlleawg made no complaint, and the strange maid remained complacent the while. Nothing in the way either of them behaved aroused the slightest suspicion. Not even Myrddin, who is ever alert to the subtlest of signs and indications, found reason to express the slightest concern.

Consequently, it was not until coming in sight of the Tor that any of us had occasion to suspect that all was not well. Llenlleawg, who might have spoken sooner, let it slip that he thought the woman bewitched. He was answering Gwenhwyvar's mild inquiry, I think, and said, "So long as she remains in sight of me, and I of her, she is meekness itself. Yet if I leave her side but a moment, she grows so distraught that it seems a wicked cruelty."

"I am sorry," replied the queen thoughtfully, turning her eyes to regard the stranger where she primly sat her horse a few paces away. "In truth, it had escaped my notice." As if sensing Gwenhwyvar's mild attention, the strange girl shifted in the saddle and turned her face towards us; the queen shivered and dropped her gaze.

"How do you sleep?" wondered Bedwyr, overhearing their talk.

"No matter where I lay my head," Llenlleawg replied, "she will not rest until she has put herself beside me."

"You mean you sleep with her?" Bedwyr said, his voice rising in surprise.

"No more than you sleep with your saddle," the Irish champion answered, glaring at Bedwyr for raising the question.

"Has she spoken to you?" the queen asked.

Llenlleawg shook his head. "Neither word nor sound has she uttered."

"I wish you had told me sooner," Gwenhwyvar chided gently. "But seeing we are so close to Ynys Avallach, I ask you abide but a little longer until we can seek the advice of Charis and the blessed Bishop Elfodd. I would trust them to know what is best to do."

Llenlleawg said no more, and no doubt the thing would have proceeded in the way Gwenhwyvar had suggested, if not for the girl's odd behavior. For as we drew nearer the Glass Isle and the abbey, the young woman fell further and further back in our ranks. When we at last reached the causeway leading to the Tor and Avallach's palace, she was nowhere to be seen. Though the queen asked after her, and many of the Cymbrogi remembered seeing her, no one knew where she had gone. A quick search of the ranks turned up neither clue nor hint of her passing. Apparently, the strange young woman had disappeared in full sight of all—and yet, no one had seen her go. It was as if she had simply faded away, leaving not the slightest trace behind.

Despite his lack of enthusiasm for the duty, Llenlleawg was abashed that he had failed in the simple task of looking after his charge. I suspect he was so relieved when she finally left his side, he simply turned a blind eye to her disappearance. We were in sight of our destination, mind. Who could imagine anyone straying away with the end of the journey so near?

Llenlleawg rode directly to find the missing woman, and even then no one doubted that we would soon see them both before the sun had so much as quartered the sky. Thus, we dismissed the matter from our minds, and were soon caught up in the gladness of our welcome. We had come to Ynys Avallach, after all, where all unhappy thoughts are banished like gloomy shadows from the trail when daylight strikes through the clouds at the end of day.

I confess, I never gave the matter a second thought until Myrddin remarked on Llenlleawg's absence the next day. I was admiring Avallach's horses in the stables. The Fair Folk's love of horses almost matches that of the Irish, and they breed a steed even our Eireann cousins could envy. I speak as a man who has spent more days on horseback than on my own two feet, so take it for a truth from one who knows whereof he speaks.

See, now: I stood stroking the long sleek neck of a handsome gray mare, when I heard the soft tread of a step behind me. I turned and Myrddin was beside me. "They are a joy to behold," he proclaimed, speaking to my thoughts. "I am certain Avallach would be happy to let you ride one if you wished." He paused, looking sideways at me in the way he has—as if looking through a body into the soul beyond—then he said, "Perhaps you might like to take this one and go in search of Llenlleawg. He should have returned by now, and I cannot think he has lost his way."

"No," I granted, "never that. But has it ever occurred to you that he may have decided to spend a night with a young woman?—beyond the gaze of prying eyes, so to speak."

Myrddin flatly rejected my insinuation. "Do you really believe he would defy his lord and queen to frolic in the forest with a maiden he has been charged to protect?"

"Well, I—"

"Something has happened to him," he declared, "or he would have returned by now."

"I will take leave of Arthur at once," I told him and started off. He caught me by the arm and stayed me.

"Take someone with you. Those who rode with you when you found the girl—who were they?"

"Peredur and Tallaght," I answered. "They are with us still. I will fetch them."

"Allow me," Myrddin suggested. "I will send for them. You can see to the horses." He turned on his heel and strode from the stable, pausing at the door long enough to add, "Swiftly, my friend; the trail is already cold."

With the help of Avallach's stablemen, I soon had three handsome horses saddled and ready to ride. Peredur and Tallaght joined me as I was tightening the cinch on the gray I had chosen for myself. I hailed the two young warriors and said, "It seems we are to be companions once more. Did the Emrys tell you what we are about?"

"No, lord," answered Peredur. "We were told to hasten to the stables to find you and bring these," he said, indicating the bag of provisions they each carried.

"Well and good," I replied. "This is the way of it: the maiden we found in the forest went missing before we reached Ynys Avallach, and Llenlleawg was sent to bring her back. He should have returned by now. Myrddin has asked us to find them . . . or Llenlleawg, at least."

"Are we to try the Fair Folk mounts?" wondered Tallaght, eyeing the animals appreciatively.

"Aye, lad," I told him. "If you can bear to sit such a beast."

"We are your men, Lord Gwalchavad," Peredur said happily. "Lead us where you will."

With that we were away, clattering through the yard and down the winding path to the marshland below. It was morning yet, and we passed a few monks toiling in the fields beyond the abbey. They sent us on our way with "God speed you!" and "Blessings of the day!"

Having seen Llenlleawg leave our company, I knew where to begin searching. Though the lake was low from the drought, the earth was still soft enough to take a fair impression, and indeed, we had no difficulty recognizing the distinctive crescent and bar of a war-horse's hoof. Arthur had long ago adopted the old Roman custom of affixing an extra crosspiece of iron to the horseshoe, which, though costly, greatly improved the usefulness of our mounts, especially on the battlefield. There was no mistaking one of the Pendragon's horses.

Taking our lead from the tracks, we rode east. Our horses, wonderful creatures, carried us over the nearer hills as lightly as thistledown borne aloft on the wind's

breath, and we were soon far from sight of the Tor. I was
so enjoying my ride that I soon forgot all about Llenlleawg and his lady. Peredur's sharp whistle brought me
up short. I halted and turned to see him pointing away
south.

"Forgive me, lord," he said, "but I think he has left
the trail just here."

Looking to the place he indicated, I saw the tracks of
two shod horses leading south. I commended his sharp
eye and confessed that I had been too much given to the
ride to notice the turning. "You have saved us the chore
of retracing our steps," I allowed, and granted him the
privilege of leading the search. "Now on with you! Tallaght and I will follow."

Thus I took my place behind the other two, and we
resumed our journey. The trail, as Peredur had rightly
espied, departed its eastward course and struck off towards the south. Once beyond the salt-marsh lowlands,
we encountered drought-dry hills and dusty valleys, passing abandoned holdings where but recently we might have
expected a drink.

Day's end found us far to the south and searching for
a stream or brook where we might make camp for the
night. The first stars were already alight when we finally
came upon a shrunken rill where a little water yet trickled.
Though I would have preferred a more private place
among the trees, I did not like to wander far from the
trail, for it seemed likely that if Llenlleawg had passed
this way, he might have camped hereabouts, too.

We gathered the few bits of dry brush to make our fire,
and pulled provisions from the bags behind our saddles
to make a quiet meal—after which we rolled ourselves in
our cloaks to contemplate the bright-spangled heavens and
wait for sleep to overtake us. I had just closed my eyes,
or so it seemed, when a strange wailing sound roused me.
I awoke and stood, stone-still and holding my breath, to
listen for a moment. The sound, similar in some ways to
that of a wolf crying down the moon, reached me from
some distance farther south.

I walked a little apart from the red embers of our exhausted fire, and looked to the low southern hills, where I saw the faintly flickering glow of a beacon flame. I watched for a while, and scanned the land round about for an answering fire, but saw none. Neither did I hear the wailing sound again. The beacon, if beacon it was, died away as quickly as a spark, and the darkness closed around the place. I waited, but the flame was not renewed, and so I returned to my rest.

The next morning, after leaving a pile of rocks to mark the trail, we turned aside to find the place where the beacon had been lit, for I hoped to discover some sign of who had made it and why. As it happened, the ride led us farther south than I anticipated, but we found the site: an immense bed of still-warm ashes surrounded by a ring of earth erected to keep the dry hillside from taking light. Here and there we saw a few footprints—though very few—and those were scuffed and featureless.

"They have taken care to leave nothing behind," Peredur observed.

"Who could have made it?" wondered Tallaght. "Llenlleawg and the girl?"

"Better to ask who was meant to see it," I replied, and then considered that the wailing began only after the beacon had all but spent itself. "Maybe they feared we would miss the signal, so they roused us another way," I suggested lightly to my companions, but neither of them deemed it likely.

"Probably it was only a wolf," suggested Tallaght. "No doubt the smell of smoke disturbed the beast."

Now, I have heard wolves howling in the night more times than either of my young friends have swung rump to saddle, and I know it was never any wolf I heard. Still, I held my tongue and let the thing go. As there was nothing more to see, I went to my horse, gathered up the reins, and regained my mount, ready to resume the trail. "The day flies before us," I called, urging them away.

"A moment, lord," cried Peredur. I looked around and saw him inside the fire-ring, squatting on his haunches, prodding the ashes with a length of branch unburned at one end. So saying, he lifted something from the smoldering ash pile and brought it to me. "What think you of this?" he asked, extending the stick towards me.

I saw that he had found a scrap of cloth—fine stuff, tightly woven—which had been all but consumed in the flames. Taking the scrap between my fingers, I looked again, more closely, and to my dismay recognized it at once.

"God help him," I moaned, my voice a low croak. "It is a piece of Llenlleawg's cloak."

Chapter Nine

"1 must have an infant—a child, my sweet. I need a child."

Loth, as I recall, merely shrugged. *"No difficulty there,"* he replied lightly. *"I will send one of the men to the settlement. There are always brats enough, and no one squeals overmuch if one goes missing."*

"No," I said. *"Not that way."* Taking up the camphor-wood box from the table, I removed the lid and dipped my fingers into the fine gray powder.

"It is nothing. Last time we—"

"This is different," I insisted quietly. *"It is not like last time."*

Young Loth hesitated in the flickering candlelight. A beautiful young man, he was the very image of his father. I dropped a pinch of the gray powder into the flame between us. Smoke puffed up, and a subtle fragrance filled the air. *"I need a child,"* I said, pressing my hands to my stomach. *"It must be bone of my bone, blood of my blood. It must be my child."*

I dropped another pinch of the powder—a potion of compliance—into the flame, replaced the camphor-wood box, and stepped nearer, lowering my voice slightly. *"And you must give me this child, my darling."*

"Me! But I—"

"I will tell you about this child, shall I?" Putting my hands on his chest, I stepped forward, drawing him to me. *"This child will grow to be a sorceress of rare and won-*

*drous powers, and she shall be called the Bane of Britain.
She will destroy that simpleton Myrddin and his tiresome
pet, Arthur. She will lay waste to the Kingdom of Summer,
and prepare the way for us to reign—you and me. Together we will establish a dynasty that will last a thousand
years."*

*I drew him closer as I spoke. "Come, my darling
Loth." My hands found his arm, and began leading him
away. "I have prepared the bedchamber for our pleasure."*

*"Mother, I—" he began, then hesitated, still uncertain.
"Morgian, it is—"*

*"Shh," I hushed gently. "I ask nothing you have not
done with other women. There is food within, and wine.
We will eat and drink and, in the time-between-times, you
will give me your seed for the making of a child."*

*He looked through the door and into the candlelit in-
terior beyond. "Come, my darling," I said, my voice like
warm mead, sweetly intoxicating and seductive, "the
night awaits."*

"I would not hear you speak so, even in jest," Tallaght
intoned ruefully.

"As I breathe, son, it is no jest. Either this is all that
remains of our swordbrother's cloak, or I know him not
at all."

Turning his gaze once more to the ash pile, he said,
"Then we best make certain there is no more of him here
than that."

And so we did. Stir the embers how we might, the ashes
revealed nothing more. Keen-eyed Peredur, meanwhile,
busied himself with searching the surrounding hillside,
and his labor bore fruit.

"See here!" he cried, drawing our attention. "They
passed this way!"

Hastening to where he stood, we saw the tracks of two
people—and possibly a third—leading away from the
fire-ring. I bent low to examine the faint markings—little
more than bent grass and scuff marks in the dirt—and
marveled once more at Peredur's ability. "Son," I said,

for he was that young, "wherever did you learn to track?"

"My father kept the game runs for King Cadwallo," he answered. "I have ridden with him since I was old enough to sit a horse."

"Well, lad, he taught you well." Tucking the burned scrap of cloak under my belt, I said, "I think it best we follow the trail we are given. Lead on."

Thus we continued on our way, pursuing our new course south and east, slowly passing beyond the lands of the Summer Realm. I took care to mark our progress, for we were moving into territory strange to me. Trusting Peredur to keep the trail, I occupied myself with watching the rocks and hills round about, keeping an eye for any sign that we might be watched. Save the occasional lonely crow, I saw no living thing.

Even so, the further we journeyed into that queer land, the more certain I grew that we were being watched. I have ridden into battle often enough to know when an enemy is lurking near, hiding and awaiting the chance to attack an unwary warrior. That was the feeling that overtook me in this place. Once, as we descended a steep defile between two overhanging bluffs, the skin prickled on my back as if danger stalked us from behind. Spear in hand, I wheeled my horse to see . . . the empty path, and nothing more.

This occurred three times before the sun reached midday, and each time it took me by surprise. Though it does me no credit to confess it, the last instance so unnerved me that I called Peredur to halt at the next opportunity, thinking to water the horses and collect myself somewhat. This he did soon after, for directly we came upon a tidal estuary and climbed down from the horses. The bank, such as it was, consisted of loose slaty shingle and wrack cast up by the tide. As ill luck would have it, the tide was out, leaving an expanse of mud wide as a battleground with only a thin rivulet of rank green water oozing down through the center.

Loath to let the horses drink this foul brack, we looked up and down either side to see if we might yet come to some better place, but were frustrated in the attempt. The

estuary stretched far inland and maintained its breadth beyond sight.

"This is an unhappy place, God knows," remarked
Tallaght, scanning the mud before us.

"It will not grow more agreeable for standing here," I
replied. Seeing nothing for it but to strike on and make
for the other side, I swung up into the saddle once more.
"The sooner we put the place behind us, the better I will
feel."

Peredur, who had ridden a few hundred paces upriver
to the first of a series of low bluffs rising from the bank,
returned to say, "The trail ends just here. There is no
better fording that I can see. They must have gone across
at high tide, or we would see the prints."

"Then we have no choice." So saying, I lifted the reins
and struck off across the muddy broad.

It was vile stuff: thick black sticky muck with a stink
that turned the stomach. The rancid slime sucked at the
steed's hooves and released a stench which assaulted the
nose and watered the eyes. I pressed on regardless, anxious to get across as quickly as possible. That was my
mistake.

For, having almost reached the slow-trickling flow in
the middle of the mudflat, I realized that my proud mount
was sinking deeper into the mire with every step. Halting,
I turned in the saddle to warn the two behind me. "Come
no further," I called. "We must go around another way."

With that I lifted the reins and made to turn the gray.
Peredur's shout stopped me. "Stay, lord!" he cried
tersely. "Do not move!"

Glancing swiftly behind me and all around, I saw nothing to alarm me and was about to say as much when
Tallaght joined in the warning. "Lord Gwalchavad," he
called, his voice tense. "Look around you!" He thrust out
his hand and pointed to the mud.

Look I did, but saw only the scum of the fetid mire
glimmering under a baleful sun. And then, even as I
watched, the whole dully glistening surface began to
shiver and then to tremble. I stared in disbelief as the
muddy flats quaked with sudden, sluggish life, and the

horror of my predicament came clear. The inrushing tide was flowing once more, and the whole unstable mass was quivering and heaving in the slow-rippling waves of quicksand.

"Go back!" I shouted. "Save yourselves!"

Both warriors turned their mounts and began struggling back towards the bank. I made to follow them, but the gray had sunk still lower and could not lift her legs.

Pulling hard on the reins, I succeeded in making the horse rear onto its hind legs, whereupon I swung the frightened animal's head and completed the turn. The gray succeeded but two further steps before sinking to the hocks once more.

Desperate to save my panicky mount, I threw myself from the saddle and instantly sank to my knees in the vile bog. The mud shuddered and heaved around me as the unseen waves lent it eerie life, but I gritted my teeth and tightened the reins around my hand, and then, with an effort, raised my foot from the mire and lumbered ahead one step.

Half turning, I coaxed my mount forward, speaking in a soft, soothing tone. Eyes wide and rolling with terror as the killing mud sucked at her hooves, the gray struggled gamely forward, rearing up and plunging, but succeeding only in sinking us both more deeply. I made to wade forward and felt my insubstantial footing give way. I now stood hip-deep in the muck, and could feel cold water seeping through the ooze and up around my legs.

Tallaght and Peredur, having reached the bank, secured their mounts, threw off their cloaks, and hastened back to help me. I saw them floundering over the mud and tried to warn them away, but they came on regardless.

"Throw me the reins!" shouted Tallaght. Having come as near as he dared, he lay himself upon the mud and stretched out his hand. "Let me take her," he called. As I could do nothing more for the beast, I threw the reins to the young warrior and concerned myself with my own fate instead.

For his part, Peredur, holding his spear above his head, waded out to me. Stretching himself flat upon the mud, he extended the butt of the spear. I leaned towards him; cold water gushed up around my thighs and I promptly sank to my waist.

Peredur wormed closer. "Take hold!" he cried.

Seeing the spear within reach, I raised my right leg and brought it down smartly so as to jump up. I did not so much leap as lurch, flinging my body forward in a sorry imitation of cuChullain's salmon leap. Though laughably awkward, the maneuver gained me a hairsbreadth of distance. I felt my fingers close on the butt of Peredur's spear, and I grabbed hold with a grip that Death himself could not shake loose.

The young warrior, by the strength of his arms alone, pulled me nearer. I slithered from the wallow and came free with a squelchy sucking sound, but there I stopped, and Peredur could not draw me further without hauling himself in as well. I tried snaking my way to him, but even the slightest movement sent the bog quivering. I lay still and began sinking once more. "We need a rope," Peredur called.

Alas, we had no rope, and well I knew it.

"A moment, lord." Peredur wormed his way to dry land, where he ran to his horse and stripped off the tack. Drawing his knife, he cut the reins from the bit and tied them together, then came to the edge of the mudflat and threw the end of the leather strap to me. It fell just out of reach, so he quickly pulled it in, took two steps nearer, leaned out, and threw it again. The second throw went wide, as did the third, but I snagged the line on the fourth try and wound it around my wrist.

"Haul away!" I called, and Peredur, holding tight with both hands, edged slowly back and back. At first I feared the strap would break, but it was good leather, and though it stretched taut as a harp string, it did not break. One step . . . and another . . . and then he reached the bank, gained his feet, and pulled hard until I was sliding smoothly over the morass.

Upon reaching the bank, I scrambled to my feet. With a whoop of delight, Peredur threw down the leather line and ran to me, grinning at his accomplishment. "Well done, lad!'' I said, clapping him heartily on the back. "That was quick thinking."

Tallaght's shout brought us back to the task at hand: "Help! I am losing her!"

I turned to see that the gray was sunk to her belly in the black ooze, and the young warrior was in over his knees, but still clinging tightly to the reins. Peredur and I ran to his aid. In my haste, I struck a piece of slate and my foot slid out from under me. I fell back, but rose on the instant with an idea.

"Here, now!" I called to Peredur. "Help me with these!"

So saying, I stooped to gather an armful of the larger slates, choosing the broadest ones I could find. Peredur saw what I was about and leapt to; digging beneath the surface layer, he found several pieces of fair size and carried them to the edge of the quicksand bog.

Placing the first slate atop the morass, he stepped out on it and found that it would support him. "It will serve!" he shouted, and I began passing him more slates, which he put down a step at a time, forming a stepping-stone path out to where poor Tallaght was now almost sunk to his waist.

"Let go of the horse!" I told him, my heart falling at the thought of abandoning my handsome mount.

"If she goes," Tallaght answered between clenched teeth, "we go together."

"Son, there is no need," I replied. "Let her go. Save yourself."

The unseen waves of the incoming tide set the mud heaving and shuddering around him. Water showed in a queasy ring around the young warrior's waist.

Peredur placed the last slate but a few paces from Tallaght. "Brother," he said, stretching forth his arm, "the tide is flowing. It is take my hand, or sink and drown."

Realizing the danger at last, Tallaght relented. With a groan he released the reins and threw out his hand. Peredur caught him and pulled him free. Though the stepping-stones were themselves beginning to sink, they yet bore up the two young men, who skittered across and clambered thankfully onto solid ground.

We three stood for a moment, panting with the exertion of our efforts and staring unhappily at the gray tossing her head and whinnying with fright. The two young men suggested throwing down more slates and somehow getting the animal to walk on them. "Even if the horse was willing," I replied, "we could never lift her onto them." Observing the eerily rippling bog, I added, "The tide is beating us besides. I am not fool enough to risk all three of us in a hopeless cause. I fear we must let the sea have its way."

Tallaght stared, and opened his mouth to protest, but Peredur took his arm and silenced him with a conclusive "Lord Gwalchavad is right."

Now, I am as steadfast as any man I know, but I could not find it in me to stand and watch that beautiful animal die. "Come away," I said to my companions. "We can do nothing more."

Tallaght resisted. "Will you not even end it with a spear?"

Glancing back, I shook my head and turned to leave.

"Lord," he called, insistent still, "let me do it if you will not."

I stopped, and though I had no wish to berate him, I addressed him with my thoughts. "Lad, a warrior should have a friendly feeling for his mount, and your affection does you credit. But this is a hostile land, and we may well be glad of our spears before another day is run. Even had we weapons to spare, killing a horse with a single thrust from this distance would take a fortunate cast ideed. I own no such skill, and will not see the poor beast suffer any more than need be. In light of these unhappy facts, I think we must leave the thing where it is." Turning away once more, I said, "I am heartily sick of this place and wish I had never seen it."

Peredur snatched up the reins of his mount and fell into step behind me, and after we had walked a few paces, Tallaght also took up his reins and came along. We moved inland, climbing up the low bluffs above the estuary, where I paused briefly to look back at my doomed mount—now plunged to her flanks in the killing bog and screaming terribly. The sound of that wretched creature cut me to the quick. I made a sorrowful farewell and moved on, miserable, wet, and stinking from toe to head. Oh, my heart was low and regretful, but there was nothing for it but to drag ourselves away.

My two companions fell into a fretful silence, from which I tried to raise them, but gave up trying after a while; I felt as bad as they did, and with the day's passing, the foreboding grew more, not less.

I found myself wondering what disaster would befall us next, for although calamity can overtake anyone at any time—especially travelers in the wilds—in my present mind I deemed our misfortune nothing less than an assault by a malevolent power dogging our every step since we had entered this accursed realm. It seemed to me that the rocks and bare hills conspired against us, and even the low, brooding sky wished us ill. I remained firm in this woeful assessment for a considerable time.

As I warmed myself by the campfire later, I consoled myself with the thought that it could have been worse. We might have lost far more than a good horse; and, to be sure, if I had been riding alone, I would have died with my horse. Accordingly, I thanked the Good God for my quick-thinking young friends and took our narrow escape as a warning, vowing to be on better guard from now on.

Chapter Ten

The search for a suitable fording place took us far out of our way. By the time we accomplished our crossing, twilight had come to that forsaken land—no wholesome twilight, mind, but a murky dusk of rising mist that made the air dank and heavy.

Our clothes were still damp and repugnant to us, but we found no clean water in which to wash and so were forced to wear them whether we would or no. And though we gathered enough twigs and brush to make a fire, the fickle flame did little to dry us. The stench of the mud took away our appetites, so we did not bother trying to cook or eat anything, contenting ourselves with a few mouthfuls from the waterskin Tallaght carried behind his saddle.

Downhearted, dejected, and tired from our ordeal, no one felt like talking, so we rolled ourselves in our cloaks and tried to sleep. Even sleep did not come easily. No sooner had we closed our eyes than the moon rose, bulging full and yellow like a great baleful eye in the heavens. The light it cast seemed filthy, mean, and pestilential—a plague moon, Peredur called it, and we agreed.

Thus we passed a wretched night and rose ill-rested to begin a day which nevertheless held the promise of coming good; after our wasted night we welcomed the clear blue sky and fine bright sun. Both sky and sun swiftly faded, however, to a dull, bleached-bone white which hurt the eyes and brought an ache to the head.

We worked our way back down along the tidal estuary in search of the trail we had followed the previous day, still feeling fairly certain that Llenlleawg, and possibly two others, had passed this way. As I had no horse, we took it in turn to ride and walk, and sometimes Peredur and Tallaght shared a mount. The bank was rough and rocky, and made for slow going—whether on horse or afoot, we could move no faster. And then, when we finally reached the place where we had tried crossing the day before, we could not raise the trail again.

For all Peredur's exemplary skill and keen eye, we found neither track nor trace of whoever it was we had been following. "The bog took them, I suppose," suggested Peredur gloomily, "the same as it took the gray." Indicating the empty stretch of slowly undulating muck, he said, "The horse is gone, and the tide is hungry still."

He need not have mentioned the calamity; carcass or no, I was only too aware of the poor beast's demise. Losing a good horse is as bad as losing an arm or a leg. And that is the end of it.

After a time, we gave up searching among the rubble rock shingle and decided to continue in the direction the tracks had been leading when they encountered the quagmire. I freely confess the plan made little sense; there was no good reason to suppose that whoever made the trail had crossed the bog when we could not—unless they knew how and where to ford, and if so, that fording was not to be found by us. Indeed, we discussed this very thing, and the two young warriors were of the opinion that it would be best to range farther downstream, since our quarry might easily have gone the other way.

But something in me urged for pressing on. As it happens, I am not a man given to whims or obscure proddings, and in any event, I seldom receive them. Yet I was seized by such a powerfully insistent urging that I threw aside all reason and followed it. Perhaps because I am unaccustomed to receiving these ethereal promptings, my own inexperience made me gullible. Then again, perhaps something beyond human ken was hard at work, but I was too blind to read the signs.

The three of us proceeded to a nearby hilltop for a better view of our position. We paused to scan our surroundings and found that we had come up out of a valley and onto a wide, hill-crowded barrens. In happier times those same stark hills might have appeared green-clothed and agreeable, a welcoming sight for man and beast alike. After a season or two of drought, however, the sight of numberless bald crests rising one after another into the distance—like so many withered, wind-grizzled heads—failed to lift a heart already laboring under the unrelenting bleakness of that desolate place.

What few trees existed were stunted, twisted things, tortured into strange shapes by the coastal wind. For, yes, I now determined that we were journeying into Llyonesse—a long, ever-narrowing spine of land thrown up by contentious seas to separate and quell their warring natures: the Irish Sea on the right hand, and Muir Nicht on the left. Long deemed an inhospitable land, it is a queer place, a realm more fitting for outcast souls and wild beasts than upright men. Ah, and I remember: it is also the unholy battleground where Myrddin fought the wicked Morgian for his life.

See, now: the disappearance of Pelleas, the Emrys' friend and servant, was but one of the misfortunes issuing from that desperate battle; another was the leaving of my twin and brother, Gwalcmai. Deeply do I miss him, for until that dreadful day my brother and I had rarely been out of sight of one another so much as a single day but that we were together again by nightfall.

While Arthur and the Cymbrogi crossed swords with the Saecsen in the north, Myrddin, warned by signs and portents, had gone alone to confront the Queen of Air and Darkness. When Myrddin did not return, Gwalcmai rode with Bedwyr to discover what had become of him. The two of them found the Wise Emrys bloodied and blind in Llyonesse. Alas! Pelleas, who had taken up the search before them, has never been seen again, and Gwalcmai, overcome with remorse and shame, undertook exile. Or, as Myrddin says, "True man that he is, Gwalcmai could no longer abide his tainted lineage and went in search of redemption.''

Tainted lineage! Truly, Morgian is no kin of mine. To speak plainly, the affair sits no more comfortably with me now than it did when I first heard of it. Allowing Gwalcmai to go away like that, however noble the purpose, has always seemed ill-advised to me. Had I been there, you can well believe I would have had a word or two to say about it. Well, I was not there, and nothing can be done about it now—save pray we are reunited one day, which I do, and so look forward to that happy reunion.

These things, then, were in my mind as we made our slow way into the empty hills. I scanned the bleak horizon, alternating this unproductive activity with picking mud-clots off my tunic and trews. After riding a fair while, we came to a small, briar-choked burn snaking along the bottom of a narrow gully. Though much shrunken from the stream it had been, the water was still good, and so we stopped to refresh the horses and replenish the waterskins. Then we washed ourselves and our clothes as best we could and sat down to rest and eat a bite of hard bread. When our clothes had mostly dried, we then journeyed on until the desultory sunlight faded and night stole in around us once more.

At the failing of the sun, a murky, tepid dusk drew over the land. Discouraged by the long and futile day, we halted and made camp in a hollow. While Tallaght busied himself with the horses, Peredur fussed at making a fire; the wood was rotten and unaccountably damp, and produced more smoke than heat. As they were about these chores, I walked a little to the overlooking hilltop to see what might be learned of the night sky.

The haze which had obscured the day yet persisted, thickening as daylight dwindled so as to keep out the light of any stars. A mournful wind from the southwest moaned over the barren hills and set the bare branches of the dwarfed trees chattering like naked teeth. Storms often attend such nights, but there was not the slightest hint of rain in the air, and the wind tasted of sea salt.

Nor was I better encouraged when Peredur called out

to advise me that he had found the source of the damp: a
small spring of water seeping from the hillside. I left off
my scrutiny and went down to attend this new discovery,
hopeful that we might get some fresh water at last. I
should have guessed my hope, like all else in that dismal
realm, would die forlorn. Though Peredur delved with his
hands into the hillside and removed several stones, the
spring remained little more than a soggy weepage soaking
up from the earth.

I dismissed the spring, saying, "Were it ten times the
trickle, it still would not serve the horses."

Peredur persisted, however, and collected enough in a
bowl to give us all a drink. As he had discovered the
spring, we granted him first draught—which also became
the last: the water tasted of spoiled eggs.

"Gah!" He spat, wiping his tongue on his sleeve to
get the taste out of his mouth.

Tallaght laughed at the pinched expression on Peredur's
face, which caused the stricken warrior to rail angrily at
his kinsman. Tallaght responded with harsh words,
whereupon Peredur took offense at this abuse. If I had not
been standing over them, I have no doubt the thing would
have come to blows.

"Enough!" I told them sternly. "It is nothing. Put it
behind you."

They glared at each other and backed away to nurse
imagined resentments the rest of the evening. I was only
too thankful to let the night smooth our ragged tempers,
but this was not to be.

The fretful wind waxed stronger with the setting sun,
gusting out of the east, blowing dust from the hilltops,
and swirling it around the hollow. At first I hoped merely
to ignore it, but the dry thunder mumbling in the distance
chased away any thought of sleep. I lay wrapped in my
cloak, listening to the storm, and thought I heard the
sound of a bell—such as monks often employ to call their
brothers to prayer.

It came to me that the sound, tolling regular and slow,
was gradually growing louder. I rose and climbed the
slope to have a look around, and in the darkness at the

summit stumbled over Peredur, who had roused himself
with the same notion. He whirled on me with a start and
struck me with his fist before I succeeded in convincing
him that he was not under attack.

"Peace, lad. It is myself, Gwalchavad."

"Forgive me, lord," he said, much relieved. "I did not
know you were awake."

"The bell woke me," I replied. The young warrior appeared so confused by this simple declaration, I added,
"The monkish bell—that," as it tolled again, "just
there."

"God's truth," he said, shaking his head, "it was the
singing that woke me. I heard nothing of the bell."

I stared at him, trying to define his face in the windy
darkness. "Singing?"

Strange to say, but even as I spoke the word, I heard
the sound of voices lifted in slow, sonorous chant. Perhaps
I had been too taken with the bell to have noticed, but I
had not heard the sound before that instant. Nevertheless,
Peredur maintained that the chanting had wakened him,
and now that he had said it, I heard it, too.

As we stood in the wind-tossed night, discussing this,
the moon broke free of the low-flying clouds and cast a
thin, watery light over the barren hillscape. The bell tolled
and the chanting grew louder, and I turned in the direction
of the sound, but saw nothing and so directed my gaze
elsewhere.

"There they are," breathed Peredur, putting his head
close to mine. "Eight of them, I make it."

"Where?" I searched the moon-shot darkness for a
glimpse of what he saw, but found nothing.

"There!" answered Peredur; placing his hand on my
shoulder, he turned me in the direction he was looking—
the same direction I had searched. Now I saw the flickering gleam of eight separate lights aglow on the hilltop.
On my honor, I swear the lights had not been there a mere
moment before. Yet there they were, bobbing gently along
the crest of the hill: torches, held aloft by unseen hands,
wafting gently nearer to the sound of chanting and the
slow ringing of a bell.

"A poor night, I think, for traveling hereabouts," I remarked.

"Who can they be?" wondered Peredur, and then suggested we take up our weapons and see.

"No," I counseled, "their course will bring them near enough. We will await them here."

We stood our ground and shortly perceived the phantom glimmer of faces beneath the guttering torches. On they came, passing out of sight briefly as they descended one of the intervening valleys—only to reappear much closer than before. Now they were near enough for us to see that there were nine of them: eight torchbearers led by one who carried the bell—monks, as I had supposed, dressed in priestly robes that billowed in the wind. They were chanting in Latin and ringing their bell so intently that they did not appear to heed us at all; had I been in their place, I doubt if I should have expected to encounter fellow wanderers on such a night.

On they came, their voices low, their steps shuffling slowly, their shapes shifting in the wind-whipped torchlight as their robes blew this way and that. Dust churned up by the gusting wind cast a filthy pall over all, so that they seemed to float along on dirty clouds. When I judged they had come near enough, I stepped forth out of the darkness, my hands upraised to show I carried no weapons.

"Peace to you, good brothers," I said, speaking boldly to be heard over the whine of the wind.

It was not my intent to frighten them, but an unexpected stranger looming out of the darkness of a storm-blown night might be assumed to set the heart racing. Curiously, the column simply halted, ceasing its chanting at the same instant, so that it seemed the monks had anticipated my sudden appearance.

"I give you good greeting," I called, stepping nearer. They turned towards me and it was then I saw that their faces were swathed in strips of cloth dressings like those that bind the wounded.

None of them spoke a word. The hiss and flutter of the torches, and the sighing moan of the wind, were the only

sounds to be heard in all the world. We all stood looking
at one another in silence—Peredur and I on our side, the
nine shrouded monks on theirs.

"What do you here on such a foul night?" I asked at
last.

The foremost monk carrying the bell deigned to reply.
"We go to worship our lord," he intoned. "The time of
our release approaches."

"We have ridden far this day, but we have seen neither
church nor chapel hereabouts," I told him. "Where is
your abbey?"

"Our temple lies beneath the hollow hills," he said in
a voice cracking like the dull, distant thunder.

"We are Christian men, too," I said, "and camped
nearby. You are welcome to share our fire."

"Christ!" spat the monk, his anger sharp and quick.
"We know him not."

Mystified by his denial, I asked, "Then who do you
worship?"

"Mithras!" he proclaimed triumphantly, and the remaining monks murmured the name in approval.

If this arrow was loosed to wound me, I confess it fell
a good way short of the mark. For the monk's revelation
so surprised me, I merely gaped at him. "Mithras!" I
cried in amazement. "That old bull-killer departed Britain
with the Romans," I replied—which was what men like
Bishop Tudno, Iltyd, and Elfodd taught, holy men and
learned, every one.

"Mithras lives!" declared the man with the bell.

So saying, he lifted his hand to his shrouded face and
drew aside the wrappings as if they had been a veil.

I beheld a visage ravaged by disease; the wretch's
cheeks and nose had been eaten away, his chin was raw,
his lips were cankered black, and on his forehead pale
bone glinted beneath scab-crusted skin. There was not a
thumb's-breadth of healthy flesh on him anywhere, for
that which was not rotted away was as dry and cracked
as the drought-blighted earth beneath our feet.

Peredur gasped. "Lepers!"

Ignoring the young man's bad manners, I swallowed

my dread and forced what I meant to be a smile of welcome. "I have extended the hospitality of our hearth, such as it is," I told them. "I do not withdraw it now."

"Fool!" said the leper, his voice a croaking whisper. "You stand on ground sacred to Mithras."

The wind tore aside his cloak and in the flickery light I saw the dull glint of an ancient lorica on his chest; a bronze-handled spatha hung from his hip, and a brooch at his shoulder was engraved with the image of a she-wolf and the words "Legio XXII Augustus."

"Hail, Mithras!" the leper hissed. "Bow down!"

These words so alarmed me, I sained myself with the sign of the cross—something the good brothers do in times of trial when seeking comfort of the Heavenly Presence—an instinctive impulse, nothing more, yet the result was staggering.

Instantly, the sky was rent by dry lightning. A searing white flash set the heavens ablaze. Thunder rolled. I threw a hand over my eyes. When I dared look around once more, Peredur and I stood on the hilltop, the wind whipping at our cloaks, curling them about our trembling legs. We were alone. The nine lepers had vanished, leaving nothing behind but the burning stink of brimstone.

Chapter Eleven

Thunder cracked over our heads as if the sky itself would fall in shattered chunks upon the ground. I felt Peredur crowding close beside me. "Devilry walks among us," I said, steadying my voice. "Come, we will hold vigil until morning."

Returning to our pitiful fire, we heaped up the small supply of brush we had put by and renewed the flame, then sat huddled close to the fire and waited out the long, storm-worried night. Tallaght slept on undisturbed.

When murky daylight finally broke over the barrens, I rose and retraced my steps to the hilltop to look for signs of what had passed in the night, but the wind had done its work too well, and there were no tracks to be seen. I did, however, see the faint smudge of smoke rising from a fire some distance away to the south. Upon rousing Tallaght, we saddled the horses and began making our way to our destination as quickly as possible.

It took longer than I imagined to reach the place, and we arrived to find the camp deserted; only the smoldering ash of a fire remained. Once again Peredur proved his skill. Forbidding us to dismount, he stalked around the camp, eyes down, squatting low now and then, searching this way and that for marks that only he could see.

"There were four of them," he announced abruptly. "They are traveling on horseback, and—"

"Which way did they go?" Tallaght asked.

"On leaving here," Peredur replied, "they rode south. But—"

"Four, you say?" interrupted Tallaght. "Where did they keep the horses? I see no—"

"Tallaght!" I said sharply. "Let the man speak." To Peredur, I said, "What else would you say?"

"Llenlleawg is with them," he answered. "Only one of the horses is wearing barred iron."

Tallaght, gazing around the deserted camp, complained, "For so many people, they left little sign of their passing. I am looking, but I see no such marks."

"You are not meant to see them," Peredur replied haughtily. "They took pains to rub them out."

"Oh, now you behold the invisible," Tallaght sneered, "and say whatever comes into your head."

Offended by Tallaght's slur on his abilities, Peredur snapped, "Perhaps if you were not so blinded by your own high opinion of yourself, you might—"

"Stop it!" I cried, exasperated and a little disturbed by their vexatious behavior. "What has come over you, Tallaght? And you, Peredur, this is not like you at all."

"He started it," sniffed Peredur.

Tallaght retorted hotly. "Liar! I only said that—"

"Enough!" I roared. Both glared at me in sullen silence, overgrown children rebuked by a disapproving elder. "Listen to you—fighting like snotty-nosed bairns, the pair of you! I will not have it." I gave them each a frown of firm rebuke, and then, addressing myself to Peredur, said, "Now, lead on. We will take it in turn with the horses as before."

"I would rather go afoot," Peredur muttered under his breath.

"Good," I replied, "then you can have the first stretch. Get on with you, now."

Tallaght allowed himself a smirk at Peredur's expense, so I rounded on him. "And you, my friend, can sift the ashes and tell us how long ago they were here."

The young warrior opened his mouth to object, then closed it again when he saw the set of my jaw. Dismounting, he stumped to the firebed and began prodding the ashes. With a sigh, he stooped and took some into his hands, felt them, tossed them aside, and put his hand flat on the still-warm ashes. "I say they left at dawn," he concluded. Rising to wipe his hands on his breecs, he added defiantly: "Unless anyone wishes to contradict me."

"No one contradicts you, Tallaght," I said, growing weary of the sour attitude. I gave a nod to Peredur, and we started off once more.

I wondered at the change that had come over the two young warriors. Previously they had shown themselves to be fast friends, quick to praise and slow to anger. Now, however, they seemed as quarrelsome as cats edging for dominion of the dung heap. I put the change to anxiety and the rigors of the journey, and let it go at that. Anyone as ill-fed and tired as we were might also be fretful. Even so, until they came to their former good spirits once more, I thought it best to keep them separated.

The path led us south and ever south. The sun waxed full, but carried itself shrouded in a white heat haze as on the previous day. We forced a rapid march all morning, stopping only to change riders. Just after midday, Peredur led us to a small, silt-choked pool a little way off the trail. We could not bring ourselves to drink the stuff, but the horses were thirsty enough not to mind. It was while we were waiting for them to get their fill that we noticed the smoke.

As it happened, I had been smelling it for some little time before Peredur brought it to my attention, but because my night's vigil over the campfire had left me with a cloak that stank of stale smoke, I had paid little heed to more of the same. "We all reek of the hearth," I replied.

"No," he said adamantly, "this is different." Lifting his head, he turned slowly around in a circle, then, stretching out his hand, pointed in the direction we had been traveling. "It is coming from that way," he said.

We continued on, following the scent of the smoke, which grew stronger with every step. Soon we came to a ridge, whereupon I ordered my companions to dismount and we crept cautiously to the crest to observe the land

below. Far off to the right, I could see the gray-green glint
of the sea, flat and glimmering like an anvil under the
white-hot hammer of the sun. To the left, the ridge descended in steep, rocky ledges to a rough, rubble-filled
valley. And there, straight ahead, rising in a thick, black
column, a pillar of smoke ascended to the heights to be
carried away on the wind.

The fire itself remained out of sight behind a low hill.
Signaling the others to follow me, I went down for a
closer look, my companions leading the horses. Upon
reaching the valley floor, we discovered the bed of a dry
stream bearing the hoofprints of four horses—one with
barred iron, the other three unshod—in the soft, fine dirt.
It did not need Peredur's eye to see that the riders had
crossed the dry stream, climbed the hill, and were now
encamped beyond.

Rather than walk into a strange camp unawares, I
thought it best to see what manner of men we had been
following all this time. "Stay with the horses," I told
Tallaght and, commanding Peredur to attend me, turned
and made my way swiftly to the top of the hill, where,
lying on my stomach, I peered over the crest and down
the slope to the valley below. What I saw astonished me.

The entire valley floor had been heaped into a mound
surrounded by ditches, and atop the mound stood a great
fortress of stone. The Romans sometimes built in stone;
however, the stronghold before me was unlike any the
Legions ever raised, save in one respect only: this fortress,
too, was a ruin. Its huge stones lay in tumbled heaps, the
remains of high walls filling the ditches. The cracked shell
of what once must have been a magnificent tower rose
over the central gateway, a tree growing up through its
empty middle. The rubble of a hundred dwellings lay
overturned and scattered within the walls; and although
the great hall itself was roofless now, several enormous
beams arched over empty space, and two of its graceful
walls stood untouched.

Hard by the mound to the south stood the blighted remains of a great wood; rank upon rank, trees of untold
age stood leafless and dead, their black trunks and twisted

limbs testifying to their tortured demise, while many more were heaped one atop the other like stout warriors fallen in battle.

At first I thought the smoke must issue from this bleak wood, but a closer look revealed that it ascended instead from the huge hearth in the center of the ruined hall.

"Truly," declared Peredur in an awed voice, "giants must have built this place."

"Perhaps," I allowed. "And did giants also start that fire?"

Peredur glanced at me to see if I was jesting with him, swallowed, and said, "I see no one."

"Then let us go down," I replied, and instructed him to tell Tallaght to leave the horses, and for both of them to follow me and guard my back.

Warily, alert to any sight or sound, I crawled down the hillside, working slowly towards the ruined gateway yawning open like a toothless mouth in the center of the collapsed wall. There I paused and waited until I saw that Tallaght and Peredur were behind me, and then picked my way through the opening. Upon entering the inner yard, I scrambled over the rubble and almost slid into a standing well; I looked in and saw my own self looking back, for though the well wall had fallen, there was yet water below.

It was the first clear water I had seen in many days, and my first thought was to drink—before caution convinced me that it might be better to wait until we could test it properly. "There is water here," I told my two shadows, and then advised, "but I would not drink it yet."

Moving on, I continued towards the hall. Here and there among the tumbled stones I caught the glint of sunlight shining up at me from the ground as I passed. Shoving aside the debris, I found bits of broken glass in the soil. Real glass, mind. The more I looked, the more I found. It was everywhere underfoot! Even the Romans who used the precious stuff with abandon were not so profligate as that.

The wrecked hall stood before me, thick, black smoke

rising above its two intact walls. I saw no one, nor any sign that anyone had set foot, much less set fire, in the place for hundreds of years. Cautiously, carefully, I crept to the hall, then worked along the wall until I came to the end. Standing against the good wall, I peered around the corner into what had been the great hall's hearth. And there I saw a curious sight: a huge iron cage, round and with a peaked roof, like a house of an earlier age.

All around this iron house, brush and branches had been piled up and set alight. As there was far more smoke than the flames themselves allowed, I supposed oil of some kind had been used to help ignite the brush. Whoever had set the fire had gone; there was no one to be seen anywhere. I signaled my two companions to join me, and was about to call out to them that once again we had lost our quarry, when I heard a groan.

See, now: I have often enough stood on the battlefield after a bloodletting to have heard the sounds wounded men make, and there was no doubt in my mind that this is what I heard—clear and unmistakable, the sound of a broken man moaning over his wounds.

"Here!" I cried. "Someone is hurt!" Darting forward, I ran to the iron house and looked inside.

Llenlleawg lay on his side, curled in a tight ball. His head was a bloody mass, and his eyes were closed. I called to him, but could not rouse him.

"It is Llenlleawg!" I shouted to the others. "Hurry!"

Desperately wishing for some way to carry water from the well, I threw myself upon the nearest of the fallen rooftrees instead. Tallaght and Peredur flew to my side as I lifted the ancient timber in my arms. It was good oak, strong still, and though broken in the middle, long enough to serve. Dragging the wooden beam to the cage, I began using it to push the burning brush away.

Peredur was first to reach me and added his strength to mine. Within a dozen heartbeats we had cleared a path to the cagework house.

"Get another beam!" I shouted to Tallaght, who returned carrying the other half of the timber I had found. Peredur saw what I intended, and before I could give the order, he ran to a nearby stone, gathered it up in his arms, and carried it to the firebreak we had cleared. There he threw down the stone and we drove in with our timbers—wedging them between the lowest bars of the cage and, using the stone, levering the ironwork off the ground.

Alas, the metal cage was heavy and the stone was not high enough to raise it much. But as Tallaght and I together applied our full strength to the timbers, Peredur leapt to the gap, digging with his hands, scraping away the dirt until he had succeeded in scooping out a hollow just big enough for a man.

Squirming on his back, his face a hairbreadth from the hot metal, Peredur wormed under the bar and into the cage. Rolling onto his feet, he leapt to Llenlleawg's side and tried to revive him. Failing that, he seized the stricken Irishman by the arms and began dragging him to the gap.

"Hurry!" growled Tallaght through clenched teeth. "I am losing my grip!"

Smoke stung our eyes and burned our nostrils, but we clung tight to the timbers as Peredur tugged the unconscious Llenlleawg to the shallow hole he had dug. Then, diving under the hot iron, he positioned himself flat on his stomach and reached back for Llenlleawg.

"For God's sake," groaned Tallaght, the cords in his neck bulging. "Hurry! I cannot hold it!"

"Stand firm, lad," I told him sternly. "It is almost finished."

"Agh!" Tallaght gasped, red-faced, his eyes shut against the strain. His shoulders were shaking.

"Steady now," I told him. "Just a little longer."

Peredur, meanwhile, had succeeded in pulling the Irish champion halfway through. The body was now stuck, however, and the young warrior could not budge it. "He is wedged in," Peredur cried. "Raise the cage higher!"

"Christ—" cried Tallaght, "—mercy!"

"On your feet!" I told Peredur. "Take him under the arms."

Scrambling up, the young warrior grabbed Llenlleawg under the arms and pulled with all his might. The uncon-

scious body moved a fraction and then stopped. Tallaght
groaned.

"Quickly!" I grunted, my own strength beginning to
fail.

Seeing there was nothing for it, Peredur raised his foot
and placed it against the hot iron. Straining, every sinew
taut, he threw back his head and gave a mighty heave,
lifting Llenlleawg and pulling him through the gap. In the
same instant, Tallaght's strength gave out and he fainted.
The sudden weight sent the timbers flying, and I was
hurled onto my side as the iron cagework house slammed
to the ground.

Llenlleawg was free. Peredur lay half atop him, panting
with his exertion. I ran to them both. "Well done!" I
cried. "Here, help me get him away from the flames."

Together we hauled the unconscious champion clear of
his would-be grave. We found a place by one of the standing walls, and I left the two of them there while I returned
for Tallaght.

I dragged him away from the fire, and marked that the
flames were already burning themselves out. The young
warrior awoke as I tried to lift him, and with my aid was
able to stagger to the wall, where he collapsed once more
and lay groaning gently to himself. I knew how he felt;
both head and heart were pounding, my breath came in
ragged gasps, my hands were raw, and my side ached
where the beam had caught me as it tore from my grasp.

"Rest easy," I told them, gulping air. "It is over. We
are safe now. All is well."

Brave words, as it turned out.

Chapter Twelve

Power as I possess is not, as many believe, given in exchange for a soul. To hear the ignorant speak, one would think it merely a simple bargain, an exchange of vows, perhaps, and the power one seeks simply flows from the fingertips for the asking. But no, it is not so easy as that! The truly great gifts are not gifts at all, but treasures obtained after long and difficult searching, prizes won only through hard-fought victories over relentless, near-invincible adversaries.

True power of the kind I possess is achieved only through the most rigorous and exhausting means, and few mortals have even the slightest notion of the enormous discipline that must be brought to bear at every step of the journey. For it is a journey—proceeding from strength to strength, adding skill to skill, eminence to eminence, following the long and arduous path to complete mastery.

The first eminence is the mastery of silence, in which the adept must forsake all communication with others. No external thought or word must be allowed to intrude or distract; no other voice can be heeded or heard. The adept must abandon all contact with other minds. This leads to the second eminence, wherein the adept gains the ability to project thoughts and images into other beings, and wherein emotional atmospheres are generated and manipulated. With mastery also comes control over animal life and the ability to command animals to one's bidding.

The third eminence allows the adept to project one's image over distance at will—to be in two places, three places at once, and in different forms. In the forth eminence, the adept acquires profound knowledge of plant and vegetable essences, the deep and intimate awareness of the nature and use of plant life in extracts and elixirs.

Gaining the fifth eminence grants mastery over the movements of air and water, and the command of fire. Weather can be manipulated and controlled in localized regions. The sixth eminence leads on to the ability to pass into etheric form, to dissolve one's physical presence— disappearing in one place and reappearing in another, whole and complete.

In the mastery of the seventh, and last, eminence, the adept achieves the ability to prolong physical life indefinitely. The adept acquires the ability to halt the normal human aging process, and even reverse it when necessary. Without this, all that came before would be too soon rendered useless.

The ignorant speak of hidden arts, but they are not hidden. Indeed, there is nothing secret about them at all; they are freely open and available to any who would pursue them. Ah, but the price! The price is nothing less than the devotion of an entire life. So perhaps the simple-minded are right, after all, in thinking of the acquisition of power as a pact in which the soul is bartered. There is no other way.

Leaving the others to restore themselves, I walked back over the hill to fetch the horses and, with some difficulty, brought them within the confines of the ruined caer. The horses shied from entering the place, and it took all my coaxing just to get them to pass through the gate. Once inside, they twitched and shivered as if they were cold, and stamped the ground anxiously. Nevertheless, I tethered them nearby and, retrieving the two waterskins from behind the saddles, hastened back to the ruined wall.

Kneeling beside Llenlleawg, I wet the edge of my cloak and dabbed it to his lips. He did not stir.

"Is he dead?" asked Peredur; he gathered his legs beneath him and came to stand over me.

Putting my face near Llenlleawg's, I felt his breath light on my cheek. "He lives, never fear," I told the young warrior. "Let us see what they have done to him."

Thus I proceeded to clean his wounds; pouring water on a strip of cloth torn from the lower edge of my siarc, I washed away the dirt and blood from his face and neck.

He had been soundly beaten, taking many blows to the head, and several of these had been hard enough to break the skin. His left eye was red and puffy; dark blood caked his nostrils and oozed from the nasty gash on his lower lip. His cloak was gone, and much of his shirt, as well as his belt and weapons. Whoever made bold to separate this Irishman from spear or knife most certainly paid a fearful price for their audacity: of that I had no doubt.

Save for some bruises on his shoulders, and scrapes on his arms and wrists, there were no other wounds that I could see. Apparently, his attackers had been satisfied to beat him senseless before throwing him into the iron house—they would never have gotten him inside it any other way.

The horses began neighing just then, so Tallaght, having regained himself somewhat, got up to see what was bothering them. He walked away shaking the cramps from his arms.

"A cruel death," observed Peredur, looking around almost fearfully. "It is fortunate we found him when we did. Who would want to do such a thing?"

"When we discover that, we will have pierced the mystery to its core," I replied, and turned once more to Llenlleawg. I tore another strip from the bottom edge of my siarc, wet it, and applied it to his battered face. This brought a moan from the Irishman's throat. He wheezed and black phlegm came to his lips. I dabbed it away with the edge of the wet cloth. "There, cough it all up," I told him. "Get rid of it."

At the sound of my voice, his eyelids flew open, and he surged up all at once as if he would flee.

"Be easy, Llenlleawg," I said, placing my hand on his

chest so that he would not do himself further injury. "Lie back. All is well. Your enemies are gone."

He slumped back with a sighing groan, then fell to hacking so hard I thought his ribs would crack. He coughed up the vile black stuff, spitting again and again, only to cough up more.

"Drink a little," I offered, bringing the waterskin to his mouth. "It will revive you."

As the water touched his lips, a troubled expression appeared on his face and he made to rise once more. "Rest yourself, brother," I said. "It is Gwalchavad here. There is nothing to fear."

Recognition came into his eyes at last; he ceased resisting and lay back, allowing me to give him a drink. He drank greedily, swallowing it down in great draughts as if he had not had any water in days. I tried to pull the waterskin away, but he grabbed my wrist and held it in place and gulped until he choked, spewing blackened water from his nose and mouth.

"Here, now! We did not pull you from the flames to drown you," I said. "Drink slowly. There is plenty."

He released my hand and slumped back. His mouth worked and he tried to speak, but it was some time before he could make himself understood. "Gwalchavad," he said, his voice raw and wispy, "you found . . . me . . ."

"We have been following your trail for days. I am sorry we did not arrive sooner—we might have saved you a beating."

"I am—" he began, then fell to coughing again, ". . . you found me . . ."

"Who did this to you?"

Before he could answer, I heard a shout. It was Peredur calling me to come running. Llenlleawg started at the sound. "Peace, brother. It is one of the Cymbrogi," I explained quickly. "Leave it to me."

"How many—" he gasped, ". . . with you?"

"Only two of the younger warriors," I said, rising. "If I had known we were going to be riding the length and breadth of Llyonesse, I would have brought the entire Dragon Flight. Rest easy; I will return directly."

I found Peredur beside Tallaght, who was standing with his arms half raised and crossed at the wrists as if to protect himself from a beating. Peredur, his hand on Tallaght's shoulder, spoke to him while shaking him gently. The horses, meanwhile, had not ceased their neighing—if anything, their distress had only increased.

"What is it?" I snapped, irritated at his failure to accomplish this simplest of chores.

"I cannot wake him," Peredur said.

I gave the young man a sour look to show him what I thought of his ludicrous explanation, and turned to Tallaght. But behold! Though he stood upright with his eyes open wide, in all other respects he appeared fast asleep, seeming neither to see nor to hear, but remaining unmoved through all of Peredur's exertions, a rapt expression on his face as if held in thrall to a dream of such pleasant aspect that he would not be roused.

Baffled and alarmed, I reached out and took the young warrior by the arm; the muscle was tensed hard, solid as wood, yet Tallaght appeared tranquil, with no sign of strain in either face or form. Next, I put my face close to his and discerned the faint stirring of his breath on my skin.

"Tallaght!" I cried sharply. "Wake up!"

The young warrior gave not the slightest indication that he had heard. Taking him by the shoulder, I shook him so to rattle his bones. As before, this raised no response. Seeing that his arms were folded, I took hold of his right arm and tried to straighten it, as if to break the spell. I could sooner have broken his arm, for, try as I might, there was no unbending that rigid limb—except by violent force, which would not have helped in the least.

After jostling and shouting some more, I admitted defeat and desisted. "I tell you the truth, Peredur," I declared, turning once more to the awestricken youth, "I have never seen the like. He has become a living corpse."

Peredur gaped. "What are we to do with him?"

"I cannot say," I replied, regarding the stiffened form before us. "But I would not leave him here like this. I suppose we must lay him down somewhere." Casting a

quick glance at the sky, I added, "Llenlleawg is not well
enough to travel yet, and we are losing the day. We will
make camp in the hall and see what tomorrow brings."

"Spend the night here?" Peredur wondered with alarm.

"Where else?" I countered angrily. "Here at least we
have stout walls at our backs, water, and a fire. It is as
good a place as we are likely to find in this accursed
land."

Too shocked to object farther, Peredur closed his mouth
and stared at me in dismay.

"Now, then," I said, "let us carry Tallaght to the hall
and make him comfortable until he wakes."

"What," asked Peredur, "if he does not wake?"

"See here," I snapped, "I am not liking this any more
than you, but there is nothing else to do."

Together we eased the young warrior onto the ground
and, lifting him between us, began carrying him to the
hall. Tallaght, gazing dreamily skyward, remained placidly unaware of his rough handling; we might have been
toting a plank for all Tallaght sagged or complained. We
moved him to a place beside one of the standing walls
and, after clearing away the stones, laid the sleeping warrior on his back. In this position, his resemblance to a
corpse grew the stronger. Tearing yet another strip off my
siarc, I wet it, folded it, and placed it over Tallaght's
eyes—as much to hide his dead, unblinking stare as to
protect his sight.

It was while I was about this chore that I saw the bite—
a small, neat circle of reddish marks on the side of his
neck where sharp-pointed teeth had broken the skin. If I
had not seen it before, I would have said it was the bite
of an animal, a small dog or weasel, perhaps. But I had
seen it before: on Rhys' arm. Rhys knew nothing of how
he had gotten it, and I was none the wiser for having seen
two, but I knew Tallaght did not have it before he went
to see to the horses.

"Now what are we to do?" asked Peredur when I finished.

"Now we make camp," I said. I saw no reason to
mention the bite to Peredur; frightening him would serve

no purpose. "Water the horses, Peredur, and—" I stopped myself, and corrected my command. "Better still, we will both water the horses, and when that is finished, we will tether them within the hall."

This we did, and our various chores occupied the fast-fading day. A gray shroud of clouds moved in from the sea to obscure the sun and cast a dusky pall over the ruined stronghold. We took wood and live embers from the remains of the fire around the iron house, and used them to make our campfire. Now and then I paused to tend our stricken brothers, but there was little to be done for either of them. Tallaght had not altered a whit since we placed him on the ground, and Llenlleawg, having drunk a little water and received dressing for his wounds, slept now—coughing from time to time, and stirring fitfully, but never waking.

While we worked, we talked, Peredur and I, for it helped to keep our courage up; I confess, I could feel the fear stealing over me as the daylight abandoned us to the long, dark night. As the shadows bloomed and spread over the ruins, I felt as if we were being stalked. I imagined cold eyes watching us from all the dark places . . . watching and waiting.

We gathered more brush and branches—enough to keep the fire during the night—and, with the dull twilight closing around us, made a simple meal from our provisions. Neither of us ate more than a few mouthfuls as we sat hunched before the fire, gazing at the rubble heaps and fallen timbers around us while the wan flames flickered over the ruins.

When we finished eating, we banked the fire and gathered our cloaks around us to sleep—if sleep were possible. With the night, a heavy stillness descended over the valley and its ancient keep—a cold, unnatural silence, which stifled all sound and made us feel as if each belabored breath we drew might be our last.

Twice my care-wracked drowse was broken by the sound of an owl. The creature's soft trilling call drifted down from the crumbling tower above. I woke and looked around to see a sickly moon rising over the broken wall.

In elder times the call of Wisdom's Bird was deemed an unchancy thing, portending ill fortune for the wretch who heard it. Some, I ween, believe it still. Now, I am of no such mind to take fright at bird sounds in the night, but this night the call made me think of winter and graves and death stealing light and life from the eyes.

After the third call, Peredur awakened. I saw him start and then leap up. The owl, startled by the sudden movement below, swooped off, flapping its broad wings slowly. Peredur crouched, his hands tensed, staring furiously around him as if he meant to take flight, too.

"Peace, lad," I murmured softly. "It was only an owl."

But he seemed not to hear. Taking two or three steps away, he stopped, then said, "No! Wait! Very well, I will go with you!"

So saying, he threw aside his cloak and started away, as if he meant to follow someone who even now led him swiftly from the camp. I thought to call after him, but held my tongue, rose, and went after him. Peredur walked through the caer and out the gate, making straight for the blighted wood. Looking neither right nor left, he ran, leaping like a stag over the crosswise boles, quickly outdistancing myself, who scrambled clumsily in the dark with only the half of a pale moon to light my way.

Avowed to the task, I pressed on, however, following the sound of his reckless flight as the cracking of dry undergrowth gave me direction. I struggled on as best I could, trying to avoid impaling myself on the ragged ends of broken branches. As I slid over a fallen trunk, I felt something soft beneath my feet and reached down to retrieve a siarc—Peredur's siarc, to be sure. I crashed on a few more paces and found his breecs dangling from an upthrust limb.

Has he gone mad? I wondered, gathering the clothes into a bundle under my arm, and running on.

A dozen paces more and the sound of his flight abruptly ceased. It took me a moment to realize I no longer heard him anywhere ahead of me. I listened, turning my head this way and that to catch any stray sound which might betray the spot where he had gone to ground. Again, I made to call out to him, but something checked my impulse. My senses, already alert, quickened as in the heat of the hunt, and I picked my way forward in stealth, stopping every few paces to listen before moving on.

In this way I proceeded, quietly, warily, my skin tingling with an eerie anticipation. I came to a place in the blighted wood where three huge trees had fallen one across another to form a rough enclosure. I crept nearer and looked over this rude wall, and there in the center of the clearing lay Peredur, sprawled naked on the ground. And on his bare chest a small, hunched black creature was lowering its flat head.

Chapter Thirteen

My heart seized in my chest. I stared at the creature, not daring to draw breath. The thing was squat and repulsive, with two long arms and a large-skulled, flat head. Its short legs were drawn up as it sat on its rump, its back curved sharply as its dark head descended towards Peredur's face.

At first I feared the thing must have killed him, for the young warrior lay with arms and legs splayed out as he had fallen. But as that ghastly head drew near, Peredur moaned. By that I knew he lived.

Instantly, my hand went to the sword belt at my side. As my fingers closed and began to draw the weapon forth, the creature halted and, quick as a cat, turned its gaze on me. A more grotesque face I never want to see: low-browed and thin-jawed, with a nose like a shriveled leaf, nostrils a-twitch as it sniffed the air; a goatlike mouth with long yellow teeth gaped open in a hiss of warning. Two wide, pale eyes menaced me from beneath the heavy brow as the head sank lower onto the shoulders and the long hands clutched at its prize.

Great King, save your servant! I thought, and the thought was answered by a low guttural growl bubbling up from the hideous creature's throat. I fell back.

With a scream, the creature leapt from Peredur's chest, charging straight at me with terrible swiftness. I stumbled back another step, tripped over broken wood, and fell down. The thing was upon me in an instant. The beast's

awful breath smelled of rotted meat and foul decay. I felt
its sudden weight upon my chest, driving the breath from
my lungs. I made to throw the creature off, but could no
longer raise my arms. It was as if all the strength had
gone from my limbs, and I could but lie and watch in
horror as the odious thing lowered its face towards mine.

Alas, for me! I could not move. I could not breathe.

The repugnant head dropped slowly nearer, and the
toothy mouth opened. Striving with all my might, I could
not so much as lift my smallest finger. I felt myself
gripped tight by a strength greater than my own.

Closer, drooling now, the evil mouth drew nearer, and
nearer yet. I saw the small, neat, sharp teeth as the mouth
opened and the creature prepared to bite.

My lungs burned. Frozen fast, I could but watch the
dread face slowly descend, its baleful eyes blotting out all
else, filling my sight, staring into my soul.

Even as I watched—I could do no else!—the face utterly changed and I found myself beholding the face of a
woman, a beauty more lovely than any other I had ever
known. Lithe-limbed and supple, she reached to gather
me in her gentle arms, her long dark hair falling down
around her white shoulders. Her breasts were full and
round, and wonderful to look upon; her shapely hips were
smooth and her long legs folded beneath her. She smiled,
and her teeth were fine and white and straight. A goddess
could not be more beautiful, I think, and despite my fear,
desire stirred within me.

She lowered herself to cover me with her fair body,
and I felt myself drawn into her embrace. My lungs
swelled to bursting, yet I could not draw breath. The
blood beat in my temples and dark mist gathered before
my eyes. God help me, I rose to meet her.

Then, even as I felt the sweet gentleness of her soft lips
on mine, and felt my breath drawn from my mouth, there
came a shriek so loud, so piercing, I feared my head
would split. In the same instant, the woman vanished, and
the beast appeared once more, its mouth open in a scream
of rage.

I sensed a swift movement above me and a dark shape

descending. The loathsome thing made to leap away, but the falling shape caught the creature full on its flattened skull with a tremendous crack. The monster threw back its head and howled. Crack! The dark shape sent it sprawling.

Suddenly I could breathe again. Good air came rushing into my mouth and lungs, and I gulped it down like a drowning man who has risen from the killing depths.

Peredur was standing over me, the broken end of a massive branch in his hands. His jaw was set and his eyes were narrowed. Still gasping, I turned my gaze to where he was looking, and saw the black beast writhing on the ground, biting itself in agony.

"Blessed Jesu," I gasped, "save us."

At these simple words, the vile thing loosed a shriek yet more terrible than any I had ever heard. There came a sizzling sound and it vanished into a sudden vapor, leaving behind only the echo of its tortured scream, and a stench of bile and vomit.

Peredur turned to me. He tried to speak, but lacked words to equal the event, and so closed his mouth and gazed in wonder at the place where the beast had disappeared. Then he raised the club in his hand and looked at it as if he did not know how it had come to be there. He threw the weapon aside with an expression of disgust. "I feared it might have killed you," he said, almost apologetically.

"You did the right thing," I assured him.

Peredur shivered and glanced down. Only then did he realize that he was naked. He glanced guiltily at me, but I turned away so he would have no need to make the explanation he was struggling to find. I knew well what had been in his mind when he shed both siarc and breecs.

"Your clothes are here," I told him, gathering up the bundle where I had dropped it. He accepted the clothing with shamefaced gratitude. "I did not see what happened to your boots."

"I—I mean, it was—" he stammered.

"Save your breath, lad," I advised gently. "You owe me neither explanation nor confession. We were attacked, and fought it off. There is nothing else to say."

Peredur closed his mouth and began drawing on his breecs. We then picked our way back to the ruined hall. Our camp, I was relieved to find, remained undisturbed; both Llenlleawg and Tallaght slept soundly.

"Lord, let us leave at once," said Peredur. "Let us get far away from here before we are attacked again."

Though it was the dead of night, and darker than the inside of a burial mound, I agreed. "We may not get far in this darkness," I told him, "but at least we will get away from here."

We quickly saddled the horses and prepared to depart, then turned to wake the sleepers. Despite our vigorous attempts to raise them, however, the two slept on. Nothing we did made the slightest difference. "Let us put them on the horses anyway," suggested Peredur in desperation.

"We would have to tie them to the saddle," I replied, "to keep them from sliding off at every step. No, Peredur, as much as I wish to be gone from here, we could easily come to greater harm stumbling around like blind men in the dark. If we are going to be hauling men like mealbags on horseback, I think we must wait until daylight." Indicating his feet, I said, "You cannot walk back to Ynys Avallach barefoot."

With great misgiving and greater dread, Peredur set about building up the fire and together we stood watch for the rest of the night, weapons in hand, our backs to the flames as we searched the darkness, talking to one another to keep fear at bay.

Dawn seemed a long time coming. When the sun finally rose, it cast but a wan gray light over us—as on those days in the north when the mist comes down and lingers on the heathered hills, but there was no cooling mist, and the hills hereabouts held only dry scrub and thorns.

As soon as it grew light enough to see the path, we broke camp. Peredur retraced his steps to the blighted wood, returning quickly with his boots, anxious to get away from the ruined caer as soon as possible. We turned to the sleepers and tried again to wake them. Tallaght had finally lost the unnatural rigidity of his limbs, and now lay peacefully asleep. I bent to remove the strip of cloth from his eyes and the young man came awake at my first touch. Up he charged, as if from a bed of live coals. He flew into me, fists flying, kicking, biting, shouting incoherently.

"Here! Here, now!" I cried, fending off the blows as well as I could.

Peredur leapt to my aid and pulled him off me. "Peace!" he bellowed. "Peace, brother!" Wrapping his arms around Tallaght's torso, he threw him to the ground and fell on top of him to hold him down, all the time shouting, "Peace! We are your friends."

Kneeling beside him, I struck the struggling warrior sharply on the cheek. "Tallaght, wake!"

At the sound of his name, the fight went out of him. He looked from one to the other of us with frightened eyes as recognition slowly came to him. "Oh!" he said, squeezing his eyes shut.

"Let him up, Peredur," I said, and we raised him between us, where he stood wobbling on his feet like a man with a headful of ale.

"It is over, Tallaght. You are back among the living," I told him.

He lurched towards me and seized my arm with both hands. "Lord Gwalchavad, forgive me. I thought . . . I thought you were—" He released my arm and clutched his head as if it hurt him. "Oh, Jesu save me, I had the strangest dream."

"It is over, lad," I said. "Are you well?"

"I feel as if I have slept a thousand years," he answered dreamily, "and yet, as if I had closed my eyes but a moment ago." He then began babbling about his curious dream, but I brought him to a halt before he could gallop any futher. "Plenty of time to talk once we are on the trail," I told him sharply. "The horses are ready; we are leaving at once."

I left him to Peredur and turned to Llenlleawg, who, though stiff and aching from his beating, at least had his natural wits about him. He roused himself slowly when I woke him, and made to sit up, wincing with pain at the effort. I put my arm beneath his shoulders and raised him. "How do you feel, brother?"

"Never better," he rasped, his voice raw as a wound. He then hacked up a gob of blackened gall and spat it on the ground. "Have I been long asleep?"

"Not long," I allowed. "Only all night and half the day besides."

"I see." He licked his dry lips. "How did you find me?"

"We saw the smoke. Can you sit a horse?"

"I will sit a goat if it bears me from this place," he answered. "Bring it on, brother, and the sooner we quit this accursed ruin, the better I will be. Have you seen the girl?"

"We have seen no one here but you," I told him. "Was she with you?"

When he made no reply to this, I said, "Llenlleawg, was she with you? Did she have a hand in this?"

Llenlleawg attempted to sit up again; his face contorted against the pain. "Wait a moment," I told him. "Let me help you." So saying, I retrieved a spear and put it in Llenlleawg's right hand. Then, squatting behind him, I took him under the left arm; the Irish champion gripped the spear shaft and pulled himself up as I lifted, and with much groaning and clenching of teeth we got him standing—shakily, and swaying like a wind-tossed sapling, but standing all the same. Then he was racked with coughing; I steadied him as he cleared his lungs of yet more black muck.

"It is not as bad as I thought," Llenlleawg gasped, squinting and pressing his left hand to his side as he leaned on the spear. "At least," he wheezed, ". . . there is no blood."

"The young woman, Llenlleawg—was she here?" I asked again.

"I cannot remember."

"But you were following her," I insisted. "You must have followed her into Llyonesse. She must have led you here."

Llenlleawg regarded me dully, then turned his face away. "As I said, I do not remember."

"What do you remember?"

"Nothing much," he said, shaking his head slowly. "I remember following the trail and crossing into Llyonesse. There was a beacon, and I went to see what it meant, and"—he paused abruptly—". . . and I cannot remember anything after that."

Obviously, there was more he would not say, but I did not know how to make him tell me. "Well," I conceded, "you are safe now, and we are returning to Ynys Avallach. No doubt you will remember more later." He nodded grimly, and I shouted for Peredur to bring one of the horses. "Come," I said, taking Llenlleawg by the arm, "lean on me; I will bear you up."

Together, Peredur and I lifted the tall Irishman between us, boosted him to the saddle, and put the reins into his hands. "Let us be gone from here," I said, leading the horse forward.

We quit the ruined fortress, passing once more beneath the crumbling tower and out through the gate. We crossed the ditches and headed north, hastening back along the trail that had brought us, traveling quickly and quietly—at least as quietly as four men might, and as quickly as possible when two of the four must go afoot. Peredur and I walked beside our two ailing companions to help steady them in the saddle and keep them from falling. We allowed ourselves but little rest, so, despite the footling pace, we made good distance on the day.

Indeed, by the time the gloomy twilight gathered round us, we were well on our way home. We camped in the dry streambed of a little cramped glen, and ate from our dwindling store of provisions, took turns at the watch through the night, and pushed on at first light next morning. No further disasters befell us, nor did anything out of the ordinary give cause for alarm. However, when we came in sight of the estuary where I had lost my horse to the quicksand some days before, a sense of dire foreboding came upon me.

There was, of course, no visible reminder of that terrible event, but the place seemed steeped in dolor and gloom. I could almost feel its spirit, restless with anguish, sad and hungry and forlorn. I felt cold and unhappy, and thoughts of death and desolation swarmed in my head.

There was nothing for it but to continue on, and to put as much distance as we could between us and the sinister place before turning aside to make camp for the night. The rest of the journey to Ynys Avallach proved uneventful, and Tallaght so improved that, though we traveled no more swiftly, at least we were able to share the horse between us. Thus, on the evening of the sixth day, we came in sight of the Fisher King's stronghold—glinting like white gold in the dusky light, its fine walls and towers reflected in the reed-fringed pool below. Weary, and more than a little footsore—I suppose I have spent too much time in the saddle these past years—we paused to gaze upon that tranquil sight and let it fill our souls with the pleasure of its serenity.

Then, our hearts lifted, and the vision of our destination lending speed to weary feet, we hastened on, arriving just as the abbey bell tolled for evening prayers. I know the good monks have a word for this, as they have a word for everything else in their peculiar world, but I know not what it is; or if I have been told, I remain ignorant of it. No matter what its name, this prayer at the closing of the day has always seemed to me one of the finer things of their occupation. Perhaps one day, when sword and spear no longer rule my days, I may give myself to such pleasant contemplation as those good brothers now enjoy.

As the slow-tolling bell rang out over the Summer Realm, we passed the silent shrine and put our feet to the upward-winding path leading to the Tor, pausing at the top to look out upon the land below, softly fading into the pale blue shadows. Then, as we turned to enter the yard, I heard a cry of welcome. Rhys came running, bursting with questions I had no wish to answer more than once.

"Peace, brother," I said, gripping his shoulder. "All will be told—and there is much to tell—only let us get a drink down our throats first."

"Leave the horses," Rhys said. "I will send someone to attend them." Turning to the others, he called, "Come inside. The Pendragon has been waiting for you, he has given—" It was then that he caught sight of Llenlleawg—head down, slumped in the saddle, almost fainting with exhaustion—and Peredur holding the reins and walking beside him. "What is this?" Rhys exclaimed, dashing to his side. "Is he wounded?"

"Help us get him down," I said, and explained that we had found him beaten and left for dead. "He will recover, never fear. However, a few days' food and rest would not be wasted on him, I think."

We hauled the unresisting Irishman down from the saddle, whereupon he seemed to come to himself once more, insisting that he could walk and would not be lugged into the hall like a sack of grain. He grew so adamant that we let him have his way. Truly, I think he had been nursing his strength for this moment; he was that proud he did not wish to be seen in his weakness by his swordbrothers, nor could he bear causing his beloved queen even a moment's worry.

As it happened, he need not have concerned himself. The hall was empty: no Cymbrogi to be seen, and few of Avallach's folk, either. Rhys, to all appearances, was king of the rock, and held dominion over the few who came and went. He called a command to one of the young Fair Folk lads I saw hurrying away on some errand; the fellow spun on his heel and raced to obey.

Had I given the matter more than a fleeting thought, I would have expected our arrival to occasion greater interest than we had so far received. "Where is everyone?" I asked as we stepped into the empty hall.

"The plague has worsened in the southlands," Rhys replied. "Charis and most of the monks have gone to Londinium to join Paulus in the fight. Lord Avallach is at his prayers. As for the others, they will return when it gets dark."

"Well and good," I told him. "But where are they now?"

Rhys called for the welcome cup, and then turned to look at me. "I thought you knew."

"How should I know?" I countered sourly. "And unless someone tells me, I fear I shall die in ignorance."

"They are at the shrine," Rhys replied, as if we should have known.

"We saw no one at the shrine," I told him bluntly, "or I would not have asked."

"Not *that* shrine," Rhys said, "the new one—Arthur's shrine. The king is building a shrine to the cup."

Llenlleawg, flanked by the two young warriors, drew up beside us. "What cup would that be?"

"The Holy Cup." Rhys paused and regarded us dubiously. "Do none of you know any of this?"

I reminded him that we had journeyed all the way from Llyonesse—on foot most of the way—and were not of a mood to appreciate riddles.

"It is to be the Grail Shrine," Rhys announced tersely. "The Pendragon has decreed a shrine to be built to house the Holy Cup, which he has taken as the sign and emblem of his reign. Arthur believes a great blessing will flow from this Grail to the benefit of Britain, and of all the world."

"Is this the same cup that healed Arthur?" asked Peredur.

"One and the same," confirmed Rhys.

"I know the cup you mean," I said, as the memory came winging back to me as from a great distance. "You mean to say that you have seen it?"

"No one has seen it," Rhys replied, "save Avallach, Myrddin, and, now, Arthur. Avallach knows where it is—he keeps it hidden somewhere, I think. Now you know as much as anyone else about it."

The boy appeared bearing the requested welcome bowl. Rhys took it, raised it, spoke a word of greeting, and delivered the bowl into my hands. I passed it at once to Llenlleawg, and waited for the others to finish before taking it up once more. The ale was cool, dark, and frothy, soothing my parched tongue and throat like milk mixed with honey. I drank a long draught and, with great reluctance, passed it along once more. The bowl made the round again, and Rhys said he would have food brought so that we might refresh ourselves while we waited for the others.

"Now I must send for Myrddin," he told us, preparing to dash away once more. "He has spent the last three days telling everyone to bring word the moment you returned."

Chapter Fourteen

"No doubt this new shrine has everyone occupied," Tallaght mumbled, staring into the empty cup as into a fresh grave.

Alone with a dry bowl in a deserted hall, we sat glumly considering our sorry homecoming. Haggard and harried, gray with dust, bone weary, we wore every step of our peculiar journey on our clothes and on our faces.

"Well," remarked Peredur, "it is not as if anyone knew we would be returning just now. Even so . . ."

Llenlleawg, above remarking on his disappointment, said nothing, but closed his eyes and bowed his head, fatigued and dispirited. The one welcome he sought above all others—that of his king—and for which he had rallied his dwindling strength, was denied him, and exhaustion was rapidly overtaking him.

"There will be time enough for glad greetings," I told them, trying to put a more favorable face on the thing. "As for me, I can think of nothing better than a bite to eat and a quiet drink before meeting the others."

The food arrived a few moments later, and upon sending the serving boy back to refill the bowl, we fell to eating, content with a little peaceful quiet to soothe our wearied souls. We ate in silence, and I was just reaching for a second barley loaf when I heard quick, purposeful footsteps enter the hall. I knew before raising my eyes to his greeting that Myrddin had found me.

"At last!" he said, gliding to the table in a single swift

motion—like a hawk falling upon its unsuspecting prey. "You have returned at last. Is the woman with you?"

"And it is Earth and Sky to see you, too, Wise Emrys," I replied. "I do hope you have fared well while we were away."

He regarded me sharply, and dismissed my lackluster attempt at scorn with an impatient flick of his hand. "Tell me what happened."

"I will, and gladly," I replied. "But it may be best if we permit my companions to leave now—I know they are anxious to wash and rest."

Myrddin's quick golden eyes turned to Llenlleawg, and he perceived in an instant what I meant. "Forgive me," he said, stepping smoothly to the Irishman's side. "I have been too distracted to notice your distress. How can I help you, Llenlleawg?"

The champion raised his head and forced a waxy smile. "I am well, Emrys. Only let me rest a little and I will greet my king and queen in a better humor." He made to rise, but lacked the strength and fell back in his chair.

"Here!" said Peredur, jumping up. "If you will excuse us, Lord Emrys, Tallaght and I will see to Llenlleawg."

The two of them raised Llenlleawg between them. Too tired to pretend otherwise any longer, the proud Irishman allowed himself to be helped to his feet. Once steadied, however, he pushed away their offered hands and moved from the hall with a slow, sore gait. The young warriors respectfully took their leave and hurried off to the warriors' quarters to find a bath and change of clothes.

When they had gone, I returned to the table. Myrddin seated himself on the bench opposite me, folded his arms on the board, and leaned close. "Now, then, there is no one to overhear," he said, leveling his keen hawklike gaze upon me. "Your confessor waits before you. Tell me everything."

"There is trouble," I told him bluntly. "I cannot say what it is, but, Myrddin, I deeply fear it."

I then began to relate all that had happened during our sojourn in Llyonesse, and it did me good, for I felt the burden lift from my soul as I told him about the strange trials we had endured in that godforsaken realm—from losing my horse in the false sands to our encounter with the beast in the night. Myrddin listened all the while, nodding to himself from time to time, as if the incidents I relayed confirmed something he already knew or suspected. At last I concluded, saying, "That we escaped with only the loss of one horse is a wonder. Indeed, we were beset from the moment we entered Llyonesse. God save me, Myrddin, it is a desolate region—with but one settlement that I could see, and that a ruin."

"Llyonesse. . . ." He muttered the word as if it hurt his mouth to say it. "A wasteland by another name. The dead rest uneasy there."

"In truth," I replied, and confessed to seeing the Mithrian lepers.

"I have not heard of them for a long time," Myrddin mused.

"You know them?" I wondered.

"When I was a boy, my grandfather Elphin used to tell me stories about the Lost Legion. I never thought to hear about them again." He paused for a moment, reflecting unhappily. Then, glancing at me again, he said, "This fortress—how did you find it?"

"From the smoke," I replied, then described coming upon the ruin and finding Llenlleawg trapped in the ironwork house inside the caer. "Do you know the place?" I asked.

"From what you tell me, I believe the stronghold you found was Belyn's."

I had never heard the name before, and said so.

"Belyn was Avallach's brother," Myrddin explained. "When the Fair Folk came to Ynys Prydain, they settled first in Llyonesse, but the land was not good to them, so Avallach and his people came here. Belyn, his brother king, would not leave the southlands, so he and his people stayed, and now they are no more."

"The place was more cairn than caer," I pointed out. "Could this have happened so long ago?"

"Yes," the Emrys answered, nodding at the memory, "long and long ago." Turning once more to the subject at hand, he said, "The woman—you never saw her?"

"I never did, Emrys, and I do not know whether Llen-lleawg can tell you more. He said she led him into Llyo-nesse, but seems to remember little else."

"Leave it to me," Myrddin said, rising. "I will speak to him when he is better rested. Now, then, I have kept you from your bath long enough. Go; we will talk again later. I want Arthur to hear what you have to say, but that can wait until tomorrow. Until then, Gwalchavad, I would have you say nothing to anyone else of these matters. I believe treachery stalks the Summer Realm, and I would not care to alert the enemy that we are on his trail."

"Treachery?" His use of the word brought me up short. "Emrys, are you saying one of the Cymbrogi is a trai-tor?"

"Just so," he replied solemnly, moving away. "He has yet to show his hand, but I sense dire purpose in this— no doubt that was why you were allowed to find Llen-lleawg."

"Allowed to find him?" I challenged, jumping to my feet to follow him. "In truth, Myrddin, they meant to kill him! And would have succeeded, too, if we had not seen the smoke and arrived in time to save him."

"If the enemy had wanted him dead, a quick thrust of a blade through the ribs would have sufficed," Myrddin replied, calmly deflecting my objection. "The smoke, on the other hand, was meant to lead you to our Irish friend so that you could rescue him. That, I am persuaded, is one of the few certainties in all of this twisted tale. You rescued him because you were meant to rescue him— nothing more."

"It is absurd!" I concluded, stopping in my tracks. "You make it seem as if we were on a fool's errand."

The Emrys turned back and regarded me with a slow, solemn shake of his head. "Never say it," he intoned gravely. "Never say it, my friend. Something brutal, cruel, and sinister is at work among us—I feel it."

"But why?" I demanded. "To what end?"

Myrddin, troubled now, and hesitant, answered, "In truth, I wish I knew. Still, we would all do well to re-

member this: where great good abides, there great evil
gathers. It is ever so, and we have been warned. We must
all tread very carefully from now on.''

With that he turned and walked away. I glanced uneasily around the hall—feeling unseen eyes on me, watching me—then fled the great empty room and proceeded
at once to the warriors' quarters. Though I expected to
join the others, they had finished by the time I arrived,
and so I had the entire bath to myself.

The room was warm and damp, the air heavy with
steam. Two torches burned in tall stands either side of the
square pool, their flames shimmering and dancing on the
water. I stripped off my filthy clothes and slipped gratefully into the bath. The hot water, heated from the ovens
in the old Roman way, did much to restore me. I confess
I stayed overlong, and perhaps the heat and steam went
to my head, for as I lay back in the soothing water I saw
a black mist gather before my eyes.

I pressed my eyes shut for a long moment and drew a
deep breath, and when I opened my eyes once more, the
mist was gone, but I felt light-headed and queasy. Con-
cluding that I had had more than was good for me, I rose
and was about to climb from the pool when I heard my
name.

"I have been looking for you, Gwalchavad!"

I felt an icy breath on my naked skin and turned. A
woman stood opposite me across the room. Dressed in
long, loose robes of blue and deepest green, her fair hair
shimmering in the feeble torchlight, she was tall and slender, and possessed of the beauty men see only in their
dreams. She was watching me intently, an expression of
approval on her face.

"Woman, who are you?" I said.

"You were but a boy when I last saw you," she said,
drawing a step closer. Her feet made no sound on the flat
stones. "But look at you now—what a fine, handsome
man you are. The very figure of your father. Lot would
be pleased."

Strange to say: until she uttered my father's name, I
did not recognize her. But the instant she invoked Lot,

my heart clutched and my strength flowed out of me like water poured out upon the sand. It was all I could do to hold myself upright.

"Morgian!" I gasped, trembling inwardly as with cold, or with frozen rage.

"My son," she said nicely, extending her arms to me. "Have you no welcome kiss for your mother?"

"You are not my mother," I replied, revulsed. "My mother is dead."

"Poor Gwalchavad," she pouted, folding her hands prettily before her. "And to think I always treated you like a son of my own blood."

"Get away from me, witch," I said. I made to turn away, but could no longer make my limbs obey.

"I would speak to you, dear Gwalchavad," she replied, her voice growing as smooth and sinuous as a serpent coiling around its prey. "There is something I wish you to do."

"Never!" I spat. "I would sooner cut off my hand than lift a finger for you."

"Oh, I think I may find a way to change your mind," she said, her smile beguiling with concealed treason. "Men are such simple creatures, after all."

I tried to speak, and felt my tongue clench in my mouth. My jaws seized up tight.

"You see, I am not to be denied," she continued, stepping nearer. She raised a hand and absently described a figure in the air. I felt my throat constrict and I could not breathe. "It is a small thing—a trifle of no particular consequence. I think you may find it far easier to obey than to refuse."

"I will die first!" I forced the words out through clenched teeth, my jaws aching as if to break.

She raised her head and laughed, her voice warm and lovely. "Charming!" she said, pressing her hands together beneath her chin. "That is exactly what your brother said," she informed me cheerfully. "Alas, poor Gwalcmai. He forced me to take him at his word. Still, I do not expect you to make the same mistake."

"No!" I shrieked, pressing my fists to my eyes. "Jesu, save me!"

There came a fluttering sound like that of wings in flight, and when I opened my eyes, I was once again lying in the water, still alone. One of the torches was out. I rose and looked at the stone floor where Morgian had stood, but despite the steam and damp, there was no trace of any footprint, nor any sign of her at all. I shouted and received only the dull echo of my own voice in return.

Frightened now, I left the bath and fled to the warriors' quarters. There was no one around, and as I dried and dressed, I gradually calmed and convinced myself that it was only a bad dream brought on by fatigue and the uncanny experiences of my recent journey.

When I emerged at last, I had put the thing firmly from my mind and was ready to greet my king and sword-brothers in better spirits. I returned to the hall feeling certain I could devour my weight in roast meat and drain a lake of ale. The babble of voices echoing along the passageway gave me to know that the shrine-builders had returned and a celebration had commenced.

Indeed, the hall was bright with torchlight and full of friends. Laughter and high-spirited talk flowed like a wave out into the night; cups were being passed, and the hearth fire had been laid. Pausing at the threshold, I stood for a moment and counted myself most fortunate among men to behold such a noble gathering. When men and women such as these pass from this worlds-realm, I thought, the world will be a colder place.

Rejecting the thought as unworthy of the occasion, I drew myself up and entered the glad gathering. On the instant, I was hailed and a cup thrust into my hands. I felt a hard clap on my back as I raised the cup, and Cai's voice loud in my ear. "Here!" he cried. "The wanderer returns! How went the hunt, brother?"

Before I could answer, Cador appeared and said, "If my two young kinsmen are to be believed, disaster dogged your trail from dawn to dusk."

"Ah, well," I allowed, following Myrddin's request, "it was never more than a nip at the heel."

Cai laughed, but my careful reply caught Cador's attention. He stepped nearer. "There was trouble?"

"Aye," I replied reluctantly, "there was." Then, raising the cup, I said, "But there is ale in the bowl, and fire on the hearth. Let us talk of happier things." I drank and passed the cup. Wiping foam from my mouth, I said, "Tell me, now, what is this I am hearing about Arthur's new shrine?"

"Och!" cried Cai. "Only a few days, but so much has happened while you were gone, you will be kicking yourself you were not here."

He then plunged into an enthusiastic recounting of the heady events of the past days. The account grew somewhat in the telling, but was well seasoned with remarks from various others who came to greet and welcome me once more into their company. The short of it was that Arthur, having returned to the place of his miraculous healing, had been wakened in the night by a vision of a shrine wherein the Cup of Christ shone forth with a light like the morning sun. The Pendragon took this vision as a sign from the High King of Heaven that he should build a dwelling for the Grail. The abbot and monks were consulted, and for two days, Arthur and Bishop Elfodd sat head-to-head over bits of slate on which the Pendragon scratched drawings to represent the shrine he had seen in his vision.

Elfodd and Arthur . . . I wondered at this pairing, but kept my thoughts to myself and allowed Cai to finish, which he did eventually, saying, "We have sent to Londinium for men who know how to work with stone."

"Stone?" I asked. "The shrine is to be of stone?"

"Stone, aye," replied Cai. "Arthur wants it to last a thousand years!"

"Ten thousand!" offered a nearby listener.

"Forever!" put in another.

"The work has begun already?"

"It has that," confirmed Cador. "The site has been chosen and the ground has been cleared. We have been cutting trees all day, and pulling up stumps. I tell you the truth, Gwalchavad, you have had the easier time of it. I was never born to drive oxen.''

When talk turned again to how I had fared on my journey, I made the excuse that I was starving and suggested we join those at the board, where the food was now arriving. I looked for Arthur and Gwenhwyvar, but did not see them anywhere among the throng—made up of Cymbrogi, for the most part, with a few monks and a smattering of Fair Folk as well. Neither did I see Myrddin, and held the absence of these three together as yet one more misfortune to be borne along with all the rest.

I might have wallowed in my melancholy, but then, overcome by the aroma of roast meat and warm bread, and by the sight of bubbling cauldrons being carried from the kitchens on wooden poles, I devoted myself to eating instead. When the rough edges had been smoothed from my hunger, I gazed along the benches, down the length of the board to see who my supper companions might be. I saw, farther along, Tallaght and Peredur, and many others I knew, heads down over their platters as if nothing in all the world could trouble them. I saw this, and I wished I could discard my unpleasant memories so easily.

And then it came again into my mind—the unwanted intrusion of my waking dream—as if Morgian herself had burst boldly into the room to taunt me with fresh terrors.

Suddenly too upset to eat any more, I pushed my bowl from me, stood, made some excuse to my companions, and started towards the entrance of the hall. I had walked but halfway across the great room when the doors swung open and Arthur and Gwenhwyvar entered. Myrddin swept in behind them, saw me, and beckoned me to him.

At my approach, the king smiled and held out his arms for me to embrace him. ''Gwalchavad!'' he cried. ''Here you are!''

''God be good to you, my king,'' I said, gripping his arm.

''Myrddin told us you had returned safely.''

''That I have, lord.''

''Welcome, Gwalchavad,'' said Gwenhwyvar, her voice soft and low. ''I was hoping you would be here. Is

Llenlleawg with you?'' She looked quickly past me into the hall for sign of her kinsman.

''No, my lady, but I have no doubt he will join us as soon as he is rested.''

''Come, now, Gwalchavad,'' said Arthur happily, ''sit with me at table. Much has happened while you were away, and I have much to tell you.''

''Nothing would give me greater pleasure, lord,'' I replied, nor was I disappointed. Truly, his zeal was irresistible as he described the great work he had undertaken. A few moments in Arthur's company and I had all but forgotten the harrows of my journey, and the queer menace of the dream.

See, now! This is the mark of the Pendragon of Britain: a man whose ardor for life is so compelling that others find their lives in him, a man whose natural nobility extends to everyone he sees, so that all others are ennobled in his sight. Truly, he is one of the Great King's sons and wears his sovereignty with such easy grace that all who will bend the knee to his authority are raised up and exalted by it.

Know you, I have lived alongside Arthur for many years, and have served him and followed him into battle more times than bear remembering, so believe me when I say that I have rarely seen Arthur in such joyous good spirits. It was as if all the hurt and pain of the past troubled years had been wiped away and his spirit restored to its true and natural state—fine and unblemished by the harsh tolls of kingcraft and war. That night he was more himself than even the day of his marriage to Gwenhwyvar, and that is saying something.

We talked and laughed together, and I felt my own heart rise to bask in the warmth of his friendship. When at last we parted for the night, I found the vision of the Kingdom of Summer burning in my heart, although the name never passed his lips. Ah, but that was not necessary. Arthur was aflame with it!

Like a Beltain fire, he scattered sparks in all directions and set the night alight. Anyone who spoke to him would have been likewise dazzled, and I count myself blessed to have sat at his right hand and listened to him describe his plans for the Grail Shrine. It was no rude hut he meant to build, but a perpetual beacon of goodness to all who walked in darkness, a wellspring of blessing to all who thirsted for righteousness, an endless feast to all who hungered for truth and justice. The completion of the Grail Shrine would commence a season of peace and plenty which would last a thousand generations.

How all this would come about was still somewhat vague. Indeed, the means by which Arthur would come into possession of the Holy Cup was not, as I recall, ever mentioned. But one thing was very clear in the Pendragon's mind: the deeds we performed now would become a song which would endure so long as men had tongues to speak and ears to hear.

Oh, and when we rose from the table at last, the night was far spent and the dawn, gleaming like red-gold on the eastern horizon, seemed not the beginning of a day only—no, it was nothing less than the inauguration of a magnificent Golden Age.

Chapter Fifteen

The first of the stoneworkers' tribe appeared three days later—eight or so men with huge ox-drawn wagons full of tools and provisions. They did not come to the Tor, but went straightaway to the site and occupied themselves with establishing their camp in the valley at the foot of the hill where the new shrine would be built.

Arthur, eager to see the work begun, rode out to greet them, and some of the Cymbrogi went with him. We watched as they went about their chores, and by day's end five large leather tents of the kind the Romans used to make occupied the little plain; five more were raised the next day. These, they said, were to house their fellows and families, who arrived in four days' time. The numbers at the site swelled to perhaps forty in all, though that included the children, who seemed always to be everywhere at once.

Over those first few days, I had ample opportunity to observe the masons as they went about the chores of ordering their camp. They were odd men: small of stature, with broad backs and tough, sinewy arms and short, thick, muscular legs. They were a hard-handed, ready-tempered crew, and loud with it—when they were not shouting at one another, they were singing to make the valley ring— much like seamen in their ways. I would be surprised if a single one of them had ever sat a horse or gripped a sword, much less thrown a spear.

The next days were given, with considerable pointed

discussion, to the preparation of the site. The stonemen
grumbled endlessly at how poorly the land had been
cleared, and they complained about the chosen placement
and the disgraceful paucity of suitable stone in the region.
Nothing was good enough for them, and they spared no
breath letting the whole realm know it.

"God's truth, Arthur," muttered Cai, quickly tiring of
their surly opinions, "if complaints were stones, the
shrine would be raised by now—"

"And a cathedral besides," added Bedwyr tartly.

"Pack the lot of them back to Londinium and be done
with it, I say," put in Rhys. "We were doing well enough
before they came."

But Arthur took the carping and complaining in his
stride. "They are hounds without a handler," he said.
"When their chieftain arrives, he will bring them to
heel."

The chieftain he meant was a bandy-legged, bald man
with a beard like a bearskin. His skin, blasted by years of
toil in sun and rain and wind, was as thick as the leather
of his tent and just as brown. His name was Gall, and he
walked with a limp and chewed hazel twigs, which he
kept in ready supply in a leather pouch at his side. Tough
as an old stump, he had but to speak a single word and
his men leapt to obey.

Arthur liked him instantly.

Once Gall and his small brown wife arrived, the complaining subsided to a tolerable level and the work began
in earnest—despite the appalling stone and lamentable situation. Again we were favored with occasions aplenty to
observe them, for the Cymbrogi were put to work cutting
trees to supply the timber they needed. I never imagined
masons required so much wood for their curious craft.

"That which you would build in stone," Gall informed
us, "you must build first in wood."

Nor could I help noticing that Myrddin seized every
opportunity to go alongside the master mason, questioning
his every move and thought in order to learn all he could
of the stoneworker's craft.

When we were not fetching logs to the site, we were

occupied supplying water for their camp. Though the drought continued as the long, dry summer wound slowly to its close, the spring below the Tor remained as sweet and cool and plentiful as ever, unaffected by the lack of rain. We filled empty ale vats and trundled them back and forth to the stonemasons' camp using their oxen and wagons. Were we ever thanked for this singular service? Ha!

In the midst of this turmoil, a strange and unsettling event occurred which should have served as a warning to us all. It was a Sabbath day, when the monks perform their holy offices and many of the Christian folk in the realm come to the chapel to observe these services and worship with the clerics. The masons, as it happens, do no work whatsoever this one day in every seven, and so they were free to join in the worship, which they did—singing out the hymns and psalms with unrestrained vigor.

Arthur so enjoyed this display of religious fervor that he went along to observe the vespers in the evening, and then invited everyone—monks and masons together—to the Tor to sup with him in Avallach's hall. Thus, we were all there together and enjoying the mood of festive cheer when I felt a queer sensation course through the hall. Beginning at one end of the great room and sweeping through to the other, I could see it ripple through the crowd as it passed, and felt a fluttery queasiness in the pit of my stomach. This was instantly followed by a peculiar numbing tingle like that of a winter chill on cheeks and nose and fingertips.

The hall fell silent with the kind of queasy anticipation that follows a sudden change in the wind just before the storm breaks. Illumined by the subtly shifting radiance of torchlight and hearthglow, the entire company stood motionless and staring, some with mouths open as if to speak, some with bowls halfway to lips as if to drink. I saw Arthur and Gwenhwyvar, half turned towards the doorway with laughter still on their faces, but frozen now. In everyone's expression and demeanor were the fast-fading remnants of a last, interrupted happiness.

I looked again and saw the cause of this interruption: a few paces inside the doorway stood a young woman;

tall and slender, her long hair a mass of fiery curls flowing
over her shapely shoulders like glistening water, her wil-
lowy form clothed in a deep green robe over a hooded
mantle of shining gold, she stood imperious and erect—
a monarch receiving the homage of her people.

For a long, frozen moment, silence reigned in the hall;
suspended between one breath and the next, no one
moved or spoke. And then I heard footsteps outside the
hall. The approach must have surprised her, for she turned
her head towards the sound, and in that instant the hall
sprang to life once more as if on command and Myrddin
appeared in the doorway behind her.

She faced Myrddin, and he halted—stricken in mid-
step. I saw the smile of welcome freeze even as the words
of greeting died on his lips.

The green-robed lady moved swiftly to his side and laid
her hand gently on his arm. Then she turned and, together,
beaming their good pleasure, they crossed the threshold
into the hall—for all the world a regal couple entering
their marriage feast.

My amazement at Myrddin's curious behavior was immediately swallowed by an even greater astonishment,
for, as she drew nearer, I realized that this lady was the
woman I myself had discovered wandering barefoot in the
forest. It was she whose pursuit had almost killed Llenlleawg—and three more besides. Gone were the rags,
gone the fearful expression; gone, too, the bare feet, dirty
hands, and unkempt hair. She appeared in every way the
very likeness of a queen, from the hem of her robe to her
curled and henna'd hair.

I stood rooted in surprise, but the crowd surged forward, exclaiming all at once. Myrddin, with a single word,
silenced the tumult. "Peace!" he said, his voice filling
the hall from hearthstone to rooftree. He stood with upraised hand and halted the commotion as quickly as it had
begun.

Then, turning to the young woman, he said, "So! You
favor us with your presence once more. I would know
who it is that we would welcome. Lady, I command you,
tell me your name."

His tone was firm but gentle, and there are few indeed able to defy his commands. Still, I knew full well the young woman lacked the power of speech ... and therefore was my astonishment compounded when she answered, "Forgive me, Lord Emrys, I am called Morgaws."

Excitement rippled through the gathering: "She speaks!" some exclaimed. "What does it mean?" asked others.

Arthur pushed through the throng to join them, Gwenhwyvar at his heel. "It is a wonder!" he proclaimed, beaming his pleasure at this unexpected turn. "How has this transformation come about?"

Myrddin, still watching the young woman narrowly, made no move as Morgaws stepped before the king. "Thank you, Lord Arthur," she said, inclining her head prettily. "I am beholden to your kindness." She spoke in a voice both hoarse and low, as if rusty from disuse. "A year ago a curse was laid on me by a woman of our holding and I lost the power of reason and speech. Since then, I have wandered where I would, a captive within myself, neither knowing who I was nor where I belonged."

"Yet you appear to have recovered yourself most remarkably well," Gwenhwyvar observed, pushing in beside her husband. "I would hear how that came about."

The two women eyed each other with cool appraisal. Morgaws put her hands together neatly and said, "I have indeed, noble queen. Yet I am at a loss to explain it. All I know is that, upon coming in sight of the Tor, I felt a great confusion overwhelm me. I knew nothing but that I must get away."

"You left us all too suddenly," Gwenhwyvar pointed out crisply. "We worried for your safety, and sent good men in search of you. They faced dangers and endured severe hardships for your sake—one is suffering still. It would have saved us great pain and no little trouble if you had but given us some small sign. We might have helped you."

Morgaws lowered her eyes demurely. "Alas, I can but

beg your forgiveness, my queen. My imprudence was
poor reply to the great benevolence you had shown me. I
was not in my right mind, I confess. I fled into the wood
nearby, and rode until I could ride no more. Then I slept,
and when I awoke, the confusion had left me and I was
myself again. After so long a time, I could not rest until
I returned home and restored my fortunes.'' She smiled
prettily. ''I have come to thank those who cared for me
in my affliction.''

A doubtful frown played on Gwenhwyvar's lips. ''And
where is your home?''

''Not far from here,'' Morgaws answered. ''My home
is near Caer Uintan—and . . .'' She paused, as if reflecting
unhappily, but then resumed: ''Upon restoring myself, I
could not rest until I had returned here to thank you for
the kindness you have shown me.'' Although she answered the queen, I noticed her eyes never left Arthur;
and when she finished, she smiled at him.

''You returned to us alone?'' said Myrddin. ''After all
that has happened to you, I would have expected your
people to take better care of you than that. Certainly, it is
unwise for a young woman to travel unaccompanied.''

The question appeared to unnerve Morgaws somewhat.
Her glance shifted away from Arthur, and she bent her
head, hesitating—as if searching for a suitable answer.
The king saved her from her predicament, however. Arthur, expansive and generous, said, ''I, too, am interested
to hear your tale, but there is plenty of time for explanations later. You are healed now, and that is cause
enough to be thankful. Come, let us sit down together and
celebrate your safe return.''

With that the king then led his elegant guest to the
table, where he seated her near him. Gwenhwyvar, catlike
in her wariness, stayed close and nothing passed that she
did not see or hear. As ever, the Wise Emrys kept his own
thoughts to himself; but I could not help noticing he did
not join them at table that night.

For the next few days, talk of Morgaws' unexpected
return was exceeded only by discussions about the Grail
Shrine. Though I listened to all that was said, further en-

lightenment was not forthcoming. Regarding the lady, some said one thing, and some another. Various speculations about her plight and marvelous restoration became hopelessly tangled, and genuine facts seemed difficult to come by. She was a noblewoman, some said, whose settlement was destroyed and her people slaughtered by the Vandali. Others had it that she was the daughter of a Belgae tribe whose people had fled to Armorica because of the plague, leaving her behind. Still others held other ideas, but no one seemed at all certain which of the various stories were true.

All the while, work on the shrine continued apace, and the days settled into a peaceable rhythm. Safely back at Ynys Avallach among friends and swordbrothers once more, I considered the fearful events in Llyonesse increasingly trivial; with each passing day the memory faded, growing more and more distant and insignificant. I even convinced myself that my dream of Morgian was the result of light-headedness brought on by fatigue, worry, and too much time in a too hot bath.

It is, I suppose, only human to put aside fear and pain, to move away from all unpleasantness as quickly as possible. I was no different from anyone else in this respect. Even Morgaws' return failed to kindle any lasting suspicion. After all, Gwenhwyvar and Arthur accepted her; the queen's wariness having given way to genuine welcome and affection, they all but doted on her. Who was I to question their sentiments?

I told myself: the lady has obviously suffered greatly, and her release from her affliction is cause for celebration. I told myself: we have no proof she has done anything wrong. I told myself: she has every right to enjoy the attentions of Arthur's court. These things I told myself repeatedly, and half believed them. Still, from time to time, doubt crept up on me—little more than vague twinges of misgiving—so, despite my repeated self-assurances and the excitement and gaiety bubbling around me, I could not make myself feel glad for her. Nor was I the only one to take a sour view of the matter. Peredur, too, held himself distinctly apart from the merrymaking.

One night, some while after Morgaws' return, I saw him sitting at the board, cup at his elbow, watching the king and queen with their enchanting guest. Sliding onto the bench beside him, I said, "Why the scowl, friend? I thought you would rejoice at the wanderer's return like everyone else."

"I might," he muttered darkly, "if everyone else was not smitten blind with adoration. I find little enough to admire in that woman."

"Morgaws?"

He regarded me with suspicion, and slowly turned his scowl back to the crowded hall. "Morgaws," he said, his voice so low I could hardly hear him.

"You do not like her much, I see."

Peredur shrugged. "I do not think of her one way or another." Reaching for his cup, he drained it in a draught. "Why should I?" he demanded. "She is nothing to me. I wish I had never laid eyes on the slut."

I wondered at this uncommon vehemence, but instead replied, "I know what you mean, brother. I, too, feel uneasy about our mysterious guest."

"You were the one who found her." His tone suggested that every misfortune in the world flowed directly from my hand. "You did not seem uneasy about her then."

It was true, I suppose. When we first came upon her in the forest, I had felt nothing but sympathy for her plight. Peredur, as I recall, had been dismayed by her from the first moment he saw her.

"Well," I allowed, "it may be as you say. No doubt my view has been altered by our sojourn in Llyonesse. And I will tell you something else: we are not the only ones to harbor misgivings."

Peredur merely grunted at this.

"Myrddin, too, withholds his blessing."

"Then perhaps Myrddin Emrys is as wise as men say." With that the young warrior threw aside his empty cup; it struck the board with a thump, whereupon he stood abruptly. "You must forgive me, Lord Gwalchavad, I find myself out of temper tonight. I assure you I meant no offense. Please, take no notice.''

He left me then, and stalked away. I saw him disappear into the throng gathered at the hearth, and so I determined to see who else might be less than complete in enthusiasm for the honored lady. After a time, I located the elusive Llenlleawg, who I expected would feel something akin to the distaste Peredur expressed. If anyone had reason to distrust Morgaws, Llenlleawg certainly did. Much to my amazement, however, I could not have been more wrong.

''She is a wonder, is she not?'' he said as I came to stand beside him. There was no question about whom he meant: he stood staring at her from a distance across the hall, where she, all smiles and demure replies, conversed nicely with Arthur, Gwenhwyvar, and Elfodd, who had joined us from the nearby abbey.

''She is that, I suppose,'' I answered, regarding him closely.

Ignoring my ambivalence, Llenlleawg continued. ''Truly, she is one of the Tuatha DeDannan.'' Happy with his comparison, he said, ''Indeed, she is a very Sidhe. How her face shines beneath her flaming locks! And her eyes . . .'' His voice drifted off in tones of such rapture I turned and looked my friend full in the face. Had I ever known him to speak so? No. Never.

''Can this be the same man,'' I said, ''who suffered so much in her pursuit?''

''She had nothing to do with any of that,'' he declared. ''Nothing at all.''

''Does that mean you have remembered something of your ordeal?''

''No,'' he said flatly, ''I remember nothing about what happened. But she was not the cause of it—that much I know.''

''If you cannot remember, how can you be certain?''

The tall Irishman gave me a darkly disapproving look, and stalked away.

Unable to make sense of his reaction, I took my search elsewhere. At the entrance to the hall, I found Myrddin, standing alone, watching the regal diners at the board.

Seeing where his attention lay, I put my head close to his and said, somewhat carelessly, "Well, it seems Morgaws has won a place among us."

"Oh, she is adept at insinuating herself into men's affections," Myrddin replied, his mouth twisting wryly. "Mark me, Gwalchavad, there is no end to the question of Morgaws. I look at her and see only questions begging answers. Why did she leave us only to return like this? Her fine clothes—where did she get them? She speaks with the easy loftiness of a noblewoman—but who is her family? Why does everyone forget themselves whenever she is near?"

"Llenlleawg has certainly forgotten himself," I replied, intending to tell Myrddin of my conversation. "Did you know that he—" I began, but the Wise Emrys was no longer listening. He had turned and was gazing at Morgaws. The frown had vanished in a look of rapture.

"Ah, but she is beautiful, there is no denying it," he murmured. This simple remark filled me with greater anxiety than anything else he could have said. I stared at him, but, heedless of my presence, he moved away.

I slept ill that night, and the next morning rode early to the site of the new shrine, hoping to take my mind from the problem of Morgaws. Once at the site, I was amazed to see how much had been accomplished since Gall's arrival.

As it happened, the hill chosen for the shrine was a low, humpbacked mound within sight of both Avallach's Tor and the abbey, and roughly equal distance from each. Early as I was, as I came in sight of the place I could see the workers swarming over the hillside. Wagons trundled to and fro, some with stone for the shrine, some with stone for the path leading to the shrine; still others, having delivered their loads, were rumbling away for more.

I dismounted, tied my horse on the picket line, and walked to the base of the hill, stopping now and then to talk to some of the Cymbrogi who were helping construct the path of stone cobbles. They all worked with cheerful vigor beside the masons, their banter high-flown and easy; the Cymbrogi fetched the stones, which the masons selected with deft efficiency, tapping them into place with wooden mallets. I greeted those I knew, commended their zeal, and walked on, slowly mounting to the top of the hill, which had been leveled to provide a precise, and striking, site for the shrine.

Pits had been dug at the four corners and filled with rubble stone; then an extensive bed of small stones had been laid down on which the foundation would be placed—the first few stones had been placed the previous day. Now the laborers were busily erecting a rough timber support along the proposed line of the wall.

I found the affable Gall blissfully employed shouting commands to a group of Cymbrogi endeavoring to drag a wagonload of stone up the hill. "Stop the wheels!" he was crying. "Use the timber to stop the wheels!" Turning to me, he said, "They fill them too full, you see. I tell them half loads are easier on the oxen. The shrine will not be raised in a day, I tell them, but they refuse to listen." Then, regarding me more closely: "Do I know you, lord?"

"I am Gwalchavad, and I am at your service," I replied, warming to the man at once. Open-faced, his features glowing with health and good-natured exasperation, he looked out upon the world through a pair of mild brown eyes, the sun glinting off his rosy bald pate.

For a moment he stood blinking at me, sturdy arms folded, mouth puckered in thought. And then: "Good lord! Gwalchavad, of course. Yes. One of the famed Dragon Flight. In the name of Christ, I give you good greeting." He smiled, his agitation at the heedless volunteers already forgotten. "My name is Gall. If it were not for the fact that the High King of Britain presses me daily to know when the work will be completed, I would invite you to break fast with me. But there is no rest for the wicked!"

Though his speech was couched in the form of a complaint, he seemed not to mind his hardship in the least. "You have no end of helpers," I observed.

He peered at me doubtfully. "Have you come to help me, too?"

"Fear not," I replied lightly, "for unless you discover some task requiring my particular attention, I will happily stand aside and watch from afar."

"Good man."

The overloaded wagon crested the hill just then and the master mason bustled off to order the deposition of the stone. I walked around the site, looking out at the surrounding fields, blasted by heat and drought. How much longer could the land survive without good, ground-soaking rain? I could not help thinking that, despite the late warmth, harvest time was soon upon us, and what a poor harvest it would be. At least the dry weather hastened the masons' work. But would the people hereabouts view the king's shrine in any kindly light when both grainstore and belly were empty?

Before I could wonder further, my meditations were arrested by a call from below. I turned and looked down the slope of the hill to see Cai trudging up to meet me. Upon exchanging greetings, he said, "I have been looking for you, brother. This is the last place I expected to find you."

"Yet find me you did."

He nodded, glanced quickly around the hilltop at the work in progress, then said, "Arthur has summoned the Dragon Flight to attend him in council."

"This is sudden. Do you know why?" I asked, already starting down the hill to where the horses were waiting.

"As it happens," said Cai, falling into step beside me, "I believe he is going to tell us about his plans for guarding the shrine." At my questioning glance, Cai continued, in tones suggesting he felt it beneath him to explain the obvious. "Once the Holy Cup is established in the shrine, it must be guarded, you know. Who better than the Dragon Flight, the finest warriors in all Britain?"

"Who better indeed?" I replied. "But where is the cup now?"

"Avallach has it, I expect. But soon it will belong to everyone."

"Maybe Myrddin is right," I countered, "and we

should leave it alone. It seems to me Avallach has kept it safe enough all these years.''

''Worrier!'' Cai scoffed. ''What can possibly happen to the cup with us guarding it?''

Chapter Sixteen

It is one of mortal humans' more curious traits, that the appearance of a thing is more greatly esteemed than its true character. This is invariable, I find. Perhaps it is that a pleasing image evokes the beholder's best sympathies and the desire to be united to the thing admired; then again, fools that they are, perhaps they simply believe that nothing which attracts them could ever bring them harm.

They are woefully wrong in this, of course, as in so much else. Be that as it may, it is precisely this oddity which has served me so well. That Morgaws is beautiful, there is no doubt. I made her, flesh and blood, for just this purpose. Fairest of creatures, she is nevertheless my creature. I taught her everything she would need to know to accomplish my will and desire. I taught her everything, and taught her well. She is that empty vessel which can be made to contain whatever its owner requires.

Born of the union between my dutiful son, Lot, and me, Morgaws is truly bone of my bone and blood of my blood. From the moment she came into the world, I have molded her to my will. Like all infants and children, she was born with a desire to please those in authority over her, those who controlled her food and shelter, warmth and security. With consummate skill, I manipulated her childish desires to serve my purpose, and she responded magnificently. Morgaws is my finest creation: revenge made flesh.

Together with the rest of the Cymbrogi, we hastened back to the Tor to prepare ourselves for the council to take place at midday. In the warriors' quarters, men rushed to and from the baths while others shaved and dressed in their finest clothes. Still others were busily burnishing their swords, spearheads, and shield bosses.

Thus inspired, I washed and shaved, too, and put on my better clothes, and by the time I had finished scouring my sword, the Cymbrogi were already gathering in the great hall. I found Rhys and Cador, and walked with them to join the rest. The tables and benches had been removed from the hall, and everyone was pressed tight at one end of the huge room.

We three pushed our way to the front of the assembly, as was our due—only to find that the Pendragon was already in attendance. He was sitting in Avallach's throne-like chair, facing the Dragon Flight, who formed a loose circle around him, beginning with Bedwyr at his right hand and continuing around to Llenlleawg at his left. Gwenhwyvar stood behind the throne, her hand resting on Arthur's right shoulder, and Myrddin beside her, tall and as silent as the oaken staff in his hand.

Cador, Rhys, and I quickly took our places at the bottom of the circle opposite the king, who acknowledged our arrival with a slow nod of approval. Seeing that all were assembled, he raised a hand to Myrddin, who then stepped forward to stand before the king. Taking his staff, he raised it high and brought it down sharply with a loud crack, and then twice more.

Planting the staff firmly, he made a circuit around it, passing once, twice, three times, gazing steadily into the face of each man as he passed. This done, he lifted the staff and held it lengthwise across his chest and, in a voice both solemn and profound, began to speak:

"Fortunate among men are you! I say again, fortunate are you, and all men alive to hear what passes in this hall. I tell you the truth: many generations of men before you have lived and died longing for this day."

Myrddin paused, his golden eyes scanning the company before him. "Heed the Head of Wisdom: this day, the sun has risen upon the Kingdom of Summer. Henceforth, and until the stars fall from the sky and the sea swallows our island, the kingdom now begun shall prevail. You, who stand before your king, bear witness: the Lord of Summer has taken his place upon the throne, and his reign is commenced.''

At these words, the assembled warriors gave out a tremendous cry—a joyous roar to alert all Ynys Prydain that a new kingdom had come into existence at the High King's command. It was some time before the Emrys could make himself heard. Finally, when the acclaim had abated somewhat, he continued.

''The praise of true men is a boon of great blessing, and the inauguration of the Summer Realm is right worthy of praise,'' he said. ''Yet the Kingdom of Summer will not be honored in word only, but in deed. For this reason, and for this purpose, the Fellowship of the Grail is begun.''

If the first proclamation brought forth cheers, this last brought a hush of anticipation as deafening in its way as the shouts of praise. I held my breath with all the others as the Pendragon rose from his chair and came to stand beside his Wise Emrys. Arthur, wearing his golden torc and serpent armband, Caledvwlch gleaming naked at his side, raised his hands in lordly laud of his decree.

''The Fellowship of the Grail,'' Arthur said, his voice echoing the strangely stirring words, ''is the first expression of the Summer Realm. But what is it? Is it a brotherhood dedicated to the service of the Most Holy Grail? Yes, it is that, and it is more: it is an alliance of true and kindred spirits, kinsmen united not by blood, but by devotion to a common duty. That duty is to guard and protect the Grail and all those who will come as wayfarers and pilgrims to the shrine of the Blessed Cup.

''Hear me, Cymbrogi! It is a high and holy duty to which I have called you. For many years the Grail has been guarded in secret, hidden for its protection and watched over by its keeper, Lord Avallach. Soon, however, the Holy Cup will be unveiled for the blessing of Britain and her people. A secret no longer, it will be de-

livered into our keeping, and we will become its guardians
and protectors. The skills we have learned in war, and
honed in constant battle, those selfsame skills will be
turned to the nurture of peace. Our swords will become
the weapons of our Lord Christ on earth. No longer will
our adversaries be mere flesh and blood, but the powers
and rulers of darkness.

"The Fellowship of the Grail is begun in you, my loyal
friends. You will be the first, and those who come after
will follow the path you mark out with your steps.
Therefore, I charge you, my Cymbrogi: walk worthy of
your calling."

So saying, he lowered his hands, turned, and seated
himself once more. The Dragon Flight, inspired by high-
sounding words and the prospect of glorious deeds,
greeted the Pendragon's declaration with loud acclaim.
They cheered and cried pledges of loyalty to the new Fellowship. When, after a time, the cheering began to die
away, Cai shouted to be heard.

"Lord and Pendragon," he said, his brash bawl of a
voice loud above the clamor, "I know full well that I am
one with my swordbrothers in welcoming the inauguration
of the Summer Realm, and like them I pledge sword and
self to the cause you have just proclaimed. Your words
are fine and high, as befitting the occasion, and I suppose
you are loath to demean the noble Fellowship with tiresome explanation. Yet, though I chance the scorn of those
blessed with keener wits than mine"—Cai turned this
way and that, as if to acknowledge those he held above
him—"even so, I deem it worth the risk to ask: how are
we to accomplish the duty which you have laid upon us,
and which we right readily accept?"

This brought good-natured laughter from all those looking on. Cai, ever practical, could not hear a cause proclaimed without knowing how it would be accomplished.
Of course, once Cai had cracked the wall, the rest came
pushing through the breach, all of them demanding of the
king, in one way or another, what they were meant to do,
and how they were meant to do it.

I could not help noticing that Myrddin made no move

to aid the king, but stood leaning on his staff and observing the clamor with cool indifference, as if to say, Who would stir the hive must brave the buzzing.

Arthur merely smiled and stood, taking his place in the center of the circle once more. "Lord Cai, fearless friend, I bend the knee to your humble entreaty." Turning to the assembly, Arthur declared, "Your approval of the Fellowship is as gratifying as your zeal is heartening. If I have not revealed my thoughts fully, it is for this reason: the Fellowship of the Grail is to be a true union of hearts and minds, and this, I am persuaded, can only be brought about by the willing dedication of those so called, and not by kingly decree.

"Therefore, I would that you, my noble friends, select from among your own number those who will determine the ordering of the Fellowship on your behalf. Holding that in mind, I urge you to pray, seeking wisdom, and choose your leaders well—for the rule they proclaim will be the law from this day forth and forevermore."

In this I thought I saw the hand of Bishop Elfodd, or at least the example of a monastic order as a guide for establishing the Grail Fellowship. Be that as it may, Arthur gave no instruction about how we were to go about our determinations, and seemed unwilling to say more. Indeed, having delivered himself of his address, he took his leave of us, bidding us to proceed with our deliberations and bring him word when we had chosen our leaders.

Soon we stood in our circle, regarding one another with glances of shrewd and thoughtful appraisal. Here was an activity to which we men of war were least suited. The best that could be said was that, while it might have been an unequal battle, at least we did not down weapons and surrender the field. Shouldering our responsibility as best we could, we embarked on what amounted to a long and fruitless wrangle.

In the end, the Dragon Flight, unused to cultivating decisions of this kind, turned expectantly to their battle-chiefs. First to speak was Bedwyr. Perhaps, as the one who enjoyed the High King's closest confidence, he had gleaned greater knowledge of Arthur's intentions than we had heard, for he said, "Brothers, if you will permit me to break into your meditations, I would offer a suggestion."

"Speak!" cried Cai, impatient to get on with the proceedings. "By all means, we will be forever beholden to you. Unless someone takes the tiller, we will be circling these waters forever."

Everyone laughed at this, and our burden was eased considerably. The stiff awkwardness of our high calling—as Arthur had deemed it—disappeared, and we became merely comrades with a duty to discharge.

"My suggestion," Bedwyr continued, "is simply this: that each man among us should declare three choices, and those whose names come most often to the lips of their comrades will scout out the path by which we are to proceed."

A fine plan, I thought, but one of the younger Cymbrogi made bold to amend Bedwyr's proposal. "If you please, noble lord," he said, seizing his chance in the outcry of approval that followed Bedwyr's address, "it is in my mind that the issue before us is both sacred and profound—and no less portentous than battle, where life and limb are placed at hazard beneath the rule of those who lead us."

Leaning near to Cai, I whispered, "He speaks well, this one. Who is he?"

"He is one of Cador's kinsmen," Cai replied. "He goes by the name of Gereint, I think."

"Ah, yes." I vaguely remembered the fellow, although, in truth, so harried were we in our battles against the Vandali, I had yet to fully acquaint myself with the more recent additions to our number.

Gereint continued: "Thus, I would gladly submit in peace to those I willingly trust in the heat of the fight. Perhaps I may be so brazen as to propose that we bestow the honor of ordering this Fellowship upon those to whom we have already sworn our loyal submission, namely, the Pendragon's battlechiefs."

Well, the proposal was carried forth on a rolling wave

of noisy enthusiasm. Bedwyr's eminently sensible, if less valiant, suggestion was forgotten in the eager rush to advance the proposition. The Cymbrogi gave voice to the plan, and all departed in high spirits, assured at having discharged their duty properly and well—all, that is, save the five battlechiefs who were now saddled with the task: Bedwyr, Cai, Cador, Llenlleawg, and me.

What happened next shames me to confess, so I will simply say that we fell to long and fevered discussion about how the thing should be accomplished. Oh, it was thirsty work, too, for as the day drew on and the weighty task conspired to steal our strength, we sought refreshment in Avallach's good ale—a dubious remedy, perhaps, but if it did little to ease the burden of decision, at least it helped us think better of our chore—for a short while anyway.

After a long, wandering discussion, we arrived once more precisely where we had started. Taking Arthur at his word, we framed this modest proposition: that the Most Holy Grail, rarest of treasures, must be guarded. "That means," Cai maintained over the rim of his bowl, "a perpetual guard."

"Well and good," replied Bedwyr. "But the Grail Fellowship is to be more than guard duty. Arthur said it is to be a sacred calling—"

"We are to protect pilgrims and wayfarers, too," Llenlleawg pointed out. "That means we must have warbands to ride the land."

"He did not say anything about riding the land," said Cador.

"He said very little at all," retorted Bedwyr, growing impatient.

"What is so difficult?" demanded Cai. "We are given a free hand to order the Fellowship how we will, and all you can do is find fault with Arthur for allowing us the honor."

"The onus, you mean," muttered Cador.

"Onus!" Cai flapped an impatient hand at Cador, who took a deep draught of the cup. "Man, where do you get such words?"

"It is Latin," Cador informed him loftily.

"Are we to be monks now," Llenlleawg inquired sourly, "spouting Latin and psalms at one another?"

"A sad day has dawned when a man cannot say what he thinks," sniffed Cador into his cup.

"And I say: give me a sword and I will guard this Grail," Llenlleawg declared.

"See! See!" cried Cai, almost upsetting the ale jar in his eagerness to clap Llenlleawg on the back. "Llenlleawg agrees—the Holy Cup must be guarded. We are to be Guardians of the Grail."

"Easy, brother," Bedwyr said, saving the jar. He poured another draught and took a long pull from the bowl and put it down with a thump. "I say we have talked enough for one day." He pressed his fingertips to his temples. "My head hurts."

Drink and frustration had worn us down, and tempers were beginning to fray at the edges. I did not like to see my swordbrothers quarreling, so determined to end the discussion before we were at one another's throats. "I agree with Bedwyr—we have talked enough for one day," I suggested. "Let us part while we are still friends and come at this again tomorrow."

"Aye, and what do you suggest we tell the king?" asked Cai. "Arthur is awaiting word from us."

"Tell him," I replied, "that our deliberations are well begun, but that a duty of such significance takes time—a day or two more at most, I should think."

The others liked the sound of that, and agreed that another day or two should give us ample time to complete our task. It was decided that we should come together again the following morning with a mind to setting matters to rights. Cai hastened away to tell Arthur, and Cador retreated to his bed for a nap; Llenlleawg quickly departed on errands of his own, leaving Bedwyr and myself to contemplate the ruin of the day.

"We must finish tomorrow," Bedwyr confided. "I could not bear two more days like this. Is everyone always so contentious?"

"Always," I assured him.

He shrugged. "I never noticed before." Looking towards the empty doorway through which Llenlleawg had just disappeared, Bedwyr said, "Our Irish friend has something on his mind."

"You mean there is somewhere else he would rather be?"

Bedwyr favored me with a knowing look. "The mysterious Lady Morgaws."

"Oh, aye," I agreed. "I have seldom seen anyone so afflicted."

"Those who fly highest fall hardest," Bedwyr observed, shaking his head slowly. "Not that I know anything about it." He paused, growing pensive. "I can almost envy him."

Chapter Seventeen

That evening at table, I watched for Llenlleawg and Morgaws, but neither of them appeared. I thought this highly suggestive, but if anyone else noticed their absence, I heard nothing about it. Then again, neither did Arthur or Gwenhwyvar join us for supper, and no one thought ill of that—why would they? The king and queen often took their supper in each other's company, and that is only right.

Still, I determined that a word with Myrddin would probably not go amiss. Also, I wanted to ask him what he thought about Arthur's shrine-building venture, and now there was the Grail Fellowship to discuss. Making quick work of my meal, I took myself off to find the Emrys—a chore far easier said than done, for it is a commonplace that Myrddin is seldom to be located where one first thinks to search. His errands are many, and as varied as they are obscure. One moment he is at the Pendragon's side, the next he is away to Caer Edyn in the north, or sailing back from Ierna, visiting this lord or that one, consulting bishops and abbots, testing the wind for portents, delving into Druid lore . . . and who knows what else besides.

Consequently, it was not until very much later that I was able to find the ever-elusive Myrddin. "A little sudden, this Fellowship—is it not?" I said, coming upon him as he poled the small boat to the shore. He had been fishing on the lake below the Tor, a pastime much favored from his childhood, I believe.

"Is it?" Myrddin wondered. "Walk with me, Gwalchavad."

Taking me by the arm, he steered me onto the narrow lakeside path. Night was seeping into the still, quiet evening. The sky was fading gold, and the first of the stars were already alight.

"I think it sudden," I replied.

"Whenever was there ever a better time?" he asked, stooping to pluck a reed from the bank. "Must goodness stand forever in the shadows, waiting for her opportunity to shine?"

"Heaven forbid," I answered. "Yet it seems to me that no sooner have we made peace with the Saecsen than we are forced to fight the Vandali. And if that were not enough, we must also face a season of drought and plague which drives our people to abandon their homes and quit these shores for foreign lands. I had thought we had enough to occupy ourselves without . . ."—the words eluded me—"without all this!" I waved my hand vaguely in the area of the Tor to signify what had taken place there.

Myrddin regarded me with his keen golden eyes for a long moment. When he spoke at last, he said, "You speak my thoughts exactly."

"Truly?"

"Does that surprise you?"

I confessed that it did, and said, "But you are his Wise Counselor."

"Our king has a mind of his own, or have you never noticed?"

"Yes, but—"

"He is impatient!" Myrddin retorted before I could finish. "He is impetuous and stubborn. I tried to tell him. 'Wait just a little, Arthur,' I said. 'We have come so far. The quest is nearly at an end. It would be wrong to force our way now.' Will he listen? No, he will not. 'The Summer Realm is aborning, Myrddin,' says Arthur. 'We cannot hold it back. The world has waited long enough. It would be a sin to withhold that which can do so much good.' And so it is as you have seen,'' Myrddin concluded. ''He rushes from one thing to another, full of holy zeal and heavenly ambition. And no one can tell him anything, for he will not hear, much less heed.''

''What of Elfodd?'' I asked. ''The king seems to have more than enough time for the good bishop. Perhaps Elfodd might prevail—''

''Save your breath,'' Myrddin interrupted. ''Elfodd is just as bad as Arthur. After Arthur's healing, the bishop is convinced that the Kingdom of Heaven is at hand, and that the High King is God's instrument for establishing it here and now. It is hopeless; the two of them goad each other.''

''And Gwenhwyvar? Might the queen find a way to persuade her husband to reason?''

Myrddin sighed wearily. ''Ah, she might—if it were not that she had seen her husband lying at death's gate in this very place not so very long ago. Gwenhwyvar is only too pleased to have Arthur hale and whole once more, so, in her eyes at least, this overzealous Arthur is preferable to the other. No, she cannot bring herself to reproach him.''

Well, it was no worse than I suspected. Arthur, miraculously healed and delivered of his enemies for once and all, was suddenly ablaze with virtue and good works. Where was the harm? Who was to say he was wrong? Might not Arthur, the one to whom the miracle had happened, possess a keener insight? Might not the one who had seen the vision be best able to describe it?

''I thought the Summer Realm was earth and stars to you, Myrddin,'' I said as we resumed our walk. ''I thought you wanted it above all else.''

Swift as a hawk swooping from the sky, the Emrys fell upon my remark. ''I do! I do!'' he exclaimed. ''No one knows how much I crave it, nor what its advent has cost me. Truly, Gwalchavad, I desire it more than my life,'' Myrddin said, growing solemn. ''But not like this.''

I waited for him to continue, and he did, after biting the tender end off the reed and sucking the juice. ''The

Kingdom of Summer is near, Gwalchavad, nearer now than ever—of that you can be certain. But it will not be compelled. If we try to force it, I fear we can only do great violence to it and to ourselves. We have a chance now—a chance that may never come again—and my best instinct tells me we must proceed with all caution."

"It does seem the soundest course," I concurred.

"Ah, but what if I am wrong?" Myrddin murmured, and I heard the anguish in his voice. "What if I am wrong, and Arthur is right? What if God's hand is on him to accomplish this great and glorious feat? To oppose it, even by so much as the merest hesitation, would be to hinder God himself. I ask myself: does God now perform his works in this worlds-realm only with Myrddin's permission?"

I let the question hang.

Myrddin continued, slashing the air with the reed in his hand. "Can it be that I, who have labored so long to advance the Summer Kingdom, cannot recognize it now that it is upon me? Is it possible that it is God's good pleasure to reward his faithful servants even before they have completed their labor?"

I did not know what he meant by this last statement, but before I could ask him, he declared, "There is one certainty, or none at all: if this thing flows from God, nothing can stand against it."

"And if it is not of God?"

"Then it cannot stand," he concluded simply, flinging the reed into the lake.

Wise is Myrddin, and keen of insight. He had not only discerned the heart of my own feelings and perceived my objections, but offered lucid consolation as well.

Moving to the matter uppermost in my mind, I said, "Have you discovered anything more about Morgaws?"

"Only that she is a noblewoman of Caer Uintan," he replied, his face hard in the dusky light. "Or so it is said." I could almost hear the gates slamming shut to keep me out. Why? Ignoring his reluctance, I pressed on regardless.

"Llenlleawg seems to have reversed his opinion of

her," I observed. "Before she disappeared, he could not
abide her. Now that she has returned, he cannot bear to
have Morgaws out of his sight."

"Yes, it is all very strange," agreed Myrddin.

"Is that all you have to say? You seemed more than
concerned before."

"Was I?"

That was all he said, but I suddenly felt foolish for
having involved myself in matters that did not concern
me. After all, if there was anything amiss, the Wise Emrys
would know; ever alert to the subtle shiftings of power
and the hidden meanings of events, Myrddin would know.

"Well," I conceded, "no doubt I was overhasty in my
judgment. She has done no harm."

Nodding, Myrddin resumed walking, turning back the
way we had come. The palace atop the Tor was black
against the pale purple sky. "Watch and pray, Gwalchavad," Myrddin said absently. "Watch and pray."

He returned to the Tor then, leaving me to my thoughts.
It came into my mind to visit the shrine—the old shrine
where the tin merchant Joseph erected the first church in
the Island of the Mighty, and where the Grail was first
seen in this worlds-realm. No more than a hut made of
sticks and mud, it stands on the place of that first small
church on the hill above the lake.

The good brothers of the abbey often say prayers in the
shrine, and I wondered if I should meet any of them, but
as I approached, I saw that I had the place to myself,
which is how I much preferred it. See, now: I am faithful
in my own way. It is not that I dislike the good brothers,
God knows, but I have not their learning, and I always
feel a pagan whenever I encounter monks at prayer. The
brothers are not to blame for this; I own the fault right
readily. Perhaps the purity of their example shames me;
such virtue and devotion as they demonstrate is to be
lauded, but I am not cut of that cloth. My days are spent
on the back of a horse with a shield on my shoulder and
a spear in my hand. So be it!

The shrine was black against the fading sky, and I stood
for a moment just looking at its looming shape and feeling

the immense age of the place. Slowly, and with mindful reverence, I mounted the slope of the hill and went inside the shrine. It is a simple, bare room, large enough, perhaps, for three or four, but no more. A single, narrow window opens above the altar made of three shaped slabs of stone. There was a candle on the altar, but it was not lit, and the interior of the shrine was dark as a cave.

Dark it might have been, but I was aware only of an immense and restful peace which seemed to fill the tiny chapel with a serenity as deep and wide as the sea. Entering, I knelt and closed my eyes, plunging myself into this ocean of calm; the irresistible tide pulled me down and down and down into its fathomless depths.

I did not pray—that is, I said no words aloud—but allowed my mind to drift along on the deep-flowing current of peace. If I had any thought at all, it was merely to bathe myself for a while in the calm of all calms, and perhaps touch for a moment the source of all serenity. Perhaps this is prayer by a different name; I do not know.

Neither can I say how long I remained like this; time was swallowed in eternity, I think, for it seemed to me that I had inhabited the shrine for a lifetime of lifetimes— in all that time knowing nothing of earthly strife and clamor, knowing nothing of desire or striving, knowing nothing but blissful contentment, and the desire that I might abide like this forever. To stay just as I am, I thought, would be joy surpassing all pleasures.

I held that thought in my mind, clung to it, and, clinging, cried out in my heart of hearts: Great King, cast me not aside! The cry arose unbidden, but I knew it as my own, for I had uttered my deepest fear. Nor was the reply long in coming. For all at once my hands and face began to tingle with an exquisite sensation, and I imagined beams of light, or flames, dancing over my flesh. I was immersed—not in water, but in living light! The notion grew so strong in me that I opened my eyes, and saw the shrine awash in a pale, golden luminescence, shifting and shimmering over the interior walls like the reflection of light on water.

Another time I might have been amazed at this wonder,

but not now. In my present mind, it seemed wholly natural
and expected that this should be. The only curiosity was
that the dancing light had no point of origin: it simply
shone of itself, and was everywhere manifest, gilding the
rude-built shrine with glimmering gold. Ah, but to see it
gleam and shine was pure delight, and I was seized by an
inexpressible rapture. My heart soared and I felt as if I
were a child once more, enfolded by a bliss which sur-
passed all understanding.

And then . . . and then: a miracle. The light intensified,
its radiance growing bold and sharp, taking substance, as
it were, and I felt a warmth steal over me—like that which
arises when the sun breaks through the concealing cloud
and all the earth warms of an instant beneath the all-
pervading strength of its rays. At the same time, I heard
the sound of silver bells hung from the branch of a tree
for the wind to strike one against another. The sound was
the light, and the light was the sound; I understood that
they were both but emanations of a thing I had not yet
perceived.

The sound, like the light, grew and hardened, too. And
when I thought all the world must hear the ringing of the
unseen bells, a word formed. I heard it as a word breathed,
not spoken, a resonant word which seemed as much a part
of me as my very bones.

Behold!

I searched within myself what this command might signify, but I saw nothing save the bare stone altar. And then,
even as my eye lit upon the stone, it began to gleam with
a golden sheen, the rough stone gilded by the light. The
bellsong quickened and I heard again the breathless command: *behold!*

Even as I looked, it seemed as if something like scales
fell from my eyes and I saw, radiant upon the altar, the
Grail.

Chapter Eighteen

The Grail!

My breath caught in my throat. I stared at the sacred object, ablaze with the fiery light of glory. The intensity of its radiance burned my face; it felt as if my eyes were coals of fire. I held my breath for fear of singeing my lungs should I dare inhale the searing air. Blood pounded in my ears with a roar like that of the ocean; beyond the throbbing pulse in my ears was a sound like that of a harp pouring out a heavenly sound, the incomparable melody falling like holy rain from heaven.

Transfixed by the beauty of the Blessed Cup, I made to raise my hand to shield my eyes, but could not lift so much as a finger. Neither could I look away. The Grail filled my vision, was all my vision. I began to see as I have never seen before. I saw the path of my life stretching out before me, and it went on forever.

I thought within myself to follow the path to discover where it might lead next, and suddenly I felt a presence with me in the shrine—a mighty force, towering in the strength of its vitality, majestic in its power—like a storm at sea where gales blow and great waves clash. Oh! the weight of it! The weight! It was as if a mountain had shifted and settled upon my pitiable frame, and I was being crushed out of existence. I could not endure.

I knew my last living moment had come. My poor heart labored in my chest, faltered, and then stopped. I closed my eyes.

Mercy! I cried inwardly. Mercy, Lord.

These words had but fled my mind when the weight vanished. My heart began beating, and I could breathe once more. Cool air, like a soothing balm, rushed into my lungs and I drew it deep, almost choking on it. No longer gripped by the power that had held me, I fell on my face before the altar.

My chest ached; my limbs quivered. I lay gasping like a fish flung from the water. But, oh, the air revived me wonderfully well, for it tasted as sweet on my tongue as the richest mead; the delicious scent filled my head and mouth and I gulped it down in great, greedy draughts, feeling as if I had never drawn breath before. When I at last raised my head, I was dizzy with the fragrant intoxication of the air.

The Grail had gone, as I knew, but the shrine still held a glimmer of the heavenly radiance of the sacred vessel, though that, even as I watched, faded quickly away, leaving the room in darkness once more. I lay for a time, placid, unmoving, my spirit at ease with the stillness of the night. And when at last I heard, as a summons from another realm, the abbey bell toll the midnight prayer, I rose unsteadily to my feet. At the doorway, I paused and looked back, hoping, I think, for a last fleeting glimpse of the holy object, but the altar was bare stone, hard and cold. The Grail had moved on.

I did not return to the Tor that night, but remained on the hillside near the shrine, wakeful and curiously agitated; I could not hold a thought in my head for a single moment before it slipped my grasp and flew away. Try as I might, my thoughts scattered far and wide like birds a-frighted from the field. Now and then, one of them would return to roost—I must tell someone! I would think—and then flit! . . . It would vanish, and another would take its place. I have seen it! I have seen the Grail!

In this way the night passed. At last, as the sun rose above the line of tree-topped hills to the east, I rose, too, and made my way back to the Fisher King's hall. The inner yard was already stirring as the Cymbrogi made ready to go out to their day's labor at the shrine. I entered the yard to the open stares of those who were preparing to leave; most of those gaping at me smiled, some laughed outright and I wondered what they thought amusing. Was it that I had, as they imagined, lost my way in the dark and was forced to spend the night outside? Or did they believe me to have slept in a serving maid's bed?

Ignoring their derisive smirks, I proceeded to the hall, and was met while crossing the yard by Bedwyr and Cai as they came to see the work party away. "Good day to you, brother," said Bedwyr; then, looking at me more carefully, added: "Though it appears you have had the best of the day already."

Cai was more direct. "Man, next time get yourself beneath a bush to nap," he advised, and they both walked off, shaking their heads and laughing.

I stared after them; the inexplicable behavior of everyone around me was rapidly sapping my lingering tranquility—I could feel my pleasant, peaceful mood melting away like dew before the midday sun. I vowed to myself that the next person to make jest of me would answer for it. As it happened, the next person was Arthur.

The king came bolting out the doorway as I stood watching Cai and Bedwyr. He slapped me on the back and said, "Greetings, brother! I have missed you these past days. I am going to the shrine. Ride with me."

"Nothing would please me more," I said, took two steps with him, and remembered that I must attend the council instead. "Forgive me, Arthur, I am forgetting myself," I said, and explained that, owing to my duty to the council, I could not accompany him.

"Ah, well, tomorrow, then," he said, then stopped abruptly and looked me in the face. "The Fellowship is important, Gwalchavad. It will soon take on an eminence of the highest order. Wherever men hear of the Grail Fellowship, their hearts will burn within them. It will become a beacon fire, and all Britain will be illumined by the blaze."

He smiled suddenly. "Speaking of fires, it seems you have stood too near the flame, my friend. Farewell!"

Bewildered and annoyed by my baffling reception, I

proceeded into the hall in search of bread and a little ale.
The Cymbrogi had broken fast, but there was plenty of
their leavings to make a meal, so I gathered a bit of this
and that onto a platter and settled on one of the benches
to eat in peace, and to see if I might recover my former
good cheer. I took up one of the small loaves, tore it, and
began to eat—only then remembering that I had missed
my supper last night and was famished. I was washing
down the bread when I saw Myrddin sweep past the entrance to the hall. Hurrying as he was, I had time but to
shout his name as I leapt to my feet and started for the
door, thinking to catch him before he vanished again.

But before I had taken half a dozen paces, he reap-
peared at the doorway. "I have been searching for you,"
he said, hastening to meet me. "They told me you did
not return from our walk last night, and I thought—" He
broke off, staring at me as he stepped nearer. Then his
golden eyes widened and his face assumed an expression
of knowing wonder.

"What?" I asked, suddenly reminded of my curious
treatment at the hands of my comrades. "Will no one tell
me what is the matter?"

"You have seen it," observed Myrddin sagely. "You
have seen the Grail."

I seized him by the arm and drew him further into the
hall as if to keep the secret from being overheard. "What
makes you think that?"

"Your face," he replied, raising a hand to my chin and
turning my head to the side. "You have the look of someone who fell asleep in the sun—your skin is red."

"Red!"

"Sunburnt," he said. "Only, you and I both know
there was no secret rising of the sun last night."

"Sunburnt," I said, "but—" I touched my fingertips
lightly to my face; the skin was as dry, with tiny raised
bumps like sun blisters, but there was no pain or discom-
fort, and the flesh felt cool to the touch. Nevertheless, I
believed him.

"As you did not return to the Tor, I surmise that you
spent the night at the old shrine," the Wise Emrys ex-

plained. "That is where I first saw the Grail."

Reluctant still to demean the radiant vision with poor words, I replied, "I cannot rightly say what I saw."

He smiled knowingly. "There is no need, Gwalchavad. I have seen it, too, remember."

"But why me, Myrddin?" I asked. "I am not the most devout of men—far from it! There are better Christians than me, and a good many hereabouts. Why me and not one of them?"

"God knows," he answered. At my disapproving frown, he said, "That is to say the Spirit moves where it will, and no man may make bold to let or hinder."

"But I thought the Grail was real—a real cup, that is. What I saw was . . ." I faltered. What had I seen?

"Oh, it is very much a real cup," Myrddin assured me quickly. "But the hallows of this world, the holy and sacred objects given to us for our blessing and edification, are never limited to mere physical manifestation."

At my confused and baffled expression, the Wise Emrys went on to explain. "The Grail is no ordinary material object—a cup of bronze or silver, as you suppose. Although it is that, it is also a spiritual entity with a spiritual existence."

"A hallow—is that what you called it?"

"Indeed. What you saw last night in the shrine was the hallow. That is, the spiritual manifestation of the Grail."

"A vision of the real cup."

"If you like," Myrddin allowed. "But one is no less real, as you say, than the other."

"I saw the hallow, then, but what does it mean?"

He shrugged. "I have no idea."

"But it must be a sign," I insisted. "It must betoken something—something important."

"God alone knows the why and wherefore."

"That is no answer," I growled.

"Then ask God for another."

Myrddin made to move off, but I followed him with my questions. "What am I to do, Myrddin?"

"Watch and pray," he advised, repeating his homily of the day before.

"Is that all?" I demanded, losing patience with his irksome reticence. I suppose I should have known better than to demand of a bard the meaning of a vision. They delight in posing riddles, but answers interest them not in the least.

"What more would you have me say?"

"Perhaps you could tell me this, at least," I said. "Why were you looking for me?"

"When I learned you had not returned to the Tor, I feared for you."

"You thought that what happened to Llenlleawg might have befallen me."

"It was in my mind," Myrddin allowed, but said no more. A moment later, Bedwyr and Cai returned to the hall, saw us talking, and joined us. The Emrys greeted them and said, "You must be about your business. Come to me when you have finished, if you like." He left then, and we took our places at one of the tables to wait for the others, and I finished my meal.

To my relief, neither Cador nor Llenlleawg mentioned my reddened skin, and we began our deliberations where we had abandoned them the day before. We talked throughout the day, and with better resolve; no one, I think, wanted to spend a third day grappling with the others over fine points of custom and ceremony.

Accordingly, we all agreed with Cai's observation of the previous day that, yes, the Grail was a rare treasure requiring protection. Therefore, the first rule of the Grail Fellowship would be to protect the shrine wherein the holy vessel was contained. The five of us—Arthur's battlechiefs, that is—would choose the guards from among the members of the Fellowship. Further, in order to ensure proper reverence and vigilance, each member of the Fellowship would be required to swear sacred oaths of loyalty and allegiance, not only to Arthur, Lord of the Summer Realm, but also to the Lord Christ, whose cup it was our sworn duty to protect.

That much was easy to agree upon, which we promptly did—and then our swift forward march quickly bogged down in the mire of minutia. Questions arose which we had not anticipated, and for which, once raised, answers must be found. What, for example, if a member of the Fellowship should disobey his duty, or fall into disgrace? How should the remedy be determined? Should there be orders of rank among the members of the Fellowship? If so, how should these be comprised?

All these and more beset us, and for each one we answered, two more sprang up to take its place. Thus the day passed, and I began to fear we would be at our task forever, when Bedwyr, who observed what was happening, suggested a compromise: that we begin with what we had agreed upon, but retain the right to amend or add rules to the ordering of the Fellowship whenever the need arose.

By this time, tempers were frayed and it felt as if we had been treading on eggs all day long. We were fairly panting for a cool drink, and Cador went off to fetch it. No sooner had he gone than Llenlleawg, having grown increasingly peevish as the day wore on, pushed himself to his feet and declared that he was not so thirsty that he could not wait until supper. "If we have finished," he said curtly, "I will beg to be excused further discussions. A matter awaits my attention elsewhere."

"Yes, go, by all means," Bedwyr told him. "We have finished, God willing. Unless you have any objection, I will inform Arthur that our deliberations have borne fruit, and that we have reached an end for the time being."

The tall Irishman inclined his head in assent and took his leave at once.

"He could not wait to get free of us," Bedwyr observed. "It is not like him to be so hasty."

"Especially with ale in the offing," Cai added meaningfully.

"No doubt the cut and thrust of a blade is more suited to his nature," I allowed. "This wordful striving is tedious; it makes my head ache."

"Aye," agreed Cai, "it does that." He thought for a moment, then added, "I say we should ride out to the new shrine and take word to Arthur. After sitting in this hall the whole day, I could use a breath of fresh air."

"After the ale," amended Bedwyr.

"Oh, aye, after the ale," replied Cai, surprised that there should be any question about that.

"I am for it," I said. Consequently, when Cador returned bearing the jug and cups himself, we all hailed him a hero, drank up, and raced out to join the work party at the shrine.

Nothing much had changed since the last time I visited the site. A few more stones had been placed along the line of the circular wall, and additional timbers erected. The heap of stone was somewhat larger, but that was all—despite the many eager hands available, for all the Cymbrogi were employed.

"The work is going well," Arthur said happily, dragging his forearm across his sweating brow. We found him standing atop the hill, bare to the waist and covered in rock dust. The sweat made little muddy rivulets where it had trickled down his back and sides. "Indeed, far better than I hoped. I think we will be able to hold the rites of consecration at the Christ Mass."

"Look at you, Bear," Bedwyr commented. "Gray as a ghost, and filthy with dust. Have you been rolling in the stuff?"

That the Pendragon of Britain should be toiling in the dirt did not surprise me in the least. Arthur was so eager for the Grail to be enshrined so that the Summer Realm might commence in full, I think he would have moved whole mountains with his bare hands if that would have helped. We all agreed that if the work continued at pace, the shrine would certainly be finished in time to mark the turning year.

"Now, then, have you anything to show for your labors?" the king asked.

"We have indeed, lord," Bedwyr replied, and began relating all we had discussed, and the decisions we had reached. We each took it in turn to supplement Bedwyr's admirably succinct, if somewhat flat-footed, report with comments of our own.

Arthur listened, nodding from time to time, and when Bedwyr had finished, declared himself well pleased with the result. "It is just as I hoped," he said, his smile quick and warm with approval. "You have done your king good service."

As he turned his gaze towards the heap of stone and timber, I saw the light come up in his eyes, and he said, "Guardians of the Grail . . . I am pleased." Facing us once more, he added, "To you is granted the highest honor of a warrior in this worlds-realm. So be it."

Over the next days, a few embellishments were added to the ordering of the Fellowship, but the basic structure we had erected remained intact. The Cymbrogi expressed enthusiastic support of the Fellowship, and as the work on the shrine slowly proceeded, so their zeal increased; it seemed their ardor, like the king's, knew no bounds.

With the passing days, something akin to religious fervor took hold of all who labored on the new shrine. It seemed as if faith raised the circle of stone. Indeed, curious happenings became commonplace: a heavy stone slipped and fell onto a man's hand as he tried to lift it onto the wall, but instead of his fingers being crushed, he received not so much as a pinch or scratch. Two workers, using nothing but their bare hands, stopped a wagon laden with rubble from rolling downhill when the wagon hitch broke—it had taken two oxen to pull the wagon in the first place. Another man, who had worked himself into such a frenzy that his hands became blistered, had his blisters healed overnight while he slept, so that he was able to renew his exertions the next morning.

There were several minor accidents as well, mind: a fully laden horse stepped on the foot of one poor fellow and crushed two toes, which then had to be cut off. Another unfortunate slipped in the mud and hit his head against one of the lower steps; he bled like a stuck pig from an ugly gash, and had to have his hair shaved off in order to dress the wound. Neither of these, nor one or two others, were blessed with any miraculous cures, however, and instead had to be carried to the abbey for the monks to tend.

Once out of sight, the afflicted were swiftly forgotten in the general excitement. Thus the small miracles loomed larger than perhaps they ought, which served to heighten the euphoria. Bishop Elfodd said that the miracles were signs heralding the dawn of a peace to last a thousand years. Once the Grail Shrine was consecrated, he said, the Age of Peace would begin, and all Britain would be blessed with signs and wonders.

Strange to say, then, that as the elation of those around me waxed the greater, my own fervor waned. Perverse creature that I am, the intense, almost ecstatic jubilation of my comrades combined with my own sinful pride to produce the opposite reaction in me. I quickly came to view both the shrine and the Fellowship with distaste; what I once held in kindly favor became offensive to me. I could not bear to look at the shrine without shrinking from it. The very mention of the Grail Fellowship put my teeth on edge. Well, the fault is mine; I own it and confess it freely, so that you will know what manner of man I am.

See, now: I do not shrink from the truth, even when it tells against me. Indeed, though it brings me no pleasure, I write this so all may believe me when I relate the horror of what is to follow.

Chapter Nineteen

In Llyonesse I learned my art—Annubi possessed a great store of wisdom, all of which I devoured, and in that way devoured him—but in the Dark Islands I practiced it. Orcady provided the solitude I required, and also the resources of a wealthy and powerful husband to protect and indulge me while I perfected my craft.

Poor Lot knew little of my labors because I allowed him to see very little—only enough so that he would respect my long seclusions. His headstrong son despised me, but his grandsons, Gwalcmai and Gwalchavad, might have proved valuable to me—ardent men have their uses, after all—and I could easily have bent them to my purposes. But they had forsaken their birthright to follow that ox-brained Arthur. So I persuaded the old king to give me a son of my own, a child I could train to my will, who would rule the realm after his father.

I might have reigned in Orcady myself, but I have greater ambitions, and was already laying my designs for Merlin. Once, I offered him the choice of joining me—united, we would have created a force more powerful than any since Atlantis was destroyed! But the self-righteous idiot had the temerity to spurn me. He styles himself a bard like his father, and holds to the ancient bardic ideals —that and the pathetic notion of his which he dignifies with the name "The Kingdom of Summer."

Since Merlin would not join me, he must be destroyed. I had, through various means, watched his progress and knew that he had acquired a rough art of his own, which, if allowed to thrive, might cause me trouble. I had paid dearly for that which I possessed—great power comes at great cost—and I could not easily afford to let anyone interfere in my plans. So I lured him to Llyonesse, where I could more easily control the confrontation.

Killing him would have been child's play, of course; and looking back on it now, I know that is what I should have done. What I wanted, however, was not only to strip him of his power, but to do it so completely and absolutely that he would abandon every hope and ambition he had ever had for his ridiculous Summer Realm.

I misjudged him, however; he was more canny than I expected; the encounter went against me and I was forced to break off the attack. Merlin imagines that he bested me; moreover, he believes my power was broken. In that, however, he is desperately mistaken. When I saw I could not win the encounter outright, I abandoned the attempt in order to preserve the power I had labored so long to gain. In truth, I permitted the little weasel to escape, or he would have been crushed and annihilated—just like the smarmy lickspit Pelleas; I destroyed him just for spite, and to show Merlin just how fortunate he was to escape.

Yes, I allowed Merlin to slip away that time, but he will not elude me again. He has made it his life's labor to raise the oafish Arthur to prominence. It will be a singular pleasure to wipe out that work, to obliterate the both of them. In fact, it is better this way. The sight of them squirming in their death throes is a sight I will relish forever.

Oh, they will die in disgrace with curses between their teeth; that is inevitable, inescapable. They will die in shame and despair, but not before they have seen everything they valued laid waste. This I have promised myself. It will be.

Morgaws is now in place. She has beguiled the entire court in one way or another, and she has chosen the one who will become the agent of betrayal. Rhys, I thought, would have served us admirably in this. Indeed, we tried to seduce him, but met with unaccountable resistance.

*Nevertheless, his influence has been abrogated; he will
not trouble us. Gwalchavad, too, might have provided a
pleasantly ironic choice, but I knew he would be difficult.
We will keep trying, of course, but whether we win him
or not makes no real difference. Others have been cor-
rupted to the cause, and only await the command to strike.
That command will not be long in coming. Only one or
two details remain, and then the destruction will commence.*

*The day of Morgian's revenge is at hand. Behold, all
you people, your doom swiftly approaches! Weep with
black despair, for there is no escape.*

The seasons passed. Harvest came and went: a dismal
business, best forgotten. The long, dry summer had done
its worst. There was nothing for it but to trust winter rains
to bring a better spring. Though we looked to every gray
cloud that drifted overhead, the rain did not come.

The lack of rain meant, however, that the work on the
new shrine could continue without interruption, and people began to look upon its completion as the salvation of
the land. "When the Grail Shrine is finished" became the
litany which began every conversation, as people turned
hopefully to a brighter future. Each day the Pendragon
and Cymbrogi rode out to their labors, and each night
returned delirious with exhaustion and companionship.
Accordingly, the day of completion, hastened by favorable weather and the unquenchable ardor of the Cymbrogi
laborers, arrived far sooner than expected.

Though I did no work myself, I often rode out to watch
as the builders, seized with the fervor of creation, vied to
outdo one another in the quality of their work. And despite my inexplicable aversion, I will say that it grew into
a fine and handsome place: six-sided, with neat straight
walls rising from a tiered base and topped by a steep-
peaked roof of wood covered with red Roman tile—God
knows where they got that!—and a series of curved steps.
It was not large, but Arthur allowed that it was, after all,
only a beginning; in time, the shrine could be expanded,
or attached to a much larger structure, which he had in

mind. "But this will do for now," he declared, well pleased with the result.

As the turning of the year approached, Arthur began making plans for the Grail Shrine's consecration. He called for messengers to summon those he wished to attend the august event. I volunteered at once, since the errand provided me a welcome escape from what I had begun to think of as the delirium which had overtaken almost everyone.

I say "almost" because there were others, like myself, who regarded the absurd euphoria with increasing suspicion. Myrddin, as ever, pleased to garner whatever he could of the builders' craft, would speak no word against the shrine or the Grail, but his praise was ever guarded and he held himself aloof from any talk of miracles, or thousand-year reigns of peace, and such. Likewise Bedwyr, who always seemed to find one important concern or another to occupy him—I know he often fished with Avallach. Llenlleawg, I believe, never so much as rode out to the site; it was whispered that Lady Morgaws demanded his constant attention. Cai helped often, however, and Cador only now and then, as it pleased him.

Thus, Bedwyr, Cador, and I, along with a score of Cymbrogi, rode out one cool, bright morning to our various destinations, far and wide throughout the realm and beyond. I was sent to Londinium to bring back Charis, who yet labored there in one of the plague camps. Before leaving, I asked Llenlleawg if he would ride with me—for all he appeared so haggard and ill at ease that I reckoned a little sojourn away from the overheated mood of the Tor would be no bad thing—but he declined. "No," he said, "my place is here with Arthur."

"Of course," I replied lightly, "no one doubts it. But Arthur himself has commanded me to go and escort Charis home."

"Then go. It is nothing to do with me."

I watched him as he stumped away, and could not help thinking that he was no longer the man I knew. I resolved to bring the matter to Myrddin's attention at the first opportunity when I returned. Be that as it may, it was with a sense of relief that I left the Tor—relief that I might be quit of the tedium and hypocrisy of maintaining a pretense of support when my heart was not in it.

Taking an extra horse, I departed, pausing at the abbey to inquire where I could find Paulus. Some of the brothers had just returned from a long stint away in the south, just outside Caer Lundein, where Paulus had established a camp off the old Roman road. Charis was there, along with a good many monks from neighboring monasteries, helping to combat the yellow death. "It has ravaged Londinium terribly," one of the brothers told me. "I believe it is far worse there than it ever was here. Paulinus is easy to find, and you will not have to enter the city."

"Perhaps you would not object," suggested Elfodd, "to taking a few supplies to them. The need is great, and it is the least we can do. Would you mind?"

"Not at all," I assured him, and then watched as the good monks piled bundle after bundle upon the horses: supplies for making medicine, cloaks and winter clothing for the brethren, dried meat, and casks of ale and mead to help their fellows celebrate the Christ Mass, which was drawing near. When they finished at last, I took my leave and made for the Londinium Road. I thought it a long time since I had been on that highway; the last time was for Arthur's crowntaking and wedding. So much had happened since then, it seemed a lifetime ago. Perhaps it is as Myrddin says: time is not the passage of an endless succession of moments, but the distance between events. That was nonsense to me when I first heard it. Now, looking back, I think I begin to know what he meant.

The swiftest way to the Londinium Road lies through a stretch of forest—an old, old trackway, used from ages beyond remembering. The forest is older still, of course, and there are yet many of the great patriarchal trees to be seen: elms on which moss has grown so thick that they appear gray-green with age, and oaks with trunks large as houses. The forest fringe, where light still penetrates to the ground, evokes no fear; but when men must go into the dark heart of the ancient wood, they go in haste, passing through as quickly as possible.

This I did, hunkering down in the saddle with one of the Wise Emrys' saining runes on my lips. As I rode, I said:

Be the cloak of Michael Militant about me,
Be the cloak of the Archangel over me,
Christ's cloak, Blessed Savior, safeguarding me,
God's cloak of grace and strength, shielding me!

To guard me at my back,
To preserve me from the front,
And from the crown of my head
*   to the heel of my foot!*

The cloak of Heaven's High King between me
*   and all things that wish me ill,*
*   and all things that wish me harm,*
*   and all things coming darkly towards me!*

In this way I passed through the darkest part of the forest. After a while, the path lightened ahead of me, and I knew that I was reaching the end. I emerged from the wood at a gallop and gained the hills above the road, where I paused to look back at the Tor's blue-misted shape in the distance. I rode until nightfall, whereupon I made camp and spent the first of several mild nights under the winter stars.

The journey remained uneventful and four days later, through the murky brown haze of evening smoke—as if the plague were a visible cloud under which the city suffered—I glimpsed Londinium, cowering behind its high walls. Those walls, erected long before Constantine was Emperor, were collapsed in several places and falling down. It was amidst the rubble of one such breach outside the northern gate that Brother Paulus' camp had been established.

Rather than trust to the hospitality of that plague-ridden city, I happily made camp beside the road and waited until the next morning to proceed any farther—and anyway, the gates were already closed for the night.

At dawn the gates opened and people emerged, bringing the plague victims with them: some they carried, some they dragged. I resumed the saddle and as I drew near, the odor of the place reached me—a foul stench of sickness, rot, and death that made the gorge rise in my throat.

I swallowed hard, crossed myself, and rode on.

A pall of smoke rose from a great refuse heap to hang like a filthy rag over the camp, and I saw what appeared to be bundles of cast-off clothes scattered in their hundreds all around. Closer, I discovered that these were not bundles, but bodies. I tethered the horses on a patch of withered grass a short distance away and approached on foot, picking my way carefully among the Yellow Ravager's victims.

There were so many! Everywhere I looked, I saw more, and still more. I believe the numbers shocked me more than the sight and smell, which were both appalling. I gazed in dismay at the scattered bodies of men, women, and children—in their hundreds, mind, and more being brought out through the gates—many, if not most, to be dumped beside the road like so much refuse, discarded and forgotten. Those who had given up the fight lay still and silent; but those in whom life yet warred cried in their torment, moaning and mewing as they twitched and writhed.

The groans of these unfortunates filled the air with a low, queasy keen. Their faces were spotted and distorted, their eyes red, their sores pus-filled and running; they vomited and defecated and bled over themselves, and lay rotting in their own filth. I had not witnessed the devastation of the Yellow Ravager before, yet judging by what I saw around me, I knew it was well named: the poor wretches mewing and crying in their throes were uniformly cast in a lurid shade of yellow—as if their flesh had been tinted by noxious dye and wrung out while wet—their skin was bloated, and vile mucus ran from nose and eyes to choke them; they sweated and panted as if being consumed from within by fire.

Many reached out their hands to me, crying for help, for release, but I could do nothing for them.

I knew the plague had worsened in the south; I had heard the bleak tidings like everyone else, but had no idea it was this bad. If it did not end soon, I reckoned, there would be no one left in Londinium to even bury the victims, let alone care for them. Oppression hung over the camp like the nasty smoke from the smutty little fires that had been lit here and there to burn the plague sufferers' clothing. This served to heighten the feeling of gloom and foreboding and misery into a sensation so palpable that I could almost see Death hovering over the camp, black wings outspread, gliding slow.

I also saw scores of monks at work among the plague victims, for the church had shouldered the burden of caring for the diseased and dying. These stalwart clerics carried water to the fevered and warm cloaks to the shivering; they prayed with the distressed and comforted the dying. And though they strove valiantly against an insidiously powerful adversary, their struggle was in vain. There were far too few of them to sway the course of battle. The cause, so far as I could see, was lost—yet they fought on.

The good brothers had used the rubble stone of the fallen wall behind them to erect hundreds of small enclosures over which cloth and skins were placed to form hovels in which the more curable of the sick might lie. Need had far outstripped the monks' kindly provision, however, and they had begun laying the plague-struck toe-to-toe, rank upon rank in endless rows beneath the crumbling wall. Meanwhile, the busy brothers hastened among the sprawled bodies on urgent errands.

I caught one brown-robed cleric and asked of him where I might find Brother Paulus. The monk pointed to a tent beside the wall, not far from the gate, and I made directly for the place. Once, when stepping over a body of one I thought a corpse, I felt a hand reach out and snatch hold of my foot. A pitiful voice cried, "Please!"

Revulsion swept over me. I jerked my foot free.

"Please . . ." the wretch moaned again. "I thirst . . . I thirst."

Ashamed of my harsh reaction, I glanced around to see

where I might find some water to give the poor fellow, and saw a monk carrying two flasks. I ran to the brother, told him I had need of the jar, and returned to the man on the ground, then knelt beside him, put my hand beneath his head, and raised him up a little to drink. His hair was wet and his skin damp and cold; his rheumy eyes fluttered in his head when I put the jar to his lips. I watched in horror as a black tongue darted out to lap at the water.

"Bless you," he whispered, his breath sighing out between his teeth.

"Drink," I urged. "Take a little more."

It was only after entreating him a second time that I realized I was clutching a corpse. I put aside the jar, lowered his head to the ground, and stood, wiping my hands on the ground. Hardening my heart, I walked on, ignoring the pleas of those I passed. God help me, I walked on, lest through their defiling touch I should become like them.

What if Arthur is right, I thought, and the most Holy Grail can end this suffering? What if it could bring about the miracle Arthur believes? Then he must try. Anyone with half a heart would try. Indeed, the king would have to be either a coldhearted fiend or insane not to attempt anything that held out even the slightest hope for healing his people. Certainly, a king of Arthur's stamp must do everything in his power to bring this healing about.

These things I thought, and began, at last, to understand Arthur's obsession with the shrine. I regretted my doubt and mistrust, and repented of my disbelief. Who was I, an ignorant warrior, to question the things of God? Thus, as I walked along, I found myself praying: Great Light, let Arthur be right. Hasten the completion of the shrine, and let the Grail do its work. Let the Grail do its saving work, Merciful Lord, and let the healing begin.

I reached the tent and ducked gratefully inside, where I found Paulus hunched over a low table, pouring his healing potion from a large jar into smaller vessels for distribution to the afflicted. "Brother Paulus," I said, and he looked up, recognized me, and smiled. It was the tired,

forlorn smile of an exhausted man. His hair was lank and
his eyes were sunken; his flesh had the wan, pallid look
of a person too long confined.

"God be praised, it is Gwalchavad!" he said, genuinely
pleased to see me. "Greetings!" He took two steps towards me, then caught himself. "You should not be
here," he warned. "Tell me quickly what you have to
say, and then leave."

Taking him at his word, I said, "Greetings, Paulus. I
bring supplies and provisions from your fellow monks. I
also bring word that Lady Charis is required at the Tor.
The Pendragon has sent me to fetch her. If you will tell
me where she may be found, trust that we will depart as
soon as the horses are unburdened."

"That would be best," the haggard monk agreed, re-
placing the jar and drawing his sleeve across his damp
forehead. "Come, I will show you."

"Please, I would not disturb you. Just tell me where
she is, and I will find her myself."

The dutiful monk waved aside my offer. "It will be
quicker to show you," he insisted.

He led me out along the wall, passing the burning refuse heap on the way—where I saw to my horror that it
was in fact an immense pit which had been dug in the
earth, filled with logs, and set alight to burn the dead. By
twos and threes the corpses were thrown onto the sputtering heap. The smoke stank and the corpses sizzled.
Down in the lower depths of the pit, black, grinning skulls
nestled among the red embers. I turned my face, held my
breath, and hurried by.

"I am sorry," Paulus said, calling over his shoulder;
"we have no other choice. The plague is far worse in the
city, where people live close together—that makes it more
virulent, I think."

"Everything is worse in the city," I concurred, then
inhaled some of the stinking smoke and was overcome by
a fit of coughing.

Paulus led me past the pit and along the wall to another
section of the camp and still more hovels and still more
bodies lying on the ground. But here, at least, robed

monks passed among the plague-struck bearing jars of healing elixir. "Not all die," Paulus told me. "Many of these may yet recover. Those who have that chance are brought here, where we can care for them."

Just then a figure emerged from a nearby hovel, moved to one of the victims on the ground. I saw that it was Charis, Lady of the Lake, her fair hair bound in a length of cloth and wound around her head, her tall, elegant form clothed in a simple coarse robe such as the monks around her wore. Kneeling beside the sufferer—a young woman with waxy yellow skin—she placed her hand gently on the young woman's forehead. The stricken woman came awake at the touch and, seeing the one who attended her, smiled. Despite the agony of her distress, she smiled at Charis and I saw the killing plague retreat, if only for a moment.

Charis offered her charge a few words of comfort, at which the young woman closed her eyes and rested again, but more comfortably, I think, for her features appeared serene as Charis rose and continued on her way. Paulus made to call Charis, but I stopped him, saying, "Please, no. I will go to her."

I watched for a while as Charis moved among the stricken and suffering, here stooping to touch, there stopping to offer a word. Like the monks, she carried a jar of the elixir, which she gave out, pouring a few precious drops of Paulus' healing draught into the victims' bowls and cups, then helping the sufferer to drink. Wherever she went, I imagined peace and solace followed—a healing presence, like a light, clearer and finer than sunlight, which soothed and calmed, easing the pains of disease and death.

Upon reaching the last of her charges, Charis stood, smoothed her robe, turned, and looked back along the ranks of victims. She closed her eyes and stood there for a moment, head bowed, lips moving slightly. Then she opened her eyes and, glancing up, saw me and smiled in greeting. In that smile she became the Fair Folk queen I remembered. Oh, they are a handsome race, there is no doubt. I saw the light come up in her eyes, and the breath caught in my throat.

I watched as she approached, feeling both humble and proud to be accounted worthy to converse with such nobility. "You have come from Arthur, I think," she said upon joining us.

"I give you good greeting, Lady Charis," I replied, inclining my head in respect. "The Pendragon has indeed sent me to find you."

"Have you come to help us?" she inquired with a smile. "Or brought supplies, perhaps?"

"Bishop Elfodd has sent a fair store of provisions, but I have come to escort you back to Ynys Avallach."

"I see." The smile faded instantly, and I watched as gray fatigue repossessed her features.

"Forgive me," I said, and explained about the Grail Shrine and Arthur's concern to have it consecrated at the Christ Mass observance. I must have told it poorly, for a frown appeared, grew, and darkened, like a shadow of apprehension, as she listened.

"So," she said with crisp indignation when I had finished, "Arthur deems the building of this shrine more important than the saving of lives. What of my son—does Merlin encourage this enterprise?"

"Lady," I said, "it is the king's hope that the consecration of the Grail Shrine will drive both disease and war from our land forever. Arthur believes it will be the saving of us. Myrddin, as ever, aids his king."

Charis regarded me with a keen eye. "You avoid my question. I wonder why."

"Forgive me, Lady Charis, but the Wise Emrys does not often vouchsafe his confidences to me."

"But you have eyes, do you not? You have a mind to question what you see. Do you think this Grail Shrine will end plague and war?" she demanded. "Do you believe it will be the saving of Britain?"

My mind whirled, searching for a suitable reply. "I believe," I answered slowly, "that the Swift Sure Hand is upon our king to accomplish many things. Who am I to say whether the Good God should bless Arthur's efforts?''

Charis relented. ''You are right, of course. My question was unkind. I am sorry, Gwalchavad.'' She smiled again, and again I saw fatigue in her clear eyes; like Paulus, she was on the knife-edge of exhaustion. She glanced along the long row of hovels and shook her head. ''You see how it is here. I cannot leave.'' She spoke softly, as if to herself. Then, turning to me, she said, ''At the risk of incurring the king's displeasure, I fear you must tell Arthur that I cannot attend the ceremony. I am needed here.''

Paulus stepped forward and laid his hand on her arm. ''You have been summoned by the High King; you must go.'' His tone became quietly insistent. ''Go now, and return to us when you have rested.''

''I have brought a horse for you,'' I told her, glad to have the monk's approval. I had seen enough of pestilence and death and was anxious to get away. ''If you are willing, we could leave at once.''

Charis hesitated. ''Go,'' Paulus urged. ''Gwalchavad is right. Arthur's new shrine may be just as important in this battle as your presence here. He would not have summoned you otherwise.''

''Very well,'' Charis decided. To me she said, ''Tend to the horses. It is best for you not to linger. I will join you as soon as I am ready.''

I thanked Paulus and asked him where he would like the supplies to be stored. ''Just leave them,'' he advised. ''That would be best. We can collect them when you have gone.''

I hastened to the horses, removing myself from the hateful camp as swiftly as possible. I carefully stacked all the bundles and casks in a neat pile, and sat down to wait. In a little while, Charis joined me, and without a backward glance we were riding for Ynys Avallach. Earlier, I had marked a stream—one of the few I encountered that had not yet dried up completely—and stopped there for the night. I was heartily glad to have left the plague behind, though it was not until I had washed myself head to sole that I felt hale again.

While I kept watch, my companion slept soundly and well—grateful, I reckon, for a respite from her unendurable duties—and the next morning we journeyed on. The return took a little more time than the outward journey, for I chose another trail, which kept us well away from the forest. Having braved the unseen watcher once, I saw no need to do so again; besides, I thought it a reproach to tax the Heavenly Host with my protection when I could so easily avoid trouble in the first place.

Thus, we skirted the forest and arrived at the Tor by another way, passing within sight of the Grail Shrine. Though I had been away only a handful of days, I found the site altered beyond recognition.

Gone were the wagons and the heaps of rock-broken stone; gone, too, the ropes and lumber and ranks of workers swarming over a half-finished building. In place of all the clutter and activity stood a silent, graceful structure of whitewashed stone, glistening in the dawn light. Elegant in its simplicity—the Master Gall had done his work well—the shrine appeared to shimmer with an inner radiance. The drought heat had long since blasted the surrounding grass to thin, withered wisps of palest yellow, so that the whole place, with hill and shrine included, glowed in the early morning with the luster and radiance of gold.

We stopped to marvel at the glorious sight. In all, it was a fitting house for the Christ's Holy Cup. What is more, for the first time since I had heard Arthur's plan, I thought he was right. It is magnificent, I thought; truly, it betokens a new and glorious reign of peace and well-being.

Upon our arrival at the Tor, we were greeted by Arthur and Gwenhwyvar, who appeared in the yard as we dismounted. Gwenhwyvar and Charis embraced one another warmly, and Arthur stood by, beaming his good pleasure. Out of the corner of my eye, I glimpsed the elusive Avallach standing beside a pillar, arms crossed over his chest. Since coming to the Tor, I had rarely seen him—most often in the long evening when he was fishing with Bedwyr or Myrddin—and then only from a distance.

I knew that the Fisher King suffered from an incurable malady which often kept him confined to his quarters. I assumed that was why we had not seen much of him since our arrival. Thus, I was surprised to see him standing in the shadows nearby. He stood for a moment, gazing at the tight group before him, then stepped out to join it.

"Charis!" he said, throwing his arms wide for his daughter. His voice boomed like friendly thunder, and he hugged his daughter and told her how much he had missed her. "You are the sun of my happiness," he said, "and now it is summer again."

"Have you seen the shrine?" asked Arthur, unable to rein in his curiosity any longer.

"I have indeed," replied Lady Charis, and pronounced the shrine the work of a master who both knew and respected the object to be protected within.

"It is that," affirmed the Fisher King—somewhat reluctantly, I thought.

"Arthur," Charis said, "are you certain this is the way?" She gripped Arthur by the arm as if to hold him to account.

"As certain as the sun and stars," the Pendragon replied, his gaze as steady as his unwavering grip. "The Summer Kingdom is here. We stand at the threshold of an age the like of which has never been seen since the beginning of our race. The nations will look up in wonder when they hear what we have done. The blessing begins here, and it will flow throughout all Britain and to the ends of the earth. People of lands far distant from these will come to witness the miracle. Britain will be foremost among the nations, and our people will be exalted."

Avallach nodded, resignation heavy in his eyes. Arthur reached out and squeezed the Fisher King's arm. "We are so close, my friend. So very close. Have faith, and watch what God will do!"

Arthur spoke with such passion and assurance that it would have been a dead heart indeed not to beat more quickly at his words. His zeal was a flame, burning away the straw of opposition. Who could stand against the Pen-

dragon when heart and will and mind were united in the
pursuit of so lofty a purpose?

Who, indeed?

As we were yet talking, others of Arthur's court came
to greet Avallach and welcome the Lady of the Lake: Cai
and Bedwyr first, then Cador and Rhys. I looked for Llenlleawg but did not see him, and it was not until we were
all gathered in the hall for our supper that the Irishman
emerged from hiding.

The hall was prepared for the Lady of the Lake's return,
and Avallach had already called for his guests to be seated
and we were making way to our places—some of us more
slowly as we hailed this one or another. Myrddin and
Charis arrived and were talking quietly just inside the
doorway while others entered the hall.

It was then I saw Llenlleawg appear in the doorway,
Morgaws at his side. The two stepped into the hall and
moved towards their places at one of the nearer boards.
As I was slowly making my way to the board myself, I
had opportunity to mark their entrance and observe what
followed.

See, now: the Emrys, his head low and a little forward,
is speaking earnestly to his mother, who listens intently.
She senses a movement beside her, however, and glances
to the side to see Llenlleawg pass by. She recognizes him,
of course, for I see it in her eyes as her lips begin a
smile—a smile that instantly freezes when she also takes
in the sight of Morgaws.

It is only the merest glance, but the queerest thing happens: as if acutely mindful of Charis' attention, the young
woman turns her head; their eyes meet. Morgaws falters,
her foot catching in mid-step. She lurches sideways as if
struck by a spear hurled from across the hall. She stum-
bles, her features twisted in pain, or rage, and I fear she
will fall. But Llenlleawg's hand is at her elbow; he stead-
ies her arm and bears her up. Incredibly, Morgaws recov-
ers both balance and aplomb in her stride; the moment
passes in a twinkling, and I, the only one to have seen it,
am left to wonder at what I have witnessed.

The two latecomers turn away and lose themselves in

the convivial mingling at the board. I look once more to where Myrddin and Charis stand. The Emrys is still speaking, but his mother is no longer listening. Instead, she stares at the place where Morgaws and Llenlleawg appeared, her expression one of horror, the color drained from her face. Strange to say, but I am put in mind of the first time Peredur laid eyes on the woman when we found her in the wood—his expression combined the same shock and terror at her appearance.

Sensing that his words are no longer attended, Myrddin looks up; his mother's stark features halt the flow of his words and he touches her arm. The Lady of the Lake quickens at his touch; she comes to herself once more— as if suddenly starting from a dream—sees her son, and smiles, her hand rising to her face. Myrddin, ever alert, turns to see what has so shattered his mother's composure. But there is now nothing to see; Morgaws and her escort have disappeared in the crowd. Myrddin takes his mother by the arm and walks with her to their places at table with Arthur and Gwenhwyvar.

I settled in next to Bedwyr, and noticed his dark brow furrowed in serious rumination. Thinking to lighten his somber mood, I said, "It seems friend Llenlleawg has become champion to the mysterious Morgaws. I wonder if Arthur kens this shift of loyalty."

"Never have I seen a man wear a more haunted look. He is sick with it, our Llenlleawg. I fear what may become of him."

"Well, no doubt he will recover. Love seldom proves fatal—so I am told."

Bedwyr gave a mirthless, scornful chuckle.

"What? Has something happened while I was away?"

"Ah," he replied, his smile as bitter as his tone, "Arthur's shrine races to its completion, and we are all deliriously happy, of course."

One of the serving boys appeared just then and placed cups before us. Bedwyr raised his cup to me and took a deep draught.

"And yet?" I prodded, nudging him with an elbow.

"Yet," Bedwyr continued, "the Pendragon communes

with God and the angels, and the concerns of earthly mortals are not to be mentioned." Bedwyr's rueful smile turned sour. "In short, our king stands with his head in the clouds and his feet on the dung heap. The odor, he imagines, is meadow-sweet, but it smells like manure to me."

"You surprise me, brother. If anyone can bring the Summer Kingdom to fruition, it is Arthur. It could happen just as he says."

Bedwyr drank again, put aside his cup, and said, "Do not mind me, Gwalchavad, I am only mourning the past. Or maybe I am jealous—she is a beautiful young woman, is she not?" He laughed, forcing himself to rise above his melancholy, yet there was a bitter edge to his voice when he said, "Two days, my friend—two days and all doubts and suspicions shall be swept away. In two days the shrine is consecrated and the Grail is established, and the Kingdom of Summer begins. I am certain all will be well."

Despite his dubious assurance, Bedwyr's conviction appeared as shaky as my own, but after my harrowing visit to the plague camp, I had tried to believe the miracle could take place. What if, as Myrddin had said, the Swift Sure Hand was on Arthur to bring about the restoring of this worlds-realm? Who could oppose God?

Chapter Twenty

Dreams of spitting cats and hissing snakes kept me thrashing on my pallet all night. I heard strange laughter, and awoke to the sound of someone calling my name. The warriors' quarters were quiet, however, and, as the sun was rising on a new day, I thought to banish the night's malignant cast with a cold plunge in the lake.

I crept from the palace and made my way quickly down the twisting path. The mist rising off the lake as the dawnlight struck the surface of the water made it seem as if I descended from the pure heavenly heights to the cloud-bound earth below. At the lakeside, I stripped off my clothes and waded out from the shore—some little distance, for, owing to the drought, the level of the water was much lower now.

Gathering courage, I dove in and swam quickly to the center of the lake before I lost my nerve. The water was clear and stinging cold, but not as cold as it should have been for the season. Here the Christ Mass was upon us, and winter winds should be howling from the frozen north; yet, save for a few chill evenings, the days, though short, remained warm as midsummer, and dry. The warmth nobody complained of, but the lack of rain scoured the land to dust.

Ever since I was old enough to walk from my father's caer down to the water's edge, I have loved swimming. Lot insisted that anyone bred and born on a rock in the sea should be able to swim to save his life, so my brother

and I learned early and learned well. This thought was in
my mind as I swam to the center of the lake, took a deep
breath, and sank down into the cold, spring-fed depths.

Down and down I went, the icy water tingling on my
skin, pricking like ten thousand needles. When at last I
could stay under no longer, I rose to dive again and again,
trying to go deeper each time. The last time, I simply
bobbed to the surface to float on my back, gazing up at
the sun-streaked morning sky, letting my thoughts drift as
idly as the clouds above.

While I lay floating, the sound of someone singing
reached me—a lightly lilting, wordless melody. Silently,
without so much as a ripple, I sank down into the water
and turned my eyes to the bank, where I saw a hunched
figure hurrying along the lakeside pathway leading to the
Tor: a woman, dressed all in black. I did not recognize
her, for a cloud had passed before the sun and her features
were hidden by shadow. Curiously, this shadow moved
with her, covering her, so that I could not see who it might
be.

It was then I remembered having heard that same
strange song before—it had led me a chase the day I
found Morgaws in the wood. The thought had no more
flitted through my mind when she stopped—halting in
mid-step, much as someone might when hailed from behind by the shout of a friend. In the same instant, the
shadow vanished and I saw that it was, indeed, Morgaws,
and what I had taken for black was, in fact, her customary
green, which I could see so clearly I wondered how I had
mistaken it before. That aside, I thought it odd she should
be astir so early in the morning, and naturally wondered
where she had been.

She stood stock-still for a long moment, and then
turned slowly towards the lake. Something in me urged
secrecy, so I allowed myself to submerge once more.
Strange to say, but as my head sank beneath the water, I
felt a peculiar warmth where her gaze swept the water. It
passed in an instant, like a wave washing over my head,
and then all was as it had been before. When I surfaced
again, Morgaws was gone. I watched for a time and

thought I saw her on the Tor path just before she entered the palace gate, but owing to the brightness of the sunlight, I could easily have been mistaken.

I swam to the bank, dried myself, and dressed, then made haste to find Myrddin; I had it in mind to tell him what I had seen. But by the time I reached the Tor, I had convinced myself that my concern was mere foolishness. What had I seen, after all? Only someone taking an early-morning walk. She sang, yes, as any young woman might, delighting in her own company and the simple splendors of the new day. In any event, Myrddin was occupied with the ordering of the ceremony, and would not care to be bothered.

Along with the rest of the Dragon Flight, I spent the day in preparation for the consecration ceremony. Beginning with a fast, we assembled in the hall to learn our duties for the ceremony, and to hear how our ranks should be ordered. We then attended to our clothing and weapons: siarcs and breecs were washed and cloaks brushed, swords and spears were burnished, and shields were washed white with lime and painted with the cross of the Christ. That night, in place of a meal, we gathered in the hall and held vigil; led by one of the abbey priests, we prayed through the night for the Good Lord's blessing on the new realm.

Then, as dawn broke upon the eastern horizon, we dressed in our finest clothes, and arrayed ourselves as for battle. The participants assembled in the yard, each one taking his place as we had been instructed: Arthur and Gwenhwyvar first, Myrddin and Charis following, with various priests and monks and nobles from the region coming after, and behind them, the Dragon Flight and the rest of the Cymbrogi. Walking slowly, crosier held high, the procession was led out through the gate by Bishop Elfodd; beside him walked Lord Avallach, carrying a fine wooden casket in his hands.

Thus, we walked slowly down from the Fisher King's palace to the lakeside path, two by two. Upon reaching the lake, the monks commenced chanting a psalm, softly, quietly at first, but louder and with more spirit as we went.

When we passed the monastery, its lone bell tolled, the plaintive voice ringing out over the countryside, calling the world to witness the changing of the age.

Much of that world seemed prepared to take notice, for there were many hundreds of people already gathered in the valley, awaiting the ceremony. The stoneworkers and their families were there, of course. Also, I suppose the monks had spread the word throughout the region, and many, despite the plague—or, indeed, perhaps because of it—had come to see the Lord of Summer begin his reign.

The Grail Shrine gleamed like white gold in the morning light, the cool stone shimmering and radiant against the fair blue of the sky. The procession reached the foot of the hill and stopped, whereupon Bishop Elfodd turned and spoke a prayer. We then continued up the hill—followed by the crowds, which pressed in all around us to see and hear what was taking place—and paused at the hilltop for another prayer; a third prayer was spoken as the Grail was carried around the perimeter, and a fourth at the entrance to the shrine. At each place, Avallach, accompanied by the bishop, presented the casket to the four quarters, while the good bishop offered up a prayer; together they sained the earth with the presence of the holy object.

In a loud voice Bishop Elfodd called for all present to bear witness. "From this day the ground whereon you stand is holy ground. Let it here be known, and proclaimed throughout all Britain, that the Lord Christ has favored this place and has claimed it for his own. Henceforth and for all time, this place shall be a refuge and sanctuary for any and all who come here, and no one shall be turned away, nor shall anyone be compelled to leave, nor carried away by force. Thus, no one shall prevent another from entering God's peace."

Then Myrddin, his dignity and noble bearing never greater, ascended the steps of the shrine, turned to the mass of onlookers, and stretched forth his hands. If anyone had forgotten that Myrddin was once a king, the memory was reawakened now. I have lived my life in the presence of kings and noblemen, and I saw a king now, lordly in manner and mien. Tall and erect, his head high, his expression grave and proud, his golden eyes ablaze with the light of righteousness, Myrddin gazed out over the upturned faces of the throng, and silence descended over the hill as all upon it strained forward to hear what he would say.

"My people!" he cried in a loud voice. "This is a day like no other in the long history of our race."

He paused and I felt the air quicken around me with anticipation. The crowd, as a solitary creature, keen with yearning, held its breath.

"Rejoice!" the Emrys shouted suddenly, and I swear I heard his shout echoing across the surrounding hills like thunder.

"Rejoice!" he cried again, lifting his hands high. "For this day begins the Kingdom of Summer, may it endure forever.

"Listen! Hear the words of the Chief Bard of Britain, Taliesin ap Elphin ap Gwyddno Garanhir: 'There is a land shining with goodness where each man protects his brother's dignity as readily as his own, where war and want have ceased and all races live under the same law of love and honor. It is a land bright with truth, where a man's word is his pledge and falsehood is banished, where children sleep safely in their mothers' arms and never know fear or pain. It is a land where kings extend their hands in justice rather than reach for the sword; where mercy, kindness, and compassion flow like deep water, and men revere virtue, revere truth, revere beauty, above comfort, pleasure, or selfish gain—a land where peace reigns in the hearts of men; where faith blazes like a beacon from every hill, and love like a fire from every hearth; where the True God is worshipped and his ways acclaimed by all.'

"Thus Taliesin spoke, bequeathing his bright vision to a world ruled by the Powers of Darkness. Today, it pleases the High King of Heaven to honor the words his servant uttered so long ago. People of Britain, hear me! Rejoice and be glad, the long-awaited day has dawned."

The High King took his place beside Myrddin then. As

I gazed upon Arthur, tall and strong, his handsome face
lit by golden morning light, the white stone of the shrine
fairly glowing behind him, I knew that the Wise Emrys,
as ever, had spoken the truth. The High King drew his
sword, Caledvwlch, and raised the naked blade like a
cross and held it before him.

"Today, in your hearing, Taliesin's prophecy is fulfilled," he said. "My friends, the Kingdom of Summer is
begun. Taliesin's fair vision has become reality. Here we
begin, and may the Living God crown our efforts with
every virtue."

Arthur lofted the blade-cross, and the host of people
gave voice with a great cry of acclaim. "Pendragon! Pendragon!" Their shout became a flood rolling down the
hillside to spread throughout the land. "Pendragon!" In
that moment, the High King, bold and bright before them,
became the long-awaited Summer Lord.

After a time, the cry died down, allowing Arthur to
continue. Lowering the great sword, he placed the point
of the blade against the stone at his feet, and folded his
hands one over the other atop the pommel. Then, gazing
out over the people and the valley beyond, as if into the
far-distant future, he said, "What is begun this day will
burn in the hearts of all who hear of it. What is begun
this day will be a boon of rich blessing to the people of
every race and tribe.

"What is begun this day," Arthur Pendragon said, his
face shining in the morning light, "will last to the end of
the world, when God shall roll up the heavens like a
parchment and return to Earth to reign in righteousness
for all eternity. So be it!"

Delivering his sword to Myrddin, the king turned,
stepped to where Avallach stood waiting, and, with a bow
of acknowledgment to the Grail's first Guardian, placed
his hand on the casket and opened the lid. The world was
lit with a sudden flash of radiance—as if lightning had
been shut up inside the box to be released at this moment.
The onlookers gasped as Arthur reached in and withdrew
the Grail and raised it high. I do not know what others
saw, but I beheld a footed cup which glittered and shone

in the bright sunlight as if it, too, were alive to the light
that danced over and around it. A row of rubies and em-
eralds glittered around its foot, and the rim was set with
pearls; a broad band of impossibly ornate scrollwork bent
around the bowl, catching the light and throwing it off
like sparks from a golden flame.

My heart soared as I filled my gaze with that rapturous
sight. I felt myself grow stronger and, yes, more noble—
as if the light revealed the man I was meant to be, but so
rarely was. And I was not the only one to feel this way:
from the murmurs of amazement around me, I guessed
that all who beheld the Lord Christ's bowl were in that
selfsame moment granted a vision of the Good God's redeeming grace.

It happened in the blink of an eye, the narrow space
between one word and the next—for yet was Arthur
speaking. "Behold! I give you the Cup of Christ, which
shall be the emblem of the Summer Realm, and a perpetual reminder of the source and sustainer of our good
fortune."

So saying, he stepped to the entrance of the shrine and
placed the Grail on the altar stone which had been prepared for it. This done, he reverenced the cup with a bow
and stepped away from the altar. Outside again, he retrieved his sword from Myrddin, raised it, and declared:
"From this day I have done with war and killing. Strife
and violent contention have no place in the Kingdom of
Summer. Henceforth shall Britain be called a land of
peace." Stepping into the shrine once more, he laid Caledvwlch before the Grail, point on the floor and hilt resting against the altar stone, so that the blade looked like
Bishop Elfodd's cross. The High King then knelt before
the altar and offered up a prayer.

Father in Heaven, never let me forget that sight: Arthur
on his knees before the altar, his head back, face tilted
upwards, his strong arms outspread, palms upwards to receive the blessing he sought. And above him, shining with
the brightness of the sun itself, filling the shrine with a
high and holy light, the Grail.

How long he remained in the shrine, I cannot say—for

the moment was eternal and all creation held its breath. When he emerged, it was to a world subtly, but surely, changed. Arthur himself seemed fairer, stronger, more noble—as if all those lordly qualities which he already possessed in rare abundance had been expanded, increased, multiplied within him, and he now assumed a greater stature than before. If anyone doubted his own perception, he had only to look at Gwenhwyvar; the expression of admiration and love commingled in her eyes would have convinced the hardest skeptic that here before us stood a lord transfigured.

The High King, his face shining with the reflected glory of the Holy Cup, slowly raised his hands in a gesture of benevolence and said, "May the Grail which we have established in this shrine serve as a beacon of hope to all mankind. Let it hereafter be said that once upon this Island of the Mighty, men and women loved virtue more than their lives, and sacrificed themselves to the rule of truth and justice.

"Friends," he said, "we have kindled a flame that will burn to the end of the world. We are men still, but God's own Cymbrogi stand in awe of the things we shall do. Even now angels are gathering to assist us on the journey we have begun. Signs and wonders will become commonplace, miracles will multiply in abundance, and peace will wash over the Island of the Mighty like a great sea wave lifted on the wings of the storm.

"I ask you, who can stop the waves? Who can tame the ocean's fury, or harness the sea's colossal strength? Who can bid the sun to halt in the sky, or stay the steady march of the seasons?

"I tell you the truth, we shall do all these things and more who pledge fealty to the Kingdom of Summer and its Eternal Lord. For if we remain loyal through all things, Britain will be the wonder of the world: a torch that is never quenched, a holy fire that cannot be extinguished. And all the nations that dwell in darkness will lift up their eyes and will behold the light of their salvation, burning as a beacon in the night. They will look up, and they will rejoice, and so great will be their rejoicing that the sound of celebration will overwhelm the sound of war. That hateful craft will pass away, never to be remembered.''

If the acclaim before had been thunderous, the roar of approval which met this pronouncement was deafening; it seemed to go on and on and on. During this exuberant and joyous outpouring, Bishop Elfodd stepped forward and, lifting holy hands to the Lord of Hosts, began saining the shrine with prayers of consecration. But the ceremony was effectively finished; even as he prayed, people came crowding forward for a better view of the sacred cup.

Arthur signaled the Grail Guardians to take their places, which we did, standing in a wide double rank to form a narrow pathway through which the people might pass into the shrine. Men and women, young and old, hastened forward, jostling one another in their eagerness to kneel before the Grail and offer up their own heartfelt prayers.

Once begun, the flood became a tideflow which washed up the side of the hill and into the shrine. We Guardians stood and watched them come, some anxious and halting, some so a-tremble with awe that they could hardly move, some with touching reverence, others bold, as if they would lay hold of the kingdom and claim its mighty promise for themselves.

No matter how they went in, all emerged changed— some more, some less, but no one who entered the shrine remained the same after having seen the Grail. I saw one old woman with a withered hand emerge with her hand restored, and a man on a wooden crutch walked out on two strong legs to throw the stick as far away as he could hurl it. Another man, so ill he lacked the strength to walk, was brought to the altar by his friends, only to emerge leaping and jumping for joy.

These were but the first of many healed that day. I saw men and women bent double by grief and care enter the shrine, and leave with heads high and the fire of hope shining in their faces. Many emerged with tears glistening in their eyes and on their cheeks; more than a few had to be removed from the shrine: dazzled by the glory of the Blessed Cup and overcome by the holiness of the moment, they were transported into a rapture of bliss and were borne out by kinsmen and friends.

The evening stars were shining in the eastern sky when the last of the worshippers departed. Bishop Elfodd lit the torches either side of the doorway, and replaced the Grail in its wooden casket. Only then were we able to sit down and rest our aching feet. Despite watching all day, Bedwyr, Cai, and Cador volunteered to take the first night's watch. Llenlleawg and I were allowed to return to the Tor—with Cai's admonition to remember the watchers their supper.

The first night passed peacefully in the Summer Realm, and the next day remained so tranquil and serene it was easy to believe that the world had indeed changed. The few folk who visited the shrine went away manifestly blessed—one crippled woman, a girl given to fits, and two boys with skin diseases were healed. The prevailing mood of peace and elation made our guard duty pure pleasure. We ended the second blissful day full of brotherly love and kindly thoughts for all mankind.

Ah, but word of the miracles accomplished in the presence of the Grail was spreading through the land. Already the news had gone out beyond the borders of the realm, and like a spear hurled from the hand, there was no calling it back.

Chapter Twenty-one

All night long, visitors streamed into the valley. To everyone's surprise, there were more than a few Saecsens among them. How word had flown so far so fast was more than I could credit. Obviously, they had been traveling day and night to reach the Grail Shrine and, once arrived, they waited patiently, sitting in groups on the ground, or sleeping on the hillside. The monks brought food and water, and cared for the sick through the night until they could be admitted to the shrine the next morning.

Arthur, upon receiving information that Saecsens were coming to the shrine, was visibly delighted, and declared that the Grail was already fulfilling its highest purpose. "One day," he said, "every citizen of Britain will have made his way to this place to see the Most Holy Grail, and the world will be made new."

There was much in what the Pendragon said. For on the third day more people came to the shrine, and the arrivals did not stop at dusk, when the Grail Shrine was closed; the people kept coming, and were contented to wait through the night to be admitted the next morning. On the fourth day the numbers swelled; a steady flow of visitors trickled into the valley all through the day and into the night. By the fifth day it was clear that the numbers were steadily rising; thus, the chore of guarding the shrine was growing increasingly wearing for the five Guardians.

Admittedly, if even one of us had thought beyond that

first day's duty, we might have seen how inept our scheme
really was. If we had not been distracted by the blissful
exhilaration of our position, and if we had properly understood the nature of the object we were guarding, we
might have anticipated the eagerness of the people, driven
by desperation and need to obtain healing.

Thus, it did not take a bard's wisdom to see that our
simpleminded notion of five Grail Guardians standing perpetual watch was—after only a few days—breaking down
under the sheer weight of numbers. Clearly, a new plan
was needed.

"Brothers," said Bedwyr as we looked out upon the
gathered pilgrims in the fading light—so many had arrived through the day that they would not now get in to
see the Grail until the morning—"you are mighty men
all, and far above me in every way. No doubt you could
stand before the shrine day and night for a thousand years
and never feel the strain, but I cannot. In short, I am
tired."

As if to demonstrate his point, he yawned, and said,
"We must have help, and I see no reason why the Cymbrogi should fritter away the days in idle pursuits while
we labor on. It is neither fitting nor right."

"Are you suggesting that we compel our swordbrothers
to help shoulder this duty?" I asked.

"I am suggesting that very thing," confirmed Bedwyr
with another yawn.

"Man, why did you not speak up the sooner?" blurted
Cai. "It is all I can do to put one foot in front of the
other, and here am I thinking you enjoy standing like a
pillar all day long."

"As much as I enjoy it," Cador remarked, "I yet might
be persuaded to let a few of the Cymbrogi take my
place—if my brother Guardians were so disposed."

"That is the Cador I know," Bedwyr replied, adopting
an admiring tone, "generous to the last. As for myself, I
deem it no less an honor for sharing it among my swordbrothers. Let them have it, I say!"

"Then it is settled," I said. "We all agree that the duty
should be shared out among the Cymbrogi."

"Llenlleawg has not said what he thinks," Cai pointed out, indicating the tall Irishman standing silent as a pillar.

"Well?" inquired Bedwyr, swinging towards the Irishman. "What say you, Llenlleawg?"

Arthur's champion shrugged. "If everyone else agrees," he muttered, glancing away and down, "I am for it."

Bedwyr stared at him for a moment, as if trying to decide what ailed the man. "So!" he said, turning away abruptly. "We have made our first addition to the rules of order."

As the last of the day's visitors made their way into the shrine, we then fell to discussing how to divide the watch, and it was quickly decided that one Grail Guardian should stand as overseer to eight of the Cymbrogi. To further ease the hardship of the duty, the day guard would be relieved at sunset by those who were chosen to watch the night. Thus, we would only be required to stand one watch in every five—an obviously superior arrangement, for we would enjoy a day of rest between. We then drew straws to see who would begin the new order of rotation. As luck would have it, I drew the next day's watch, but Llenlleawg drew the short straw and was forced to stand watch that very night, after having stood guard all day. Though luck went against him, he made no complaint.

While there were still many people waiting in the gathering twilight, we had no choice but to declare the shrine closed. Bedwyr told the people the Grail Shrine would open again at dawn, and the attending monks bade those in need to come to the monastery for food and shelter. One old man became agitated at this announcement and began shouting. "I have waited all day!" he said. "I cannot wait any longer."

"Just until tomorrow, friend," said the monk firmly, but not unkindly.

"Tomorrow will be too late," the man insisted, his voice and shoulders shaking with the effort. He carried a long stick, which he leaned on for support. "Please, I must see the Cup of Christ tonight."

"Come to the abbey and we will take care of you,"

the monk told him. "You can come back in the morning."

"I am old and sick. I may die tonight!" the man said stubbornly, and turned to appeal to Bedwyr. "You there! You are the king's man—you can let me see the cup before I die. Please!"

The monk took hold of the old man's arm and made to lead him away. Bedwyr intervened, however. "Wait! Let him in. But no more today—he will be the last."

The monk relented and led the old man forward. They entered the shrine and Bedwyr undertook to inform all the other visitors that food would be provided at the abbey for any who required it, and that they were welcome to return to the shrine at dawn, when they would be cheerfully admitted. The people muttered over this, but accepted their lot and began making their way down the hill to the valley below, where most of them would spend the night.

The rest of us, meanwhile, fell to discussing who should make up the watch for the night. We quickly chose the guard and informed Bedwyr when he rejoined us; a moment later, the old man emerged from the shrine. He walked directly to Bedwyr, seized his hand, and kissed it, saying, "Bless you, son. Bless you. Bless you," ducking his head with each benison. "I can die a happy man," he said, and then walked away, carrying his stick in his hand.

"A friend for life," Cai observed. "Now let us be gone."

Llenlleawg wished us a restful sleep in our good, soft beds, and bade us remember him his supper. He then urged us to haste lest he starve before the food should reach him.

We promised to send his supper along with those who were to take the watch with him that night, whereupon Bedwyr, Cai, and I rode back to Ynys Avallach. We passed through the gate to find the yard alight with torches and filled with people and horses. "Someone important has come," one of the Cymbrogi told me as I dismounted.

"Who?" I asked, but he did not know.

Thinking it might be Gwalcmai, I threw the fellow the

reins and commanded him to take care of my mount. While Bedwyr called for volunteers to stand guard duty, I ran to the hall to welcome, not my brother, alas, but someone almost as dear and good to me: Bors.

See now: I have known Bors for a long time. He and his brother, King Ban of Benowyc, were among the first of the Pendragon's advocates. Having supported Aurelius and Uther—Arthur's father and uncle, the first High Kings of Britain—they had aided the young Dux Britanniarum in his struggles to unite the lords of Britain and conquer the Saecsens. For Bors, that meant more than merely providing men; he had joined the Cymbrogi and lent his sword to the cause.

For seven years he, like all the rest of us, fought alongside Arthur. Following the defeat of the Saecsens at Baedun, and Arthur's kingmaking and wedding, Bors returned home to help his brother out of some difficulty or other. Summoned from Armorica to help fight the Vandali, he had at last arrived—just in time to help celebrate the enshrinement of the Grail—and now stood drinking ale and laughing with Arthur and Gwenhwyvar. "If you could not resist finishing off the Black Boar," the prince of Benowyc was saying, "you might at least have saved one of his piglets for me. Here I have come to feast on pork—only to be given cakes and ale instead."

"Did you think to fight the Vandali alone?" I remarked, striding up beside him.

"Where is your warband?" asked Bedwyr.

"Welcome, brother," said Cai. "We feared your pilot had lost his way on that ocean of yours."

"Gwalchavad! Bedwyr! Cai!" he shouted with husky heartiness, embracing us with his free hand. "Bless me, but it is good to see you again. I tell you the truth, we met Arthur's messenger halfway, so I sent the warriors home and came on alone."

He did not say it, but with Britain sore beset by plague and drought, no doubt it was safer for his men to remain in Armorica. Turning to Arthur, he said, "I am heartily sorry I could not come to you sooner, Bear. But the Frencs grow ever more contentious and will not be appeased so easily as in the past. We had our hands full through the summer, I tell you. Still, Ban would have me beg your pardon for the delay.''

''There is no need,'' said Arthur, waving aside the apology. ''Tell me, how fares your brother?''

''Ban sends his greetings to one and all, and asks to be remembered by his former swordbrothers. As ever, he is desirous of coming to Britain one day soon, 'when kingly duties weigh less heavily upon the crownéd head,' as he says.''

''If that is the case,'' I ventured, ''then he will likely remain in Benowyc forever. I have never known a man so able at producing work out of thin air.''

''Too true,'' agreed Bors. ''I tell him the same thing myself, but he can always find a thousand things begging to be done, and it is 'Who will do them if I leave?' and thus he keeps himself busy year to year.'' Turning to Arthur, he said, ''Now, then, what am I hearing about this Grail of yours?''

''It saved Arthur's life,'' Gwenhwyvar replied. ''If not for the Grail, Britain would be in mourning now. The Holy Cup healed his wounds and restored his life.''

''Then it is true?'' Bors wondered, turning wide eyes towards Arthur. ''From the moment we made landfall, I have heard nothing but talk of this Holy Grail. I thought it must be one of those peculiar rumors that surface from time to time—like that enormous serpent living in the lake up north.''

''Afanc,'' I told him. ''I know a man who saw it snatch one of his cows from the shore of the lake where it was grazing. I myself have seen it.''

''The serpent?'' asked Bors in astonishment.

''No, the lake.''

They all laughed at this, and Bors thrust the cup into my hands. ''Drink, brother! Ah, but it is good to be back among true friends.''

Rhys arrived while Bors was speaking and whispered something to the king. ''I fear, Lord Bors,'' said Arthur, ''Gwenhwyvar and I have been called away. We must speak to Myrddin before he disappears again. But you will sit with me at table tonight,'' Arthur promised, ''and I will tell you all about the battles you have missed.''

The Pendragon and his lady moved away then, and Bedwyr made excuses, too, saying he must see to the night watch and supper for Llenlleawg. He hurried off to order the Cymbrogi, leaving Cai and me to help Bors with the welcome cup. ''Where is our Irishman?'' wondered Bors.

''At the shrine,'' I answered, and went on to explain about the Fellowship of the Grail. ''We each take it in turn to guard the shrine,'' I concluded. ''It was Llenlleawg's bad luck to draw the short straw—he has the watch tonight.''

''Alone?'' asked Bors, passing the cup to me.

''Nay,'' replied Cai, ''there are eight Cymbrogi with him—or soon will be—so he will not lack for company.''

''When did you arrive?'' I asked, taking a drink and passing the cup to Cai.

''At midday, just,'' Bors replied. His features grew keen. ''But tell me, have you seen this Grail?''

''Man,'' Cai hooted, ''for three whole days I have done little else save stand beside it from dawn to dusk.''

''Where is this shrine?'' Bors asked, excitement growing. ''Take me.''

''Now?'' said Cai. ''We have just this moment returned from there.''

''Now,'' Bors insisted. ''I want to see this marvel for myself. If it is as you say, even a moment is too long to wait.''

''But the shrine is closed now,'' I explained. ''Even if it were not, people in their hundreds have waited through the day to see it, and now must wait through the night as well. They stand ahead of you, brother. But never fear, I have the watch tomorrow, and I will take you and make certain you get to see it.''

Bors yielded with good grace. ''Very well,'' he said, ''if I must wait, then at least I tarry in good company. Bless me, but I am sorry I missed the fighting. Was it bad?''

''Bad enough,'' I replied. ''The Saecsens were worse,

of course, but the Vandali were nearly as bad—fiercest
when backed into a corner. Fortunately, Arthur saw to it
that did not happen very often. Mostly, we chased them
up and down the valleys. They had their women and children with them.''

"God in Heaven!" He shook his head in disbelief.

"Truly," I declared. "It seems they had been forced
to flee their homeland in the southern seas somewhere,
and they were looking for new lands for settlement."

"They chose the wrong place when they chose Britain," Bors said.

"They tried Ierna first," I said, "and when we chased
them away from those green hills, they came here. It took
the whole summer, but we vanquished them at last. Even
so, they have not done too badly."

"No?" He regarded us dubiously.

"For a truth," Cai declared, nodding. "In return for
peace and sworn allegiance to the High King, Arthur gave
them lands in the north."

"He never did!"

"Did and done," I told him, and related the story of
how Arthur had undertaken single combat with the Black
Boar, and received the deadly wound which ended in the
miraculous healing. "I believe it is for the best," I concluded. "The Grail is established, Britain is at peace, and
the Kingdom of Summer is begun. Never has there been
a better time to be alive."

Bors regarded me curiously, trying to determine if I was
sincere or not. Unable to decide, he reached for the cup
instead, took a long draught of the ale, whereupon one of
the serving men appeared to say that Avallach called for
his guests to take their places at the board. We hurried
into the hall, where we were joined at table by Bedwyr
and Cador, and some others eager to renew their acquaintance with Bors. The talk was fine and amiable, the ale
flowed freely, and we spent the evening pledging and re-
pledging our undying friendship to one another.

"I wish Llenlleawg were here," Bedwyr said at one
point. "This is just the tonic that would do him good."

"To Llenlleawg!" proclaimed Cai grandly. "The finest

warrior who ever drew sword or sat horse.''

''I will drink to that,'' declared Cador cheerfully, raising his cup high.

''To the finest warrior that ever drew sword!'' echoed Bedwyr, and we all acclaimed the sentiment with a noisy rattling of our cups.

We were then overtaken by a sudden and irresistible urge to drink the health and virtue of every single member of the Dragon Flight, fine men each and every one. Night was far gone when I finally found my bed. The warriors' lodgings were full, so I took off my boots and curled up in the corner. It seemed that I had merely closed my eyes when I was roughly roused by someone shaking me by the shoulder.

''Wake up!'' said a voice loud in my ear. ''Lord Gwalchavad, please, wake up!''

I opened one eye, and recognized the face hovering above me in the dark. ''Tallaght, what are you doing?''

''I am trying to wake you, lord,'' he said.

''You have achieved your ambition,'' I replied, and made to roll over. ''Now go away and let me sleep.''

He started shaking me again. ''Forgive me, lord. You must come with me. There is trouble.''

I sat up. ''What trouble?'' I demanded, pulling on my boots.

''I cannot say,'' he answered. ''Rhys says the Pendragon has roused the Dragon Flight. We are summoned to the yard at once.''

As we were no great distance from the hall, I could hear men moving quickly and quietly in the corridor beyond. By the time we joined them, the yard was in turmoil: men rushing everywhere at once to saddle horses and procure weapons by torchlight. I caught sight of Rhys, leading Arthur's mount from the stables.

''Rhys!'' I shouted, running to meet him. ''Are we attacked?''

''The shrine,'' he shouted breathlessly as he passed without slowing. ''Something has happened at the shrine.''

''Well, what is it, man?''

"How do I know?"

He hurried on, so I concerned myself with saddling my horse and arming myself. I had just strapped a sword to my hip and got hold of a spear when Rhys' hunting horn called us to be mounted. I swung into the saddle and saw Arthur across the yard, his face set in that expression I have come to know well: the serene, unhurried calm of a skilled craftsman assembling the tools of his trade. Unlike other men when riding into battle, the Pendragon becomes more himself rather than less.

Even-tempered by nature, in a fight Arthur is never uneasy or alarmed, never worried or distressed, never fear-fraught nor less yet unnerved. Myrddin has said that he believes Arthur truly lives only in the fight. "Many warriors live to fight," Myrddin told me once, "but Arthur comes alive in battle—the way an eagle only comes alive when it takes flight."

"He is courageous," I agreed.

"What is courage but the mastery of fear?" said the Wise Emrys. "But there is no fear in Arthur. Tell me, does the eagle fear the wind that frees him to fly?"

Well, the Eagle of Britain was ready to soar, and those who recognized the sight knew well what it meant.

We rode through the gate and pounded onto the winding Tor path in the dark—there must have been fifty or more men clattering down the hillside at Arthur's back. Gaining the lakeside path, we flew past the monastery, scrambled over the lowland, and made directly for Shrine Hill, where we found the place in chaos.

People were stumbling around in the darkness, for the moon had set and dawn had not yet come, and they were shouting at one another; the women were wailing and children were crying, but I could not see what had happened to cause such distress. There was a crush of confusion at the foot of Shrine Hill; Rhys gave forth blast after blast on the horn, and we forced our way through the clinging throng and rode for the hilltop.

The shrine itself was peacefully quiet, and we swiftly discovered why: the warriors charged with guarding the shrine were dead. They lay on the steps leading to the entrance to the shrine where they had fallen. All had been attacked with a sword and suffered horrific wounds—several had lost limbs, and one had been decapitated.

Arthur took one look at the carnage and said, "Who had the watch tonight?" His voice was tight, as if he were speaking with immense difficulty.

"Llenlleawg," I answered.

Without another word, the king turned and mounted the steps to the shrine. He stepped inside, only to emerge a moment later, his face frozen in a rictus of shock and dismay.

"Arthur?" said Bedwyr as the king strode past. "Is he inside?"

But the king made no reply and, without so much as a backward glance, walked back down the hill.

Seizing a torch from the hand of a nearby warrior, Bedwyr dashed to the entrance of the shrine. "Well?" Cador shouted at him.

When Bedwyr did not answer, Cador cleared the steps in a bound and dashed inside. I could see the torchlight playing over the interior of the shrine, and then Cador appeared in the doorway looking shaken and unsteady. Thinking to see Llenlleawg dead in a pool of blood, I leapt up the steps to the door of the shrine and looked inside—but there was neither blood nor body. Indeed, the shrine was completely empty. . . .

Owing to my relief at not finding Llenlleawg's corpse, it took a moment for the awful significance to break over me. But when it did, it burst with all the fury of a tempest: the shrine was empty . . . the Grail was gone, Caledvwlch was gone, and Llenlleawg was nowhere to be found.

Chapter Twenty-two

"Rhys! Cai!" cried the Pendragon upon reaching the throng at the bottom of the hill. "Find someone who saw what happened!"

The two were already moving to his command as Arthur, having mastered his shock, swiftly turned to the waiting Cymbrogi. "The Grail is gone, and Caledvwlch with it. The guards are dead. Get more torches. Search the hill. I want to know how many were here, and which way they went." In the moment of stunned hesitation that followed, he roared, "Now!" and men scattered in twenty directions.

Seizing a torch from one of the sconces at the entrance to the shrine, I began searching the outside of the building and was quickly joined by Cador bearing another torch. We walked slowly, crouching low, examining the soft, dusty earth for fresh footprints, or for any other sign that the attackers might have crept up from behind the shrine to take the watchmen unawares.

There were all sorts of marks in the dust—the tracks of masons and the imprints where stone and tools had lain—but all these were old and scuffed about. "Nothing fresh here," Cador concluded.

Still, just to make certain we had not missed anything or overlooked any possible trace, however small, we made a second circuit of the shrine. This time, the only new tracks we saw were those Cador and I had made during the first circuit; I could identify them readily enough on the dry, dusty ground—which gave me to know that had there been any new tracks the first time, we would have recognized them. There were none.

"Go tell Arthur," Cador said. "I will look over there." He pointed to the broad slope of the hill's rearward side.

Hurrying to the front of the shrine, I found the hillside ablaze with the light of torches as the Cymbrogi scoured the path and surrounding area. Arthur and Bedwyr were standing halfway down the hill talking to Myrddin, who was still on horseback. After a few brief words, the Emrys turned his mount and raced away again. Hearing my footsteps behind him, the king whirled on me. "Well?" he demanded.

"We found nothing, Pendragon," I told him.

"Look again," he commanded.

"We have already searched twice, and—"

"Again!" The order was curt, and brooked no reply.

Bedwyr, grim in the softly fluttering light, nodded. "We must be certain," he said.

As it was easier to comply than to argue, I walked the shrine perimeter for the third time, more slowly and painstakingly, to be sure. Again I saw nothing I had not seen before. Nor did Cador's scrutiny turn up any traces that the shrine had been approached from the rear. Cador met me at the hilltop, shaking his head. "Nothing," he said. "Whoever did this did not strike from behind."

We hurried back, reaching the king just as Rhys and Cai came hastening up the pathway, dragging two others between them.

"There are at least three more dead down there," Rhys informed us bleakly. "Skulls split ear to ear. Another four wounded."

"These two saw what happened," Cai added. "They are father and son—arrived after nightfall from east of—"

Arthur raised a hand and cut him off. Addressing the two men, he said, "What did you see?"

The older of the two swallowed, then glanced sideways at Cai, who urged him on with a sharp nod. The man licked his lips and said, "It was dark, Lord Pendragon. I

fear my eyes is not what they was—'specially in the dead
of night.''

"Just say what you saw,'' urged Arthur impatiently.

The man blinked, his face squirming in the torchlight;
he licked his lips again, and worked his jaw. The second
man, a youth with a club foot, blurted, "It were terrible,
Lord Pendragon. Terrible. The first thing I knowed something's amiss was when up there comes a shout—like a
death cry, it were. We had just got ourselves a piece of
the ground and rolled up in our cloaks to sleep, and this
brought us up again something quick, I can tell you.''

The elder man nodded his agreement at this. "Aye, the
very truth.''

"Yes, yes,'' growled Bedwyr testily. "But what did
you see!''

"Tell them and be quick about it,'' coaxed Cai in a
low tone, with another nod of encouragement.

"Up there,'' the youth said, pointing to the shrine,
"men was all asudden fighting for their very lives. All of
them at it, eh, Da?''

The man nodded. "Every last one,'' he murmured.

"They was fighting something fierce,'' the youth continued, "and must have been six or more against one—
but the one, he were a fighter. He flew this way and that,
slashing and slashing. And what with the shouting and
slashing, I never seen such a sight. He killed them all, he
did.''

"Every last one,'' repeated the father.

"Who?'' demanded Bedwyr.

The young man looked at Cai for help.

"His name!'' said Arthur tersely, holding him to the
task.

"I never heard his name,'' the youth replied. "But he
were tall—taller than the rest, at least.'' He hesitated,
glancing around quickly, then added, "And the queen
were with him.''

The words hit me like a spear in the gut. Llenlleawg
and Gwenhwyvar? Can it be true? I looked to Arthur to
judge his reaction, but, save for a tightening of his jaw,
saw no appreciable change.

Bedwyr, however, had gone red in the face, and was almost shaking with frustrated rage. "How could you see all this from down there?" he shouted, pointing angrily down the hill at the place where they had stood.

"For the torches on the side of the shrine," the young man explained. "We saw it all. He killed them, and then he comes running down here, running like his legs is afire. We see him waving that great sword in one hand, and carrying something under his other arm."

"What was he carrying?" demanded Bedwyr roughly.

The youth shrugged. "A wooden box."

"Is that what you saw, too?" Bedwyr turned his withering gaze on the elder of the two.

"Tell the truth, man," Arthur cautioned, his voice tight.

The man licked his lips and said, "Some of the people down here, they started shouting: 'The Grail! The Grail! He has got the Grail!' I do not know about that—all I saw was the box, and him running away with it."

"You said you saw the queen—where was she?" Cai asked.

"Well, now, the tall one runs to where the horses is picketed over there." He pointed to where the guards had tethered the animals. "The queen was waiting there—I never seen her at first for all the battle going on up the shrine. But I reckon she was waiting there all along."

"What happened then?" said Arthur softly, almost trembling with rage.

"Well, they go to ride away. Some of those nearest by make bold to lay hold of the killer. Everyone is shouting, 'He stole the Grail! He stole the Grail!' and they try to stop him."

"And it is dead they are for their troubles," asserted the older man.

"That sword is up and he strikes them all down who lays hand to him. And then they both ride off that way." The youth pointed to the east.

"Is that all?" said Arthur.

"That is the last I seen," the youth answered. "We never seen anything after that until you all came."

The older man nodded and spat, adding, "We feared you was coming to kill us, too."

"There is nothing else—you are certain of that?" Bedwyr glared hard at both of them, daring them to add to or take away anything from what we had already heard.

The two shook their heads and remained silent, whereupon Arthur dismissed them, charging them to say nothing of this to anyone else until more could be learned. As soon as they had gone, we all turned to one another. "It cannot be Llenlleawg has done this!" Cai insisted vehemently. "It was never Llenlleawg and Gwenhwyvar."

"Who, then?" snarled Bedwyr. "Llenlleawg is the only one of us missing now—why is that, do you think?"

"It was someone else!" Cai maintained. "Someone who looked like him."

"Those two are confused," I suggested quickly. "It is dark. They were asleep when it started. They could not possibly have seen everything that happened."

"Truly," agreed Cai. "Maybe they caught sight of Llenlleawg riding off in pursuit of the attackers, and assumed he had done it."

"Aye, he rode off," asserted Bedwyr, his voice an ugly sneer, "taking the Grail with him."

"What of Gwenhwyvar?" Cador wondered.

"Gwenhwyvar was with me," Arthur said bluntly.

"Llenlleawg could not have done it," Cai insisted. "Anyway, Llenlleawg was sworn to protect the Grail with his life. If he rode in pursuit of the killer, he could never leave it behind."

Bedwyr dispatched this lame suggestion without mercy. "Then why not ride to the Tor? He could bring the Grail for protection and raise the alarm. If word of the massacre had not been brought to us by those confused people down there, we still would not know of it."

"Since the queen was with Arthur," Cador suggested, "it must have been Morgaws with him."

Arthur glared hard in the dim light. "Yes," he agreed sourly. Turning to Cador, the king said, "Ride to the Tor and tell the queen what has happened; then find Morgaws—if she is there, bring her to me.''

Cador leapt to the saddle at once and raced away into the darkness. Swinging towards Bedwyr, Arthur commanded, "You and Rhys take eight men and see if you can raise the trail."

Bedwyr made to protest, but the look on Arthur's face warned him off and he departed, calling for men and torches.

"Gwalchavad," the king ordered, "you and Cai see what is to be done for those who have been wounded, then take word to Elfodd and remove the dead to the abbey."

"I do not like this, Arthur," Cai muttered under his breath.

Arthur ignored him, saying, "I will talk to the people here. Someone may have seen something more."

The king stalked off towards the distraught crowd. Cai made to follow, but I put a hand on his arm and said, "Come, there are injured needing help. If you would go to the monastery, I will see to matters here."

"You go to the monastery," Cai said, staring at Arthur as he walked away. "I want to talk to some of the others and see if anyone saw anything different."

Thus, I found myself hurrying to the abbey to summon Bishop Elfodd. Owing to the fact that a few monks had been at the shrine tending folk through the night, word had reached the abbey before me. I rode into the yard to meet the bishop and five or six monks as they rushed from their lodging hall.

"I pray there has been a wicked mistake," Elfodd said.

"It is no mistake," I told him. "There are dead and wounded. The king wants you."

"Yes, yes," Elfodd replied quickly. "We will do whatever we can. Are you returning to the shrine?"

"At once."

"I will go with you." Laying a hand on the shoulder of the nearest monk, he said, "Brother Hywel, I leave you in authority." He then ordered the monks to fetch balms and bandages and hasten to the shrine.

"Ride with me," I said, putting down a hand for him.
"The way is short and we are soon there."

Two monks hurried to the bishop's aid, and we were
soon hastening back across the night-dark valley. Upon
dismounting, we proceeded directly to the shrine, where
Arthur was holding council with Myrddin and Bors by
fluttering torchlight.

"As much as it pains us," the Emrys was saying, "it
may be the truth."

The High King stared at his Wise Counselor, his face
grim in the fluttering light of hissing torches.

"At least," Bors said, softening Myrddin's pronouncement, "what passes for the truth—until we find Llenlleawg and learn why he has behaved like this."

"Then it is true?" I asked. "Llenlleawg is gone?"

Myrddin replied, "He is not at the Tor."

"It is a tragedy," Bishop Elfodd said, breaking in. "I
am shocked beyond reason. I thought the shrine well protected. I never imagined one of the Guardians—"

"We are no less dismayed than you, bishop," Myrddin
said pointedly. "What this moment requires, however, is
your sympathy and support, not your reproach."

The bishop accepted his reprimand with good grace. He
inclined his head in acknowledgment of his error and said,
"I am deeply sorry, Lord Arthur, and I want you to know
that I am placing myself and my brothers under your command. We will do all in our power to assist you in any
way we can."

Arthur thanked him and said, "Your skills would best
be employed aiding the wounded and praying for Llenlleawg's swift return."

"The wounded will be cared for, of course," the cleric
replied, "and I will immediately establish perpetual
prayer for the recovery of the Holy Cup." Glancing at
Bors and Myrddin, he said, "Please, send word if you
need anything." With that he hurried off to direct the
monks who were helping with the injured and dead.

Cador returned from the Tor, lashing his horse up the
hill at full gallop. Without even pausing to dismount, he
leaned from the saddle, putting his head to Arthur's ear.

Even while he spoke, the Pendragon's face changed. Now, I have seen the Bear of Britain in his rage before, but have never seen him like this: his face darkened, his jaw bulged, and the veins stood out on his neck and brow.

Seizing Cador by the arm, the king almost hauled him bodily from the saddle. "My wife—gone?" he cried.

"She is nowhere to be found," Cador replied, trying to keep his saddle. "I stopped at the stables—the queen's horse is gone, along with Morgaws' and another." He hesitated. "The stablers were asleep, but one of them says he thinks he saw the queen take the horses. Mind, he was half asleep at the time."

Added to what Myrddin had already said, it seemed the two witnesses were right: the king's champion had murdered his swordbrothers and stolen the Most Holy Grail. What is more, it appeared he had been aided in this atrocity by none other than the queen.

That Llenlleawg could perform such a treacherous act was unthinkable; that Gwenhwyvar should be party to it was impossible. Yet there it was—a double betrayal of such abhorrence the mind shrank from contemplation of it. There must be some other explanation, I determined. Morgaws is involved somehow; find her, and no doubt all would be explained.

I stepped quickly to join those at Arthur's side and await his command. Cador was saying, "Avallach wanted to come here, but I persuaded him to remain at the palace. He instructed me to say that he will await the Pendragon's return in his chamber. Charis has gone on to the abbey to help the monks." Duty discharged, Cador continued. "It cannot be what it seems, Bear. We will find them, but until we do, we cannot know what really happened."

"He speaks my thoughts entirely," I said, speaking up. "We should not judge by the appearance of the thing alone. It cannot be what it seems."

"I pray you are right," said Bors. "God knows, I have trusted that man in the thick of the fight more times than I remember, and I cannot find it in my heart to doubt him now."

"Until we find Llenlleawg," said Myrddin, "we will

not discover what happened. Therefore, our best efforts are given to the search.''

''Rhys and Bedwyr have already begun,'' snapped Arthur angrily.

''It will be daylight soon,'' Bors observed, striving to sound brisk and confident. ''They will raise the trail, never fear. We will learn the truth before the day is out.''

Away in the east, the sky was graying with the dawn. ''Come, Arthur,'' said Myrddin, taking the king by the arm, ''I want to see the shrine.'' Together they started towards the shrine to examine the empty building and, I believe, to speak to each other alone.

''What would you have us do now?'' Cador called after them.

''Bury the dead,'' came Arthur's terse reply.

Silent with our own thoughts, we stood and watched the thin gray line turn to silver, and then blush bright red as the sun rose on the worst day I have known since Baedun Hill.

Chapter Twenty-three

*N*ow the battle begins. I have made the first strike. It is greatly to Morgaws' credit that no one saw it coming. She chose her servant well, and bound him to her with strong enchantments. He is ours, and a more potent weapon would be difficult to find.

Oh, it would have been pure joy to have seen their faces when they discovered the traitor in their midst. I wish I had been there to savor it to the full. But it is not time to reveal myself just yet. I must content myself with the knowledge that my glory will be all the greater for remaining so long undiscovered.

Still, the shock of betrayal is an exquisite pleasure. And that it followed so quickly upon the birth of the Summer Kingdom is especially poignant. Simple treachery, when applied with such swift and thorough proficiency, can be simply devastating. Trust is, I think, the most fragile of the virtues; ever brittle, it shatters easily and, once broken, can never be completely repaired. In a single stroke, I have broken Arthur's most deeply held trusts. There is no force on Earth that can compel a heart to continue trusting when cruel, hard facts fly in the face of faith.

Doubt and fear are ever-faithful allies, I find, and, when joined with suspicion, can become wonderfully debilitating in an enemy. They are like twin hounds baying for blood. Relentless and merciless, they will chase and bite and howl, wearing down the prey until mind and *heart and will are spent, and the helpless victim drops from exhaustion.*

I do not expect Arthur to surrender easily; nor less yet Myrddin. They will prove stalwart adversaries, I expect. Thus will my eventual triumph taste the sweeter.

And what is this? Morgaws tells me she has come into possession of a certain talisman—a treasure of some kind, by which Arthur and Merlin set great store. An object of power—healing power, apparently, among other things— she used it to bait her trap. She does not tell me what it was, but I suspect the Grail.

That would be a treasure indeed. There were rumors in the wind about this Grail years ago—the miraculous cup of such power, it is able to work wonders of its own accord. Well, these tales are always stirring up the poor folk. Superstition has its uses, I find. Still, I never would have thought Merlin would have anything to do with it; he fancies himself above the common herd and its bovine beliefs.

Dear nephew has surprised me before, however. Therefore, I will make it my affair to find out more about this treasure Morgaws has discovered. In the meantime, I have a little talisman of my own to reveal. Come, enemy mine, the chase awaits you.

"Is this the last one?" wondered Cai, shoveling dry earth onto the body in the grave.

A bright, red-gold dawn had given way to a pale gray monk's-mantle of a sky—a gloomy day to match the mood of death and doom. The dirt was hard-baked and the graves shallow. We worked away in silence, thinking about the horrific events of the previous night. Twelve had been buried, and three more bodies brought from the hillside to the little yard near the lake below the abbey. Cai and I, along with Cador, Bors, and some of the Cymbrogi, had buried our swordbrothers first, before turning to the pilgrims. Many of the dead had families with them, some of whom stood nearby, weeping quietly as their kinsmen were laid to rest.

"One more," I told him, indicating the last of the three.

Together we dragged the last body to the newly dug grave, and rolled it into the narrow hole. I put my shovel into the mound of dirt and dragged part of the pile onto the body. Cai likewise bent his back to the task, then hesitated. "God bless him," he muttered under his breath. "I know this one." I glanced up, and he said, "Is this not the old man who raised the commotion when we closed the shrine?"

I turned and looked into the bloodless face of the corpse in the grave. "So it is," I confirmed. The last time I had seen him, he had been striding away with an expression of rapture on his battered old face.

"He said he wanted to see the Grail before he died," Cai remembered.

"Then at least he died happy," I replied, and began pulling dirt over him.

A moment later, a rider came from the Tor. "Arthur wants you," the warrior said. "Bedwyr has returned. You are to come at once."

Leaving the mourners to the care of Elfodd's monks, we rode back to the Tor to face the king's wrath. Arthur was standing behind his camp chair—the chair Uther had used as a throne—waiting for us in Avallach's chamber at the Fisher King's palace. Bedwyr and Rhys were standing before the chair, arms folded and unhappy.

"He betrayed us!" Arthur said, his voice the growl of a wounded animal. "He has betrayed the Summer Kingdom, he has betrayed his king, and he has betrayed Britain."

"We do not know what happened," Rhys pointed out.

"Do we not?" demanded the High King, his voice hard and flat and cold. "Do we not? We know the Grail is gone, and Llenlleawg with it; we know eight Cymbrogi were slain by his hand and fifteen pilgrims as well; we know the Summer Realm lies in ruins; we know he has stolen, murdered, and destroyed. If that were not condemnation enough, he has taken the queen with him—whether by force or by deception, I know not—the queen he has vowed to protect through all things. He shall be hunted down like the treacherous dog that he is, and he shall be killed.''

''Bear,'' pleaded Bedwyr, ''be reasonable. We will find him and then we will discover the truth.''

''Let it not be said that Arthur Pendragon was ever less than reasonable,'' replied the king icily. ''We shall be a very paragon of reason. If a servant betrays his master, it is reasonable that he should expect to receive punishment. It is reasonable that the murderer should forfeit his life for his crime. It is reasonable to seek justice and demand retribution.''

''Justice, yes, by all means,'' agreed Bedwyr. ''But what of mercy?''

''Ah,'' said Arthur, ''you think us too harsh. Then let us temper our justice with mercy as you suggest. Know this: the same mercy granted those who were slain shall be granted the one who murdered them.''

Bedwyr glanced at Rhys uneasily. Clearly, they wanted to say more, but, owing to Arthur's poisonous mood, felt their intercessions were only making matters worse. In the strained silence, Cai and I took our places beside our swordbrothers and waited for the storm to break.

''Twenty-three dead! The Grail gone!'' the Pendragon roared suddenly, striking the back of the chair with his fist. ''My sword taken, and my queen abducted!'' That was the first time I heard that word uttered, but no doubt he was right. The king glared around him, defying anyone to dispute his reading of events. ''Is that not the shape of things?''

No one made bold to answer. Arthur glowered murderously at us; I had never seen him so angry. ''You!'' he shouted, pointing at Bedwyr. ''Have you nothing to say?''

''In truth,'' intoned Bedwyr wearily, ''I thought we could not fail. We raised the trail at first light, but—''

Arthur cut him off. ''Save me your excuses. You failed.''

''Yes.'' Bedwyr shut his mouth and stared ahead.

''A short while ago,'' Arthur continued, pacing behind his chair like a caged bear, ''I told Avallach that his worst fears had been realized. He was against enshrining the Grail, but I persuaded him that it would be safe. I pledged my honor to it: 'The best men of the Dragon Flight will protect it. Nothing will happen to it.' But now—'' He glared at us with true contempt and loathing, and I felt the depth of his anger, restrained now, but dangerously close to flaring. ''Now it has been stolen by one of our own, and we are no closer to recovering it than we were when the alarm roused us from our beds. The blame will fall on me, and rightly so. But, God help me, I will not—''

''Make no vow you cannot keep,'' Myrddin declared. He had entered the chamber so quietly, no one noticed.

Arthur swung angrily towards this ill-opportuned interruption. Glaring at his Wise Counselor, he drew breath to vent his rage anew, but Myrddin said, ''Morgaws, too, is gone. Or have you forgotten?''

I confess that I did not at first understand the significance of Myrddin's insistence. Preoccupied with what we considered far more weighty matters—such as the dire betrayal of the king by his own champion—what did the disappearance of a foundling guest matter?

Arthur stared hard at Myrddin. ''It can wait,'' he growled at last. ''We have more important affairs before us—or have you forgotten?''

Impatient and angry though he was, he should not have said that last. ''Do I weary you with my prattling?'' Myrddin demanded tartly. Drawing himself up full height, he took breath and let fly. ''I am a True Bard,'' he said, his voice a very lash. ''If I speak, know that it is worthy of your regard, O Lofty King. Question me, if you will, but doubt me at your peril.''

''Peace, Myrddin,'' Arthur grumbled. ''I meant no disrespect.''

But the Wise Emrys would not be appeased so easily. ''While you have been busy with your grand and glorious schemes, the secret enemy has quietly invaded the innermost treasure-room of your stronghold. Find Morgaws and you will find the Grail.''

Arthur gazed grudgingly at his counselor—as if trying

to weigh the implications of his next decision. "Ready the Dragon Flight," he said at last.

Bedwyr remained unconvinced. "Do you think Rhys and I would have returned so soon if we had found anything? With so many people coming and going in the last days, it was impossible to see anything."

"Might it be possible you were looking in the wrong place?" inquired Myrddin smoothly.

Bedwyr opened his mouth to protest, then clamped it promptly shut. He knew better than to argue with Myrddin when the Wise Emrys was in a mood to cross swords. Thus, we were very soon riding out from the Tor in force. At my suggestion, the king agreed to allow Peredur to lead the search. I knew and valued the young warrior's abilities as a tracker, and he was eager to be of service.

The day was no longer fresh when we set out, but our hopes were kindled when, upon reaching the lakeside, we found the tracks of one unshod horse leading away west. All of Arthur's horses are iron-shod, of course, and so are Avallach's. "It might be Morgaws' mount," suggested Peredur doubtfully. "Then again, there have been many visitors to the Tor of late. It could be any one of them."

"True," Myrddin allowed, "but did any of the visitors ride west in the last day or so? Can anyone say that they saw anyone riding alone?"

That was good enough for Arthur. "Let us see where this leads. We will quickly discover whether we have made an error."

Well, the trail was good to begin with, and we flew along the wooded pathways, confidence growing through the day, only to be cast down abruptly when it ceased. I do not mean that we merely lost the trail, for we did not: the tracks—those of a lone horse and rider—led us all the way around the lake, thereby avoiding the abbey, and then bent towards Shrine Hill. According to the tale of the tracks, the rider came within sight of the Grail Shrine but did not approach, paused, then moved off at speed east, in the direction of the wood.

We followed the trail without the slightest difficulty; the tracks were good and the dry ground took a ready

impression. Eventually, the trail came to a small clearing
in the wood where stood a stone; there the rider had
stopped.

"It appears she met someone here, lord," Peredur said,
rising from his examination of the tracks. Even without
dismounting, I could see the place where two other horses
had stood, chafing the dry earth here and there with impatient hooves. "They rode on that way." Peredur
pointed into the trees on the opposite side of the clearing.

We resumed our pursuit, but not for long; at the other
side of the clearing—no more than two or three hundred
paces away—the hoofprints of the three horses simply and
suddenly stopped. The marks were there in the dust for
everyone to see, and then they were gone.

"It appears they have vanished between one step and
the next," Bedwyr observed, pressing a fingertip into the
last print. Not trusting completely to his eyes—less yet to
Peredur's or anyone else's—Bedwyr had dismounted for
a closer look, and now turned from his scrutiny of the
prints in the dirt to regard the jagged circle of sky showing
through the close-woven branches above. The short day
was far gone, the wan light already fading.

Meanwhile, Cai had carried the search farther along the
trail, and some others had quickly scoured the perimeter.
Finding nothing, they all returned to await the Pendragon's pleasure.

"What would you have us do, lord?" asked Bors. Arthur stared at the broken trail and said nothing, so we fell
to discussing what, in view of this unhelpful discovery,
might be the best course.

In the end, it was decided that Rhys and Cador would
continue the search with Peredur and a company of men;
the rest of us would return to Ynys Avallach—which we
did, reaching the Tor long after dark, having ridden in
dejected silence all the way back.

Nothing had happened in our absence: the dead were
still dead, the Grail was still gone, Llenlleawg had not
returned to explain his behavior, nor had Morgaws been
seen. Neither had Gwenhwyvar returned to welcome the
search party and tell us we had worried for nothing, that

all was well. Exhausted and edgy, we stared blear-eyed at the prospect of another long, hopeless night, and an endless succession of hopeless days to follow.

Thoroughly dejected, we dragged ourselves to the hall to get a bite to eat and a drink, and to rest ourselves from our strenuous, if futile, exertions. More disturbing news awaited us there, however. We entered to find the great room empty save for one of Avallach's servants, who approached us the instant we crossed the threshold, greeted the High King, and said, "If you please, lord, I have been instructed to tell you that Lord Avallach and Lady Charis have left the palace and returned to work with the good brothers at Londinium. They wish you God's aid in your search."

Arthur stiffened. "I see," he said. "Was there anything else?"

"No, lord," the steward replied. "That is all I was to say."

While some might have considered this circumstance a blessing in disguise—after all, facing a still-angry Avallach would not have been the most pleasant end to a day already rich with disaster—Arthur took it hard. "I am disgraced," he murmured, then, remembering himself, dismissed the servant with a command to bring some food and drink for his men.

We collapsed onto the nearby benches, a sorry-looking group once more. The only good that could be said of this day was that it was soon to end. Well, it could not end soon enough for me. Even so, too tired to eat and too disheartened to sleep, we prolonged the torment; we sat like gloomy lumps on the bench, clenching our cups in unfeeling hands, the bread tasteless in our mouths, each one nursing his disappointment as best he could.

Bors made a halfhearted attempt at lightening the desultory mood with a tale about a hunt in Benowyc. When the effort failed, he dragged himself away to sleep. Bedwyr followed soon after, leaving only Cai, Myrddin, and myself to sit with the king.

After a while, Myrddin rose, drained his cup, and said, "This avails nothing," he said. "Tomorrow's troubles can wait until tomorrow. Rest while you can."

With that he left, and Cai and I stood to go, too, but hesitated when Arthur made no move. Cai sat down once more. "Go on," he whispered to me. "I will see him to his bed when he is ready."

I did not like leaving them like that, but I was swaying on my feet and could not keep my eyes open any longer. "Very well," I said, relenting. "Only see to it that you both get some sleep."

"Oh, aye," agreed Cai, turning his gaze to the dejected king. "Soon."

I have no doubt they sat there all night, for Cai was red-eyed and irritable the following day, and the Pendragon's disposition had not improved. Nor did the morning light serve to brighten our circumstances.

The day ended in dismal waiting, Arthur's spirits sinking ever lower with the slow, relentless arc of the sun. He fretted and fumed, chafing at the tedium, and then, as the long shadows stretched across the yard, subsided into a wretched silence.

"Cador and Rhys had better appear tomorrow," muttered Bedwyr as we abandoned the vigil for the night, leaving the king to his misery. But they did not return, and Bedwyr, refusing to endure a third endless day of anxious inaction, took six Cymbrogi and rode out to see what he might find.

He returned at dusk, having done nothing more useful than tire seven horses. Finally, toward evening of the following day, Cador appeared, alone, with ill tidings on his lips.

"We searched in all possible directions," Cador informed us, his clothes begrimed, his face gray with fatigue, "and could not raise the trail again. But Peredur found this—" He put his hand to his belt and withdrew a circlet of silver.

In our eagerness we all gathered close for a better look, and I saw, on Cador's extended palm, a silver brooch of the kind used to fasten a cloak. The metal had been worked into the shape of a torc, with two small rubies at the ends. The pin was missing and the brooch was bent—

as if a horse had stepped on it—but still it was a handsome piece, no doubt belonging to a man or woman of noble rank. I had never seen it before—at least not that I could remember.

But Myrddin took one look and almost swooned. His knees buckled and Cai took him by the shoulders and bore him up. "Emrys, are you well? Here, sit you down."

But Myrddin pushed away from him and staggered forth. "Give it to me!" he shouted, snatching the brooch from Cador's hand. He studied it closely, then folded his fingers around it and pressed his fist to his forehead. "Great Light!" he groaned. "No . . . no . . . no," he murmured in his anguish. "Not again."

We stared at him, apprehensive, uncertain what to do, ignorant still of the trouble. What could he see in this simple ornament?

"Is it Gwenhwyvar's?" asked Bors, his voice creaking with apprehension.

"No," said Arthur. "It was never Gwenhwyvar's—or Llenlleawg's, either."

"Then whose?" wondered Cador, as mystified as the rest of us. "I thought it must be—"

Myrddin gave out a groan. "Ah, fool . . ." he said, more to himself, I think, than to anyone else. He looked around, his face ashen. "It belonged to Pelleas."

Chapter Twenty-four

See, now: the Fisher King had two daughters—Charis, the elder, and Morgian, the younger, by his second wife. There was some trouble between the two daughters—I never learned what it was—but it led Morgian to reject her kinfolk. She left Ynys Avallach long ago and took refuge in the wild north, as far away from Charis and Avallach as possible. In time, she came to the Orcades and, in that clutch of smooth-hilled islands, made for herself a fortress amidst the ancient standing stones and barrows.

God help me, this selfsame Morgian became my grandfather's wife. She was not my mother, nor even my father's mother. Heaven forbid it! Hear me, I am the son of Lot ap Loth, King of Orcady. My father rode with Arthur against the Saecsens and Vandali. Let all men remember that. It was my grandfather's misfortune to fall prey to Morgian's lust for power. He was a king, and she wanted a kingdom. The match was set before anyone knew the danger.

Poor Loth, in his dotage, imagined himself a lord of vast wealth and influence, and she was very beautiful. Some say that even then she was a canny sorceress, and laid an enchantment on my grandfather. Under the sway of Morgian's corrosive influence, he believed Lot, his loyal son, plotted to steal his throne. He harried my father and tried to kill him, but Lot escaped with most of the warband, and established himself on one of Orcady's many unassailable rocks. Gwalcmai and I were raised there, coming south to serve with Duke Arthur. No more than boys, my brother and I, and Arthur no older; we were among the first of the young war leader's Cymbrogi.

I have no doubt that it was Morgian who had turned Loth against Arthur in the end, but, true lord that he was, Arthur never counted our kinsman's rebellious ways against us. Still, the infamy is never far from me—every time I take the field, it is to restore some luster to our tarnished name. The Good Lord willing, we may yet be remembered as something other than the twin grandsons of wayward Loth, the mad king who made wicked Morgian his queen.

In the years we were fighting for our lives, Morgian delved deep into the Dark Arts that now ruled her. Myrddin says she has been consumed by the power she sought to command. Evil, he says, cannot rest and is never satisfied; it is a guest that always devours its host, a weapon that wounds all who would wield it. And Myrddin should know: he faced her and defeated her; she fled the field, her precious power shattered, her sorcery overthrown.

That victory did not come without a price, however; it cost Myrddin his eyesight and his closest friend. When Myrddin rode out to confront Morgian, he went alone. Pelleas, Myrddin's faithful friend and servant, feared for his master and followed. Alas, Pelleas has never been seen again, nor his body ever found. In all the world, there is only one person who knows what happened to Pelleas, and that person left Pelleas' brooch behind.

"You ask what this means!" said Myrddin Emrys, clutching the silver brooch. "Do you not know the darkness of the tomb when you see it? Do you wake in the night and think it bright day?"

He pressed the back of his hand to his mouth, and stared around him with wild eyes.

"Calm yourself, Myrddin," said Bors, attempting to soothe. "We do not understand."

"Death and darkness!" he said, his voice raw in its torment. "Morgian has returned!"

"Morgian!" whispered Bedwyr.

At the sound of her name, the hairs on my neck prickled and my mouth grew dry.

Myrddin, his face ashen, his hands shaking, swept from the chamber, leaving us stunned and bewildered. As soon as he had gone, everyone began talking at once. Most knew something of the Queen of Air and Darkness—aside from Myrddin, I think Bedwyr and I knew her best—but Bors knew her not at all. He pulled me aside and said, "This Morgian—she and Morgaws are the same, yes?"

"No," I answered, but in my heart I wondered: was it possible? Had Morgian taken the shape of Morgaws? I shuddered at the thought.

"But you know her?" he persisted. "Who is she that she wields such power?"

"She is a sorceress, and the sworn enemy of the Emrys and all his works," I told him. "Her powers are as vast as her ways are subtle, she is shrewd and she is cunning, and the Ancient Adversary himself is not more fearful than she."

"Myrddin fought her once and nearly lost his life," Bedwyr informed Bors. "She blinded him and left him for dead. I think if it were not for Pelleas, he would have died."

"I remember Pelleas . . ." Bors said, his voice trailing off.

"Maybe it is nothing to do with Morgian," Cai suggested weakly. God love him, if the sea and sky ever changed places, he would be first to question it, and last to believe it.

I wished I had some of Cai's dogged obstinance. As hardheaded as he was bighearted, he refused to believe the worst about anyone or anything. But I believed—more the dread—for I had some small experience of Morgian's powers, and it chilled me to the marrow to think she was somehow involved in the theft of the Grail.

We fell silent. No one believed Cai was right, but no one had the heart to dispute him, either. After a time, Arthur turned quietly to Cador. "What of Rhys?" he inquired softly.

The change in the Pendragon astonished me. The fire

of his anger had been quenched utterly. Cowed by Myrddin's revelations, he appeared shaken and defeated.

"I did not like to keep you waiting any longer," Cador replied. "I thought best to bring word, but also to begin spreading the search. Rhys and the Cymbrogi are riding to the nearby settlements and holdings to ask their aid."

"Soon the whole world will know of my failure," mused Arthur ruefully. The king dismissed Cador then, charging him to rest and return to the court when he was once more refreshed.

When Cador had gone, the Pendragon turned to the remaining Grail Guardians and Bors, who had in all respects taken Llenlleawg's place. "This is what your negligence has wrought," he said, "the ruin of a kingdom." He glared around the ring of faces. "If you have anything to say, I beg you say it now, friends. For I tell you the truth, unless the Holy Cup is restored, Britain is lost."

We all stared in silence, loath to make matters worse for saying the wrong thing. Alas, it was true; the Guardians had failed in their sworn duty and now the kingdom was imperiled. Who could answer that?

Unfortunately, the king read our reticence the wrong way. Taking a step backward, he collapsed into the throne-like chair. It was as if a blow from the flat of a sword had struck him down. "Even my friends desert me," he groaned. I could but gaze in wretched misery at his anguish now made painfully visible.

Then, as if to fight the despair that even now ensnared him, the Pendragon heaved himself up once more and stood defiant—a man confronting his accusers. He spoke, and there was fire in his voice. "Every day more and more pilgrims arrive at the shrine, only to find it empty. The word of miracles has gone out: 'Come!' they say. 'Come to the Summer Realm, and there you will see miracles!' And so the people come expecting a marvel, but instead see only Arthur's folly." His grotesque smile was terrible to see. "Ah, perhaps that is the greatest marvel of all: one man's arrogance and pride transformed into a hollow shell of lifeless stone."

He regarded us dully, then flicked a hand at us. "Leave me!"

No one said a word, and no one moved. "What?" the king demanded. "Are you become stumps? Leave me, I said. Get you from me! I cannot bear the sight of you!"

Bors, standing with his head down, arms wrapped around himself, made no move. Lost in thought, he seemed no longer to heed anything taking place in this world. But Bedwyr, dour in his silence, turned on his heel and led the retreat, abandoning his king to his misery.

Oh, it was a hard, hard thing, but what else could we do? With Arthur in this vile humor, there was nothing for it but to quit the chamber. To stay would have served no good purpose. Bedwyr and the others went to the hall, but I could not bring myself to join them.

I went my way alone, wandering wherever my feet would take me, and soon found myself out on the high parapet above the gate—the inner yard on one side, the sloping hill with its twisting path on the other and the lake beyond. I watched as the dull twilight deepened, and with it a dreary fog rose from the marshes and lake to clothe the Tor in a thick, damp, silent cloak—the silence of the grave, Myrddin would say.

My thoughts flittered here and there, restless birds that could find no friendly roost; when I looked around, night had settled uneasily over Ynys Avallach, ending another foul day at last. I noticed, without pleasure, that though the year had turned, the change brought no rain; the drought persisted.

Aching with fatigue and thoroughly dispirited, I left the battlement, but not before casting a last glance towards the woodland to the east where the Grail, and all our brightest hopes, had disappeared. A bank of low cloud, darker even than the night sky, rose over the wood—as if the darkness Myrddin feared was drawing down upon us. I shivered with a wayward chill and hurried inside.

The next day, Arthur did not receive us. Bedwyr went to him for instructions, but returned saying that the king had shut himself in his chamber and would not see anyone.

"This is not right," Cai asserted.

"Do you blame him?" Bedwyr snapped. His anger flared instantly. "None of this would have happened if not for us. The fault is ours." He struck himself on the chest with the flat of his hand. "The fault is ours!"

"I am going to him," said Cai, stalking from the hall.

He returned a short while later without having seen the king, and we spent a dismal day in an agony of bitter despair. Cymbrogi came and went throughout the day, anxious for a good word, but there was nothing to tell them. Dispirited, dejected, discouraged, we slipped further into the besetting gloom. At last, unable to stomach the bile of guilt any longer, I left my woeful companions and went in search of Myrddin.

Quitting the hall, I moved along the corridor towards the warriors' quarters, passing by Avallach's private chamber. The door was open slightly, and as I passed, I heard the moan of a man in pain. Pausing, I listened, and when the sound did not come again, I went to the door, pushed it gently open, and stepped inside.

Arthur yet sat in his chair, his head bowed upon his chest, the feeble glimmer of a single candle casting its bravely futile light into the close-gathered gloom. Oh, and it tore at my heart to see him, who was Earth and Sky to me, sitting alone in that darkened chamber. I regretted at once that I had intruded, and turned to go away again. But the king heard the sound of my soft footfall and said, "Leave me."

His voice was not his own, and the strangeness of it filled me with dread. I cannot leave him like this, I thought, so turned and advanced. "It is Gwalchavad," I whispered, approaching the chair.

At this he raised his head slightly; black shadows clung to him as if to drag him down into the depths. The room had grown chill, and the king sat with neither cloak nor brazier to warm him—a dragon torpid in his winter den. Even so, the eyes that gazed at me from beneath the grief-creased brow were fever-bright.

"Go away," he muttered. "You can do nothing for me."

"I thought I might sit with you," I said, wondering how it was possible for a man to decline so swiftly and completely. A short while ago he had been aflame with righteous anger, and now it had burned to ashes, and those ashes were cold.

There was no other chair in the room, so I stood awkwardly, certain that I had made a mistake in coming and, for Arthur's sake, regretting the intrusion. I was just thinking how best to make my retreat when the king said, "He has raised me up only to dash my head against the rocks." The hopelessness in his tone made me shudder, for I knew whom he meant.

After a moment, he continued, saying, "I thought the time had come, Gwalchavad. I thought the world would change, and that we would bring peace and healing to the land. I saw the Kingdom of Summer so clearly, and I wanted it so—" Arthur's voice became a strangled cry. "God help me . . . I wanted it so."

He was silent for another long moment, as if considering what he had just uttered. I stood quietly, and he seemed not to heed my presence any longer. "Perhaps that is my failing—wanting it too much," he said at last. "I thought he wanted it, too. I was so certain. I was never so certain of anything."

The king sank further into his chair, only to start again out of it as rage suddenly overswept him. "Three days!" he shouted, his ragged cry ringing in the empty chamber. "Taliesin's vision! Myrddin's work of a lifetime! The promised realm of peace and light—and it lasts all of three paltry days!" The cry became a moan. "God, why? Why have you done this to me? There was such good to be gained . . . why have you turned against me? Why do you scorn me?"

As if remembering my presence once more, Arthur shifted in his chair and looked at me. "I was betrayed," he spat, his voice harsh and thick. "Betrayed by one of my own. I loved him like a brother and trusted him. I trusted him with my life! And he repaid my trust with treachery. He has taken the Grail, and he has taken my wife."

"If Morgian is at the root of this," I ventured quietly, "then Llenlleawg was likely bewitched. He could not have done it otherwise."

The king seemed not to hear me, however. Clenching his hand into a fist, he struck it hard against his chest, as if to quell the inner pain. He did it again, and I stepped nearer so as to prevent him from injuring himself, should he persist. But the fit passed and he slumped back in his chair, weak with misery.

"Arthur's folly . . ." he muttered, closing his eyes once more. "They come—they come to see a miracle, and find nothing but a heap of stone raised by a fool of a king."

I could no longer bear to see him berate himself so harshly. At risk of rousing his wrath against me, I spoke. "You could not know any of this would happen," I said, trying to soothe him.

"King of Fools!" Arthur mocked. "Hear me, Gwalchavad, never trust an Irishman. The Irish will stab you in the back every time."

"If it is as the Emrys believes, it was Morgian, not Llenlleawg, who did this," I said. "You could never have foreseen that."

"You hold me blameless?" he sneered. "Then why has destruction befallen me? Why am I forsaken? Why has God turned against me?"

Fearing I was making matters worse, I hesitated. Arthur seized on my reluctance as confirmation of his failing.

"There!" he shouted. "You see it, too! Everyone saw it but me. Oh, but I see it now. . . ." He slammed his head sharply against the back of the chair with a cracking thump. "I see it now," he said again, his voice breaking with anguish, "and now it is too late."

"Arthur, it is not too late," I countered. "We will find Llenlleawg and recover the Grail. Everything will be made right again. The Kingdom of Summer has not failed—it must wait a little longer, that is all."

"I saw it, Gwalchavad," he said, closing his eyes again. "I saw it all."

He was exhausted, and I thought at last he might allow sleep to overtake him if I kept his mind from wandering along the more distressing paths. "What did you see, lord?"

"I saw the Summer Realm," he replied, his voice growing soft and dreamy. "I was dying—I know that. Myrddin does not say it, but I know I must have been very near death when he prevailed upon Avallach to summon the Grail. Avallach was against using the Blessed Cup in that way."

He paused, and I made bold to suggest that he should rest now. "Sleep, lord, you are tired."

"Sleep!" Arthur growled. "How can I sleep when my wife is in danger?" He pressed his fingertips to his eyes as if to pluck them out of his head. In a moment, his hands dropped away and he continued. "Gwenhwyvar came to me. She was so brave—she did not want to let me see her crying. She kissed me for the last time, as she thought, and left me—Myrddin left, too—everyone left the Tor and then Avallach came into where I lay. . . ."

I realized that I was about to hear how Arthur had been healed and restored to life by the Grail, so said no more about resting just now.

"I did not see either of them at first," Arthur said, his voice falling to a whisper at the memory, "but I knew Avallach had entered the room, and that the Holy Grail was with him, for the bedchamber was suddenly filled with the most exquisite scent—like a forest of flowers, or a rain-washed meadow in full blossom—like all the best fragrances I had ever known. The scent roused me, and I opened my eyes to see Avallach kneeling beside me, his hands cupped around an object that appeared to be a bowl. . . ." Arthur licked his lips as he must have licked them at the time. "And I opened my mouth to receive the drink, and tasted the sweetest flavor—the finest mead is as muddy water compared to it—and this was merely the sweetness of the air I tasted, but he had not brought me a drink as I supposed. It was the Grail itself infusing the very air with its exquisite savor."

Arthur drew the air deep into his lungs now as he had then. His tormented features smoothed as, in memory, he relived the marvel which had saved him.

"I breathed the redolent air, and the vapors of death which had clouded my mind parted and rolled away. I came to myself again, and knew myself in the presence of an eminent and powerful spirit—not Avallach only, for though he is of great stature in the world of the spirit, this Other was more immense, more profound, more potent by far. My own spirit, hovering between life and death, seemed a feeble, fragile thing—a bird caught in a bush weakly fluttering wings for release. I was nothing beside them . . . nothing. My life had been wasted—"

Here I interrupted. "Arthur, it is not so. You have ever held true to that which has been given you."

But the king would not hear it. He shook his head in denial. "My life has been wasted in the pursuit of things mean and ordinary—insignificant matters, meaningless and swiftly forgotten."

"Peace and justice are not insignificant," I countered, alarmed to hear him talk so. "Winning freedom for our people and our land is not meaningless, nor will it be quickly forgotten."

This brought a wan, pitying smile to the king's face. "Dust," he said. "Nothing but dust carried away by the first wind that blows, lost forever and forever unknown. Who but a fool regards the dust beneath his feet?"

I made to protest again, but he raised his hand, saying, "Let it be, Gwalchavad. It matters not." Returning to his recounting, he closed his eyes and lowered his head. "Shame," he said. "I have never known such shame: it burned—how it burned!—as if to consume me from within. My guilt overwhelmed me. Guilt for the misuse of my life and the lives of so many, many others. I stood adjudged and knew myself condemned a thousand times over. Neither Avallach nor the Other with him so much as raised a finger in accusation. They had no need—my own spirit damned me. To die before making atonement filled me with such remorse, the tears flowed from my eyes in a flood as if to wash away the mountain of my guilt.

"But, oh, the Grail! The Grail was there, and even as the world dimmed before my eyes, Avallach held the sacred bowl before me, dipped in his finger, and touched his fingertip to my forehead. He sained me with the cross of Christ. It was, as I thought, the last rite for a dying man. Soon my soul would stand before the High King of Heaven, and I would face my judge.

"Yet even as Avallach touched me with his fingertip, I felt life surge within me. I was alive! What is more, I was forgiven. At Avallach's touch, I was at once healed and released from the guilt and shame of my squandered existence. My former ways dropped from me like a sodden cloak, and like an eagle borne up on the winds of a gale, my soul rose from the pit and soared.

"The joy, the rapture, the delight overwhelmed me and kindled within me a fire which blazed with the love of goodness and right. And it was as if I stood on a high mountain, looking down at the world far below. I looked and saw a green and peaceful land spread out on the breast of the blue-green sea.

"I looked to see whence came this light, and lo! it was the Grail. I saw a shrine of stone set on a hill and, established within this shrine, the Blessed Cup of Christ. Even as I beheld the cup, a voice from Heaven said, 'Feed the people, heal the land.' The voice spoke these words three times, and I saw Britain shining like gold in the radiance of a light brighter than the sun.

"What could this mean but that I should build the shrine and set the Grail within it to shine as a beacon of truth and right throughout the land. From Britain would flow every good and perfect thing for the succor of the world; all men would look to the Island of the Mighty and hope would be renewed. Ynys Prydain would become that vessel through which great blessing would flow to all mankind.

"I vowed that this would be my work hereafter: to build the Grail Shrine, that the Blessed Cup might begin transforming the world. Thus, I stood up from my bed of death, fully healed, and possessed of an ardor to bring the vision granted me into living reality. I went out and greeted my wife—Myrddin and Llenlleawg were there, too, and all the Fair Folk.

"The next day I took the work in hand, and began laying plans for the Grail Shrine. From that day I have held but one thought uppermost: to honor my vow for the glory of God and the good of Britain and her people. This I have done"—he paused, raising his eyes briefly, only to turn them away again—"and for this I am brought down."

Arthur lowered his chin to his chest once more and lifted a hand to his forehead. "Leave me," he said, the glorious vision vanishing in the hollowness of his resignation. "I am tired, Gwalchavad. Leave me."

I stood for a moment, longing to speak a word of solace to ease his hurt. "I am sorry, Arthur," I said at last, then crept away, leaving the king to the cold misery of his woe.

Chapter Twenty-five

How many realms had Morgian ruined? How many men had she killed? In her relentless pursuit of power, how many lives had she destroyed?

Myrddin said she had returned, and I did not doubt it. Indeed, it was not difficult to believe the relentless, ever-vindictive Morgian had somehow preserved a portion of her power when she fled to her stronghold. Safe in the distant fastness of her dark dominion, she has been tirelessly assembling the remnants of her broken art from the wreckage. Even if Morgian was not as strong as before, she was still far more powerful than any other adversary mortal man could face. Dread Morgian was yet a force to be reckoned with, an implacable enemy as sly and deadly as any serpent and more wicked, more hateful, more vicious and rapacious than a whole host of demons.

These things I thought, and my thoughts were true. But no matter how hard I tried, I could find no good explanation for Morgaws. Who was she? What was her part in the cruel treacheries breaking upon us?

Myrddin, I thought, might hold the answers, so to Myrddin I went. After a search that took most of the day, I found him, not with the king, but in the old wooden shrine beside the abbey. One of the monks had seen him enter the shrine at break of day. "I never saw him leave, lord," the monk said. "Perhaps he is still there even now."

Entering the shrine quietly, I found him flat on his face

before the tiny altar, arms outstretched in the priestly attitude of prayer practiced by the brown clerics.

"Lord Emrys?" I said, loath to speak at all—but he was so still I feared him dead.

At the sound of his name, he shifted. "Gwalchavad," he said, raising his head. He made to rise, and I helped him to his feet. "How did you know to find me here?"

"I knew you had to be here," I replied. He lifted an eyebrow inquiringly, and I added, "I have searched everywhere else—this was the only place left."

He smiled at this, and I saw the light in his eyes, sharp and clear, the fire restored and burning bright once more. "I have been praying," he said.

"All day?"

He shrugged. "I did not mark the time."

"I wish Arthur had been with you—instead of gnawing out his heart in his chamber." I told him of my conversation with the king the night before.

"Is he there now?" asked Myrddin as we stepped outside.

"I think so. He has shut the door against us and will see no one."

Myrddin turned his farseeing eyes to the sky. The sun was going down and a chill twilight was swiftly drawing a veil of mist over a dismal day. "Will you go to him now?" I asked. "He needs you, Myrddin."

"I will go to him," promised the Wise Emrys, starting down the path towards the lake. "But not yet."

"He needs you now," I insisted, darting after him.

"Let him imbibe his despair," Myrddin said. "Truly, until he has drained that cup to the dregs, he will not hear a word I say."

"How long must we wait?"

"God alone knows." I frowned at this answer and he saw it. "Concern for the king is not what sent you looking for me, I think."

"No," I confessed, "though that is reason enough. It is Morgaws."

"Yes?" He stopped abruptly and turned to me. "Have you remembered something?"

The question caught me unawares. "Remembered? What do you mean?" The Emrys made a sound of mild disgust in his throat and started walking again, and I chased after him. "I was thinking who she might be," I said quickly. "I know she is not Morgian."

"Why do you say that?"

"No matter what guise Morgian took, I would always know her," I answered confidently.

"So would I," Myrddin declared.

"Besides," I continued, "she appeared to me."

Myrddin stopped walking again and I almost collided with him. "Morgian appeared to you?" His eyes were daggers keen and bright, and leveled at me. "When?"

"Not long ago," I said, more hesitant now.

Myrddin seized my arm and squeezed it hard. "Why have you waited until now?" he demanded angrily, releasing my arm and pushing it away.

"She came to me in a dream," I explained quickly. "At least I thought it was only a dream."

"Fool!" cried Myrddin. "Only a dream, he says! You should have told me."

"I am sorry, Emrys. Believe me, I never meant to keep anything from you."

Myrddin stared at me hard, then looked away and began walking again; we had almost reached the lake. We continued on in silence for a time before he spoke again; when he did, he said, "Morgaws is Morgian's creature— whether daughter or foundling, I cannot say, but she serves her mistress well."

Though I did not doubt him, I asked, "Then why did we never suspect her before?"

"It is the simplest of all enchantments," he replied, and I waited for him to explain, but he merely said, "We see what we think to see."

"And Llenlleawg?"

"Again, it is not difficult to bewitch the weak and willing," he replied.

Something in me bristled at the suggestion that the Irish champion joined in the betrayal voluntarily. "What of

Gwenhwyvar? It seems to me the queen was certainly neither weak nor willing.''

"Who knows what they told her?" Myrddin answered simply. "Morgian is duplicity itself. Her powers of deception are astonishing.''

"Then you are certain Morgian is involved.''

"If there was any doubt, finding Pelleas' brooch removed it.''

"You are convinced the brooch belonged to Pelleas?''

"How not?'' he said. "I gave it to him.''

Upon our return to the Tor, Myrddin went his way alone. I took myself off to the parapet, where I held vigil deep into the night, thinking about Llenlleawg's betrayal, and why everyone seemed so eager to hold him at fault for all that had happened, when clearly, if Morgian was involved, he was no doubt bewitched, and bent to Morgian's evil purpose. I was still struggling with this when, toward dawn, Myrddin summoned the Dragon Flight to the king's chamber.

I hurried to join my swordbrothers—many of whom, myself included, appeared to have spent another sleepless night wrestling with the guilt and shame of their failure. No one spoke as we made our way along the corridor and to the door of Arthur's chamber. There, waiting in the dimly lit passageway, was Myrddin, carrying his staff, his golden torc gleaming in the torchlight.

"Good,'' he said and, pushing open the heavy door, strode boldly in to confront the Pendragon. He advanced to the foot of the throne, raised the oaken staff, and struck it smartly on the stone floor. Crack! "Rise up, Arthur!'' he cried in a loud voice, and struck the floor again.

"The time has come to rouse yourself from your sleep of despair. Wake, and rise!'' He raised the staff and struck the floor again. The crack resounded like a peal of thunder as the Wise Emrys said, "The foe is at the gate, and your queen is taken away. She cries, 'Where is my deliverer? I cry out in my cruel captivity. Where is my salvation? When will my king arise?' ''

Arthur started. The shock of the bard's words struck

him to the core and jolted him from his self-pitying misery. "Gwenhwyvar!"

Lofting his staff, Myrddin advanced to stand before the throne. The Bard of Britain lifted his voice and kindled the hearts of all who stood mute and dejected in that room.

"Why do you languish here when the Treasure of Britain is despoiled by the enemy? Why do you cover yourself in gloom while your noble wife is ravaged by her captors? Why do you yet delay while wickedness lays waste your realm?"

Arthur's shoulders slumped and his head fell. But Myrddin did not allow despair to reclaim him; he stood before the king, lifting the stricken monarch from the pit with the strength of his words.

"Stiffen your spine, O King! Take up your spear and shield," he cried. "Gird yourself for battle, and take your place at the head of the Dragon Flight. The name of the enemy is known: Morgian has returned! The Queen of Air and Darkness is moving against you, and her aim is destruction."

A murmur, like a tingle of fear, flitted through the gathered ranks of Cymbrogi. "Morgian . . ."

Crack! Myrddin struck the floor with his staff. "Rise up, O Mighty Pendragon! Save your kingdom and your queen. For I tell you the truth: if you sit by and do nothing, you will lose all you hold most dear. And when that is gone, Dread Morgian will take your life as well. Your enemy will not be content until she has destroyed you body and soul."

I looked to the king and saw the color flooding back into his ashen features. The Heart of Britain was stirring again.

"Arise, Arthur! Bind steel to your hip and courage to your soul. The time has come to choose: fight or die; there is no middle ground!"

I felt within me the familiar rising to the call as Arthur gripped the arms of his chair and heaved himself to his feet. He yet appeared haggard and ill-disposed, but there was a glimmer of purpose in his eyes.

"Behold!" cried Myrddin Emrys with a flourish of his

oaken staff. "The Chief Dragon arises in his strength. Tremble, all who would oppose virtue and right! Flee to your dens in Hell, you citizens of corruption! Let all who practice evil beware: your days are no more. The High King of Britain has set his face against you and the day of your doom is at hand."

Arthur drew himself up and gazed upon his Cymbrogi. With a small movement of his hand, he gestured the Emrys to his place beside him. "Cai," he said quietly, "call the Dragon Flight to arms."

Stalwart Cai turned on his heel and shouted aloud to one and all. "Brothers! You have heard your king! Take up your swords and prepare for battle!"

With one voice the Cymbrogi gave out a mighty shout, and the chamber rang with the sound of their battle cry. Everyone fled the chamber in a chaos of haste to be the first one ready and waiting for the command to ride out.

"Bedwyr," the king said, "find me a sword."

Bedwyr's hand fell instantly to the hilt of his own sword. He drew the blade and laid it across his palms, stepped to the throne and offered it to Arthur. "Take mine, Bear. It will serve until we recover Caledvwlch."

The king hesitated, but Bedwyr extended his hands insistently, so Arthur took up the sword, stepped from the throne, and walked out of the chamber. We fell into step behind him, resuming our long-accustomed places, battle-chiefs to the Pendragon once more.

Horses were saddled, and wagons loaded with provisions. We raced through our preparations as if to banish the days of misery and gloom. When all was ready, we assembled in the palace yard to await Arthur's command; it was not long in coming. The king appeared before us, bathed and shaved, his hair scraped back and bound at his neck. Calm, resolute, he wore his red cloak and good mail shirt, and carried Bedwyr's sword at his side. Two daggers were tucked in his belt, and his shield was on his shoulder. It was a sight I had seen a hundred times if once, and it ever lifted my spirits.

"Brave Cymbrogi," he said when the cries of acclamation were quieted, "the battle we join will not be won by strength of arms alone. Therefore, heed the Head of Wisdom and take his words to heart.''

With this Myrddin Emrys came to stand beside his king. "Hear me, Sons of Prydain," he said, raising his hands in the ancient way of the bard. "Morgian is as deadly as she is evil. Wherever we are weakest, she will find that place, and that is where she will bring her powers to bear. Therefore, let each man beware. Look to your souls, my brothers, for it is a spiritual battle that we undertake. Though we search for the Grail Cup and seek the release of the queen, know you this: it is nothing less than a quest for the restoration of holiness and the blessing of God's good favor.

"I tell you the truth," he continued solemnly. "Morgian's powers are great and many of us may die. But though we lose life to her, our souls remain in Christ and forever beyond reach of the Evil One. We will do well to remember that when the day of travail is upon us. Therefore, if any man is unshriven, let him confess now and receive holy absolution for his sins.''

Indicating a row of brown-robed clerics across the yard, he said, "The bishop and his priests even now stand ready to hear our confessions and offer forgiveness.''

At this, the good bishop stepped forward. "My friends, brave ones, I would have you ride into battle secure in your salvation. Remember, the incorruptible cannot abide corruption, and in the quest before you, none but the pure of heart can succeed. Come, then, and purify your hearts of all unrighteousness.''

Any awkwardness in coming forward for shrift was quickly dispelled when Arthur, wholly without thought for his sovereign dignity, stepped before the bishop, knelt at the churchman's feet, crossed his arms over his chest, and bowed his head reverently. If the High King of Britain could humble himself in this way, no man of lesser rank need feel belittled in the sight of his friends. Indeed, more than one warrior who held himself begrudged made peace with his swordbrother so as to enter God's presence reconciled.

It is no disgrace to tell you that I myself, concerned for

my soul and the tribulations ahead, knelt on the cold
stones of the dusty yard and made my confession, knowing full well it might be my last.

After the confessions, we received assurances of our
forgiveness, and the bishop invited us to share the bread
and wine of Christ's table in a last meal of holy communion. We did eat the bread of the Blessed Jesu's body
and drink the wine of his blood, and then fifty warriors
rose as one man to face a relentless, subtle, vicious, and
implacable foe.

Thus we rode out from the Tor, a fighting force
equipped for battle against a foe unlike any other we had
faced. Upon reaching the trail beyond the abbey, we
turned, not east, but south. Myrddin Emrys held it a gesture of futility to attempt raising the days-old trail. "I
believe the only traces we would see are those Morgian
desired us to see," he declared. "We have been her playthings from the beginning. Mark me, Arthur, Llyonesse is
where battle will take place."

Llyonesse . . . I shuddered inwardly at the word. Dread
stole over me, and it took a very great effort of will to
hold fear at bay. Courage, Heaven's Bright Warriors stand
ready to aid us; God's own servants go before us to prepare a way in the Wasteland.

Chapter Twenty-six

With every step closer to Llyonesse, apprehension mounted within me. As the short winter day faded to the chill of a damp twilight, I found opportunity to speak to Myrddin. While the Cymbrogi set about making camp, I saw the Emrys laying a fire outside the king's half-raised tent, and went to him. "Allow me, Emrys," I said.

"There is no need," he replied. "Once of a time, if there was to be warmth at all, it was my chore to provide the fire. I do little enough providing these days." He glanced up at me quickly, then continued arranging the twigs and breaking up the larger branches. "Sit down, Summerhawk," he said—no one else save my father called me that—"and tell me what is on your mind."

Folding my legs under me, I settled on the ground before the fire-ring. I watched as he deftly snapped the branches and placed them onto the carefully stacked pile. After a few moments, I saw a thin tendril of smoke rising from the tinder—although I never saw him strike steel to flint.

"You seem certain Morgaws has fled to Llyonesse," I said, watching the smoke waft slowly upward in the still evening air. "How do you know?" I little doubted the Emrys would have sound reason for his judgment; I merely wished to hear it.

"I know because Morgian is guiding her, and Llyonesse is the one place in all this worlds-realm where Morgian can move at will," he replied.

"She seems to have no difficulty moving anywhere she pleases," I observed morosely.

"No," Myrddin countered. "That is why she needs Morgaws. I believe Morgian no longer commands all the power she once possessed, and now she must use others to further her dark purposes. Morgaws leads us to Llyonesse, where Morgian waits, like a spider spinning her webs, surrounding herself with lies and deceit."

"And yet, Llyonesse is where her power was broken," I pointed out, referring to the time he had last faced the Queen of Air and Darkness.

"Yes," he agreed, sitting back on his heels as a yellow flame fluttered to life among the dry twigs. "In Llyonesse Morgian's power was broken, and I think she has returned to that heaven-forsaken land in order to reclaim it through our defeat."

Considering the theft of the Grail and the easy abduction of the queen, I said, "Perhaps she has reclaimed her power already."

"Perhaps," Myrddin allowed, showing neither fear nor surprise at the thought. "Either way, Llyonesse is where we will stand or fall."

"Where will we find her?"

"I believe she will find us," answered the Wise Emrys. "But I suspect she will draw us to the place where she met her defeat. I know the place, a hill not far from the western coast—there was a Fair Folk settlement on that hill long ago. If she does not attack us on the way, that is where we shall go."

"Do you fear her, Myrddin?"

He watched the fire for a moment before answering. "I fear her greatly, Gwalchavad," he said quietly. "Abandon any hopes you harbor that we shall escape the full impact of her malice. We will not. Morgian has determined the fight, and chosen the battleground that suits her best. The Queen of Air and Darkness will not spare us the least torment or travail. Our journey will be an ordeal of suffering."

"Yet we go to meet her."

"We go to meet her," he replied, "because we have no other choice."

Arthur did not join us at the fire that night—his usual custom when we were encamped—but took food in his tent, admitted no one save Rhys, who served him, and emerged only at dawn the next morning when we moved on. We continued as before, riding in a long double rank south and west, slowly leaving behind the friendly hills of the Summer Realm and passing into the arid, drought-blasted barrens of Llyonesse.

The Pendragon, with Myrddin at his right hand, led the way, and I, who had already traversed this perilous path, rode with Rhys just behind them so as to be close to hand if needed. Bors rode behind me, followed by long ranks of warriors stretching back and back, fifty strong. Bedwyr, Cai, and Cador were given command of the rearward forces and took their places far down the line.

The sun, never bright, passed low over the southern hills before sinking once more. The dreary day dwindled away to a long, lingering dusk. Mist gathered thick on the trail and dull clouds lowered above. The voices of the men grew quieter by degrees until we moved in a netherworld between two skies, a world devoid of color, light, and any sound—save the steady clop, clop, clop of the horses' hooves, hollow and slow on the bare, hard ground.

As the last fleeting glimmer of light faded in the west, we glimpsed a rise of fog on the trail ahead. The closer we came, the more dense it grew, billowing higher and higher until it resembled nothing so much as a massive wall towering over us.

Unwilling to enter the fog blindly, Arthur halted the columns a few hundred paces away so that he might observe for a time. "Strange that it does not move," Myrddin said to Arthur. Though he spoke low, his voice carried on the unnaturally still air. "I advise caution."

"The day is going and we are losing the light," the king pointed out. "We might make camp here and hope the weather clears tomorrow."

"There is no wood for a fire," Bedwyr put in.

"Then we will do without," Arthur said, making up

his mind. "It makes a cold night for us, but that is better than risking our necks on a trail we cannot see."

At a nod from the king, Rhys raised the hunting horn and signaled the Cymbrogi to dismount. We made camp and spent a chill, damp night on the trail. Dawnlight the next morning revealed that the bank of fog had not shifted or dissipated. Indeed, it now appeared more solid and imposing than before: a vast, gently seething eminence, beyond which neither eye nor ear could penetrate. The wall of mist lay across our path as if marking out the line of battle—as if an enemy had thrown up a defensive rampart and carved upon it the words, "cross over if you dare."

We crossed, of course. Having no better choice—there was no riding around it, and waiting was pointless—we formed tight columns and marched forward, breasted the wall, and passed into the mist. I could make out Rhys beside me, but Arthur and Myrddin ahead and those behind were hazy, half-formed figures floating at the perimeter of sight, and beyond that I could see nothing.

As the fog closed like a tight woolen glove around us, I spared a fleeting thought for the phantom legion. Was this how Legio XXII Augustus met its uncanny fate? Had they, like us, marched into the mist, and into the realm of the undead, never to return?

The mist, so close and thick, stole away every sound, even the hollow plod of the horses' hooves and the dull jingle of the tack. The world seemed still and cold and silent, as if offering us a foretaste of death. I ignored the damp chill and gazed staunchly into the quiet, unchanging void, and was surprised when, after a time, I began to hear an odd, rhythmic drumming. Looking around, I could not locate the source of the disturbing sound—until I realized it was the very blood pulsing in my ears with every beat of my heart.

In addition to banishing sight and sound, the fog was heavy and wet. Within moments of entering the mist, I felt the chill weight settle on my shoulders and the cold trickle of water along my spine. Water beaded on my face and mustache, and ran down my head and neck. I gathered my sodden cloak around me, lowered my head, and rode on, thinking, I have been cold before. And I have ridden in mist many times, and will again. It is winter, after all, and mist and fog are to be expected. This is just poor weather, nothing more.

We journeyed an eternity, or so it seemed. With neither light nor shadow to mark the passing day, time dwindled and stretched, and then stood still. Once, my horse stumbled over a rock and I came awake with a cry. Glancing quickly around, I found everything as it was before: dense, cloying fog pressing in on every side. Nothing had changed; nevertheless, I felt vexed at having slept, for, try as I might, I could not remember falling asleep.

"Gwalchavad?" said Rhys, his voice close.

I could make out my companion as a disembodied head peering anxiously back at me as if through a depth of clouded water—the face of a drowned man, bloodless and cold, and pale as a fish. All at once it came into my mind to warn Arthur . . .

"The river!" I shouted, surprising even myself with the sudden outcry. "Arthur! Stop! There is a river ahead!"

Arthur's reply was quick and decisive. "Rhys, the horn," he said. "Sound the halt."

An instant later came the blast of the horn, signaling the column to stop. Arthur passed word back through the ranks to dismount and rest the horses. I slid from the saddle and walked a few paces ahead to where Myrddin and Arthur waited. "The river is treacherous with quicksand," I told them. "I lost my horse to it last time."

Arthur regarded me with a bemused expression on his face. "We can see nothing of the trail ahead; how can you be certain we are anywhere near the river?"

His question brought me up short. Before he asked, I had been sure we were ready to topple over the brink. But now, as I observed their expressions of perplexity and concern, the certainty, so solid and secure just a moment before, crumbled away to nothing. I looked to the track before us and saw only the dull blankness of the all-obscuring fog.

I was saved from having to explain when Myrddin, calmly concerned, said, "Come, it will not hurt to walk ahead a little." He and Arthur dismounted, and we proceeded up the trail.

We had moved only a few paces, however, when my feet began sinking into soft mud. Arthur, beside me, took another step and his foot splashed into shallow water. He stopped at once, turned towards me, and opened his mouth to speak; but before he could say a word, his feet were sucked down into the quagmire. He threw out a hand, which I seized and pulled towards me. We stumbled backward together onto solid ground.

"Well done, Gwalchavad," he commended.

"The first rider in would have been lost," Myrddin observed.

"That first rider would have been me," Arthur declared, shaking cold mud from his feet. "And others would have followed me in.

"Stay near," said the king, gripping my shoulder. "I have need of your discernment."

That was all he said, but I sensed urgency in his touch. "What little I have is yours, lord," I said lightly.

"How do we get across?" wondered Cador, coming up behind us.

"There is a fording place some way up the valley," I told him.

"Lead on, Gwalchavad," the king commanded; "we will follow you."

As before, by the time we reached the fording, the day was spent. Rather than attempt the crossing in the dark, we made camp and waited to cross the river until morning—hoping against hope that the mist might lift during the night. There were thickets of bramble and furze abounding along the riverside, and the Cymbrogi set about hacking at the roots with their swords, quickly gathering whole bushes into a great heap which Myrddin promptly set alight. The resulting flame burned with a foul black smoke, but the heat and light were welcome nonetheless. We hung our wet clothes over the prickly branches of low-growing gorse and stood basking in the warmth, trying to drive the cold and damp from our bones. Some put their boots on sticks and held them near the flames to dry them.

When the fire died down to a comfortable blaze, we prepared our supper, glad for a hot meal at last. We ate in small huddles of men, hunched over our bowls as if afraid the cold and darkness might try to steal away the little warmth and light we held. Still, it was good to get something hot inside us, and our spirits improved immeasurably—so much so, in fact, that Cai, having finished his meal, set aside his bowl, stood up, and called for a song.

"Are we to allow the dolor of the day to gnaw at our souls until there is nothing left but a sour rind?" He raised his voice as if to challenge a foe. "Are we to sit shivering before the fire, muttering like old women taking fear at every shadow?"

Several of the older warriors, knowing Cai, answered him in kind. "Never!" they shouted, rattling their knives against their bowls. "Never!"

"Are we not the Dragon Flight of Arthur Pendragon?" cried Cai, his arm raised high in the air. "Are we not True Men of Ynys Prydain?"

"We are!" called the Cymbrogi, more joining in with every shout. "We are!"

"Well, then," Cai declared, his broad face glowing with pleasure in the firelight, "let us defy this ill-favored night with a song!"

"A song!" the Cymbrogi cried; every man was with him now, shouting for a song to roll aside the gloom and woe.

With that, Cai flung out his arm towards Myrddin, sitting a few paces away. "Well, Myrddin Emrys? You hear the men. We would have a song to bind vigor to our souls and courage to our hearts."

"A song, Myrddin! A song!"

To the hearty acclaim of all, the Emrys rose slowly, motioning to Rhys to fetch his harp. He took his place before the fire, and the Cymbrogi crowded in around him. "If you would hear a tale," Myrddin began, "then listen well to what I say: the enemy encircles us and dogs our every step. Therefore, let us take up whatever weapon comes to hand. Tonight we raise a song, tomorrow a prayer—and one day soon a sword. In the darksome days to come, let each man resolve within himself to hold to the light that he has been given.''

So saying, Myrddin reached for the harp Rhys had brought him, and began to pluck the strings. He bent his head and put his cheek against the smooth, polished wood of the instrument, and closed his eyes. In a moment, the seemingly idle strumming became purposeful. Everyone, Arthur included, leaned forward as the Bard of Britain opened his mouth and began to sing.

Chapter Twenty-seven

"When the dew of creation was still on the ground," Myrddin sang, his voice rising like a graceful bird taking flight, "a great king arose in the Westerlands, and Manawyddan was his name. So mighty was this king, and of such renown, that all nations held him lord over them and sent their best warriors to his court to pledge their loyalty and serve him at arms. And this is the way of it:

"Manawyddan, fair and true, received the warriors and bade them wait upon him in his hall. When all were gathered there and ready, the noble lord arrayed himself in his fine cloak, took up his rod of kingship, and mounted his throne. He gazed out upon the assembly and thought to himself: A thousand times blessed am I! No man ever wanted better companions. In truth, each man among them could have been king in his own realm had he not chosen to pledge faith with Manawyddan.

"The great king's heart was touched by the glory of his warhost, and so he bade them stay a while with him, that they all might enjoy a feast he would give in their honor. When the feast was prepared, the warriors, noblemen all, came and filled the benches at table, where they were provided with the best food that was ever placed before men of valor from that far-off time to this. What is more, whatever food any warrior preferred—whether the flesh of deer, or pigs, or beef; or the delicate meat of roast fowls, or succulent salmon—he had but to dip his knife into the bowl before him, and that food was provided.

"The warriors were delighted with this wonder, and acclaimed their host with loud approval. So clamorous were they in their praise that Manawyddan was moved to decree another wonder. He ordered golden ale tubs to be set up in all four corners of the hall, and one beside his throne. He then summoned his serving boys to bring drinking bowls of silver and gold to his noble guests, and invited them to plunge their cups into the foaming brew. This they did, and when each man raised bowl to lips, he found the drink he liked best—whether ale, or mead, or wine, or good dark beer.

"When they had drunk the health of their sovereign host, the noble guests accorded such vaunted praise that Manawyddan's great heart swelled to hear it. He pulled his golden torc from around his throat, put aside his fine cloak, and stepped down from his throne to join in the feast, moving from table to table and bench to bench, eating and drinking with his guests, sharing the feast as one of them.

"When hunger's keen edge had been dulled against the bounty of the groaning boards, King Manawyddan called for his bards to regale the company with tales of mighty deeds, songs of love and death, of courage and compassion, of faith and treachery. One after another, the bards appeared, providing a feast for the soul, each one finer and more accomplished than the last.

"The last bard to sing was Kynwyl Truth-Sayer, Chief Bard of Manawyddan, who had just begun the Tale of the Three Prodigious Quaffings when there came a shout from outside the hall; the shout became a cry, and then a keening, beginning loud and growing louder and louder still until it shook the entire stronghold to its deep foundations, and every mortal creature within the stout walls covered his ears and trembled inwardly.

"Then, when the bold company thought they must be undone by the terrible sound, it stopped. The warrior host looked at one another and saw that they were covered in the sweat of fear, for none of them had ever heard a cry like this: tortured beyond endurance, beyond hope.

"Before they could wonder who might have made a cry of such wounding torment, the high-topped doors of the hall burst open and a tremendous wind swept through the hall—a fierce gale like those which rage in the wintry northern seas. The warrior band braved the icy blast and when it had abated at last, they looked and saw a lady standing in their midst. The stranger had the look of a queen, and she was dressed all in gray from crown to heel; her face was hidden beneath a hood of gray, and she had three gray hounds beside her.

"Manawyddan was first to recover his wits. He approached the woman, his hands open and inviting. 'I give you good greeting,' he said, speaking in a kindly voice. 'You are welcome here, though you may find the companionship of women more to your liking. If so, I will summon the maidens of my court, that you may be made comfortable in their presence.'

"'Think you I have come seeking comfort and pleasure?' the Gray Lady snapped haughtily.

"'I was merely offering you the hospitality of my court,' replied Manawyddan. 'Unless you tell us, we will never know why you have burst in among us. Was it to put an end to our enjoyment?'

"'You may keep your hospitality!' remarked the woman tartly. 'I have done with all kindliness and generosity. The gentle pursuits I once enjoyed are more bitter to me now than death and ashes.'

"'Indeed, I am sorry to hear it,' Manawyddan replied sadly. 'Tell me what I may do to restore warmth and tenderness to your heart, and rest assured that before the sun has set on another day, I will have done all anyone can do. What is more, the men who even now fill this hall are no less ready to aid me in this endeavor.'

"This handsome offer was thrown back in the king's face, for the lady offered only a grim, mocking laugh in reply.

"'Lady,' said Manawyddan, 'why do you persist in this uncouth behavior? I have made a king's vow to do all that can be done to aid you in any way you desire. I am certain that my men and I can meet and overcome any difficulty, end any oppression, right any wrong, and thus redress whatever hurt or harm has befallen you.'

"This heart-stirring speech received the acclaim of all who heard it. The noblemen lauded their monarch and pledged themselves to the Gray Lady's service.

"But the strange woman scorned their pledges. 'Can you raise the dead, O Great King?' She laughed, and her laughter was bitterness itself. 'Can you restore life to a corpse on which the carrion crows have feasted? Can you make the blood flow once more in the veins when that blood has soaked the earth, and the living heart is but a lump of cold meat in the breast? Can you, O Wondrous Manawyddan, return the warm gaze of love to an eye which has been cut out and thrown to the dogs?'

"Hearing this, Manawyddan's great heart surged with grief for the lady's plight. 'Lady, your sorrow has become my sorrow, and your woe my own. But know this: the full weight of the sadness you feel now, seven times that much will be visited upon the one who has caused your lament.'

"At this, the mysterious lady bowed her head and professed herself well pleased, knowing Manawyddan would honor his vow to the last breath in his body. She then began to tell the king what had transpired to bring about her ruin. The warriors pressed close around to hear—and between the telling and the hearing, it was difficult to say which was the more distressing.

" 'I was not always the gray hag you see before you now,' the lady said. 'Once I was beautiful, but mourning has made me old and dry before my time. Listen, then, if you would learn the reason for my travail.

" 'I am the daughter of a mountain king called Rhongomynyad, a ruler both wise and good, who fell ill of a night and died not long after. I was left alone to rule in his place until I should marry and my husband relieve me of that tedious duty. As one might expect, from the moment my father's demise was made known in the world, the path to my stronghold was crowded with suitors seeking to win my approval. Truth to tell, though I never found any of these hopeful young men remotely to my liking, still I did not grow weary of the chase.

" 'One day, as the customarily disappointing flock of suitors ambled through the fortress gates, my eye chanced upon a tall young man fair in face and form: slender, but not too thin; handsome, but not vain; proud, but not arrogant; kind, but not simpering; generous, but not profligate; canny, but not conceited; friendly, but not flighty; trustworthy, but not dour. In short, my heart kindled with love for him the moment his eye met mine.

" 'We spent the day, and all the days to follow, in close companionship, and my love grew greater each time we met. Before the summer was over, we were betrothed. Our wedding was to be held in the spring, and I could turn aside from the duties of sovereignty which weighed so heavily upon me. Like all betrothed couples, we made our plans and dreamed our dreams, and my love for my beloved was as all-consuming as the flame of an ever-burning fire.

" 'Then one day, while my beloved was tending to affairs in his father's realm, a dark-clothed man came striding into my court. Without so much as a tender glance in my direction, he declared himself king by virtue of his skill at arms and challenged any who would dispute him to draw sword or heft spear, and have at it. To my shame and outrage, no one would defend me. All the young men who stood in my court shrank away, shaking with fear.

" 'For, like a man in most respects, in stature this dark foe was nothing less than a giant! Standing two men high, he was broad of shoulder and long of arm. His weapons were black iron, and his shield iron, too. It took two men just to heft his axe, and three to raise that weighty shield.

" 'Nevertheless, my beloved soon heard what had happened. And up he jumped, calling for his sword belt and spear; he called for his horse to be saddled and his shield to be burnished. He mounted his horse and rode straightaway to take up the challenge. The two met on the path leading to my fortress, and the narrow valley between two mountains became the battleground.

" 'Alas! They fought! The combat was fierce and, alas, my best beloved was killed!

" 'The Black Oppressor fell upon the body of my beloved, plucked the eyes from his head, and threw them to the hounds. Then he hewed the eyeless head from those fair shoulders and stuck it upon his iron spear. He set the spear over the gate of my fortress as a reminder to all who passed beneath the bloodless head that he now ruled the realm. That same day, he claimed me for his wife, and had me bound and borne to my chamber, which he had taken for his own. He then demanded a meal to be prepared and served him in the hall; he said it was to be our marriage feast. The glutton devoured seven pigs, three oxen, nine lambs, and drank four vats of ale, while I touched not a morsel.

" 'While the Black Giant feasted in my hall, I bound courage to my heart and determined that when he came for me, I would either be dead or gone. I struggled free of my bonds, and then sought my escape. Alas, the door was securely barred, and there was no other way out. I bade farewell to life. Taking up the ropes that had bound me, I knotted the lengths together to make a noose, which, with trembling hands, I placed around my neck.

" 'I was even then tightening the noose when one of my serving maids entered the chamber. She had come to light the fire in the hearth so that the chamber would be warm for my hideous bridegroom and me. When she saw the killing ropes around her lady's neck, she threw herself upon me and vowed to help me escape if I would only take her with me. I agreed at once, and we stole that instant from the chamber, pausing only to set fire to the bed.

" 'From that dire day to this,' the Gray Lady concluded, 'I have wandered where I would, seeking justice and retribution. Most miserable of women am I! Never has any creature shown himself man enough to meet the Black Giant in combat and rescue my realm and my people.

" 'Even so, to show you I am in earnest and virtue is with me wherever I go, I offer this promise: any man who

slays the Black Oppressor shall that day have me for his
bride—and my kingdom and all I possess. Fortunate is
the man who takes me to wife,' she added, 'for I know
well what I am worth.'

"Great Manawyddan cast his gaze upon the gathered
warriors, each one more accomplished and stalwart than
the last. 'You have heard the lady's tale of woe,' he said.
'Who among you will take up the challenge? Who will
slay this vile being and restore the lady's kingdom? Who
among you will cover himself in glory and bring honor
to this court?'

"At once there arose a tremendous outcry as the
doughty warriors strove to make themselves heard each
above the other. But the man who carried the day was the
king's own champion, a warrior of vast renown, and Llencellyn was his name. 'My king and lord,' said Llencellyn
when he had gained his sovereign's ear, 'may I be bound
in chains and hurled into the sea if I do not avenge this
lady and restore her realm before three days have passed.'

"The Great King smiled, for he expected no less of his
champion. Manawyddan extolled the warrior's resolve,
saying, 'Go, then, Llencellyn, with my blessing. I charge
you to remember that though all the fiends of Hell stand
against you, yet with the help of the Swift Sure Hand,
you must surely prevail.'

"Up leapt Llencellyn and called for his weapons and
his horse. When he had armed himself, he then mounted
his fine steed and called to the lady to lead him to her
realm, that he might kill the giant without delay and win
himself a wife and kingdom. The Gray Lady mounted her
yellow mare and led the king's champion away.

"The men of Manawyddan's court were not content to
stand idly by and await the combat's outcome. 'How can
we stay here while our swordbrother faces this peril?' they
cried. 'O, King of Might, let us follow them to the place
of combat so that we might see how Llencellyn fares.'

"This they did, following the champion's trail to the
battleground, arriving just in time to see Llencellyn strike
the first of many stout blows—any one of which would
have been enough to fell the strongest enemy. Curiously,

the more Llencellyn fought, the stronger grew the giant.
With every well-placed stroke of the champion's sword,
the Black Giant's strength increased and Llencellyn's
grew the less.

"The king and all his warhost looked on in horror as
their renowned champion's strength waned, until, no
longer able to lift the blade, Llencellyn's arm faltered. The
Black Oppressor, keen for the kill, drove in the instant
the sword blade fell. Up went the cruel iron axe, and down
without mercy, striking the champion squarely in the center of his helm. The giant's blade sliced the warhelm and
passed through skin and flesh and bone and brain as if
through empty air, cleaving the dauntless champion's
head in two.

"All the host stood bereft and watched in agony and
grief as the Black Oppressor leapt upon the corpse and
hacked poor Llencellyn's body into small pieces and then
trampled those pieces into the ground—those, that is,
which the hounds did not devour. He then turned to the
stricken company, and jeered, 'Who will be next to
chance with death?'

"When no one made bold to answer the evil lord, Manawyddan cried out, 'If my men have lost their courage,
so be it! Far better for me to die fighting than to go to
my grave a coward and the king of cowards. Bring me
my sword and shield!'

"This speech shamed the assembled warriors—though
not enough for any to overcome their terror of the giant.
They all looked at one another and shrugged as if to say,
'If that is the way the king wants it, who are we to disagree?' Meanwhile, the king's weapons were brought and
the king began to gird himself for the battle which would
certainly be his last.

"Yet while the king was strapping on his sword belt,
a slender young man approached, knelt before him, and
said, 'Please, lord, I am your servant.'

"The king had never seen the youth before, and said,
'Forgive me, lad, but I have no time for tact. Too soon I
shall be feeding hungry ravens and quenching the parched
soil with my blood. Who are you, and what do you want?'

" 'My name,' replied the stripling youth, 'is of little importance. I am new to your court and have not yet distinguished myself in arms, and thus I have doubtless escaped your notice.'

" 'Yes, yes,' snapped Manawyddan irritably. 'If you have something to say, say it quickly.'

" 'I beg the boon of trying my hand against the Black Oppressor,' the youth said simply.

" 'Well, your courage is sound, but I misdoubt your intelligence. Fine and mighty warriors who have tried to slay this Black Oppressor now sleep in turf houses. What makes you think you, little more than a boy—and a skinny boy at that!—can succeed where battlechiefs the like of Llencellyn have failed so miserably?'

"To this the lad replied, 'Young I may be, but I have never yet met an enemy who can stand against me.'

" 'Clearly, you cannot have faced many foemen,' the king declared sadly. 'That, I suspect, is the secret of your success.'

" 'Regard me not too lightly,' the youth warned, his assurance undimmed. 'For I have succeeded by reason of a strange endowment with which I have been favored.'

"Manawyddan leaned on his spear and sighed. 'Am I ever to learn the end of this? Perhaps it was pointless conversation that laid all your adversaries low.'

" 'Not at all,' the youth assured the king solemnly. 'I owe my triumph to the fact that, having no strength of my own, whenever I take the field the might of my opponents is granted me in double measure.'

" 'Son,' Manawyddan replied, shaking his head sadly, 'I have lived a very long time in this worlds-realm and have heard many strange things, but I never heard of anything like that.' He paused, regarding the slender youth with great suspicion. 'If I believed even the smallest part of what you said to be true, I might allow you to try your hand. As it is, I fear I would merely be delaying my own death with the purchase of yours. As a king of renown and a leader of warriors, I consider it far beneath me to even contemplate such a thing.'

" 'Well,' answered the youth happily, 'there is something in what you say, of course. But from where I stand, it appears your vaunted warhost has made the selfsame bargain with your life as you fear making with mine. Indeed, your warriors, fearless to a man, no doubt, have given you up for dead before you have even lofted spear or lifted blade.'

" 'Tread lightly here,' the king growled in warning, 'for you are talking about men tested in the straits of battle. Nevertheless, I find myself sorely tempted to grant your entreaty, though it be your last. I could always fight the giant tomorrow, I suppose.'

"The shaveling youth smiled and bowed to the Great King. 'Truly, you are a sovereign worthy of the name,' the lad replied. 'You have but to grant my plea, and reap the reward.'

"Manawyddan sighed. 'Would that it were so.'

" 'Rest assured, you will never hear a word of reproach from me,' said the youth. 'Give me a sword only, then stand aside and watch what I will do.'

"Lord Manawyddan, Chief Dragon of the Island of the Mighty, gave the youth the sword from his hand, and called for his shield-bearers to arm the lad with spear and dagger, helm and belt as well. But the young man shook his head firmly, saying, 'Either this blade will suffice, or it will not. If it will, then nothing else is needed; if it will not, then nothing else will help. Summon the giant, and let us set to. The day stretches long, and I am growing hungry.'

"The Black Oppressor, who had long since retired to his hall to gloat over his loathsome triumph, was duly summoned by a blast of the king's horn. 'What is this?' the giant grumbled in a voice like low thunder, 'Who disturbs my rest? Can it be the Mighty Manawyddan has finally gathered his courage into a heap and wishes now to weigh its worth against the standard of my blade?'

" 'Say nothing you wish not to regret,' the valiant lord advised. 'It is not myself who is judge over you, but whatever god made you—and that soon. Before you stands the youth who will do for you as you have done for so many others.'

"The Black Giant laughed long and hard at this. Then he looked upon the youth, standing white and naked before him, armed with nothing but a sword that was so overlarge, he had to clutch it tight in both hands just to raise it.

" 'Lad,' rumbled the giant, wiping tears of mirth from his eyes, 'of all the warriors I have slaughtered, I cannot remember killing any as foolish as you.'

"The slender youth stepped smartly forward, dragging the sword with him. 'Only sow what you wish to reap,' the lad replied evenly. If there was the slightest quiver of fear in his voice, no one heard it.

"In his eagerness to kill again, the giant licked his thick, foul lips and grinned down at the fair youth. Hefting his war axe, and testing the keenness of its blade with his thumb, the Black Oppressor said, 'Come, then; it will be a joy to send you hence.'

" 'Beware, I am not so easily killed as you might think.'

"Angered by the youth's indifference, the Black Giant gave a roar that curdled the marrow of all who heard it for twelve hides around. He raised the iron axe high above his head and brought it down with such a vicious chop that everyone looked away lest they see something they devoutly wished later to forget. When the axe made no sound, they opened their eyes and turned once more to where the youth stood—expecting, no doubt, to see his body halved like a carcass for the spit.

"But no! The young man was still standing. What is more, he appeared more hale than before. Indeed, he seemed to have grown a handspan taller, and his slender limbs were thicker. The giant gaped in amazement, and looked at the axe in his fist as if he expected it to offer an explanation. Rage bubbled up like molten lead within him, and he roared again, shaking the ground with the blast. Up swept the axe blade, and down. The youth, effortless as a willow in spring, stepped lightly aside as the wicked blade shaved the empty air.

" 'My father always taught me that war is a bane, and the chief of man's afflictions,' the youth intoned mildly.

His voice had deepened and his arms, well muscled now, raised the blade and held it steadily before him. 'Perhaps it is a lesson you should have learned.'

"Glowering murderously, his black face growing blacker in its fury, the giant screamed, 'How dare you condemn me! Just you stand still, and we will see who is the master here.'

"The giant lunged wildly at the youth, who met his charge with a swift kick which stopped the black enemy in his tracks. The giant, stunned by the blow, doubled over in pain. The youth stood leaning on his sword a few paces away as his adversary heaved his dinner onto the ground. 'It is a shame to waste a good meal,' taunted the youth, 'but then you were always a wastrel and a destroyer. Tell me, how does your victory taste now? Is it still as sweet in your mouth—or has it all gone sour?'

"With a cry to crack the sky, the Black Oppressor heaved up the iron axe. The cruel weapon seemed much heavier now, and it took all his strength just to raise it and balance it above his head. The blade hung in the air, its honed edge glinting sharp in the sunlight.

"The youth, head and shoulders rising level with those of the Black Oppressor's, raised the king's sword and flicked the axe blade away as if it had been a feather. The ease with which he had been disarmed inflamed the giant beyond all restraint or reason. Lowering his head, he threw wide his arms and ran at the young man, intent on crushing the youth in his all-encircling grasp.

"The giant made but three paces before his legs gave out and he toppled face-first onto the ground. The collision drove the breath from the wicked foeman's lungs, and caused the earth to tremble and shake as if to draw the mountains down. But the young man, towering over the giant now, stepped to the Vile Enemy and lopped off his head with an easy stroke of Manawyddan's sword, saying, 'Never more will you trouble the good people of this realm.'

"The king and all his tribe stood blinking in astonishment at what they had seen. For the space of six heartbeats, not a sound was to be heard in all the world, and then, with a great shout of relief, they all rushed forward to acclaim the wonderful youth and his astounding triumph over the Black Oppressor.

"Manawyddan was first to laud the youth, and led his people in a song of praise in the young man's honor. The Gray Lady threw off her hood, ran to the youth, and put her arms around his neck—for, as soon as the giant was dead, the lad had assumed his former shape and size. The lady kissed him, and declared loudly for all to hear: 'Truly, you are a champion among men. This day you have won your kingdom, and your queen.'

"Abashed by the tumult, the young man blushed crimson from top to toe. Taking the lady's arms from around his neck, he said, 'Though your offer is kindness itself, I must ask your pardon and decline. My course is set before me, for I am directed by another hand.'

"Lord Manawyddan was saddened to hear these words. 'What?' he cried. 'Will you not stay with us? My champion is slain, and I have need of another. You, I think, more than deserve that place.'

"The youth only smiled, and begged to be excused the honor. 'Alas, I cannot stay even a moment longer,' he said, and explained how it was his geas to roam the width and breadth of the world and offer his aid wherever it was needed.

" 'Leave if you must,' said Manawyddan, 'but please do not go away empty-handed. You have but to name your reward and, to the half of my kingdom, it is yours.'

"Smiling still, the young man declined once more. 'I have what is needful, and more would avail me nothing.' Looking at the warriors gathered close around, the young man said, 'Good king, honor me instead in these who have been given you. Do not hold their fright against them—men are only dust, after all.'

"The king marveled the more at these words. 'Go, then,' said Manawyddan, 'and with my blessing. Yet, I would not have you leave us before I learned your name.'

"The young man smiled at this. 'Do you not know me yet?' he asked.

"The king answered, 'Son, I never laid eyes on you before this day. Who are you, lad?'

"To which the stranger replied, 'I am the Youth of a Thousand Summers.' He then bade everyone farewell and, passing among them, disappeared in much the same way as he had arrived: unseen and unguessed.

"When he had gone, the Gray Lady threw open the gates of her stronghold and invited Manawyddan and his warrior host to feast with her and her people in celebration of their deliverance. The king, though still less than elated with the fainthearted behavior of his warband, accepted. They all went into the queen's hall and feasted for three days and three nights in the most pleasant fellowship they had ever known. Men and women sat down together and soon found themselves sharing the feast with the one they loved best. One by one, each couple came before their ruler to beg the boon of marriage. All were duly married, and the celebration continued as a wedding feast, and their joy was made complete.

"Gazing out upon all the feasting couples, the queen observed, 'It is right and good that our people should unite our kingdoms in this way. I only wish that I could share their happiness and increase it with my own.'

"To this Lord Manawyddan replied, 'God knows I am setting a poor example for my people if all of them are married and I myself have no queen.' Turning to the lady beside him, he said, 'I may not be a giant-slayer, but I know I would be a better king than I have ever been if you would be my wife. Lady,' he said, taking her hand in his, 'will you marry me?'

"The Gray Lady smiled easily and said, 'And here was I thinking you would never ask. Yes, my king, I will marry you.'

"This pleased the king greatly. 'Here we are to be married,' he declared, 'and I do not even know your name.'

" 'My name is Rhiannon,' the Gray Lady answered. So saying, the queen threw off her gray hood and cloak to reveal a dress all of gold, with jewels—each more costly than the last—and tiny pearls sewn with thread of braided silver. Her hair was red-gold and braided fine, her skin white as milk, her flesh supple, and her smooth-cheeked face lovely to look upon. The sight of her pleased Manawyddan well, and he married her at once lest she somehow slip from his grasp.

"The king then presented his new queen to the people, and the noble couple made their way through the hall, giving gifts to one and all. The celebration was renewed to the delight of every creature, high or low, living in the realm.

"Behold! When they rose from the table, three hundred years had passed them unawares. Nor had they suffered the predations of age, for every man and woman was as hale as the moment he or she had first sat down. Indeed, not so much as a single silver hair was to be seen on any head, and even those whose brows had been creased by care were seen to be as smooth and cheerful as the day each was born.

"From that moment, the combined kingdoms of Rhiannon and Manawyddan became known as the Isle of the Everliving. The realm flourished as never before, producing a bounty of all good things, and becoming the envy of all the world.

"Many tales are told of this enchanted island, but this tale is finished. Let him hear it who will."

Chapter Twenty-eight

The Grail is mine! The single most potent talisman in all the world, and it is mine!

Oh, Morgaws, my lovely one, you have done better than you know—better, even, than that simple sot of a nephew of mine will ever know. And to think Avallach had it all this time! All these years, Avallach kept it hidden away, never sharing the secret with anyone.

Of course, if I had so much as imagined Avallach possessed such a relic, I would have taken it long ago. He would never have given it to me; when did Avallach ever give me anything? Truly, if he had ever favored me with even the crumb of consideration he shows the hound sniffing around his stables, things might be far different now.

But did the mighty Fisher King ever lift a finger for me? Never! It was all for Charis, always for Charis. She had everything, and I had nothing. Taliesin should have been mine! Together, we would have ruled Britain forever.

Charis, Goddess of the Stinking Masses, will yet curse the day of her birth. I might have killed her any of a thousand times—it would have been so easy! But death would merely end her suffering, and I want her torment to linger long.

No, it will not be Charis who dies; it will be the wretched Merlin and his clumsy creature, Arthur, swiftly followed by his simpering slut of a queen and her ox-brained champion. They will all go weeping and wailing

*to their graves—but not before they have seen their ri-
diculous dream destroyed by the one real power in this
world. They had the Grail, the fools, they had it in their
hands and failed to discern what it was they held.*

*Well, before I am finished, they will rue their ignorance.
They will gnaw out their own bowels with regret. They
will claw out their own eyes as they watch their absurd
Kingdom of Summer, all sweetness and light, shrivel away
like dung on a hot rock.*

*This will cause Avallach no end of pain—literally. For,
now that I have the Grail, the pain will truly last forever.*

Rising the next morning, we formed the columns and
journeyed deeper into the Wasteland. The wind was cold
out of the northwest, but the sky stayed clear and bright,
and I took heart, for the Pendragon was in better spirits
than I had seen him since the Grail disappeared. This, I
surmise, was to Myrddin's credit; his song had put everyone in fine mettle. Though far, far ahead on the horizon
I could see the dark gray-blue cloud line of a winter storm
rising in the south, I considered we were more than a
match for whatever came our way.

By midday the storm had made little progress, and I
began to think it might pass us by, or hold off altogether.
When we stopped to make camp for the night, I walked
with Myrddin to a nearby hill to see what we might learn
of the region. The sun was setting in a violent blaze of
red and gray. Pointing to the heavy band of blue-edged
darkness clearly visible on the horizon, I said, "I have
been watching it all day, but the storm has not advanced
a whit."

"Yes," he murmured absently. Squinting his golden
eyes against the glowing sky, Myrddin surveyed the long
blue-black line. I observed that the wind, which had been
at our backs through the day, had died down now, and
the land was quiet—save for a small, distant rhythmic
rumbling, like that of ocean waves pounding against cliffs.

At last, the Wise Emrys said, "When we discussed
your sojourn in Llyonesse, you said nothing about a forest. Why was that, Gwalchavad?"

"Lord Emrys," I said, turning my face towards him, "I mentioned no forest for the simple reason that there was no forest."

Lifting a hand to the squat stripe sitting thick and dusky on the far horizon, Myrddin replied, "There is a forest now."

"How can this be?" I wondered aloud; doubting him never occurred to me. "I did not think we had come so far out of our way. We must have wandered further astray in the fog than I imagined."

"No, Gwalchavad," Myrddin said, "we have not wandered out of our way." He turned and began walking back to camp, leaving me to ponder the more subtle implications of his words.

Did he mean, I wondered, that the forest had grown up since I had last passed this way? Or that the forest was always there, but I had not seen it? Could I have ridden through a forest and never noticed a single tree?

Either alternative was as unlikely as the other. Possibly, some bedevilment had blinded me to it, or caused me to forget. I decided to ask Peredur about this, and discover what he remembered.

I found the young warrior helping raise the picket line for the night. As when in war, Arthur had commanded the horses to be picketed, rather than tethered, so they might be readied more quickly should need arise. I called him from his work. "Follow me. I have something to show you," I said, leading him away.

He fell into step beside me, and I asked, "Do you remember when we were here last time?"

"I have been trying my best to forget."

"Well, I would ask if you recall passing through a forest during our sojourn in Llyonesse."

"Forest!" he exclaimed. "Why, the place is barren as a desert—as you very well know. If we had—" Realizing that I was in earnest, Peredur stopped and regarded me strangely. "Lord? Forgive me, but I thought you in jest. Why would you ask such a thing?"

We gained the hilltop where Myrddin and I had just stood. There, I pointed to the bruise-colored line hugging the gently undulating southern horizon, and said, "See now! A forest where none was seen before."

Peredur gaped at the sight, glanced at me, and then returned his gaze to the tree line, visible now as a blue-black band below a swiftly fading twilight sky. "It might be clouds only."

"The Emrys is in no doubt," I replied. "Trees—not clouds."

The young man's face squirmed into a frown. "Myrddin cannot be faulted, I suppose," he allowed reluctantly. "It must be that we strayed far from the trail when we rode in the fog."

His tone did nothing to quell my suspicions, but I agreed and we returned to camp and helped finish the picket by tying horses to the central line, before hurrying to one of the four large fires that had been lit to keep us warm through the night. There was a stew of salt pork, black beans, and bread for our supper: bland-tasting mush, but hot and substantial after a cold day in the saddle. When the meal was finished, some of the warriors tried to get Myrddin to sing again, but he would not. He said a sword is made dull by dragging it out all the time, and he wanted a keen blade when next he reached for it.

So we huddled near the fire and talked and dozed instead, and night tightened its grip on us. One by one, the Cymbrogi succumbed to the all-pervasive silence of the blighted land. We wrapped ourselves in our cloaks, closed our eyes, and tried to sleep. Sometime during the night, the wind rose again, this time gusting from the south, colder. I tasted snow on the icy air, and edged closer to the fire.

We awoke to a hard frost and wind like a knife cutting through our cloaks. There was no snow, but a low gray sky spat dry sleet on us, making for a miserable slog as we began the day. We broke fast, and started out, only to halt again as we crested the first hill.

Myrddin flung out his hand, and Arthur pulled hard on the reins; his mount reared. The company stopped behind us, alert to danger. I heard the dull ring of weapons being readied. The Emrys glanced over his shoulder and motioned me to draw alongside.

I was beside the king and Myrddin in an instant, and saw what had brought them up short. The forest, last seen as a thick line on the far southern horizon, now rose directly before us—a dense growth of hornbeam, elm, and oak standing just across the valley.

Astonished beyond words, I stared at the wood as if never having seen a tree before. There was, so far as I could determine, nothing at all to suggest that the trees I saw before me were not what they appeared: solid and thick and, like all trees everywhere, deeply rooted to their places through years of slow, inexorable growth.

Gazing in disbelief at the dense woodland, I slowly became aware of a strange, unsettling sound. I think the sound had been there from the first, but I noticed it only after the first shock of seeing the trees had passed. Nor was I the only one to hear it.

"What is that?" asked Arthur, his voice low. He half turned his head, but his eyes did not leave the dark wood for a moment. "It sounds like teeth clicking."

Truly, it did; it was the sound of many teeth, large and small, gnashing against one another—not fiercely, but softly, almost gently, in a low, gabbled muttering.

Arthur's eyes swept left and right along the stout line of trees for any break in the wood. The line met us as a timber wall, and there was no breach to be seen anywhere along its thick-grown length save one only: directly ahead, a gap opened between the close-grown trees.

The trail we pursued led straight into the heart of that dark wood. What is more, the mist was rising again; it was already filling the valley between us and the wood's edge.

Bedwyr and Cador reined up beside us then. Having observed the forest from their rearward places, they now joined us to learn what the king and his Wise Counselor made of it. "Unless it was hidden by mist," Bedwyr declared, "I cannot think how it has come to be here otherwise."

"Perhaps," Cador suggested, "like the warriors in your

story, Myrddin, we have slept a thousand years, and the wood has grown up around us.''

Bedwyr frowned at Cador's frivolity, and reproached him with an indignant grunt. But Myrddin said, ''In this place, that is as sound an explanation as any other.''

''If that is what passes for reason,'' Bedwyr said darkly, ''then folly is king, and madness reigns.''

''A wall before us, a wall behind. There is but one way through,'' Arthur said, ''and there is no turning back.''

So saying, he raised his hand and signaled the column to move on. I returned to my place behind Myrddin. ''Well,'' I said to Rhys as we urged our horses forward once more, ''we are going in.''

''Was there ever any question?''

''No,'' I answered. ''*Alia jacta est.*''

''What does that mean?'' he asked.

'' 'The die is cast,' '' I told him. ''It is something old Caesar once said.''

''Who told you that?''

''My father used to say it—I never knew why. But lately, I begin to think I know what he meant.''

We crossed the valley and entered the wood in silence. No one spoke, and all kept a keen eye for any sign of attack, though many, I noticed, cast a last glance at the sky before the intertwining branches closed overhead. It was like entering a tomb—so close and dark and silent was the unchancy wood. The trail narrowed as it passed among the broad boles of the trees, but rather than ride single file, the men urged their horses together and rode shoulder to shoulder and flank to flank.

Like all the others, I cast a longing glance behind me as we entered the wood and saw the same look of sick apprehension on one face after another. But there was nothing for it. We clutched our weapons more tightly and hunched lower in the saddle as if to escape notice of the tight-crowded trees.

Keeping my eyes on Myrddin and Arthur ahead of me, I remained alert to the sounds around me, but there was little to hear; a thick mat of pine needles cushioned the horses' hooves, and the men made no sound at all. Neither was any birdsong heard—nothing, in fact, but the incessant clicking, and the hush of muffled breath passing into the dank, dark air.

As to the ceaseless clicking and clicking and clicking, after a time I discovered what created that unsettling sound: the wind twitching the bare upper branches. Fitful and gusty, the wind did not penetrate the forest at all, but continually mumbled and fretted overhead, stirring uneasily in the high treetops and making the thin branches quiver. So close were these limbs and so entangled, they chattered against one another in endless motion. Even this, however, did not strike the ear with any vigor, but reached us as a faint muttering falling from high above, sinking down and down into the soft forest floor below.

The forest swallowed everything that came into it—sunlight and wind, and now the Pendragon and his warband. Everyone who comes into a woodland wild feels something of this oppressive enclosing; it is what causes a traveler to skirt the shadows and stay to the trail, proceeding with wary caution. What is more, this uncanny sensation seemed to increase with every step deeper into the wood until it took on an almost suffocating aspect, becoming a thing of towering proximity and ponderous weight.

We came upon a stream—little more than a muddy rivulet dividing the trail—and stopped to water the horses, taking it in turn by twos, and then moving on to allow those behind to get at the water. We rode a fair way farther, whereupon Arthur halted the columns, turned his horse, and sat looking down the long double line of warriors. Without a word, Myrddin rode down the center, passing between the warriors.

"What do you see, lord?" I asked, turning in the saddle to learn what held his attention.

"It is what I am not seeing that causes me concern," the king replied, still gazing back along the trail.

The trees along each side and the branches thickly interwoven above made of our trail a shadowy tunnel, like the entry shaft of a cave or mine. The Cymbrogi, riding close to one another, sat their horses, awaiting the call to move on. Owing to the dimness of the light and the narrowness of the trail, I could not see past more than twelve or fifteen riders as I looked down the line. Yet I could discern nothing amiss.

I was about to say as much when Myrddin shouted something and came pounding back along the trail to join us.

"Well?" said the king.

"I cannot see them," Myrddin replied. "They should have rejoined us by now."

Only then did I realize what they were talking about. The fifteen or so pairs that I saw behind us were, indeed, all that remained of the long double column. The others were not lost to the shadows—they were gone completely. Obviously, we had become separated from the rest of the warhost. The warband led by Bedwyr and Cador had vanished.

"Lord, allow me to ride back and find out what has happened," I volunteered. "No doubt meet them before I have gone a hundred paces."

"Very well," Arthur agreed, "but take Rhys with you—let him signal us when you have reached them. We will wait for you here."

I returned to my horse and informed Rhys of the king's command as I swung into the saddle. We passed down the line of warriors and back along the trail. I counted thirteen pair: twenty-six warriors out of fifty, I thought, and wondered what had become of the rest. Could twenty-four mounted warriors simply disappear?

Once past the last of the Cymbrogi, we urged our mounts to speed and raced along the close-grown track. When, after a fair ride, we still caught no sight of the stragglers, I halted. "We should have seen them by now," Rhys said as he reined up beside me. "What could have happened to them?"

"Until we find them, we only waste our breath asking such questions," I pointed out. In Llyonesse, anything might happen, I thought, but kept the thought to myself.

"Well, what do you suggest, O Head of Wisdom?" Rhys gave me a sour frown.

"Either we keep riding until we find them, or we go back," I suggested, and Rhys rolled his eyes to show how impressed he was with my reckoning. "Which is it to be?"

Before he could answer, there arose on the path behind us the strangest sound I have ever heard. If you were to imagine the sound of a bull stag belling out his rage as a pack of baying hounds raced in for the kill—imagine that, and then increase it tenfold and add to it the roar of a stream in full spate, and you will have some small idea of the sound that broke upon us as a single blast, like that loosed from a horn.

A seething, restless silence reclaimed the trail. The horses shied and tried to bolt, but we held them tight. In a few moments, the sound came again, closer. The bare-limbed trees quivered, and I felt the dull tremble of the earth in the pit of my stomach. Whatever made that sound was coming our way, and swiftly.

Chapter Twenty-nine

The next sound I heard was the sharp slap of leather against the withers of Rhys' mount as he wheeled the frightened animal and gave it leave to fly—nor was I slow to follow, pausing only long enough to cast a fleeting backward glance. I saw nothing but the shadow-crowded path and darkness beyond. Even so, the shudder of the trees told me that the thing was charging towards us with speed.

I gave my mount its head, and a heartbeat later, I was racing along the forest trail, trying to catch Rhys.

It took us longer to reach our waiting companions than I expected, and I feared we had somehow lost king and Cymbrogi along with all the rest. But then Rhys slowed and I saw, just beyond him, two horses in the track ahead. The Cymbrogi had dismounted to rest the horses while awaiting our return. They called out to us, asking what we had discovered, but we did not stop until we had rejoined Myrddin and Arthur.

Rhys slid from the saddle before his horse had come to a halt. Arthur and Myrddin had risen to their feet, the question already on their faces. "We did not find them, lord," Rhys was saying as I dismounted.

"Then what—" began the king.

Before he could say more, the creature behind us loosed its bone-rattling cry. The forest trembled around us and the horses began rearing and neighing. The waiting warriors leapt to their mounts, stretched for their dangling reins, and retrieved spears from beneath their saddles.

Arthur, sword in hand, ordered the battle line and, an instant later, we were armed and ready to face whatever came our way. The trail was too narrow for horses to maneuver, so Arthur ordered the fight on foot. "It will come at us on the trail," the king cried, his voice taking on the vigor of command. "Let it come! Open a way before it—make a path—two men on each side. Let it come in—then close on it from either side."

It was a desperate tactic, borrowed from the hunt, most often used when a man finds himself unhorsed during the chase. Arthur established himself at the forefront of the line. Myrddin stood to his right, with Rhys and me to his left. The Cymbrogi led the horses to safety well up the trail, and then quickly filled in behind us in ranks four across.

We stared into the gloom, tree limbs quivering on either side and overhead. I could feel the trembling of the ground as the shudders passed up through the earth and into my feet and legs. A hundred horses pounding hard down the path could not drum the earth so. What could it be?

The unnerving cry thundered again. Closer. The entire forest seemed to ripple like a wave. The unnatural sound sent a cold flash of fear snaking through the ranks.

The drumming thud in the ground grew louder. The Cymbrogi stood gripping their spears in silence, staring hard into the gloom ahead.

The roar sounded again. Closer still: an unearthly howl that pierced to the heart. Cold, sick dread spread through me and the wood seemed to undulate; a black mist gathered before my eyes as the ground shook with the pounding of unseen hooves.

I tightened my grip on my spear and shook my head to clear it, thinking, The thing must be nearly on top of us now . . . but where is it?

And then I saw, looming out of the murk of shadows, the form of a beast: a great dark mass racing with impossible speed directly towards us. God help us, it was enormous!

Out of the shadows it came. I heard several stifled cries behind me, and others gasped and muttered hasty prayers.

Curiously, the creature had no substance, no solidity. Even as it swept swiftly nearer, I could get no clear notion of its appearance. The thing seemed nothing but shadow and motion. Indeed, I could see the dimly quivering shapes of trees and branches through it.

And then it was upon us. The ground heaved beneath our feet, and I smelled the rank scent of animal filth. But though we stood steadfast with our spears at the ready, there was nothing substantial to fight.

The shadowshape charged through our midst and I received the distinct impression of a massive beast with the sharp spine and high-humped shoulder of a boar, its foul hair long and flowing in matted shreds like the tatters of a rotten cloak. I imagined two huge yellow eyes glaring balefully out from a flattened piglike face, beneath which bulged a massive jaw from which two great, curved brown tusks jutted in upward-sweeping arcs like a pair of barley scythes. Short, powerful, stumplike legs pummeled the earth, driving the creature forward on the cloven hooves of a stag.

This, as I say, was merely an impression, an image that burned itself into my mind. There was no actual creature, nothing corporeal at all—just a dark-gathered mist of churning shadow and motion.

Some of the warriors let slip their weapons, and one or two dropped to their knees.

"Courage!" shouted Arthur, his voice a steady rock amidst the rising flood of fear. "Stand firm!"

The vile thing drove down on us with the speed of a falling mountain, shaking the ground with every flying step. I gripped my spear and hunkered down, ready to let fly should anything tangible present itself.

The beast came on. The monster loosed its earsplitting scream. The chill air shivered to the sound of a thousand slavering hounds and the belling of a hundred stags at bay.

The cry carried the creature into our midst.

"Hold!" called Arthur. "Hold, men . . . stand your ground."

Beneath my feet, the ground rumbled hollow like a drum.

"Stand firm . . ." Arthur called, straining to be heard above the sound of the onrushing beast. "Stand . . ."

My stomach tightened in anticipation of the terrible impact. The air shuddered and I had the explicit sensation of a great hairy flank heaving past me—like a rippling black wall of muscle.

Spear poised, I drew back my arm and prepared to strike.

The warrior opposite me let fly—too soon! The spear sailed over my head; I ducked under it and in the same instant heard a short, sharp cry as the creature whirled in mid-flight and struck. I saw merely a sudden surge, a quickening of the darkness, and the monster thundered past.

I leapt to the stricken warrior's aid, and a stink like that of rotting meat struck me like the blow of a fist. The gorge rose in my throat and I gagged on the stench. I put a hand over my nose and mouth to keep from vomiting. The Cymbrogi round about groaned, coughed, and spat, and the wounded man writhed on the ground.

His side had been laid open from chest to hip, and blood gushed dark and hot from the wound. "Help me!" he screamed. "Help me!"

"Tallaght?" I said. In the dim light, his features twisted with pain, I did not recognize him at first. "Lie still, brother. Help is coming.

"Myrddin!" I shouted. "Over here! Hurry!"

Tallaght clutched my hand; his grip was slippery with blood, but he clung to me as if to life itself. "I am sorry, lord," he said, his voice already growing weaker. "I did not mean to disgrace . . ."

"Shh," I said gently. "It does not matter. Just rest easy."

"Tell Arthur I am sorry . . ." he whispered, and fell to coughing and could not catch his breath. He died, choking on his blood before Myrddin could reach him. "Go with

God, my friend,'' I said, and lay his hand upon his chest.

Just as swiftly as it had come, the apparition vanished. The ground continued to drum and tremble for a time, but the creature was gone. Myrddin appeared at my side and bent over the fallen warrior. "It is Tallaght," I said as the Emrys stretched his hand towards the young man's face. "He is dead."

Some of the warriors nearby repeated this pronouncement, and it was passed along the ranks. A moment later, there came a cry from farther up the trail. "Stop him!" one of the warriors shouted. "Someone stop him!"

Glancing up, I saw a mounted warrior burst forth from among the horses. Rhys shouted for the man to stop at once, and several others tried to head off the horse, but the rider was too quick and the horse had already reached its stride. He gained the trail at a gallop, and disappeared into the shadows.

Arthur quickly ordered men to go after him, but Myrddin counseled against it. "It is too late now," he said. "Let him go."

"We can catch him still," the king protested.

"We have just lost one warrior to the beast," the Emrys informed Arthur. "How many more will you risk?"

Arthur frowned, but accepted his counselor's advice. "Did you see who it was?"

"No." Myrddin shook his head slowly.

"I saw him," I told them. "It was Peredur. No doubt he has gone to avenge his kinsman's death."

"The young fool," Arthur muttered.

"He is God's concern now," Myrddin said. "Put him from your thoughts, and instead think how to find your missing warriors."

Night was hard upon us, and rather than risk losing the rest of the warband in the dark, Arthur decided to make camp and wait until morning. We buried Tallaght's body where he had fallen, and Myrddin spoke a prayer over the grave. I would have liked to do more for the boy, but that is the way of it sometimes. The Pendragon ordered the remaining Cymbrogi to gather fuel for a fire. What with the dense wood all around us, the men had a great heap of dead timber piled up, and in less time than it takes to tell, the first snakes of flame were slithering up the tangle of old branches.

Once the horses were settled, we gathered to warm ourselves and, in crowding close, to console one another. The fellowship of loyal men is not to be slighted; it is a thing of great solace and is therefore sacred. Accordingly, the Pendragon, in ordering the fire, meant not only to warm us, but to help us to restore our confidence, which had been badly shaken. No one could have imagined that it would turn out as it did.

Comforted by the fire, the men began to talk, and some wondered aloud what manner of creature it was that they had driven off; others voiced surprise that they should have chased it away at all. Speculation proved futile and as one suggestion after another foundered, everyone turned to Myrddin, who was squatting on his haunches at the edge of the fire, arms crossed over knees, staring bleakly into the flames.

"Here, now, Myrddin," called Arthur genially. "Have you ever heard tell of such a beast?"

At first it seemed Myrddin had not heard the king's question. He made no move, but continued staring into the red heart of the fire.

"What say you, bard?" the king said, his voice loud in the sudden quiet of the wood.

The Cymbrogi watched in silent expectation as the Emrys, without taking his eyes from the flames, slowly drew the hood of his cloak over his head and rose. He stood for a moment as if entranced by the flames, then stooped and reached into the fire. Several of the Cymbrogi cried out instinctively at the act, but Myrddin calmly withdrew a fistful of hot ashes. Despite the heat, he held the embers in his hand, blew on them, and then gazed upon the coals.

We watched in astonished silence as he held the burning embers in his hand, his face illumined in the ruddy glow. Suddenly he cast the coals back into the flames. He stood for a moment clutching his hand—whether from pain or the shock of what he had seen, I cannot say—

then, as if in a trance, he raised his hand and licked the palm with his tongue.

No one moved or said a word as the Bard of Britain took up his staff and raised it over his head. Slowly, he turned to face us. My heart clenched in my chest, for his face was as rigid and pale as death.

The eyes gazing out from beneath the hood were no longer those of a man, but of a preying hawk, farseeing, keen, and golden. Stretching forth his hand, he held his palm level to the ground and, opening his mouth, began to speak. Or perhaps it was some other speaking through him, for the voice seemed to come from the Otherworld.

"Hear, Men of Britain, Valiant Ones," he said in the strange, hollow voice, "the Head of Wisdom speaks. Heed and take warning. The Black Beast sent among you this day was but a foretaste of the power arrayed against you. The battle is joined, and every man who would achieve the quest must face many ordeals. Be not dismayed, neither be afraid, but face the trials to follow with all forbearance, for the Swift Sure Hand upholds you, and the Holy Grail awaits those who endure to the end."

Having delivered himself of this decree, he lowered his staff and sat down again. Almost at once, he began to shake and tremble all over. Thinking to aid him, the warrior nearest reached out and took hold of the Emrys to steady him. Instantly, the man yelped and fell back as if he had been struck by a thunderbolt.

Others reached to help the man. "Let him be," advised Arthur sternly. "It will pass."

The stricken warrior quickly recovered, and the Cymbrogi set themselves the task of settling the horses for the night before lying down to rest. Though I tried to sleep, the weird events of this fraught day conspired to overthrow my best resolve and I found myself thinking about Morgian instead, and wondering when the next attack would come, and what form it would take.

Chapter Thirty

It was still dark when I awoke. Judging by the deep darkness of the forest, dawn was still very far away. At first I closed my eyes and tried to go back to sleep, but then I heard again what must have roused me: the horses were awake and whickering restively to one another, so I roused myself, thinking to see what might be done to calm them.

The fire had burned itself to a heap of ashes, and I had to stumble over the sleeping bodies of my swordbrothers, waking a few of them, who joined me at the picket with the horses. "I feel as if I have slept an age," remarked one of the warriors. "But it looks as though dawn is still far off." He gazed around warily. "Indeed, if I did not know better, I would say the darkness has only increased."

As he spoke, a thin trickle of fear snaked along my ribs. I raised my eyes to the darkness above, dense and heavy as iron. Others joined us and began offering their observations. Some held that the night had passed and we would soon see the sunrise; more maintained that the time for sunrise had passed without bringing the light.

Before the disputation could become contentious, however, Arthur brought an end to the speculation by putting the question to Myrddin directly. "Is this the enemy's doing?"

Myrddin hesitated, then glanced quickly at the warriors, who stood awaiting his answer. "Yes," he said simply.

The king nodded. "It makes no difference." Turning to the Cymbrogi, he said, "Our swordbrothers should have reached us by now. We are going back for them." He ordered the horses to be saddled and all idle talk to cease; he commanded torches to be prepared, and once we were saddled and ready to depart, the torches were lit.

Thus, we took up the search for the lost Cymbrogi, returning along the trail by which we had come the day before. Whether the sun shone beyond the cover of the forest, I cannot say. All I know is that the light of day did not reach us, and we rode in darkness as complete as that which covers the earth on the stormiest of nights.

Without the sun, however feeble, to mark time's slow passing, it seemed we journeyed an eternity, stopping only to rest and water the horses and to renew the torches, continually alert to the wood around us all the while. We traveled what must have passed for a day in the wider world, slept a little, and continued on, never knowing where one night left off and another began, moving from one march to the next without speaking more than a dozen words to anyone. And all the time the darkness wore on us; a grindstone it was, covered in darkest silk, perhaps, but a stone nonetheless, grinding and grinding us down to dust.

See, now: fear stalked the bold Dragon Flight—fear like the immense shadow beast loosed to rampage through our anxious ranks. Stouthearted men started at the smallest sound, and sained themselves with the cross whenever they thought no one else was looking.

Arthur—alas, even Arthur—who feared no earthly foe, found reason to be afraid—not for himself, mind, but for his queen. Her name was never far from his lips. From time to time he roused himself from his bleak meditations and made an effort to lift the spirits of his warband—he called encouragement to those who appeared to be struggling, and offered conversation to those who seemed most in need of distraction—but his labors went unrewarded.

At times the forest trail seemed to twist around upon itself and, occasionally, another path might be seen to diverge from the main—although there was never any question about which way we should go. The Pendragon led without wavering. Even so, it grew increasingly apparent that we would not gain our destination no matter how long or far we rode.

"Only a little farther," Arthur argued. "We must be nearing the end."

"Arthur," Myrddin replied gently, "we should have reached it long since."

"We go on," Arthur insisted, and so we did.

So unvarying was the trail, and the darkness so unrelenting and complete—and our fortitude stretched so thin and fine—that the clearing came as a shock to our benighted senses.

Without warning or sign, we simply rode out from the rooflike cover of the trees and onto a wide river mead. Even in the darkness we could tell that it was a clearing of considerable extent. The sound of rushing water could be heard from the other side of the mead, and the damp, chill closeness of the wood gave way to the sudden gusts of a cold winter wind.

As we had ridden some way since our last resting place, the king thought best to make camp, water the horses, and refresh our own water supply. Accordingly, we found a place beside the encircling stream to picket the horses and began dragging dead limbs from the surrounding wood. Glad for this change, such as it was, we fell to with a will and soon had a large campfire burning with the brightness of a beacon on the edge of the clearing.

Far better for us if we had endured the darkness and cold, our accustomed misery. Far better, indeed, if we had never set foot in the Wasteland at all!

For, as the campfire reached its height and we gathered to warm ourselves around it, the flamelight revealed a great oak tree a short distance away. At first we knew nothing of it but that it was a true monarch of the wood, ancient and lordly, supreme ruler in its domain, and that it stood alone in the center of the clearing, which, bounded by the encircling stream, formed an almost perfect ring around it.

But then, as we drew closer and looked up into those

huge gnarled boughs, we glimpsed strange, elongated
shapes twisting in the wind. We looked and courage, already rattled from the long, grinding darkness, took flight.
With nothing to halt the rout, our beleaguered imagina-
tions fled instantly to the worst.

Ah, but the truth awaiting us in those misshapen boughs
was far, far worse than anything we could have imagined.

We looked to where Arthur stood, Myrddin at his side,
gazing towards the great oak. The king stooped and took
a brand from the fire, drew himself up, and then started
for the tree. Taking up brands, we hastened after him,
crowding in close to one another so as not to be the hind-
most.

Closer, I could see the strange shapes dangling in clusters from the lower limbs like enormous bats. It was not
until we stepped almost directly underneath the foremost
bough that I realized what it was we were seeing.

Terrible silence crushed hard upon us. I could not
breathe. I could not speak. My strength flowed away like
water. A fearful drumming filled my ears and boomed in
my head. I staggered back and, God help me, I vomited
bile over my feet.

Then, forcing myself to a courage I did not possess, I
wiped my mouth on my arm and stood, taking my place
once more beside my king. Myrddin stood beside him, his
hand on the king's shoulder and the other to his eyes, as
if to shield them from the sight of that tree's terrible fruit.

Only Arthur, firebrand in his hand, yet stared up into
the tree at the naked corpses of his brave Cymbrogi.

"Come away, Bear," I heard Myrddin mutter. "There
is nothing to be done here."

Arthur made no reply, but shrugged off Myrddin's hand
and gazed full on the grisly display before us. Each of the
lower boughs bore the corpses of at least four warriors—
bound singly, or in groups of two or three—and there
were more hung high in the upper branches, and yet still
more beyond these. From what I could see in the shifting
light, most of them had died in battle. Many had lost limbs
and several had been disemboweled. Every corpse had
been shorn of both hands and feet, and these we discov-

ered placed in a ghastly ring around the roots of the tree.
Some few must have been alive when they were hung,
for I saw bloated blue faces of men I had once known as
swordbrothers among the dead: Cai and Cador and Bedwyr.

Brave Cai, his tongue protruding, swollen in his mouth,
his scalp hanging loose on his skull . . . Cador, friend and
stalwart companion, his arms bloody stumps and his legs
broken and limp, his mouth gaping in a last, silent scream
. . . and Bedwyr, hero and champion, his smashed jaw
dangling on his chest, one eye gouged out, the remains
of a spear jutting broken from his stomach. . . .

Tears rose in my eyes then, and I had to look away.
My God! my spirit cried out in grief and anguish. God,
why? Why these?

Myrddin tried again to get the king to leave, and again
the Pendragon refused. "My men are here," he said, his
voice grating in the deathly silence. "My place is with
my men."

"You can do nothing for them," Myrddin said, almost
harshly.

"I can bury them," Arthur snapped.

"No, Bear," Myrddin counseled. "It is the living you
must think of now." I wondered at this answer, but trusted
the Emrys would have a sound reason.

Thrusting a helpless hand towards the tree, Arthur said,
"I cannot leave them like this and still call myself king.
Go, if you must, and take the men with you. I will stay."

The Emrys frowned, glancing at the dread oak.

"Well?" Arthur demanded, forcing the Emrys' choice.

Myrddin hesitated, and a light came up in his eyes.
"There may yet be a way to preserve some small scrap
of dignity and courage." His voice quickened as he spoke.
"Hear me, Proud King. We will not abandon our loyal
swordbrothers in death. We will send them on their journey hence with all honor, in sharp defiance of the wickedness that has so cruelly slain them. Are you willing?"

"You know that I am."

"Then listen to me." So saying, the Wise Emrys put
his hand to the back of Arthur's neck and drew him near.

They spoke together like this for a time, and then the king drew himself up, turned, squared his shoulders, and said, ''Very great evil has been practiced here, and we, who strive towards the light, bear witness to this vile deed and condemn it before the throne of God. Yet, though life has abandoned our brothers, we will not forsake them in ignoble defeat.

''Here in the camp of the Evil One we will kindle a light, and send this light like a spear into the very heart of the darkness that oppresses us. As light shining in the midst of darkness overcomes that darkness and banishes it utterly, so we shall drive it from the hand of the enemy who would employ it as a weapon against us. And the dread tree on which hang the bodies of our friends will become a funeral pyre, and the flames that light our brothers' homeward way will become a beacon of our defiance.''

When Arthur finished speaking, I added my own voice to the acclaim that welcomed the king's pronouncement. Oh, we made that blighted wood ring with righteous adulation. And then we hastened to the edge of the wood round about to gather a bounty of dead wood for fuel, and when we had heaped the tinder man-high around the ancient oak, Myrddin caused the remnant of the Dragon Flight to make a wide circle around the tree.

He then commanded us to walk slowly in a sunwise direction. Led by Arthur, we began; meanwhile, the Emrys stepped to the tinder heap and raised his staff high. Calling in a loud voice, he cried out, ''Great Light, whose life is light and power to his creatures, hear your servant!''

Taking the staff with both hands now, he held the oaken rod above his head and cried, ''We who journey in darkness have need of your light. We who are bereft of hope and beset by evil on every side have need of your power. Lord, in our day of travail, hear our cry!

''Great Light, our kinsmen have been wickedly murdered, and their bodies given over to death.'' His voice resounded across the meadow. ''You alone, Lord, hold authority over the grave. Even as your voice quickens the spirit in the womb, so you summon the spirits of the departed to your throne. Therefore, we ask you to call our brothers home to your Otherworldly realm, and give them places of honor in your banquet hall.

"This night great evil gathers close, seeking to destroy us. Yet we will trust in you, Lord, to deliver us. If this cannot be, then we trust you to meet us on the way and guide us to your halls. In token of our trust, we light this pyre to hold the darkness at bay. Let it burn as a beacon to light the homegoing of our swordbrothers and put evil to flight."

Holding the oaken rod above his head, he stood for a long moment and then slowly lowered the staff and extended it towards the firewood. There was a flash of blue and a sound like the tearing of a cloak between giant hands. The fire simply appeared, arcing through the air, flowing like shimmering liquid, leaping from branch to branch, and scattering in bright blue tracery through the dry wood. Within moments the flames were cracking hot and bright, licking up through the tinder heap, leaping up and up into the great spreading branches.

Turning to the Cymbrogi, Myrddin said, "Sing! Make a noise to rouse the Heavenly Host!" With that he led us in a psalm such as the brown clerics chant in the Holy Mass:

> *The Lord is my rock!*
> *The Lord is my fortress, and my deliverer!*
> *God is my refuge; He is my shield!*
> *And the horn of my salvation, my stronghold.*

The flames mounted higher, stretching into the branches, caressing the lowermost corpses. Ringed by fire, the massive black trunk began to smolder as the yellow flames stretched higher and ever higher into the tree.

Still walking, maintaining the circle, we began to sing with the Emrys, chanting the words as he led us.

> *I call to the Lord who is worthy to be praised,*
> *And I am saved from my enemies.*

The cords of death entangled me;
The torrents of destruction overwhelmed me.

The cords of the grave coiled around me;
The snares of death confronted me.
In my distress, I cried to my God for help.
From his temple he heard my voice.

The heat from the flames forced us back, making our circle larger still. The corpses, now alight, began swinging and twisting in the quickening wind created by the flames. The boughs creaked and cracked as the flames tripped from branch to branch, higher and still higher into the sky.

The earth trembled and quaked,
And the foundations of the mountains shook;
They trembled because he was angry.

There came a long, sighing crack. All at once the mighty tree slumped inwardly upon itself. Riven by fire, the trunk of the oak split, sending sparks spiraling upward on the rising air like thousands of tumbling stars. It seemed to me that these were the spirits of our friends taking flight towards Heaven.

And he looked down in his anger and said:
Because their love is set on me, I will deliver them.
I will deliver them from danger, for they know my
  name.
I will be with them in times of trouble;
I will rescue them from the grave,
And bring them honor in my courts;
I will satisfy them with eternal life
  to enjoy their rich salvation.

I said the words as Myrddin spoke them, and watched the glimmering sparks rising up and up, and I thought, Farewell, Cai, stalwart companion, faithful through all things. Farewell, Bedwyr, loyal brother, steadfast in the fight. Farewell, Cador, brave and true. Farewell, my friends, enter into the Peace of Christ. Farewell . . .

My heart rose to my throat and my eyes filled with tears, and the burning oak blurred into a blazing mass of shimmering, shifting light, and I heard a roar like thunder as the gathering wind rushed to feed the towering flames, whipping them to white heat. The light that blazed from the pyre filled the wide meadow now, forcing back the darkness on every side.

I heard the wail of the wind, and the cold air gusted, swirling around us. My back was cold, my face and hands searing hot from the blaze before me. The scream grew louder and I realized it was not the cry of the wind, but the wild scream of a creature tortured beyond endurance. What is more, the creature was coming swiftly towards us, drawn by the fire.

Myrddin heard the sound, too, and cried out, "Fear nothing! Greater is he who has heard our prayer than that which assaults heaven with its cry."

As it rose above the wind, shivering the wood all around us, I felt the wild, keening sound in my belly and then in the quiver of the earth beneath my feet. I thought at first that it must be the Shadow Beast returning to attack us again, but the trembling mounted steadily and I knew it must be something far, far larger and more deadly.

"Listen to me!" cried Myrddin, and he began instructing us on how to survive the onslaught we would soon face. We were to link arms, he said, and form an outward-facing ring, an enclosed wall with our bodies. Where men might be too far apart they should hold a spear between them, but under no condition were we to break the chain. "Though Hell itself break over you, do not let go," the Emrys said. "Whatever you may see, whatever you may hear, do not break the circle. Keep the ringwall intact and, though the Devil himself leads the attack, we will not be harmed."

I reached out to the man next to me—it was Rhys, his face grim in the lurid light. We linked arms, then clasped hands with the warriors on either side and braced ourselves for the assault. The ground began to shake, and I heard a sound like that of giants crashing through the wood, uprooting trees, and casting them aside. The very earth trembled beneath our feet, and the forest all around cracked and groaned with the snapping of branches and the twisting of limbs. What, I wondered, could cause such destruction?

Suddenly the sound stopped and the ground ceased shaking. The roar of the flames behind us seemed to still for a moment and even the wind grew calm. I have seen this before, and know it to be but the false tranquility of an enemy gathering itself for the onslaught.

"Stand your ground!" shouted Arthur. "Here they come!"

Chapter Thirty-one

We stood gazing into the darkness, the fire at our backs throwing our shadows before us like an all-encircling army of shape-shifting phantoms.

Breathless, we waited.

Across the meadow, the trees began thrashing back and forth as if in the grip of a violent storm, but the air remained still. I heard a low, grinding sound and the trees parted, lying down on either side as if divided by a giant hand.

In the same instant, the burning oak behind us gave another tremendous crack, sending sparks and chunks of flaming wood showering all around. The fire at our backs leapt high, and higher still into the night; our shadows flickered and danced out across the darkened meadow. In the newly opened gap where the forest met the river, a figure appeared—a lone warrior on a horse.

"There!" someone shouted, and from the corner of my eye I saw a movement as the speaker thrust a hand to point out the horseman advancing towards us.

"Do not break the circle!" Myrddin Emrys cried, his voice terrible in the silence. "As God is life and evil death, hold tight and do not let go!"

The rider came on, slowly. He carried a dark shield with a burnished iron rim; both the shield's rim and the honed tip of an upright spear glimmered in the firelight, and the blade on his thigh gleamed dull red. The warrior was dressed all in black from head to foot, and wore a hooded cloak, so I could not see his face; from the withers and flanks of the horse, long black strips of fine cloth rippled and fluttered as the animal moved, making it seem as if the beast were floating towards us.

The dark rider advanced to within a spear's cast of us, whereupon the Emrys challenged him. "Halt!" he shouted in his voice of command. "The Swift Sure Hand is over us. You can do no evil here. Go back."

The rider made no reply, but sat regarding us while his mount chafed the ground impatiently.

"Go back to the hell from whence you came," Myrddin shouted again. "You cannot harm us."

By way of reply, the warrior shifted the shield to cover his chest and, with the slightest lifting of the reins, turned the horse and began riding around the ring. He made one circuit, then another and another, slowly gathering pace with each pass. By the sixth or seventh circuit, the horse had reached an easy canter.

Around and around he rode, in a long, slow circle, the hooves of his mount beating the ground in a rhythmic thump like the rising beat of a drum. Around and around—the canter became a trot . . . the trot became a gallop . . . the gallop became faster, the beat of the hooves coming quicker.

The strange black strips of cloth hanging from the horse's sides rustled like wings. I could hear the beast's breath coming in snorts and gasps now as the pace began to tell. The warrior's cloak billowed out behind him and the hood slipped from his head, revealing a face I knew well.

"Llenlleawg!"

It was Arthur, crying out in surprise and dismay. He shouted again, hoping, I think, to gain his former champion's attention. Others quickly joined in, and soon everyone was calling Llenlleawg's name. I shouted, too, thinking that we might yet sway him from his course.

But looking neither right nor left, the Irish champion urged his mount to charging speed and lowered the spear.

"Stand your ground, men!" shouted Arthur. "Do not break the circle!"

Even before he finished speaking, I saw the quick flick of the reins and the horse swerved towards the ring of Cymbrogi, driving in toward the ring at a shallow angle to my right. The spear swung over the horse's neck and came level. The Cymbrogi, arms linked, shouted to distract the horse, and braced themselves for the killing blow.

But the attack was merely a feint, and he slanted away well before committing himself to the charge.

"The Swift Sure Hand upholds us!" shouted Myrddin.

The next charge came while the Emrys' words yet hung in the air—another slanting drive, the angle sharper this time. Again the Cymbrogi shouted to distract the horse, and again Llenlleawg broke off the attack—but carrying it closer before turning away.

"Llenlleawg!" the king cried. "Here I am! Come to me!"

The champion galloped on, his face set, expressionless, his eyes staring and empty as the dead.

The third attack carried him almost headlong into the line. In the leaping firelight, I saw the head of the spear swing towards me as Llenlleawg began his charge. This time he came on a straight course and I knew he meant to break us. "God help us," I breathed, tightening my grip on Rhys next to me.

The black's hooves tore the turf as it gathered speed, legs churning, closing swiftly. I could already feel the spearhead slicing into my flesh and my bones breaking as I fell beneath those crushing hooves. I braced myself for the impact.

Llenlleawg charged to within a hairbreadth of the line. I could hear the spear blade sing in the air. But at the moment when the spear should have pierced my chest and carried me off my feet, the blade shifted and the horse blew past me—so close I could feel the heat of the animal as it surged by.

The line held, and the Cymbrogi cheered in their relief.

But when Llenlleawg did not so much as break stride, I knew that the testing was over. The next charge would be in earnest; the man chosen to meet it would die, and the circle would be breached.

Around and around rode Llenlleawg, straight-backed in the saddle, shoulders square, oblivious to the jeers and taunts of his former friends. On the final pass he began his charge. The horse strained forward, hooves pounding the earth. The spear came level as the horse turned onto its course, and I saw who had been chosen. The spear was aimed at Arthur.

"Hold, men!" he cried as the deadly blade swept swiftly nearer. "Hold the line!"

The Cymbrogi, desperate to help their king, writhed in an agony of helplessness. Obedient unto death—each man willing, longing, to take the Pendragon's place in the line, yet unable to so much as lift a hand or move a step for the sake of that selfsame obedience—the brave Dragon Flight screamed their defiance at the onrushing traitor.

I could not bear to see the cruel spearhead pierce my lord and friend, neither could I look away. So, like all the others, I watched helplessly as the death-stroke hurtled swift to the mark. And, like all the others, I screamed in a futile attempt to draw the spear away from that mark.

Hooves flying, the black and its silent rider swept in.

The line tensed as if to meet the blow for the king. "Stand firm!" shouted Arthur for the last time.

As Arthur cried out, the hard-charging horse stumbled, its forelegs buckling beneath it. The animal's speed and weight carried it forward, pitching the rider over its neck and onto the ground as the beast's hindquarters sailed up, back legs still kicking.

Llenlleawg fell headfirst to land sprawling on the ground. The spear struck the earth not two paces from Arthur's feet and buried itself deep, the shaft quivering with the force.

The line held, and we cheered our king's deliverance. Doubtless we would have swooped upon Llenlleawg if Myrddin had not prevented us. "Peace!" he cried in his voice of command. "Break not the circle, for the Great King upholds us still!"

Llenlleawg was on his feet again almost instantly. Up he leapt, hand on sword. As he drew the blade, I recognized it at once. How not? I have seen it every day for the past seven years. It was Caledvwlch, the Pendragon's own blade: the last evidence, if any were needed, of Llenlleawg's vile treachery.

The traitor grasped the sword in both hands and raised it over his head as he came.

Perhaps the fall had hurt Llenlleawg, for even as he raised his arms, his steps faltered and his legs gave way. He crashed onto his knees and then sank onto his side as if he had been struck on the head.

Before anyone could think or move, thunder sounded over the meadow. I saw three more riders racing towards us out of the night. Like Llenlleawg, they were all in black from head to heel, cloaked, and hooded. The strangers rode to where Llenlleawg lay. The foremost sat with spear at the ready, while his two companions dismounted, pulled the stricken Llenlleawg upright, and, in one swift motion, lifted him onto the nearest horse. One of them took the saddle behind the stricken warrior, and the other gathered the dangling reins of Llenlleawg's mount and vaulted into the empty saddle. Without a word, they turned as one and rode away, fleeing back into the darkness to the taunts and cries of derision of the watching warriors.

The Dragon Flight wanted nothing more than to pursue our attackers, and we would have, too, but Myrddin, exhorting us with a bard's power of persuasion, held us in line. Stand firm in the circle of God's protection, he told us. Breaking the sacred ring now could only bring about the destruction we had so far eluded.

Oh, but it chafed me sore to see our enemies getting away, and not so much as a spear cast at their retreat.

The black riders reached the river, melting again into the deep shadows beyond the light of the burning oak. They gained the water—I heard the splash of hooves— and all at once the wood before them burst into flame.

Perhaps sparks from the burning oak, drifting across the clearing, had ignited the dry winter wood. Perhaps it had been smoldering for a time and we, preoccupied with Llenlleawg's attack, had failed to notice it. Then again, perhaps some other had set the wood to blaze. I cannot

say. All I know is that even as the fleeing riders gained
the water marge and splashed into the stream, a great
shimmering curtain of flame arose before them. With a
roar like a mighty wind, the flames struck skyward.

In a moment the fire was spreading outward on either
side. The enemy warriors rode through the curtain of fire
without hesitation, and disappeared on the other side.

Only then did Myrddin give us leave to break the ring.
The Pendragon called us to his side and, even while prais-
ing our valor, began ordering the pursuit. While the horses
were being brought from the picket, he turned to the Emrys and said, "Myrddin, he had it—Caledvwlch! The
treacherous dog raised it against me—my own sword!
God in Heaven mark me, that selfsame blade will yet
claim that traitor's head."

The drought-dry wood leapt eagerly to the flame. The
trail by which the enemy riders had escaped was now
impassable. By the time we were mounted, the flames all
but encircled the meadow, leaving only a narrow gap by
which we might escape.

The Pendragon raised a final salute to the dead he left
behind. Lofting his spear, he cried, "In the name of the
Lord who made me king, I will not rest until the blood
debt is paid in full. Death shall be answered with death.
Arthur Pendragon makes this vow."

Myrddin, grim beside him, frowned at this, but said
nothing. Many of the Cymbrogi supported the king's vow
with their own. Then, turning his horse, Arthur led us
away. We rode for the river and the swiftly narrowing gap
of unburned wood—not in orderly columns; there was no
time. Even so, before we were halfway to the water, the
encircling flames closed the gap.

A quick glance behind confirmed what I already knew
to be true: the forest was ablaze on every side and we
were completely enclosed in a ring of fire. Smoke rolled
across the meadow in billows like earthbound clouds.
Gusts of heat swept over us in waves like warm currents
in a freezing ocean. A sound like continuous thunder filled
the night, and we urged our horses to all speed.

Arthur never hesitated, but rode straightaway into the

river, where he dismounted, knelt in the water, and drenched himself all over, shouting for us to follow his example. The horses, smoke stinging their nostrils, jittered and shied, agitated at coming so near the flames.

Removing his wet cloak, the king flung it over the head of his horse to shut out sight of the flames. "Follow me!" he called, pulling the terrified animal after him.

There was nothing for it but to stay close and follow. Flinging my sopping cloak over the head of my mount and mouthing words of encouragement to the frightened animal, I waded through the river, splashing more water over myself as I went. Arthur, having already reached the other side, paused to exhort the men to keep together, then turned and led us into the fire.

Chapter Thirty-two

*M*orgaws has her captives well in hand. Arthur has joined his slattern queen; Rhys, royal bastard, shares his chains; and Merlin, vainglorious bard, now feels how tightly a true sorcerer's charms can bind. Alone among them, Gwenhwyvar might have made a useful friend. She had grit enough and guile, but Charis ruined her—turned her against me, just as she has always turned everyone against me. So Gwenhwyvar will go down like all the rest. The slut queen professes a great love for her Arthur, yet she went willingly from his bed, never once imagining that she is the one who leads him to his ruin. She thinks to save the Grail, and save her hulking husband. In truth, she only hastens his end.

They are so trusting. They actually believed they would be saved, that their god would rescue them. Perhaps they imagined the sky would open up and their miserable Jesu would float down on a cloud to bear them away to high, holy Heaven, where they would be safe forevermore.

Their disappointment, when the awful truth struck them full in the teeth, was too, too wonderful for words. Their expressions of despair will continue to delight me for ages to come. Indeed, I have so enjoyed the pursuit, it is almost a shame to see it end so soon.

But the end swiftly approaches. All that remains is to wring the last tincture of torment, fear, and pain from these, my woeful and wretched adversaries. This is soon accomplished.

*Morgaws has asked to use the Grail to help bring about
their destruction. A fine idea, that! We could allow them
all a Last Supper, a final communion wherein the cup is
passed and its contents shared among them. Oh, there are
some exquisitely painful poisons where death is delayed,
and the victim lingers in agony—sometimes for days.
Watching them twitch and heave in the final extremity
while cursing their ineffectual god could prove highly en-
tertaining.*

*I can already hear the voices of the dying as they
scream out the last of their lives in utter despair. True
desolation is a thing of rare beauty—the stark horror of
the grave when every hope is shattered and swept away—
what can match it, what can compare?*

*But no, I do not want them dead just yet. They have
not even begun to suffer the agonies I intend for them. I
mean to bring them to despair. I mean to make them curse
heaven for giving them life and leaving them to their torment. I mean to harry them, removing their hopes one by
one until there is nothing left but the appalling certainty
of oblivion—the unendurable silence of the pit . . . endless
. . . endless . . . endless.*

Chaos reigned. All was thick smoke and fire-shattered
darkness. Men shouted as they ran, stoking courage to
dare the flames around them. Horses, the sting of smoke
in their nostrils, screamed and thrashed, desperate to escape. We clung to the reins and pulled the terrified animals through the thick-tangled brush. The wood cracked
and rang with the sound of the fire and the shouts of men,
urging their mounts through the wall of fire.

Dodging burning branches, running, running, headlong
and heedless, we fled into the wood beyond the fire's
greedy reach. Thus we came through the flames and found
ourselves deep in the forest once more, dazed by the dev-
ilish assault and the dangers just braved. Like the others,
I called out so that we might locate one another by the
sounds of our voices, and re-form the warband.

But the forest began to exert its malign power over us,
for what should have been a simple matter of drawing our

scattered forces together soon descended into a nightmare of futility. Once beyond the curtain of fire, all sense of direction vanished. For the life of me, I could not tell where I was, or where I was going.

I heard men calling and hastened towards the sound, only to hear them again, somewhat further off, and often in another direction. Once, I heard two men shouting—they could not have been more than fifty paces away—and they answered when I called. I told them to wait and I would come to them . . . only to discover that they were not there when I reached the place. I heard them twice again, calling for me, but farther away each time. I did not hear anyone after the last.

Strange, to hear men all around me—some near, some farther off—and not be able to reach them. It was as if the forest itself were drawing us apart, dividing us, keeping us from reaching one another—either that, or some other, more powerful force for which the wood was merely a single expression. Be that as it may, I kept my head, and when I heard the jingle of a horse's tack just ahead, I rushed for the place, crashing through the wood and shouting: "For God's sake, wait for me!"

"Who is it?" called the nearest of the two as I stumbled through the entangling brush and branches.

I recognized the voice at once. "Bors!"

"Gwalchavad?" he wondered. "However did you get there? We heard you ahead of us but a moment ago."

"Stay where you are," I insisted, struggling forward and tugging my reluctant mount behind me. A ghostly shifting light from the fire some little distance behind shimmered in the low clouds above and reflected on the surprised faces of Bors and the young warrior called Gereint.

"Finally," I said, wiping sweat from my face, "I have found someone."

"We have been hearing Cymbrogi all around us," Gereint said, "but never can find them. You are the first."

"Let us hope I am not also the last," I answered. "Have you seen Arthur?"

"How are we to see anything in this murk and tangle?"

Bors growled. "Three of us came through the fire together, and held on to one another."

"I see but two before me now," I ventured.

"I know!" Bors cried. "I could not keep even the three
of us together, much less find anyone else!" He puffed
out his cheeks in exasperation. "No one will stay in one
place!"

"Listen," said Gereint, "they are getting further
away."

Even as we listened, the sounds around us dwindled.
We all shouted and shouted again, but there came no answer, and in a few moments we could hear nothing at all.
"Well," I concluded, breaking the silence after a time,
"it seems we are on our own."

"So it appears," agreed Bors. "We can either stay here
until morning and see if we can raise a trail then, or we
can go on and try to find some others."

"Morning?" I wondered. "You amaze me, Bors. Do
you even now believe that this foul night will end? I am
thinking it never will."

Stalwart Bors regarded me placidly. "Then let us rest
a little at least, for I grow weary of stumbling through
this godforsaken wood in the dark, bashing my shins at
every turn."

Seeing no harm in the suggestion, I agreed, and we
settled the horses and sat down to rest before continuing
the search. "I did not mind the fire," Bors said after a
time. "At least it was warm. My clothes are still wet."
He yawned, and added, "I am starving."

"We best not dwell on that," I said, and suggested that
we should try to sleep instead.

"I will take the first watch," volunteered Gereint.

"Very well," I agreed. "Rouse me when you get tired
and I will take the second watch."

"Wake us if you hear anything," Bors instructed
through a yawn. In a few moments I heard the gentle burr
of a soft snore as Bors drifted off. Though weary to the
bone, I could not sleep, so I merely closed my eyes and
let my mind wander where it would.

I thought again about my dead swordbrothers, and a

pang of grief cut me like a spear thrust in the heart. Great Light, I thought, using Myrddin's term, gather my fallen comrades in your loving hands and bear them safely to your strong fortress. Give them the welcome cup in your halls of splendor, and make a place for them in the forerank of your Heavenly Host. May they know peace and joy and feasting forever in your company, Lord of All, and grant me the strength to abide my trials until I, too, lay down my sword and take my place among them.

This I prayed, not as the brown-hooded priests pray, but as a cry from my own bruised heart. I felt better for having unburdened myself in this way and, though I still rued the deaths of my swordbrothers, was in some small way comforted by the thought that they would be welcomed and received in Heaven's bright hall. So I lay back, listening to Bors' soft snoring.

Here was a wonder: a man who could sleep in the midst of the enemy's camp, untroubled by fear or the frets of an uneasy heart. Here was a man so secure and peaceful within himself that he could forget his troubles the instant he lay down his head. Like a child, with a child's trust in the moment—here, surely, was a true soul.

"Gwalchavad," came a quiet voice in the darkness. "Are you asleep?"

"No, lad," I answered.

"I have been thinking."

"So have I, Gereint," I replied. I heard him shift in the darkness as he moved closer. "Have you thought of a way we might find our lost companions?"

"No," he said. "I have been thinking that it must have been difficult for the Pendragon—seeing all his men killed like that, and then being attacked by his own champion."

"I should think that would be difficult, yes," I agreed. "But Arthur has been in many a difficult place, and he has never been defeated. Think of that."

"He is the greatest lord I have ever known," Gereint confessed. There was nothing in his voice but awe and praise—as if the distress of our present adversity, and all that went before it, were nothing at all to him.

"When did you join the Cymbrogi?" I asked the young warrior.

"Cador came to us and said the Pendragon needed help to defeat the Vandali. Tallaght, Peredur, and I answered the summons and joined the warband."

"Then you are Cador's kinsmen?"

"That we are," Gereint confirmed.

"He was a good man, and a splendid battlechief. I was proud to call him my friend. He will be sadly missed."

"Indeed," the young warrior replied, "and we will lament his death when we have leisure to do so." He paused and added sadly, "Tallaght and Peredur also."

My forgetfulness shamed me. In truth, the deaths of my own friends and swordbrothers had driven poor Tallaght's demise completely from my thoughts. We fell silent, each to his own bitter memories, and I recalled the time Peredur, Tallaght, and I had gone to inform the people of Rheged of their lord's rebellion and the resulting forfeiture of their lands. It was on that errand that we had found Morgaws. Would that I had never laid eyes on Morgaws! And now Tallaght was dead, along with so many other good men, and probably Peredur, too.

Silent was the wood, and dark, as I say—dark as the night when the moon has gone to rest and the sun not yet risen. The air did not move and there was no sound. The darkness and unnatural quiet put me in a mournful mood, and I began to think about my dead swordbrothers: Bedwyr, and Cai, and Cador, and all the rest—dead and gone. I ached for the loss of them. The darkness seemed to gather me into itself and cover me over. I would have given myself to my black grief, but something in me resisted—a hard knot of stubborn wariness that refused to yield itself to either sadness or acceptance.

So long as we remained in the realm of the enemy, I would not indulge my grief. In duty to my king, I must strive through all things for the enemy's defeat. Thus, I determined to remain alert to any danger lest I, too, fall victim to the evil which had stolen the lives of my friends. When battle is done, I told myself, I will deliver myself to grief. One day soon I would mourn. Soon, but not now, not yet.

The thought gave me some consolation, and I took what solace I could. Arriving on the heels of my determination, however, came that sound which, once heard, can never be forgotten: the strange, tortured bellow of the loathly Shadow Beast. The eerie baying cry seemed to come from ahead of us, though still some distance away. Bors came awake with a start. "Did you hear?"

"The creature," Gereint said in a raw whisper. "It must be the same one that attacked us before."

"Same or different, I will kill the vile thing if it comes near me again," blustered Bors. "God is my witness: that monster will not escape this time."

The bellow sounded again, farther off this time, and in a slightly different direction. It was moving swiftly away.

"You may not get the chance, brother," I told Bors. "The creature is going away from us."

Bors grunted his disdain, and we roused ourselves and resumed the search of our lost companions. We set off on foot, leading the horses. Lest we become separated from one another, we held tight to all our bridle straps; Bors led the way, and Gereint followed, and I came last—wandering a hostile wood in the dark of a never-ending night. Less a search, I considered, than an exercise in forlorn hope.

In the silence that pressed in around us once more, I heard Myrddin's words: *In the quest before us, none but the pure of heart can succeed.*

The thought had scarcely formed when I felt a thin quivery shudder pass up through the soles of my feet and into my legs. I froze in mid-step. The reins in my hand pulled taut as Gereint, just ahead, continued walking. I drew breath to speak, but even as I called for the others to halt, the sound of my voice was lost in the weird screeching bellow of the baleful beast.

The monstrous creature was closing swiftly. I could feel the drumming of the earth in my very bowels. Bors and Gereint stopped on the path ahead. In the gloom I saw Bors turn; his mouth opened.

"Fly!"

In the same instant, there came a crashing sound as the trees directly before us snapped like twigs and burst asunder. The monster was upon us.

Chapter Thirty-three

My terrified mount reared, snapping the bridal strap that bound it to the others, and all three animals plunged into the wood. Branches and tree limbs scattered and fell around me. I glimpsed a massive black shape like a molten hillside charging towards me and knew the monster had found us again.

I threw myself into the dense brush and scrambled for my life. Branches tore at my face and hands. I heard Bors shouting, but could not make out the words. Crawling like a frenzied snake, I dragged myself through the tangled undergrowth.

I glimpsed a hole in the brush no wider than a badger sett and dove headlong for it. But even as I squirmed to pull myself inside, I felt a heavy weight seize upon my legs and I was yanked off the ground. In the same moment, the most foul stink assaulted me: a putrid stench of decaying flesh, together with vomitus and excrement.

Choking, retching, I gasped for breath. Tears filled my eyes and streamed down my face. The beast secured its hold on me and began jerking its hideous head back and forth, shaking me hard to break my bones one against the other before swallowing me whole.

Kicking and clawing, I twisted my body this way and that, trying to scratch out one of the creature's eyes. In my frenzy, my hand struck against a slick-furred neck below the massive jaw; I clenched the odious fur in my hand and hung on, screaming and screaming for help.

The pain grew unbearable. I screamed and screamed again, beating at the heavy flesh with my fists. Pain rolled over me in waves as darkness—terrible, mind-numbing darkness—gathered around me. I could feel the life slowly being crushed from me, and I knew I was breathing my last.

"God in heaven!" I cried in agony. "Help me!"

No prayer was ever more heartfelt than that one, and the words were no sooner out of my mouth than Gereint appeared.

He seemed to hang in the air above me, as if floating, or hovering. I realized then that he had somehow contrived to scale the beast's back. Plunging his knife to the hilt to secure his handhold, he began hacking at the creature with his sword.

The young fool will get himself killed! I thought, trying desperately to free my legs.

Up swung the sword, and down, striking at the back of the great beast's skull. The vile creature's neck jerked up and its mouth gaped wide. The monster roared in agony and I was sent sprawling to the ground. I fell heavily on my side and fought to get free lest I be trampled to death.

My left leg would not move. I heaved myself forward and, on arms and elbows, pulled myself into the brush. Once clear of the beast, I glanced back over my shoulder to see Gereint. He was gone now, but his sword was still stuck in the brute's bulging neck just behind the skull. The monster was belling its agonized shriek with a sound to rip the earth asunder. I threw my hands over my ears and hunkered down, trying to hold out that hateful sound.

What happened after, I cannot say, for the next thing I knew, I was waking up in the dark, silent wood. The black beast was gone, and I was alone. My side felt as if it had been raked with a spearhead and then pounded with an iron rod; my leg burned. Though it hurt to breathe, I drew great draughts to keep from passing out again.

A swirling mass of fear churned within me, but I have been afraid before and in equally trying circumstances. Forcing myself to remain calm, I lay back and listened for a moment. When I did not hear anything, I made to rise. Instantly, pain burst upon me anew, and I fell back.

Bors and Gereint are pursuing the horses and will return any moment, I told myself. They know I am here and will not abandon me. I clung to this hope, repeating it over and over.

The pain in my leg throbbed with a sharp, deep-rooted, urgent ache. It took my mind off the raw pulse of pain in my side. With an effort I pushed myself upright and leaned back against a fallen log. I reached down to touch the place where the pain seemed the worse, and my hand came away sticky and wet with blood. I tried to move my leg; the exertion sent a searing bolt of fire into my head and I almost swooned, but at least the leg could bend somewhat and no bones seemed broken.

My knife was still tucked in my belt, but my sword was missing; my spear had disappeared with my horse. Using the knife, I contrived to cut a strip from my siarc and bind my leg to stanch the flow of blood. The effort exhausted me. I tied the knot and lay back panting and gasping. A fragment of Myrddin's psalm came into my mind and I spoke it out. There in the darksome forest, lying on my back, warm blood oozing from my wounds, I said:

> *The Lord is my rock!*
> *The Lord is my fortress, and my deliverer!*
> *God is my refuge; He is my shield!*
> *And the horn of my salvation, my stronghold.*

There was solace in the words. Just saying them aloud in that dolorous place comforted me, so I continued:

> *I call to the Lord, who is worthy to be praised,*
> *And I am saved from my enemies.*
> *The cords of death entangled me;*
> *The torrents of destruction overwhelmed me.*

It was an act of defiance, I believe, to invoke the Great Light in that place, for I felt my heart stir as courage returned. In truth, I surprised myself at how much of these

songs I could remember. Feeling a very bard myself, I
sent those heaven-breathed words into the darksome
wood:

> *The cords of the grave coiled around me;*
> *The snares of death confronted me.*
> *In my distress, I cried to my God for help.*
> *From his temple he heard my voice.*

Wonder of wonders, even as I spoke those last words
I saw a light shining in the wood: so pale and dim, I first
thought I must have imagined it. I looked and the faint
glimmer disappeared, but when I glanced away again, I
saw it once more. I raised myself up and stared at the
place—as if to hold it there so that it would not vanish
again, leaving me alone in the dark.

I could not see the light directly for all the trees and
brush. Desperate to hold the fragile luminescence, I tried
to remember the rest of Myrddin's prayer. How did it go?

> *And he gazed with . . .*

No, no . . . that was not right. The pain in my leg drove
out everything else. I could not think. I took a deep breath
and forced myself to concentrate. In clumps and snatches
the words came to me and I spoke them out.

> *And he looked down in his anger and said:*
> *Because their love is set on me, I will deliver them.*
> *I will deliver them from danger, for they know my*
>   *name.*
> *I will be with them in times of trouble;*
> *I will rescue them from the grave,*
> *And bring them honor in my courts;*
> *I will satisfy them with eternal life*
>   *to enjoy their rich salvation.*

As I spoke, the faint radiance seemed to strengthen,
gathering itself into a steady gleam like that of the moon
on a mist-shrouded winter night. I thought that the light

might yet break forth, but though I continued repeating the psalm over and over again, the fragile light remained a mere pearly glimmering, and beyond that did not increase.

After a time, I felt the winter chill seeping into my bones. My clothes were damp with sweat and the air was cold, and I began to shiver. Each tremble sent a jolt of pain through me, as it meant moving my leg. I clenched my teeth and willed the gently gleaming light to stay.

I do not know how long I lay there, shivering with pain and cold, grinding my teeth, and praying for that small, thin glow to remain. It seemed a long time, however— long enough for me to begin harboring the suspicion that I had indeed lost both Gereint and Bors, and was now completely alone. Once this suspicion hardened into certainty, I decided to try to get up and move in the direction of the light.

Searching around me for a sturdy branch to use for a staff, I put my hand to a crooked tree limb; it was old and the rotten bark came off in my hand, but the wood was strong enough to support me, and so I used it to pull myself up onto my feet once more. My injured leg still throbbed with the slightest movement, but I clenched my teeth, steadied myself, and started off.

I found I could hobble only a few paces before the pain grew too great to bear and I must stop and rest. Then, after a few moments' respite, I staggered on. I saw that I was following the trail which the black beast had forced as it crashed through the wood. This made my passage somewhat less difficult, for I was able to steady myself against the fallen trees and broken branches.

Thus, by halts and starts, I proceeded along the narrow path. Despite the cold, I was soon sweating once more with the pain and exertion, my breath hanging in phantom clouds around my head. I listened all the while, alert to any sound in the forest. I strained to hear Gereint returning at any moment, or Bors. Or the black beast.

But no. I was alone. Again fear boiled up, but I swallowed it down and moved on, berating my companions for running off, as I supposed, after the horses. How I had

come by this notion, I cannot say. Consumed by my own
troubles, I had not spared a single kindly thought for
them. Indeed, they could have been lying wounded or
dead in the wood nearby and I would not have been any
the wiser.

"Blessed Jesu, forgive a foolish man," I sighed aloud,
and then breathed a silent prayer for the safety of my
friends. These thoughts and prayers occupied me as I staggered my slow way along the trail towards the faint moon-
shimmer of radiance.

At long last, the trail turned slightly and I came to a
huge bramble thicket—an infernally dense tangle of
spiked vines and thorny branches. Had it been a rampart
of stone, it could not have been more formidable. Yet the
monstrous creature appeared to have crashed into this wall
and, in its blind rage, driven a ragged gap into the close-
grown tangles. Although I could not discern the source,
the light seemed to be coming from somewhere beyond
the hedge wall.

I leaned on my crooked staff, gazing at the thicket. The
throb in my leg had become a steady pulse of pain, and
my side felt as if live coals were smoldering under the
skin. I was shivering with cold and pain, and sweating at
the same time. I closed my eyes and leaned harder on my
staff. "Jesu, have mercy," I groaned. "I am hurt and I
am alone, and I am lost if you do not help me now."

I was still trying to marshal my waning strength to attempt the hedge when I heard quick, rustling footsteps
behind me. My first thought was that the monster had
returned. This fear swiftly vanished at the sound of my
name.

"Gwalchavad!"

"Here!" I called. "Here I am!" I turned to stare back
down the narrow path that had led me to this place. A
moment later, I saw Gereint loping towards me, his face
gleaming ghostly in the pale light. He carried a sword—
mine, it was—and wore an expression of mingled relief
and wonder.

"Lord Gwalchavad, you are alive," he said as he
joined me. Out of breath, he stuck the sword in the

ground, and bent over with his hands on his knees. "I feared you were—" He paused, gulping air, then said, "I feared I had lost you, but then I saw the light and followed it."

Observing my leg, he asked, "Is it bad?"

"I can endure it," I replied. "What of Bors? Have you seen him?"

"Not since the attack," he answered.

"God help him," I replied; then leaving Bors' welfare in the Good Lord's hands, I turned once more to the thicket. "The light drew me here, too. It seems to be coming from the other side of this hedge wall."

"We will go through together," said Gereint. Taking up the sword, he stepped to the gap and began slashing at the briers. He cleared the path before us, and reached a hand back for me.

"Go before me," I told him. "I will follow."

He peered at me doubtfully, then turned and resumed his chopping at the knotted branches. He hewed like a champion, slashing with tireless strokes. The vapor from his breath hung in a cloud above him, and his hair grew damp and slick, but he stood to his work, arms swinging, shoulders rolling as he hacked at the dangling vines.

I followed, hobbling a step at a time, as the hedge parted before Gereint's blade. In this way we proceeded, until . . .

"We are through!" Gereint declared triumphantly.

Glancing up, I saw the light shining through and Gereint standing in the breach, sword in hand. Whatever lay beyond the hedge wall occupied his complete attention.

Chapter Thirty-four

I staggered behind Gereint into a wide clearing. Beyond the all-enclosing thicket, the ground was rocky and uneven, and the hedge wall stood back in a circle all around. In the center of the clearing rested a squat stone hut with a steep, high-pitched roof, also of stone. The walls were squared, solid, and without openings of any kind, and the roof was covered with moss—in all a most curious dwelling.

Beside the house stood a stone plinth of the kind the Romans used to erect for their statues and memorials. There was no memorial or statue now, but a heap of broken rubble at the foot of the plinth suggested that once there might have been.

These things I took in first, and only when Gereint spoke did I feel the calming silence of the place. "It is very peaceful here," the young warrior said, and even at a whisper his voice seemed to boom like a beaten drum.

Placing a finger to my lips, I warned him against speaking aloud until we could discover whether we were the only visitors. Gereint nodded and took my arm upon his shoulder and we proceeded cautiously towards the dwelling.

We had been drawn to the clearing by the light. Now that we were here, however, there was no light to be found and none to be seen—that is, there appeared no source of illumination: no campfire, no torches, no subtle sunlight shining down from above—yet the stone hut did stand

suffused in a softly gleaming radiance very like that of
moonlight, and what is more, this gentle gloaming bathed
the entire clearing with a fine luminescence that shimmered gently at the edges of my vision. Whenever I
looked directly at an object, this ghostly glimmering
faded, though the soft glow remained.

Wary with every step, we approached the stone hut,
moving slowly along the near side to what we took to be
the front. There we found a door both low and narrow,
its threshold overgrown with weeds and grass. So small
was this entrance that only one could pass at a time, and
that one must bow almost to his knees to enter.

Gereint cleared away the growth with a few quick
swipes of his blade, then, sword in hand, stooped and
entered.

A moment later, his face appeared in the doorway, and
he said, "It is empty, lord. There is no one here."

With some difficulty and no little pain—for I could no
longer bend my injured leg at all, and had to lie down
and drag myself through the opening—I joined him
within. Gereint raised me to my feet again, and we stood
together in a holy place.

"It is some kind of chapel," Gereint said, his voice
filling the stone-walled room.

The same weird light that played in the clearing outside
also filled the interior of the single, vaulted room, allowing us to see each detail of the rich ornamentation—for
every surface was carved with wonderful designs: intricate
knotwork panels and borders, countless triscs and spirals,
and hundreds of the elongated, much-entwined shapes of
animals and men. I recognized this adornment; it was that
which the Celts of old made with such zeal and delight.
There were also innumerable crosses carved on the walls
and floors, many with odd runelike symbols which I could
not read.

The room, unforgiving in its square, spare simplicity,
seemed to dance to the rhythm and movement of those
wonderful carvings. To stand and gaze upon floor and
walls and roof was to inhabit a psalm or a glad song of

praise. I filled my eyes with the graceful dance of the
room, and felt my spirit rise up within me.

"Truly, this is a sacred place," I said.

"An ancient place," Gereint replied. "Look how—"

"Listen!" I held up my hand to quiet him.

There came the sound of a soft footfall—someone was
moving along the wall outside. Gereint made a flattening
motion with his hand and silently stepped to the doorway,
sword ready.

I stood stock-still, straining into the silence. There came
no shouts, no cries of help or alarm. I held my breath and
heard only the rapid beating of my own heart. And then—

A quick movement at the door and a dark shape burst
into the room, straightened, and became the familiar figure
I knew.

"Bors!"

Gereint lowered the blade and fell back; he had been
that close to striking.

"Here you are!" Bors cried, lowering the sword in his
own hand. "And here was I thinking I had lost you for
good."

His relief was instantly swallowed in amazement as he
beheld the walls and floor. He turned his wondering gaze
upon the beautiful carvings, and we joined him in silent
admiration. Explanations could wait; a greater mystery
commanded our attention.

When he spoke again, it was in a voice humbled with
awe. "It is wonderful."

"That it is," I agreed. "I have never seen the like."

"It reminds me of those cells the monks make in Armorica. Look here," he said, moving towards the rear of
the chapel, "the altar still stands, and—"

He broke off so suddenly, I glanced quickly at his face,
which now wore an expression of revulsion: lips twisted
in a grimace of distaste, eyes narrowed in disgust. With
my crooked staff, I struggled across the room to join him.
"Damn them to hell," he muttered, turning his face away.

Then I saw what he had seen, and turned my face away,
too. The sight and smell brought bile to my mouth and I

coughed, feeling the burn in my throat as I swallowed it back. "Desecrated."

On the altar before us lay the severed genitals of a bull, the members placed atop a pile of human excrement. The bull's bloody horns with bits of the skull, and tail with part of the anus attached, flanked the stinking mound on either side, and the poor animal's tongue, torn out by the root, completed the repugnant arrangement.

"Have you found something?" Gereint hastened to where we stood. I tried to warn him off but was too late, and he pushed in beside Bors.

The young warrior looked at the altar. Clapping a hand to his mouth, he choked and turned swiftly away.

"That is the worst of it," I said.

"Holy Jesu," he whispered in a small, wounded voice.

"This is not right," Bors declared solemnly. "I will not allow it."

So saying, he stripped off his cloak and flung it over the obscene display. I thought that he meant merely to cover the desecration, but he had another plan, for he spread the cloak and then gathered up the defiling mass, folding it into the cloth. Holding the bundle at arm's length, he bore it from the chapel, returning a moment later with a double handful of grass in each fist.

Striding to the altar, Bors took to scrubbing the flat stone with the grass. "I need some water," he said through clenched teeth.

"Maybe there is a well outside," said Gereint, darting away.

I leaned, exhausted, against the wall while Bors put the full strength of his arms into the cleansing of the venerable stone. As he worked, a faint green sheen began to gleam where the grass, crushed by its abrasion, left some of its substance.

"See here, Gwalchavad," Bors called, motioning me nearer. "What is this?"

I hobbled closer, and only then did Bors notice I was wounded. "But you are hurt, brother. Forgive me, I should have—"

"I will live, never fear," I said, waving his apology

aside. Indicating the altar, I said, "What do you make of
it?"

"It is a circle, and words, I think." He pointed to a
broken arc of spidery lines which seemed to be etched in
the stone. "But I cannot read the letters."

"Nor can I," I told him. "Perhaps if we could see more
of it—" Bors fell to scrubbing again, as if by brute effort
he could make the words appear. But for all his muscle,
the thin, cracked lines did not mend or improve. "It is no
use, Bors. Whatever is written on that stone is worn away
and there is no reading it now."

Bors ceased rubbing, and stood with knots of grass
clenched in his fists. "I should go see what has become
of Gereint," he said, but his eyes never left the etched
surface of the stone.

"Yes, and then we should decide what to do next."

Curiously, we were both reluctant to leave the altar. We
stood staring at the fragmented lines, neither making a
move . . . until Gereint returned a few moments later. He
burst into the chapel in a rush of excitement.

"There is a well!" he exclaimed, bustling towards us.
"And I found this bowl on a chain. I had some difficulty
getting the bowl free without spilling the water, but—"
He stopped when he saw what we were looking at. "It
looks like writing."

"Aye, lad, it is," Bors affirmed. "But we can make
nothing of it."

"Maybe this will help," replied Gereint. Stepping
quickly to the altar, he raised the vessel and dashed the
contents over the stone.

The water struck the stone with a hiss and a splutter,
casting up great vaporous clouds of steam while droplets
of water sizzled and cracked—as if the altar had been
iron-heated in the forge. Bors and Gereint drew back a
step, and I threw an arm over my face and twisted away
lest I be scalded by the heat blast.

"Jesu be praised!" breathed Gereint. "Look!"

Lowering my arm, I gazed once more upon the altar.
Through the steam I could see the incised lines glowing
with a golden sheen. Even as I watched, the thin broken

lines joined, deepened, became robust and bold. The flat
altar stone had changed, too: glittering and smooth as a
new polished gem, it gleamed with the milky radiance of
crystal shot through with veins of silver and flecks of
crimson and gold.

The image on the stone resolved clearly into that of a
broad circular band of gold with a cross inside; bent
around the band was a finely drawn ring of words. Flank-
ing the circle and cross on either side were two figures—
creatures whose bodies appeared to be made of fire—with
wings outspread as if in supplication or worship.

"It is beautiful," murmured Gereint.

"The words," said Bors, his voice soft with awe.
"What do they say?"

"I have never seen writing like this," I said.

"Is it Latin?" he wondered.

"Perhaps," I allowed doubtfully, "but it is not like any
Latin the monks use. See how the letters curve and twist
back upon one another. I think it must be some other
script."

Gereint, his face illumined by the soft golden light,
gazed upon the altar figures with a beatific expression on
his face. Oblivious to all else, he sank to his knees before
the altar, his lips moving in an unspoken prayer. The purity of this simple, spontaneous act shamed me and I
averted my eyes. Then I heard a movement beside me and
when I looked back, Bors had joined the young warrior
on his knees.

The two knelt together shoulder to shoulder, hands upraised in the posture of monks. Had I been able to bend
my leg, I would have joined them. Instead, I clung to my
crude crutch, and raised my voice to heaven.

"Blessed Jesu," I prayed, my voice sounding loud and
clear in the sacred place, "I come to you a beggar in need.
Great evil stalks this forest and we are not strong enough
to overcome it. Help us, Lord. Do not forsake us, nor yet
leave us prey to the powers of the Evil One." Then, remembering the ruined chapel and its desecration, I added,
"Holy One of God, accept our poor offering of water
poured out upon the stone. Sain this chapel with your

presence, and restore the glory of your name in this place. So be it.''

Into the silence of the chapel came the echo of a song—like one of those Myrddin sometimes plays in which the harp seems to spin the melody of itself: Gift Songs, the Emrys calls them—so quiet it took me a moment to realize that it was not of my imagining. Bors and Gereint ceased their prayers and raised their eyes above.

I, too, gazed around, for it seemed as if the music derived from the heights. I saw nothing but the shadowed recesses of the high-pitched roof. The music, exquisite in its simple elegance, grew louder, and I saw the shadows fade as the carvings on the roof and walls of the chapel began to glimmer and glow.

We gazed in wonder at the old, old markings as the delicate interwoven lines filled with the same shimmering radiance that transformed the altar. Soon we three were bathed in soft golden light. Suddenly the chapel was filled with a sound like that of the wind swirling through long-leafed willows, or the rush of feathered wings beating the air when birds take flight. With this sound came music, very faint, but distinct and unmistakable: the celestial music of the heavenly realms.

A joy like that which I had experienced when I knelt alone in the presence of the Grail once more filled my heart, and it swelled to bursting for me to hear the strains of that glorious song swirling like a graceful wind, sweeping the crannies and corners of the chapel. I closed my eyes and turned my face heavenward and felt the warmth of the golden light on my skin, and knew a fine and holy rapture.

Then, more wonderful than anything that had gone before, there came to me a fragrance far surpassing that of all the flowers that ever grew. I drew the marvelous scent deep into my lungs and breathed the air of heaven itself; and on my tongue I tasted the honeyed sweetness of that rarest of atmospheres.

I tasted, and knew, even before I opened my eyes, that we were no longer alone.

Chapter Thirty-five

Gereint saw her first. Still kneeling before the altar, he raised his head, and his eyes widened slightly in surprise, but there was neither fear nor alarm in the expression, only delight. The light reflected on his face made him appear wise and good.

Bors—kneeling beside Gereint, his still head bowed—had yet to apprehend the visitor in our midst.

She took the appearance of an earthly woman; her features dark and dusky, her skin smooth and clear as amber honey, she stood before us as calmly and naturally as any mortal being, but with the dignity and grace only the heaven-born possess. Her eyes were blue as the sun-washed sky, pale against the tawny hue of her supple flesh. Hair the color of autumn chestnuts hung in long, loose curls around her shoulders, and spilled over the fine, gentle curves of her breasts. Clothed in a robe of deepest crimson, with a woven girdle of blue fretted with plaited gold, she seemed to me the very image and essence of beauty, wisdom, and dignity conjoined in the elegant, winsome form of a woman.

I could have lingered a lifetime in her presence and reckoned it only joy. I could gladly have stood entranced forever and counted it nothing but pleasure as, fairest of the Great King's servants, she bent over the altar, gazing devoutly upon the object in her hands.

Her devotion drew my own; I looked and saw what it was that the maiden had placed upon the altar: the Grail.

My first thought was that the Blessed Cup had been found, that she had somehow got it away from those who had stolen it and was now returning it to us. This notion was instantly dashed, however; as if in answer to my thought, the Grail Maiden turned her head and looked directly at me, and the fire that burned in those clear blue eyes was terrible to see.

"Turn away, Sons of Dust," the angel said in a voice unyielding as the altar stone. "The cup before you is holy. You defile it with your presence."

Speechless with shame and amazement, I could only stare at her and feel the full depth of my worthlessness in her eyes. Glancing at Gereint, I saw that he had bent his head under the weight of futility, and held his clasped hands tight against his chest. Bors had collapsed inwardly upon himself, his hands lying palm upward on the floor, his head touching his knees.

"Did you think me incapable of defending that which I have been ordained to uphold? Blind guides! How is it that you can see so much, yet understand so little?" Her words were like fire scorching my ears with the vehemence of her anger. "I do not know which is worse, your ignorance or your arrogance. Think you the Great King requires the aid of any mortal to accomplish his will? Is the Lord of Creation powerless to protect his treasures?"

Her righteous scorn leapt like a flame, withering my self-respect and misplaced honor with its indignant heat.

"O Mighty Guardians," she demanded, "where were you when the enemy laid hand to your treasure? Did you imagine the Cup of Christ would be protected by frail flesh?"

I stared in dismay and could not answer.

"Hear me, Sons of Dust! You held the Kingdom of Summer in your grasp and you threw it away. You have destroyed the one opportunity you were granted to bring peace to the peoples of the earth."

I could not endure her anger any longer. "Please!" I cried. "I am an ignorant man, it is true. If I have failed to—"

"Silence!" the angel cried, and the walls of the chapel

quaked at the word. "The Grail Cup is returning to the hand that gave it. Look upon it, Son of Dust! Look upon it and weep at your loss, for this is the last it will be seen in this worlds-realm."

Bending over the cup, she reached out to take it up once more, and I knew no mortal being would ever again know its healing presence.

"No, wait!" I said, and the Grail Keeper hesitated, the light of righteous anger flaring in her eyes again. I had braved it once, and would a thousand times over if I could but stay her hand a little longer. "Forgive me, lady. My words and ways are crude, I know, but I mean no disrespect. It is only that I do not know how to speak as I ought. Truly, I could not endure the knowledge that this Holy Cup has passed from the world of men because of my failure. If there is any way the Glorious Vessel can be redeemed, only tell me and I pledge my life and all I possess to its redemption."

The maiden regarded me with a look both piercing and pitying; her reply was blade-sharp. "Why weary heaven with your contemptible pleading? Think you to sway what has been commanded from before the earth was framed and the stars set in their courses?"

"Please," I said, summoning every grain of courage I owned to one last entreaty. "It is not for myself that I ask, less yet for those whose duty it was to defend the Grail, but for those who struggle in darkness for the light. They have so little, and their needs are so great, the merest glimpse of the Holy Cup is enough to give them courage to abide the misfortunes of their lot with hope and faith in the life to come. It is for them that I plead. I beg you, do not take the Grail away."

The lady listened to my plea, but her face remained like flint and her fierce gaze unaltered. "Words cannot atone for your sin and failure."

"Then take me instead, I pray. I will endure the fires of perdition, and that gladly, if my suffering could be accounted for the reclamation of the Summer Realm and the cup that upholds it."

"You are a man, indeed," she conceded, softening somewhat. "But it is not to be."

So saying, she reached for the cup and took it between her hands. I knew I looked my last upon the Most Holy Grail.

She straightened and made to turn away, paused, and raised her head; her gaze lifted—as if heeding a voice I could not hear.

I saw this and hope leapt in my heart.

Nodding once, she turned to me again. "Most fortunate of men are you," she said, "for the Lord of Hosts has heard the plea of your heart and has been moved to give you a second chance to prove yourselves worthy. The Grail will stay."

Joy flowed up and over me in a warm, giddy rush. But for my injured leg, I would have thrown myself to my knees before her and kissed the hem of her robe in gratitude. "Thank you," I breathed. "Thank you."

"Your petition has been granted," she told me, "for the sake of the king you serve, and those who stand in need of the blessing of this Holy Cup."

Before I could think what to say, she continued, her voice assuming a commanding tone once more. "Hear me, Sons of Dust: it has been decided that you are to be shown what you have pledged your lives to protect, and who it is that sustains you in your duty."

Placing the cup upon the altar once more, her fingers described a graceful figure in the air, and the Grail gathered radiance, drawing light to itself, shining with a rosy brilliance as if reflecting the sunrays of creation's dawn. When she removed her hands, I saw that a faint circle of light had formed in the air above the rim.

"Behold!" she said, and spread her hands wide.

At once I heard a sound like that of a struck harp, and a bright light leapt up, and the altar began to glow with a fine and holy light. I do not know how to say it otherwise, but that this radiance expanded outward to embrace the whole of the chapel. The stone walls began to shine, and the incised designs seemed to move and grow in the light, entwining with one another and spreading to form patterns of gleaming light. The next I knew, those self-same walls were not stone anymore, but gold! Still, the alteration did not end there, for the patterns continued to grow and change and the gold paled to white marble, and that gave way to crystal so pure I could see through the very walls to the world beyond—all green and lush beneath a sky of gold.

"Look upon me, Son of Dust, and know me as I am," the lady said; I do not think she spoke aloud this time, but I heard her clearly and, emboldened by the tenderness of her invitation, I looked and saw that she, like the chapel, had changed.

Indeed, the woman who stood before me now was taller and far more noble in face and figure. Her long hair was silver-white, and so, too, the robe which clothed her slender form. Her skin was pale as milk or moonlight, and she seemed, despite her aspect and the obvious maturity of her body, to manifest the spirited youth of a child. The visible manifestation of her sustaining power rose behind her in two radiant arcs, subtle, yet perceptible as a rippling rainbow in the sunlight, shimmering with vital potency, overarching and sweeping out like enfolding wings to sustain and protect. Her face, once fair to look upon, was no less beautiful now, yet it was a piercing beauty almost frightening in its symmetry and the compelling elegance of its proportions. Piercing, too, the radiance that streamed from her—almost too bright to look upon, and of a quality that penetrated the heart as well as the eye, and illumined both; for to see her was to know one looked upon a glory that partook of the heavenly and was the birthright of those who served in the High King of Heaven's celestial courts.

"Behold," she said again, and I saw that the cup had changed. No longer a vessel of jeweled metal—indeed, there was neither ornament nor design: no gold, gems, or pearls; no inscribed scrollwork; nor any other such embellishment—yet it glittered and shone with a dancing brilliance as if it were made of golden starfire, for it was garbed in its heavenly form now, and was as high above the earthly cup as the Grail Maiden was above her mortal sisters.

This! I thought. *This is the True Cup of Christ!*

These words formed in my mind before I knew what they meant. Even so, I heard in them truth's clear and undisputed ring. The Grail Maiden raised the Holy Cup from the now-translucent altar stone, turned, and, Holy Savior, offered it to me! I hesitated, glancing towards Gereint and Bors for help, but their heads were bowed and their eyes were closed as if in raptured sleep. It was to me alone that she extended the wondrous bowl. Still, I hesitated lest I defile the Holy Cup with my touch.

Take it, noble Gwalchavad, the angel urged gently, her tone melting honey and sunlight. With trembling hands, I reached out and received the Sacred Bowl.

The blood of Christ, shed for you, Gwalchavad, she intoned. *Drink deep of it and be renewed in body, mind, and spirit.*

My heart beating within me like a captive creature sensing its release, I raised the Sacred Bowl and saw the liquid glint of deep crimson as I brought it to my lips. I put my mouth to the rim, closed my eyes, and emptied the cup. The wine danced on my tongue like cool fire; it was sweet to the taste, but with a tart, almost bitter edge that revealed subtle depths of flavor. Although I am no master of the vine, I would have said that it must far surpass the finest wine ever poured into an emperor's cup.

As I swallowed, I felt the renewing warmth spread out from my throat and stomach, passing through my limbs and out to the tips of my fingers and toes. The sensation, after innumerable privations of the trail, was so pleasurable I could not help smiling. My injured leg tingled and I realized the pain was swiftly ebbing away to a distant memory. I flexed the limb and discovered it whole and hale once more.

The Grail Maiden extended her hands and I released the wonderful bowl. Inclining her head as she received the cup, she smiled at my delighted surprise, and then, holding her palm above the cup's rim, turned to Gereint.

Though I heard nothing, the instant she turned from me

the young warrior raised his head and opened his eyes as if summoned. The angel offered him the cup, in the same way she had offered it to me, and Gereint took it in both hands, lifted it, and drank, draining the cup in great, gulping swallows, as if he could not get the liquid inside him fast enough. Then, embarrassed by his immoderate quaffing, he bent his head and returned the Holy Cup to the maiden, who accepted it nicely. She must have spoken a word of encouragement to him, for Gereint raised his head and smiled.

Then it was Bors' turn to drink from the cup, which he did with his customary exuberance. Seizing the proffered vessel in both hands, he elevated it once, twice, three times over the altar, then brought it to his mouth and drained it down—much as I had seen him do on countless occasions in Arthur's hall. Tilting back his head, he swallowed and then paused, savoring the draught before returning the empty bowl to the angel. "Noble lady," he said, the only one among us to speak aloud.

The Grail Maiden bent her head in acknowledgment and replaced the Sacred Cup on the altar stone, whereupon she raised her hands to shoulder height, palms outward, and said, "Rise, friends, and stand."

This time she spoke aloud, and oh! to hear that voice was to know the intimate ecstasy of a lover when beckoned by his best beloved. She called us friends, and I vowed within myself to be worthy of the word to the end of my earthly life.

"This day you have by grace been granted a foretaste of heaven's feast," she told us. "Those to whom much is given, much is required. Draw near by faith and stand at the altar where men's hearts are tried and known."

Raising her face heavenward, she appeared to listen for a moment, and then began reciting aloud the words as she was given them. She said:

"Receive the word of the Lord! The Kingdom of Summer is close at hand, but the Evil One is closer still. He roars and raves, and roams the earthly crust ever seeking those he might destroy. Hold fast to the truth, my friends, and know in your hearts that where the King of Kings is honored, evil cannot prevail. Remember, greater is He who is in you than he who is in the world. Fear nothing, but gird yourself for the battle to come, and cling to the Sword of your Salvation.

"I tell you the truth, the greatest among you fell from grace through the sin of pride. Trusting in strength was his weakness; trusting in wisdom was his folly. Lusting after honor, he was bewitched by one who honors only lust and lies. Thus are the mighty undone. Therefore, trust not in the strength of your arms, nor the wisdom of your minds; rather, trust in Him who made them, and who with His Swift Sure Hand upholds all things.

"Heed well the warning I give you: the battle is perilous, and it is deadly earnest. Yet, in the twistings of the fight, as in the darkness of the night, you are not alone. The Champion of Heaven rides before you; seize the victory in His name."

The Grail Maiden bade us farewell, saying, "The Grail abides. For the sake of all who stand in need of its blessing, I charge you to guard it well." Raising her right hand, she made the sign of the cross, and said, "All grace, and power, and righteousness be upon you now, and forevermore. So be it!"

She seemed to grow both larger and taller as she spoke, and her form lost its solidity, becoming crystalline and sharp before fading from sight in a muted flare of dazzling starlight. The gleam lingered for a while where she had stood, and then that, too, disappeared. When I looked, the Sacred Grail had vanished, and in its place was the same vessel I had seen in Arthur's hands at the consecration of the shrine. The altar stone was merely a stone once more, and the chapel only a bare room with walls of figured stone.

We three came slowly to ourselves, like men waking from a dream we all had shared. I looked at Bors and Gereint, and my heart moved within me to see them. Good and faithful men, noble-hearted, loyal through all things—to death, and beyond. How was it possible that I should have gained a portion of such friendship?

Gereint saw my look and said, "If that was a dream, never wake me."

"It was no dream," Bors replied, stirring himself and looking around. "Did you not drink from the Holy Cup?"

"What did it taste like to you?" asked Gereint.

"It was the wine, of course," I told him. "And fine wine, too."

"Wine!" roared Bors. "I wonder at you, Gwalchavad. It was never wine. Have I lived so long not to know mead when I taste it?" He looked to Gereint to support this assertion. "What say you, brother? Mead or wine?"

"It was the sweetest, most pure water I have ever tasted," replied Gereint, blissfully ignoring Bors' lead. "Like water from a living spring."

"Wine and water!" scoffed Bors, shaking his head in mystified disbelief. "It was mead, I tell you. Mead! Sweet elixir of life, and libation of kings! How can anyone say otherwise?"

I gazed longingly at the altar. The cup remained, but not a glimmer of that wild, exultant light persisted. "How strange," I murmured to myself. "We held eternity in our hands, had we but known."

"Eh?" said Bors, glancing at me over his shoulder. "What was that?"

"We have been given another chance," I said. "Let us vow here and now to prove ourselves worthy of our charge this time."

"Aye," Bors agreed solemnly. "She called us Guardians, and I will die before I leave this place undefended."

Gereint agreed, and we all pledged ourselves to stand guard over the Grail until Arthur returned, or death overtook us. "We had best look outside," I said, starting for the door.

"Lord Gwalchavad, your leg—" Gereint began.

"There was healing in the cup," I declared. "I tell you, Bors, I feel more refreshed and alive than I have in years."

His smile was ready and wide. "I believe you, brother. For my part, I do not believe I ever felt this good." He gazed around him in expectant wonder, as if hoping to see something of the splendor that we had witnessed only moments before. "Truly, I begin to understand what Arthur must have felt when he was dragged from death's door."

With the greatest reluctance, we left the altar and crossed the chapel to the door, where, one by one, we bowed low and passed through the narrow way. In recognition of my healing, I placed my rude staff just inside the door and stepped through. Once outside, the darkness struck us like the blow of a fist. Though the clearing still glimmered as if with pale moonlight, we reeled on our feet for a moment before finding our balance again.

"All is quiet," mused Bors, gazing around at the forest, dark and forbidding as it loomed over the small circle of the clearing. "As much as I wish it, I doubt it will remain so."

I was about to suggest that one of us should make a circuit of the chapel to ensure that the clearing remained secure, when Bors said, "Shh!" He stiffened, his eyes narrowing as he stared into the darkness.

Gereint and I froze and waited for Bors to speak. "Someone is watching us," Bors said after a moment, his voice low and tight. I heard Gereint ease his sword from the strap at his belt, and wished I had something better than a knife.

"Where?" whispered Gereint, stepping closer. "I see no one."

"There," Bors replied, indicating the place with the blade in his hand. "You there—waiting in the shadows. Come out!"

"Careful, brother," I warned. Taking my place behind his right shoulder, I motioned for Gereint to guard Bors' left side. "There may be more lurking in the trees beyond."

We advanced halfway across the clearing and stopped. "You there!" called Bors sternly. "Come out and declare yourself."

From the deep-shadowed darkness a voice called out. "Bors! Gwalchavad!"

"It is Peredur!" said Gereint, starting forward.

Bors caught him by the arm and pulled him back with a warning look as a solitary figure stepped from the surrounding wood into the clearing. We waited. The young warrior stepped nearer and I recognized the familiar shape and stance at last.

"It is Peredur," Gereint insisted, and hastened to welcome his friend. "I feared you had been killed by the beast long since. Have you seen the others?"

"Is there no one else here?" Peredur asked, looking past Gereint to Bors and myself. "Arthur and Myrddin—are they here?"

"It is only the three of us," Gereint told him. "We have seen no one else since coming to this part of the wood." Raising a hand to the chapel behind us, he said, "We have seen the Grail. It was here."

"Truly?" wondered Peredur. "I would give much to have seen that."

The remark was innocence itself, but the way he said it made our holy experience seem a petty thing. If we had said we had seen a green dog, or a calf with two heads, it might have drawn the same remark.

Bors scrutinized the young man closely. "Where is your horse?" he asked.

"Oh, nearby," answered Peredur indifferently. "I have ridden hard and the animal is tired. I found a trail—I think the others used it not long ago. Come, we can find them and—"

"Did you come by way of the burning oak?" asked Bors abruptly. I noticed he had yet to put up his weapon.

"No," answered Peredur. "I came a different way."

The young warrior seemed disinclined to say more, but Bors pursued the matter. "Which way would that be, then?" he said, more in the way of a demand than a question.

Peredur turned and looked Bors full in the face. "I came by another way," the young man said, speaking plain and low. There was an edge to his voice I had never heard before.

"Who can find their way in this wood?" said Gereint.

"How long have you been waiting out there?" demanded Bors.

Peredur's eyes narrowed as he gazed at Bors, but he made no reply.

Bors did not allow the query to go unanswered. "It is perfectly simple," he said, bristling with animosity. "How long were you standing out there waiting for us?"

Gereint, who had been eager to interpose himself between the two, looked to me for help. I warned him off with a motion of my hand and he stepped back. Peredur put out his empty hands in a show of goodwill. "Your suspicions are ill-placed, my friends," he said with an awkward laugh. "Yet I bear no grudge. Indeed, I forgive you right readily. Come, now, let us put aside this contention and think what we must do to unite ourselves with our swordbrothers once again."

Peredur turned away and made to step around Bors. He had taken but one step when Bors seized him by the shoulder and yanked him back around. "Stay where you are!" he shouted. "Gwalchavad, relieve him of his sword."

Knife in hand, I stepped slowly towards the young warrior, saying, "Stand easy, brother. There is nothing to fear. We are your friends."

"You behave like enemies!" he snarled, backing away. The hate in his voice struck me like a balled fist.

"Stand!" said Bors, repeating his command with a jerk of his sword.

The man before us opened his mouth to protest, then hesitated—only for an instant, but when he spoke, his demeanor had altered completely. The hate and suspicion fell away from him and he became so mild and contrite I felt ashamed of myself for doubting him.

"Cymbrogi," he said, "it is me, Peredur. Why are you treating me so poorly?" Raising an inoffensive hand, he made to step by us. "I am so glad to see you. Truly, I thought I would never see any of you again. How long have you been here?"

"Forgive us, brother," Gereint said with a sigh of relief. "We did not mean to offend you." He put up his sword and glanced at Bors expectantly. Bors, too, lowered his blade.

"We should try to find Arthur and Myrddin," Peredur said. "They cannot be far away. I will show you the trail. Come with me, it is not far."

Instantly, my senses pricked. I felt a thin thrill of fear ripple across my shoulders. Without a second thought, I stepped swiftly to Peredur. My knife flicked up in the same quick motion, and I pressed the keen edge hard against his throat.

"Step away from us, Gereint," I commanded. "Bors, take his weapon."

Peredur gaped in disbelief. "Have you gone mad?"

"Perhaps," I replied as Bors, sword upraised, quickly snatched the blade from the young man's hand. From the corner of my eye I glimpsed the chapel, and it came into my mind how we might discern the truth. "But you will forgive us our madness, I think. We will not be deceived again."

I grasped him by the upper arm and, my knife still hard against his throat, I pulled him forward.

"Where are you taking me?" he asked, growing frightened.

"To the altar," I answered, "where men's hearts are tried and known."

Chapter Thirty-six

The Grail is gone.

Morgaws tells me that it disappeared. The lying bitch insists she had it secured, and that from the moment Llenlleawg delivered it to her, the casket never left her sight. The casket she possesses still, but the cup is gone; what is more, she claims it vanished at the moment the king's champion attacked his king.

Morgaws will pay for this blunder. Oh, yes, she will pay dearly. I taught her better than this. Could she not see how much they valued the Grail—that alone should have warned her to be on her guard. How could she be so blind?

The insolent cow insinuates that it is my fault for not warning her of the cup's true power. I remind her that whatever else it may be, the cup is just bait in a trap so far as she is concerned, and that whatever powers it might possess, the gaudy trinket certainly did not divert the doom which even now crushes our enemies in its cold embrace.

The disappearance of the cup makes not the slightest difference; it will not change anything. All is ordered as I have planned, and even now the end swiftly approaches. Already, events are hurtling towards the consummation of my plan: my crowntaking, and the reign of terror to follow. My triumph will be devastating.

Some monarchs, upon accession to the throne, declare the pardon of their opponents, and the forgiveness of sins *practiced against them. I shall do the opposite, however. The blood will flow from one end of Britain to the other! I think I shall begin with bishops, and then . . . well, all in good time.*

First, I must have that cup. Morgaws will devote her full attention to its recovery—before the fools somehow discover what it was they let slip away. The thought that they might get hold of it again does not sit well with me. It may be time for me to intervene.

"Brother," said Peredur, dragging his feet, "there is no need for this. You are anxious over nothing."

I drew the young warrior forward a few paces, whereupon he stopped. "Gereint," he said, pleading, "you are my kinsman. Tell them—tell them."

Bors stepped behind us and prodded the reluctant warrior from behind with the sword point in the small of his back. "Move along, friend."

Peredur, outmanned and unarmed, seemed to accept his lot. He nodded and proceeded docilely. "You are wise to be suspicious," he said after a few steps. "But you know me. What can you possibly hope to achieve? It is meaningless."

At this I began to doubt. What did I hope to prove by making him swear his faith and loyalty before the altar? It was, as he had said, a meaningless exercise and would prove nothing.

I felt hard bone and muscle under my hand and doubt stole over me. Fool! What are you doing? Has the enemy so confused and deceived you that you can no longer tell the difference between friend and foe? Let him go!

As if echoing my thoughts, Peredur said, "Let me go— I will not think the worse of you. Trust me; we can still find the others, but we must hurry."

If I had been alone, I believe I would have released him then and there. The urge to do so was stronger than my conviction to see the thing through. But Bors, when roused, is not easily put off. "Save your breath," he told the young warrior flatly. "It is soon over, and no harm will come to you."

With that we marched to the chapel door, whereupon I removed the knife from his throat and, shifting my free hand to the back of his head, pushed Peredur down so he could navigate the low entrance. He stooped and bent his back as he entered the narrow opening. But as his foot touched the threshold, he suddenly froze.

"No!" he shouted, and made to squirm away. I renewed my grip on his arm and held him tight. "It proves nothing. I will not do it."

Bors, close behind, put out a hand and pushed him further into the narrow opening. The young man arched his back and dug in his heels.

"Get on with it, man," Bors urged roughly. "There is nothing to fear."

"No!" he cried again, almost frantic this time, his fingers raking at the pillar stones of the entrance. "No!"

Bors, larger and stronger, pushed him further through the doorway. Twisting and turning, Peredur fought, resisting with all his strength. He shouted to be released, his distress turning quickly to rage. Bors, however, was growing ever more determined and would not be moved. He stooped and, with a mighty heave, shoved the struggling warrior through the low entrance and into the chapel.

Bors followed him through and I pushed quickly in behind them. Peredur had landed on hands and knees on the stone-flagged floor, and Bors stood over him, reaching down a hand to raise him up. I joined Bors and, taking hold of the young man's arm, said, "Here, now—come stand before the altar."

As I took his arm, I felt a tremor pass through his body. His head whipped around, mouth open to bite my hand. With but a fleeting glimpse of his face, I released my hold and leapt aside. "Bors!" I cried. "Get back!"

In the same instant, Peredur gave out a tremendous guttural growl and rose up, flinging Bors aside as if he were no more than a toddling child. Bors fell on his side, his head striking the stone floor. He made to rise and collapsed. I dove to his aid as Peredur, shaking in every limb, began howling like an animal.

"Bors!" I cried, trying to shake him awake. "Can you hear me? Get up!"

A ragged snarl of rage filled the chapel. I glanced over my shoulder to where Peredur stood. I no longer recognized him at all: his neck was bent, forcing his head down low onto his chest; his lower jaw jutted out and his mouth gaped, revealing teeth both sharp and oddly curved; his shoulders and arms were thicker, his back more broad, with humps of powerful muscle. But it was his eyes that startled me most—red-rimmed and wild, they bulged out of their sockets as if they would burst from within.

Still howling, he turned and slowly stepped towards me, long hands with fingers like claws, twitching and reaching. Bors was still unconscious, and I could not leave him. I looked for his sword, but could not see it.

"Gereint!" I shouted.

He entered the chapel at a run. Without a quiver of hesitation, Gereint interposed himself between the monstrous Peredur and me, his blade drawn. Taking no heed, the thing lurched nearer, growling and slavering like a wolf for the kill.

Gereint held his ground; the blade in his hand never wavered. Heedless of the sword, the brute lunged and made a raking swipe, which the young warrior deftly deflected. The howling thing received a quick slash on the arm. "In God's name, stay back!" warned Gereint.

At this the creature threw back its head and shrieked, gnashing its teeth and clawing at the air. Then, still shrieking, it started forth once more. Bors came awake at the sound. He pushed himself up from the floor and struggled to rise—only to slump back once more. "I am with you, brother," I said, holding to him so as to protect him.

On a sudden inspiration, Gereint grasped the naked blade and turned it in his hand, presenting the hilt upward in imitation of the Holy Cross—as Arthur had done at the consecration of the Grail Shrine. Taking the blade in both hands, he held the sword hilt before him, thrusting it at arm's length into the brute's face.

The creature roared, and staggered backward. Gereint

advanced, holding the sword-cross and calling, "In Jesu's holy name, be gone!"

The brute loosed a mind-freezing scream and began clawing at itself, as if to tear the ears from its own hideous head. It sank to its knees, wailing, keening, gnashing its teeth. Dauntless Gereint bore down upon it, calling upon Christ to drive the thing away.

The wicked thing shrieked and shrieked again to drown out all sound but that of its own torment. Then, even as we watched, the thing began to change again: its body stretched, growing thinner and taller, until its narrow head almost touched the rooftrees of the chapel—whereupon it could no longer support its height and fell, doubling over itself, to writhe and thrash, beating itself upon the floor.

Gereint, unyielding, his face hard as flint, clutched his improvised cross and stood implacable. Wailing pitifully, the creature continued its hideous transformation, its thin body becoming small and scaly and its terrible voice waning away to a high, hissing scream. It rolled in its writhing coils and then slithered for the chapel door, where, with the speed of a fleeing serpent, it slipped over the threshold and disappeared into the night beyond.

The young warrior, still clutching the sword-cross, hastened to where I knelt with Bors. "It has gone," he said, his voice hollow, his face drained.

"Well done, Gereint," I told him, and noticed the blood dripping from his hands. He had gripped the sword blade so tightly, he had cut his palms and fingers. I reached for the hilt. "You can let go now, son. The fight is over."

Gereint released the sword, which I returned to its place at his side, then helped him cut strips from his cloak to bind his hands. I tied the strips in place, and we turned our attention to Bors. Between us, we rolled the big man onto his back, bunched up his cloak, and put it beneath his head to make him as comfortable as possible. Then Gereint and I sat down together; leaning against the stout wall, we rested and talked about what had happened.

"What do you think it was?" Gereint wondered. "A shape-shifter?"

"A demon maybe," I replied. "I have heard Bishop Elfodd tell about such things."

"Is that why you thought to bring it into the church?"

"Truly, I do not know what I thought," I confessed. "I only knew that Peredur was a devout man and it would be no hardship for him to take an oath before the altar."

"But how did you know it was not Peredur?"

"Something about his manner made me suspicious. I cannot say what it was. But then"—I shrugged—"it seemed silly to hold such a small thing against him. I doubted myself and almost let him go."

"But how did you know?" Gereint asked, then added ruefully, "I was taken in completely."

"There is no shame in it," I assured him. "As to what warned me, I can but say I did not like his manner. When I spoke of the Grail, he behaved as if it were a thing of no importance."

"Yes!" agreed Gereint. "The true Peredur would have wanted to see it."

"So I thought to test him at the altar. It seemed to me no one given to evil could abide the presence of the Grail."

Gereint nodded with sage admiration. "You are a very Druid yourself, Lord Gwalchavad. I would never have thought of that."

"I only wish it had been Peredur," I replied, and thought again how very close we had come to believing the lie. It could easily have gone the other way, and now we would certainly be dead and the chapel undefended.

As if to draw me out of my unhappy reverie, Bors awoke just then with a groan and sat up holding his head. "Be easy, brother," I said, bending over him quickly. "All is well. The wicked thing is gone. Rest a little."

"Mmm," he said, craning his neck around. "It feels like a wall has fallen on my head. Here, help me stand." I took him by the arm and he made to get up, but fell back again at once, his eyes squeezed shut against the pain. "Ahh! No, no—on second thought, I think I will sit here a little longer."

"There is no hurry," I told him. "Let us fetch you a

drink. Here, Gereint, take the bowl and bring Bors some
water.''

The young warrior retrieved the bowl from beside the
altar and started for the door. "You should go with him,"
Bors said, rubbing his neck.

"It is only outside," Gereint protested.

"Go," Bors insisted. "I am well enough to sit here by
myself. Go."

"I could do with a drink, too," I said, and told Gereint,
"Come, then, show me the well."

Gereint led me out and around to the rear of the chapel.
The ground was lumpy with mossy stones, and rose to a
small, tidy outcropping a short distance away.

"Here!" called Gereint, springing up the rocks. "The
well is just here."

The well, as Gereint called it, was actually a small pool;
sometime in the past it had been edged with unshaped
stones to form a low wall around its oval perimeter. From
a metal peg driven into one of the stones dangled the
bronze chain which had secured the bowl Gereint had
used to fetch water to help clean the desecration from the
altar.

We dipped water and, as we drank, began speculating
about how the chapel and the well had come to be here.
"This must have been a joyous place once," Gereint
mused, gazing over the clearing.

"I would like to have seen it in happier times."

"Was there ever such a time?" he wondered.

"The Grail was offered here," I replied. "Whoever
built this church must have known it as a holy place."

Oh, yes, I thought, but this is Llyonesse, the blighted
land, desolate, barren, and beset with strange airs and
weird creatures. Perhaps it was not always so. This little
chapel still survives to tell a different tale, after all. Perhaps there is yet some better hope for Llyonesse.

"We should go back before Bors wonders what has
happened to us," I said and, leaning low over the water,
refilled the bowl, and we hurried back to the chapel.

Bors had moved himself to the near wall and sat against
it. Accepting the bowl, he drank his fill, set the vessel

aside, and professed himself refreshed and ready to resume his duty as Grail Guardian.

As if in answer to this declaration, Gereint cocked his head to one side, half turned toward the door, and said, "Did you hear that?"

"I heard nothing," I confessed.

"Nor I," said Bors.

"Listen!" Gereint whispered. Drawing his sword, he stepped lightly to the door and out. I followed close behind, and we scanned the chapel yard. I saw nothing, and was about to say as much when Gereint raised the point of his sword and said, "There they are."

Until he spoke, I had seen nothing but the dark shapes of the trees rising above the thick gloom of the encircling thorn wall. But even as he raised his sword I saw the heads and shoulders of three warriors emerge from the darkness of the hedge and step into the clearing. I saw the long spears rising above the large round yellow shields they carried, and knew we were in for a fight.

Chapter Thirty-seven

"**B**ring Bors," I commanded. "Tell him to prepare for battle."

"Bors is ready," the big warrior said, taking his place beside me as three more enemy warriors joined the first three already advancing towards us across the clearing. More were coming from the thorn hedge.

Within the space of six heartbeats, we were surrounded. There must have been twenty or more foemen, each armed with a spear and a shield; some wore pointed helms and others the metal shirts of Saecsen men, but most were naked to the waist, and I could see the pallor of their flesh as they advanced into the half-light of the clearing.

If it was not bad enough that we were woefully outnumbered, we had but two swords between us—Bors' and Gereint's—and I had only a knife. "Two blades and a dagger are not much against twenty," I observed, wishing I had not lost my spear.

"This blade is yours, lord," replied Gereint, delivering it into my hand.

"Keep it, lad," I told him, but he would not hear that.

Darting forth, he ran a few paces into the clearing, stooped, snatched something from the ground, and returned, bearing the sword we had taken from the false Peredur. "It is a good weapon," said Gereint, swinging the blade to get the feel of its heft and balance. "It will serve."

"Good man," commended Bors approvingly. Turning

his attention to the advancing warband, he said, "Shoulder to shoulder, brothers. Keep your backs to the chapel, and do not allow any of them to get behind us."

Silently, silently, they advanced, shield to shield, forming a bristling wall around us. Then, without so much as a whispered command, the spears swung level and they prepared to attack.

"Now!" I cried, and we three sprang forward as one, slashing with our swords and shouting. I was able to cut the spearheads off two shafts with as many chops; Bors and Gereint fared just as well. When we broke off our foray, six of the enemy had lost the use of their weapons.

If I expected the loss of their spears would daunt them, however, I was sadly mistaken, for they came on regardless, holding their headless spear shafts as if the lack of a killing blade were of no account.

We waded into them, three Cymbrogi, undaunted, united in heart and mind. Shoulder to shoulder we stood to our work, and the bodies toppled like corded wood beneath the woodcutter's axe. Time and time again we struck, the steel in our hands pealing like the ringing of bells. The enemy now clambered over the corpses of their kinsmen to reach us, and still we cut them down . . . and still they came.

"It is no use," complained Bors as the enemy regrouped for another assault. "They will not break ranks."

"Perhaps we can change their minds," I suggested. Scanning the enemy ranged before us, I saw where several advancing foemen carried the shafts of spears from which the blades had been lopped. "There!" I shouted, pointing with my sword. "Follow me!"

With that we all three ran for the spot I had marked. The foemen stood their ground, apparently unconcerned that their spears had no heads. They held their ground, but since their weapons were blunt, it was an easy matter to cut them down. Three fell without so much as a murmur, and we were rewarded with a momentary confusion as the enemy jostled one another to repair the gap in their shield wall.

Hacking hard to my right, I was able to kill another

enemy warrior, and Gereint yet another. We then turned
to help Bors, who was struggling to fend off two more.
These went down under a frenzied attack by Gereint, who
rolled beneath their shields and stabbed them as they tried
to loft their spears to strike.

Thus we suddenly found ourselves standing alone as
the enemy fell back to re-form the wall once more.

"This is the calmest battle I have ever fought," Bors
observed. "I have never been in a fight where I was not
deaf from the clatter."

It was true; even in a small skirmish the sound is a very
din, and in most battles it is a deafening roar. The shouting of combatants, the clash of weapons, the screams of
the wounded and dying—it all melds together to produce
a distinctive clamor which can be heard from far away,
and which, once heard, is never forgotten.

But these foemen stood to their grim work in utter silence—no shouted commands, not even a curse or cry of
pain when a blow landed. Whether they were attacking or
dying, the only sounds to be heard were the swishing rustle of their feet through the long grass and the dull clank-
ing of their shields where our swords struck.

Moreover, the enemy was curiously lethargic. Their actions were the lumpen, clumsy gestures of bodies with no
force behind their movements. Their faces—when I
glimpsed them from behind their shields—were grim and
gray, but expressionless, betraying neither rage nor hate.
Tight-lipped and dull-eyed, they seemed to be performing
a laborious and tiresome chore, and nothing so dangerous
or desperate as battle. Indeed, they lurched and lumbered
like men asleep, heavy on their feet and slow to react.

Even as I turned to offer this observation to my companions, Bors muttered, "I do not believe it."

He was looking at the place where the first combatants
had fallen. I turned, too, and saw the slain warriors rising
from the ground. Like men throwing off sleep, they simply arose with a start, climbed to their feet, and joined
their mute companions.

The weird, silent foe shuffled forth once more. Despair,
black and bleak, yawned before me like an open grave as

the realization broke over me: we could cut them down, but we could not kill them.

"God help us," was Bors' terse reply. He had no time to say more, for the foemen renewed the attack, and we were quickly engaged in trying to regain the small space we had carved for ourselves.

In the confusion of the next attack, Gereint succeeded in getting hold of one of the enemy shields. This he used to guard his left, affording both of us better protection on that side, for he made it a virtue to stay close to me. We fought side by side, and it put me in mind of the times my brother, Gwalcmai, and I had labored together in all those battles against the Saecsen host.

The attack—as poorly conceived as the others—soon foundered and the battle settled into a sluggish, lumpen rhythm. Thrust and chop, thrust, thrust and chop . . . I found it absurdly easy to strike them down, for the slowness of the foe and their dull reactions quickly told against them. They fell as they fought, without a sound, readily collapsing and expiring without a murmur—only to rise again after a small space, and join in the fight as if nothing had happened.

This made Bors frustrated and angry. He railed at the enemy, filling the dull, dreadful silence with taunts and challenges which went unanswered. He hewed at them mightily, slashing with powerful strokes. Once, he lopped the arm off one hapless foeman—the limb spun from the wretch's shoulder in a bloodless arc, still gripping the spear shaft in its dead hand.

The enemy fell and Bors let out a whoop of triumph. But the unfeeling creature merely picked itself off the ground and came on again—even though it could not longer wield a weapon.

This provoked the big warrior so much that he beheaded the creature next. "Shake that off, hellspawn!" shouted Bors, thinking he had at last succeeded in removing at least one combatant from the fight.

Alas, he was wrong. The headless torso lay still for a time, only to rise and resume the attack, a gaping wound on its shoulders where its head had been. As before, no

blood spewed from the wound, and it brought no dimi-
nution of persistence; the corpse stumbled forth, reaching
with empty, clutching hands.

Unfortunately, we had not the stamina of the undead,
for though they could fall and rise and fall, only to rise
again—though we hacked the weapons from their hands,
or severed the hands themselves, or heads!—we could
not. Our hands and arms were growing weary, and our
wounds bled.

"They do not mind dying," Bors observed, deftly striking the fingers from a hand stretching too close, "because
they are dead already. But when I lie down, I will not get
up again so easily, I think. What are we to do, brother?"

There was no stopping them. Despite the practiced efficiency with which we dispatched the foe, we received
only the smallest respite before they awakened and rose
to fight again.

I could feel the strain in my shoulder and arm. My
fingers were cramped from gripping the hilt, and the blade
seemed to have doubled its weight. Bors, too, was laboring; I could hear his breath coming in grunting gasps as
he lunged and thrust time after time after time. Gereint's
blade struck again and again from under the near edge of
the shield, but even his youthful strength could not last
forever. No doubt that was their sole tactic: to wear us
down until we could no longer lift a blade to defend ourselves, whereupon they would simply overwhelm us and
tear us limb from limb.

We had no other choice, however, but to stand our
ground and fight. Thus, I raised the sword again, and
again, and again, slashing and slashing while the undead
warriors stumbled ever and again into our blades. Sweat
ran freely down my neck and chest and back, mingling
with the tears of exhaustion welling from my eyes and
spilling down my face. Jesu, help us! I prayed as I cut
the arm from the wretch before me. The warrior shambled
ahead, pushing his shield into my face. Sidestepping the
clumsy lunge, I brought the sword blade down sharply on
the back of his neck and he sank like an anvil, falling
against my legs and throwing me off-balance. I tried to

kick the body aside, but could not shift the dead weight and fell.

Two enemy warriors bore down upon me. Squirming on my back, I kept my sword in their faces and tried to regain my feet as they woodenly jabbed at me with their spears. I shouted to Bors for help, but could not see him. I shouted again, and dodged a spear thrust; the stroke missed my chest, but I got a nasty gash in the side. Seizing the spear shaft with my free hand, I flailed with my sword and succeeded in getting to my knees.

Clutching the hilt in both hands, I whipped the blade back and forth, desperate to gain a space in which I might climb to my feet. But the blade struck the iron rim of a foeman's shield. My fingers, long since numb from the relentless toil, could no longer hold the hilt and the sword spun from my grasp.

The long spears drove down upon me. I threw myself to one side, rolling in a desperate effort to escape. One spear jabbed at my head and grazed my cheek. Seizing the spear shaft, I tried to wrest the weapon from my foe, but his grasp was like stone. As I struggled, another spear thrust at my side, and I felt my siarc rip as the blade sliced through the fabric, narrowly missing my ribs.

Lashing out with both feet, I kicked the nearest in the leg and he staggered back. I jumped up quickly, and was just as quickly surrounded once more. Three more warriors had joined the first two, and all pressed in on me, spears level, aiming to take me in the chest and stomach.

Just as they prepared to make their final lunge, I glimpsed what I thought to be a flash of light out of the corner of my eye, and heard Gereint cry out in a loud voice. Taking the shield by the rim, he spun around and flung it into the foremost of my attackers. The iron rim caught the luckless wretch as he turned; his face crumpled and he collapsed, taking two others down with him.

Before I could struggle to my feet, Gereint was over me, half lifting, half dragging me from danger. Bors cleaved the skull of another in two, and the enemy, beaten back for the moment, retreated to regroup and attack again.

"You are hurt, Lord Gwalchavad," Gereint said, seeing the blood flowing freely down my side.

"I lost my sword," I told him, my breath coming in ragged gasps as the pain in my side began to bloom like a flame taking hold of dry tinder.

Ignoring my protests, Bors examined the wound and said, "I do not like the look of that one. Does it hurt?"

"Not so much," I told him.

"It will."

"Just help me bind it up before they come at us again," I said.

"Let us wash it at least," Bors suggested doubtfully. "Here, lad, help me get him to the well. I could do with a drink myself."

They bore me to the well between them, and sat me down on a rock at the pool's edge. Gereint dropped his blade to the ground and fell face-first to the water and began drinking noisily.

"I think we must abandon the field," Bors said, raising the edge of my siarc to splash water on the wound.

"We are pledged to the fight," I insisted, squeezing my eyes shut against the shock of the cold water on my hot wound.

"I will die before I run from a battle," Gereint maintained staunchly. He lowered his face to the pool again and cupped water into his mouth in great gulps.

"Did I say we should give up the fight?" growled Bors, tearing a strip from my siarc to bind around my waist. "I only meant that we should retreat into the chapel. The entrance is low and narrow—they will not find it easy to get at us in there."

I recognized this as the last desperate tactic of a warband forced to the extreme. Once we were inside, there would be no coming out again. But at least we would die on holy ground, protecting the Blessed Cup we were sworn to defend.

Bors tied off the binding, regarded his crude handiwork, and said, "There—that is the best I can do for now."

"I am certain it will serve," I told him. With difficulty,

I turned and leaned painfully down to drink. I cupped water in my hand and raised it to my mouth, spilling most of it before wetting my tongue.

Gereint, having drunk his fill, was looking across the clearing to where the enemy, much mutilated and ravaged, was yet again re-forming the battle line. "We must fly," he informed us, "if we are to reach the chapel."

I took a last gulp, then leaned low over the well to splash water on my face. Bors stepped beside me and reached down a hand. As I made to stand, the dull gleam of a submerged object caught my eye.

In truth, I do not know how I saw it at all: the pale gloaming of a moonlit night lay upon the chapel clearing, and all around us bristled the deeper darkness of the forest. But I saw what I saw—the faintest glimmer of gold in the shape of a cross.

My first thought was that I had found the altarpiece. Of course! It must be the cross which had adorned the chapel's altar. In the desecration of the altar, the cross had been taken and thrown into the well. And now I had found it, and could restore it to its rightful place.

"See here!" I said, my heart leaping at the thrill of my find. "I give you the missing altarpiece."

To my companions' amazement, I reached down into the pool. My fingers closed on cold metal, and grasping the topmost arm of the cross, I drew it slowly out. The expressions of astonishment on their faces were wonderful to see, and caused me to forget for a moment the fiery pain burning in my side. Indeed, I was so enjoying their amazement, I did not myself see the object until I had pulled it from the water.

"A curious altarpiece, that," observed Bors. Gereint, wide-eyed with the strangeness of it, nodded.

Only then did I look down to see that I held not a cross, but a sword. A mass of vines and weed wrack dangled from the long, tapering blade—the weapon had been wrapped in the stuff to disguise it, I reckoned—still, I would have known the weapon anywhere. How not? I have seen it nearly every day for the past seven years.

"That was well done," enthused Gereint. "You have got yourself another sword."

"Not just a sword, son," I told him, clutching the hilt tightly in both hands. "This is Arthur's sword."

Chapter Thirty-eight

"Caledvwlch!"

Gereint knelt quickly beside me and stretched out his hands to receive the sword, which I delivered into his eager grasp. Taking up the weapon, the young warrior proceeded to tear away the slimy tangle and then plunged the sword into the well and washed it clean.

"There," he said, drawing the weapon from the water. "It is ready to serve the king once more."

Then, before Bors or I knew what he was about, the young warrior lofted the Pendragon's battle sword, threw back his head, and shouted, "For God and Arthur!"

With that he darted away, his cry echoing through the wood. Bors leapt after him to pull him back, but the youth was already beyond reach.

"Gereint!" shouted Bors. The young warrior, flying headlong to meet the undead enemy, did not even break stride.

"Go with him," I urged. "Help him."

"For God and Arthur!" came the cry again.

Pressing Gereint's sword into my hand, Bors said, "I will return as soon as I can."

He hastened away in a tired, rolling lope to engage the enemy one last time. I sat on the edge of the well, clutching my sword and praying for protection for my friends. "Great of Might," I said aloud, "we are weary and we are overcome. We have no other help but you, and if you do not deliver us now, we will surely die."

Having spoken my mind, I made the sign of the cross over my heart and then, using the sword as a staff, pulled myself up onto my feet and stumbled painfully to join my swordbrothers in the fight.

The undead warriors had regrouped and were advancing once more. Bors had almost reached the battle line, but Gereint was yet a dozen paces ahead of him. Loosing a loud battle cry, the impetuous young warrior leapt forward, the great sword a blur of gleaming steel around him as he flung himself headlong into the center of their ranks.

Oh, it was bold. It was brave. It was foolhardy beyond belief, but my heart soared to see him as he charged alone into the fray, brandishing the sword and bellowing his wild war chant.

Behold! Even before Gereint could strike a blow, the enemy's relentless advance staggered to a halt. Heedless, Gereint raced ahead and the ranks of the undead collapsed before him. He swung Caledvwlch around his head and leapt to the right and left. Everywhere he turned, the enemy fell away.

Back and back they fled, stumbling over one another in their haste to escape. Wonder of wonders, it was as if they could not abide the sight of the sword, much less stand against it!

The mere sight of the Sovereign Sword of Britain made them cry out in alarm and dismay, for whenever Gereint came near, they opened their silent mouths and filled the air with piteous wails. The thin, bloodless sound tore up from their hollow throats in long, biting shrieks that ended in raking sobs and clashing teeth. Their faces, once impassive, now convulsed in the hideous rictus of abject, mindless terror. Though rarely seen elsewhere, it is an expression common enough on the battlefield, and I had seen it more times than I like to remember—on the faces of men who knew themselves bereft of every hope and doomed to swift destruction.

That the sight of Caledvwlch should inspire such horror amazed me so, I stood flat-footed and stared as, all around me, the enemy abandoned their weapons and fled the field in a mad, futile effort to escape. They trampled one another and, falling, clawed their way over their comrades in a blind panic.

But Gereint was not daunted. Leaping and spinning, striking with clean, efficient strokes, he cut them down as they fled before him. With each stroke and every thrust, another enemy fell—and this time they did not rise again, but expired, screaming as they died.

God help me, their shrieking was more appalling than their loathsome silence. It cut me to the quick to hear it, even as I rejoiced in the victory.

The young warrior became a very reaper, cutting a wide swath of destruction and havoc through the crumbling ranks of the undead. As the last of them fell before Caledvwlch's fury, I saw Bors standing a little distance away, his shoulders bent, his sword dangling at his side. "Brother," I said, "it looks as though we live to fight again."

Gereint, exultant in his triumph, came running to where we stood, his face glowing with exertion and pride. "Did you see?" he cried, almost shaking with jubilation. "Did you see?"

"That we did, lad," Bors assured him. "You swinging that sword and cutting them down as they fled—it is a sight I will never forget."

"A glorious sight," I agreed. "Gereint, my friend, you are a very Bard of Battle."

"It was never me," Gereint replied. "It was the sword." He raised the blade and regarded it with awe. "Caledvwlch spoke and I obeyed."

"If you had not obeyed when you did," Bors declared, "I am certain we would all be drawing breath in the Otherworld right now."

We fell silent then, each to his own thoughts. I closed my eyes and breathed a prayer of thanks that we had survived our ordeal. While I was yet praying, a gurgling sound reached my ears—like that of a cauldron left too long on the hearth. It seemed to be coming from the corpses on the ground. I turned in the direction of the sound and saw that the dead were decomposing—and this with such rapidity that their bodies seemed to crumple inwardly, melting into one another, congealing into a lumpen ooze that bubbled and spurted with escaping fumes.

As we stared at the horrific sight, a stench like that of rotting entrails rose from this swiftly liquefying coagulation. All around the clearing, the corpse heaps were dissolving into a stinking mass as once-firm flesh turned into a sighing, quivering mass. Amidst the muck, I could see long, pale bones protruding—here a slender leg bone, there the twinned lengths of an arm, or the swept curves of a rib cage—and all of them sinking into miry dissolution.

The vapors gurgling from the vile quagmire hung in the air, giving off a faint, noxious glow. The air was so rank with the stink and belch of the putrid slurry, I gagged and wretched, vomiting bile onto the ground. Dragging my sleeve across my lips, I tried to wipe the bad taste from my mouth, to no avail.

"I think I preferred them when they were trying to kill us," Bors said through clenched teeth.

Retreating into the chapel, we sank down upon the cool stones. I lay there drawing clean air deep into my lungs, grateful for the peaceful sanctuary of this holy place. Exhausted from our ordeal, we rested then, content to simply await whatever should befall us. I slept and awakened some while later much refreshed; the pain in my side had eased a great deal, and I found I could move without difficulty. Leaving the others to their sleep, I got up and went to the chapel door and looked out to find that the vile heaps of putrefaction had vanished.

I roused the others and we went out.

Not a scrap of bone or a shred of clothing was anywhere to be seen; gone, too, was any sign of the battle we had fought: no splintered shafts or broken blades; no dented helms or discarded shields . . . nothing. The ground was as smooth and untrammeled as we had first found it.

"It is a wonder," Bors declared. "Not so much as a footprint remains."

"The holy ground has done its work," I replied, and was reminded of the Grail Maiden's challenge: *Think you the Great King requires the aid of any mortal to accom-*

plish his will? Is the Lord of Creation powerless to protect his treasures?

No, the High King of Heaven required nothing from us but obedience. It was for us that his gifts were given, his commands likewise. What we did, we did for our own welfare, not his.

We had been commanded to guard the Grail, and it was to secure the boon of blessing that we obeyed. Thus, we stood before the chapel, weapons drawn and ready, waiting, listening. But no sound greater than the wind whispering in the bare treetops met the ear.

I felt the first faint breath of a breeze on my face, and Bors said, "The wind is rising."

Even as he spoke, I felt a gust of cold air and the thorny hedge wall began to quiver, as the sighing in the treetops became a moan of regret for the storm to come.

We stood before the chapel, listening to the wind gather strength, gusting in the treetops, making the high boughs creak and groan. Far off, I heard the keening howl of a storm wind sweeping towards us, and I could feel the air growing steadily colder. Something was coming that despised all warmth and light, and it advanced on the wings of a storm.

Chapter Thirty-nine

Morgaws is showing signs of weakness. When I have established my reign, I will teach her the true uses of power. She must learn, as I did, how to harden her heart and bend all things to her will. Sympathy, compassion, mercy—what are they, but weakness by other names? The Queen of Air and Darkness is beyond weakness, beyond frailty, beyond all human imperfection. Morgaws will learn this, or Morgaws will die.

She denies she has made any mistakes, and in the same breath informs me that Llenlleawg has failed, the Grail has not been recovered, and three of Arthur's warriors have mounted a pitiful resistance. It is of no consequence, I tell her, but she insists they have succeeded in finding the chapel and suspects they may have regained the Grail.

All the better, I say; it saves us the trouble of finding it again. The Irish oaf will join his churlish master in the pit, and the opposition will be crushed. But Morgaws complains that the resistance is very strong—powerful enough, at least, to defeat the warriors I conjured for her.

Forget swords and spears—children's playthings. I taught you better than that, Morgaws. I suckled you on venom and bile, girl—use it!

There are other ways, I tell her . . . other ways. The end is decreed. It will be. I grow tired of waiting. I am ready to ascend to my rightful throne. Finish it!

"We should make a fire," Bors said, trying to fend off the sensation of menace flowing out of the forest on the cold wind.

No one replied, however, and we slipped back into an anxious, dread-filled vigil. The wind, fretful and restless, whined in the treetops and tore at the hedge wall.

Foreboding swirled in the dead leaves at our feet, and the long grass hissed and rippled like snakes across the clearing. Long, frosty fingers of despair sought me; I could feel them reaching, reaching, stretching out from the bleak heart of the forest to poison my spirit with their malignant touch. How long must we endure? I wondered. Will this torment never end? I would die right gladly—if only to be free of this ceaseless travail. Yes, death . . . death would be a welcome release.

The barrenness of the thought brought me to myself once more. It was not my wish, but that of the enemy seeking to unnerve me. I glanced at Gereint beside me and saw that his eyes were closed.

"Take heart, brother," I told him. "There is no solace in death. We can endure this, and we will."

He opened his eyes and looked at me. "How did you know what I was thinking?"

"Because I have been thinking the same thing myself," I replied. "But listen, we are warriors of the Summer Realm and Guardians of the Grail. I drank from the Cup of Christ; I tasted the wine of his blood on my tongue, and I was healed—we all were. And though the Devil himself and all the demons of Hell assail us, I say we shall stand. But whether we stand or fall, our souls rest in the hollow of the Swift Sure Hand, and no power on earth can snatch us from his grasp."

Bors, grim-faced, said nothing, but tightened his grip on the weapon in his hand, and gazed steadfastly into the onrushing night. The darkness surged and roiled around us like a tempest-torn sea. Clouds blacker than that of the surrounding wood streamed around the chapel clearing: rivers of darkness flowing, rising on a flood tide of foreboding, bleak and dire.

Soon it seemed as if the entire forest was in motion.

The thorny hedge tossed this way and that, as if gripped by monstrous hands intent on tearing it out. Gaps began appearing in the surrounding wall as the thicket gave way before the enemy's approach.

Meanwhile, the cold wind clawed at us. Shivering, freezing, huddled against one another, we stood our ground, awaiting the enemy's appearance.

They arrived all at once.

The wood seemed to convulse and the enemy warhost simply stepped out from the forest to the edge of the clearing—line on line and rank upon rank of dark warriors encircled the chapel. I tried to see the end of them, but their numbers stretched back into the forest and were lost to the darkness whence they came.

At the foe's abrupt appearance, the fretful wind stilled, lapsing suddenly into an eerie, menace-fraught calm. A sickly yellow radiance like that of a foul, false sunrise dawned over the chapel clearing. The bruised light gave off a putrid glow which made everything seem filthy and lurid.

In this ghastly dawn, the thronging multitude gathered, moving among the trees like a noiseless flood; the war-helms rising above the rims of their round shields looked like a great swath of rocky shore, or a beach of rounded stones stretching as far as the eye could see; the upright spear shafts in tight clusters of ten and twenty were like narrow plumes of sea grass rising ridge upon ridge.

There were so many!

"God save us," breathed Bors. Gereint made the sign of the cross over himself, and swallowed hard, but said nothing.

"Why do they wait?" I wondered aloud.

They stood in silence, but for the slight rustle of their clothing where they brushed against one another, or the hollow clink of shield rims gently touching. Line on line, and rank on rank, they stood, silent as the fog on the night-dark sea. I studied the nearest faces—more the dread, for they were cold countenances each and every one: long-featured with flat noses and mouths which were little more than bloodless slits in their pale, waxy-fleshed faces. The eyes staring back at me were large and black—indeed, the black filled the eye so that no white showed at all—like the eyes of beasts; and though the expressions remained impassive, the eyes gazing at us across the grassy clearing were baleful and malevolent. I could almost feel the coldhearted hatred burning across the short span between us like flames of a frozen fire.

One look in those unblinking eyes and I knew beyond all doubt that they wished us dead, yes, and more than dead: they willed our annihilation; we were to be completely and utterly destroyed and our souls obliterated. Yet they waited, a malign and brooding mass beneath a gruesome yellow sky.

"Why do they just stand there?" Gereint said, his voice quivering—with cold, I think, not fear.

"Perhaps their battlechief has not arrived," Bors suggested. "Or maybe they await the command to attack."

"Come on," muttered Gereint. "Let us finish it!"

"Patience, lad," said Bors. "Life is short, and death is long. Use what time you have left to make your peace."

"God knows I am more than ready," replied Gereint evenly. "Let it begin, I say."

"Look there," I said, directing their attention to a disturbance in the rearward ranks. In a moment, it emerged that the warhost was dividing along a line back to front.

"They are preparing to attack," said Bors, flinging his cloak away from his arms in preparation.

"I think their war leader has arrived," I said. "He is taking his place at the forefront of his warhost."

The ranks continued parting until a wide way stood clear. I could see several figures moving towards us along the opened course. One of them, taller than the others, appeared to be advancing at the head of the others.

I watched him stride nearer, and recognized the familiar gait. I had seen it so often, I would have known it far more readily than my own.

"It is Arthur," said Bors. "He is alive."

The Pendragon came to the edge of the clearing and stood regarding us silently. His clothes were ripped and torn—as if he had been dragged through the wood by horses. His face was lined with fatigue; he looked haggard and old. His right cheek was discolored with an ugly bruise, but he held himself erect, head high.

"Arthur!" I shouted. "Here! Join us!"

The king made no reply, but turned and stepped aside; only then did I notice that his hands were bound with chains. Llenlleawg, spear in hand, advanced directly behind Arthur with Morgaws at his side. I could also see Myrddin and Gwenhwyvar, with Rhys and Peredur coming up behind Llenlleawg; their hands were chained also, and they stood with their heads down. Their clothes, too, were ragged and blood-stained, and they wore the look of warriors who knew the battle was lost and their lives were swiftly approaching a bloody, wretched end.

At a nod from Llenlleawg, Arthur turned once more to address us. He called us by name, and said, "You have fought well, my friends. But the battle is lost. It is time to surrender."

"Is it really the Pendragon?" whispered Gereint uncertainly.

"Never!" declared Bors. "The true Arthur has never so much as breathed a word of surrender, and never will." Raising a hand to his mouth, Bors shouted, "Take your words of surrender to hell with you! We are Pendragon's men, sworn before God to guard the Grail. We will not stand down for anyone."

The Pendragon, humble and sorrowful, appealed to him, saying, "Bors, old friend, do as I say. You have pledged loyalty to me, whether in victory or defeat. It is time to end this battle."

"In God's name, Arthur," Bors cried, "what have they done to you? Join us, lord, and fight them! We will go down together!"

Ignoring this outburst, the king continued calmly. "They have come for Caledvwlch and the Grail. The fighting can stop, but you must do as I say and bring the sword and cup."

Bitterness and bleak desperation welled up inside me. I had known defeat before, but never like this. Never! This . . . this ignoble submission was not worthy of the Pendragon I knew. Myrddin would have moved Heaven and Earth before giving in, and even the least of the Cymbrogi would have fought to the last dying breath rather than be party to such a shameful capitulation.

I stared across the clearing as across a great divide; my king stood on one side, and I on the other. Could I defy my king and continue the fight? Or must I obey him, even to my shame and degradation?

See, now: one who has never served a True Lord, nor vowed loyalty through all things to the end of life, cannot know what it is to behold that lord defeated by wicked enemies, humiliated, and disgraced. Those who know nothing of honor cannot comprehend the pain of dishonor. I tell you the truth, it is a pain worse than death, and it does not end.

Thus, I stood staring at Arthur, his head bowed in defeat, and the tears came to my eyes. I could not stand the sight and I had to turn away.

"The fighting can end," the Pendragon repeated, his voice broken and weary. "Bring the Grail. Give it up."

Bors' face clenched like a fist, and his refusal was anvil hard. "Never!" he cried, shaking with rage. Taking Caledvwlch from Gereint, he flourished it, shouting, "To get the Grail, you will have to pry this blade from my dead hands."

It might have been a trick of the light, but I thought I saw the merest shadow of a smile flicker across Arthur's face as he received Bors' reply. Turning towards Morgaws, he made a gesture with his hands—as much as to say, Well, I tried—and Llenlleawg prodded him aside into line with the butt of his spear.

The Irish champion took hold of Myrddin and dragged him forth. But Morgaws, impatient with Arthur's feeble efforts at persuasion, stepped out from among the enemy warriors. Flame-haired, features ablaze like a torch with hate and triumph and spite all mingled together in her wild expression, she was both terrible and magnificent. The flames of her passion had given her a fearful, feral beauty, like that of a ravening she-wolf leaping to the kill, or lightning striking from a storm-fraught sky. Her smooth white brow fierce, fiery hair streaming from her temples, lips drawn back in a malevolent smile of rage and dominion, she appeared a goddess of destruction—the fearsome Morrighan of the old tales could not have been more appalling in aspect and allure.

"The cup! Give me the cup!" Morgaws cried in a voice swollen with exultation. Long gone was the maid I had found wandering lost in the wood that day; like everything else about her, the mute innocent was a lie, too.

I watched Morgaws now, and remembered our first meeting. I had stepped from among the trees and there she was, sitting on the ground, her carefully gathered mushrooms scattered around her. She had tripped and fallen, spilling her harvest. I helped her retrieve them, as I recall. Peredur and Tallaght were with me, and we had simply stumbled upon her, alone and lost . . . Ah, no, no, it was not that way at all. It was the song—the song led us to her. She had been singing and we heard it and followed, and that was how it began.

Had I not been so beguiled, I might have stopped long enough to wonder how it was that a maid who could sing yet lacked the power of speech. Alas, I was deceived like all the rest. I hung my head and asked Jesu to forgive my blindness.

As if in answer to my reproachful thoughts, I heard again the song that I had heard that summer day in the wood. Glancing up, I saw Morgaws standing before me, the song still fresh on her lips. She smiled and I knew at once that I had judged her far too harshly.

"Do not think ill of me, Brave Gwalchavad," she said in a voice both soft and low. She stepped closer. "I am just like you. I, too, have suffered at Morgian's hands."

It was true, I thought. Like all the rest of us, she was caught in Wicked Morgian's designs. And like everyone else, she had suffered for it. A pang of genuine regret speared my heart, and I opened my mouth to express my sorrow at her distress.

But Morgaws prevented me. "Say nothing," she whispered, placing her fingertips against my mouth. "It is over, my love. We can forget the pain and hardship, and begin again. We must make a new start, and we can. You do believe me, Gwalchavad. We can show the others, the doubters. We can show them, you and I."

She smiled again and the last particle of doubt melted away in the bright sun of her smile. She looked at me and I saw nothing but love in her eyes. "Come with me, Gwalchavad. Come away with me, my love. We can be together, you and I. Together always."

Oh, I did believe her. And I so wanted the travail to end. In that moment I think I would have done anything she asked. "Come, bring me the Grail, my love. You do not need to guard it anymore. Bring it to me, and we can begin anew."

When I hesitated, she urged me on, saying, "I want you, my love. Is the cup inside?" She glanced at the chapel expectantly. "Go get it, Gwalchavad. Bring the cup to me. Hurry! Then we can leave this place forever."

I heard Bors raise a protest behind me, but I could not hear what he said. It did not matter. Morgaws, beautiful and yielding, stood before me, and desire was in her eyes. "Come to me, my love," she said, extending her hands to embrace me. I looked at those long, lovely arms—so fine and shapely and inviting—and lust leapt like a flame within me. I looked at her rounded hips and breasts and I wanted her. I ached to hold her in my arms and to take her.

In that instant the watching world disappeared—the enemy host with its rank on rank of baleful-eyed warriors, my friends and comrades, the chapel and surrounding forest—everything vanished in the white heat of my ardor and was instantly forgotten. It was as if a dull, thick fog descended over the world, blotting out everything but Morgaws and my aching need; nothing else existed, nothing else mattered. Only Morgaws and I remained, only we two, a man and a woman. One look at the hunger burning in her eyes, and I knew she wanted me as much as I wanted her.

"Come to me, my love. Take me, lie with me—make love to me. I want you, Gwalchavad. Come to me."

I stepped nearer, my breath coming in raking gasps,

desire making me weak. I could feel the last restraining cords of will dissolving.

Morgaws smiled knowingly. Her lips parted as she put her head back to allow me to kiss her throat. At the same time, she opened her robe so that I could admire her body. I saw the white, white skin and her gently rounded thighs and rose-tipped breasts; I saw the welcome in her eyes and the temptation of those half-parted lips, and wanted so much to taste the sweetness there.

"Gwalchavad," she said, closing the distance between us with a swaying step. "Take me." Her voice was husky with longing, and she moaned with pleasure as she pressed her body against mine. I felt her hands on mine, pulling me nearer. "The Grail, my love," she whispered, her breath hot in my ear. "Give me the Grail and I am yours. . . ."

Jesu save me, I turned and started towards the chapel, intent on fetching the Grail and yielding it up to her. But as I turned, the gleam of gold caught my eye—Caledvwlch, clutched tight in Bors' fist—and I heard again the Grail Maiden's admonition to cling to the Sword of Salvation. I heard her solemn warning: *Lusting after honor, he was bewitched by one who honors only lust and lies. Thus are the mighty undone.*

"Bring me the cup," Morgaws said, subtle insistence rising in her voice. She stepped nearer. "Give it me, and I will be yours, my love, forever."

"No," I said, and the sound of my voice was harsh in my ears. "I am sworn to guard the cup."

"The Grail," Morgaws moaned, rubbing her body against mine. "I am yours, Gwalchavad. Take me now."

I felt her touch hot on my skin as she raised my hand to her mouth. "I want you," she whispered, bending her head towards my hand. I saw her lips draw away from her fine white teeth as she prepared to bite.

I jerked my hand away, as if from a serpent. This angered her. "Gwalchavad!" she said sternly. "You will give me the cup."

Confusion assaulted me. Morgaws' voice boomed inside my head, urgent and insistent. The Grail! Give me the Grail!

"No," I said, shaken, confused.

"Maggot!" Morgaws advanced, her presence overpowering. "I killed all the rest, and I will kill you, too. For the last time, bring me the cup."

"No," I said, forcing strength into my voice. "I will not."

She turned on her heel and moved to where Llenlleawg stood, spear in hand, watching the proceedings with a hostile eye. "They have the Grail, my darling," she said, her voice softly cozening once more. "Kill them, and it is ours. We can rule forever, you and I."

Llenlleawg's gaze shifted from me to Morgaws. I saw him glance down the length of her body, and an expression of loathing appeared on his face. "You said you loved me," he rasped in a voice so tight he could hardly force out the words.

"The Grail," she whispered, moving closer. "They have the cup, my love. Kill them and it will be ours!"

Llenlleawg's jaw tensed and he turned his face once more towards me. Morgaws lifted her hand to his cheek and put her face close to his. She whispered something to him, and pressed herself against him. I saw Llenlleawg's free hand come around behind her to gather her into his embrace as her lips parted in a kiss. Llenlleawg's hand moved up from her waist to her shoulders and was lost in the snaking tresses of her hair.

Morgaws kissed Llenlleawg again and, still clinging to him, turned her face towards me, her expression haughty, exulting in triumph. "Kill them, my lo—" she began, but never finished, for suddenly her head snapped back sharply.

She made to cry out, but Llenlleawg tightened his grip on her hair and pulled her head back still further. The scream stuck in her throat. Her eyes bulged in terror as Llenlleawg put his lips to her pale cheek.

"Farewell, my love," he growled, then jerked her head sharply back and to the side. The bones of her slender neck snapped with a meaty crack and Morgaws fell dead to the ground.

The next thing I heard was a queer, hushed clatter. In the same instant, the entrancing fog vanished from my head and I raised my gaze from Morgaws' corpse to see a thousand spears swinging level.

Then Dread Morgian's dark minions attacked.

Chapter Forty

"Cut me free!" cried Arthur, struggling to his feet.

I staggered towards him, amazed that I could move again.

"Hurry, Gwalchavad!" Behind him, I glimpsed Morgian's massed battlehost surging to the attack.

There was no shout of command, no battle cry. One moment they were standing at the ready, and the next they were in motion, swarming down upon us.

"Gwalchavad!" cried the Pendragon, holding out his chained hands. "For the love of God, man, cut me free!"

I was beside him in an instant. Raising the sword, I took careful aim, and brought the blade down sharply. The blow made not the slightest mark on the chain. I tried again, and yet once more—with no greater success than before—and then the enemy was upon us.

Turning to meet the attack, I put myself between the king and the onrushing foe, and shouted for the others to join me. "Bors! Gereint!"

Out of the corner of my eye, I glimpsed Bors as he raced to take his place at my right hand. Expecting Gereint on my left, I turned, and when I did not see him, I shouted for him. He did not answer.

"Gereint!" I cried again.

"Here I am!"

I heard his voice behind me as he dashed for his place on my left. He came up with me, but did not stop. Instead, he raced on ahead. I saw a flash of gold in his hands as he blew past.

"He has the Grail!" Bors shouted.

Gereint, holding the Blessed Cup between his hands, ran to meet the foe alone. Lofting the Sacred Bowl, he cried, "In the name of Christ Jesu," he shouted, "be gone!"

Confusion descended upon the onrushing host. The foremost ranks halted in mid-step and fell back. Those behind kept coming, trampling the leaders underfoot before they could halt themselves.

The young warrior, defiant and unafraid, stood in the midst of the chaos. "In the name of the Father God, the Blessed Son, and the Holy Spirit," Gereint shouted again, "I command you to leave this place. Return to Hell!"

All at once there arose the sound of a thousand wings taking flight, and the enemy host flew. They appeared to shrivel and diminish, wrinkling and shrinking like the flesh of rotten fruit in the sun. Even as we stood looking on, they became no more than husks of grain, brittle and dry, and though there was no wind, they appeared to rise up into the air as if scattering and dispersing before a mighty gale. The power that had called them and sustained them was broken, and now they fled, away from the realm of light and life, and back to the nameless pit from which they had been summoned.

Spinning and tumbling into the void, the last of them disappeared and they were no more. A great peal of thunder broke over us and I looked up to see the leaden vault of the sky crack open and a single shaft of light stabbed down into the gloom of the forest. Like a spear thrown from on high, the beam struck the chapel, transforming the stone to silver, dazzling our light-starved eyes. In the same moment a scream pierced the air high above us—a wounded cry, dying away even as it was born. Myrddin lifted his head at the sound and said, "Morgian is defeated." His voice sounded tired and old, but the light in his eye was undimmed. "We have driven her back to her darksome lair and, God willing, she will not trouble us again for a very long time."

The thunder cracked once more and I felt something wet on my face. "It is raining!" someone shouted, and as the word was uttered, the heavens opened and down poured the precious water. The blessed rain fell from the sky, striking down through the empty air to bathe the long-parched earth.

We raised our faces to the glorious water and drank it down. "The chains—" called Gwenhwyvar, holding up her hands, "I am free!" Myrddin and Arthur held out their hands, and Rhys and Peredur. As with Gwenhwyvar, wherever the rain touched the links, the chains parted and the pieces fell to the ground, the shattered links melting like ice.

Standing in the rain beneath that low, leaden sky, I looked around and understood that we alone had survived; of all the multitude, only we were left: Arthur and Gwenhwyvar, Bors, Gereint, Peredur, Rhys, Myrddin and me, and, alas, Llenlleawg. Dazed and bewildered, we all gazed at one another, trying to comprehend our miraculous survival.

Arthur moved to where Bors and Gereint and I stood. Falling to one knee, he put Caledvwlch point downward on the ground and held the bare blade in both hands. Then, as if swearing a solemn oath upon the Holy Cross, he said, "Most noble friends, I owe you my kingdom and my life. No king was ever served by more loyal and honorable men, and no king was ever more aware of his failing. I beg your forgiveness, and offer my pledge, as I would offer it to Jesu himself, that I will never forget the debt of gratitude and honor that I, and all Britain, owe you."

Bors, touched by the king's words, rushed forward and embraced him, saying, "Rise, Arthur, rise. You owe me nothing, and there is nothing to forgive. I did only what I have ever done in your service."

Gereint, shamed at the sight of his king kneeling to him, bent his head nervously and looked away. I stepped forward and prostrated myself before Arthur. "Lord Pendragon," I said, "it is I who must beg your forgiveness. It is through my weakness that this evil has befallen us."

Arthur stood, reached down, and raised me to my feet. "Where is the fault? You have remained steadfast through all things. What lord could ask more?"

So we stood together, my king and I, the rain falling over us. Gwenhwyvar, Rhys, and Peredur joined us and, in delight and eagerness, everyone began talking at once.

"God love you, Bear, but it is Earth and Sky to be with you again," Bors said, his grin wide and handsome. "I thought I would never see any of you again."

It was exactly what Bedwyr would have said, and grief awakened at the words. "Lord," I said, turning to Arthur, "I fear the answer, but I must know. What happened to the rest of the Cymbrogi?"

"I never saw any of them after the fire," replied Arthur sadly. "We all became separated in the forest. I fear they are dead. Rhys, Myrddin, and I somehow stayed together. I thought we were the only ones left until we saw you."

He then told us how they were ambushed in the darkness while they slept; Llenlleawg, leading a host of the foe, delivered them to Morgaws, with whom they found Gwenhwyvar and Peredur bound and waiting. "There was nothing we could do," Arthur said. "You saw how many warriors she commanded. We fought, but were overwhelmed from the start."

We then told Arthur how it was with us: how we had come upon the chapel and had cleaned away the defiling filth. We told how the Grail Maiden had appeared and returned the Holy Cup, how we had found Caledvwlch in the well and fended off each attack made on the chapel.

"You have done well," Myrddin declared. "Heaven has blessed your efforts. Your reward is assured." Lifting a hand to the chapel, he said, "Come, let us thank God for the victory he has given us."

"You are right to remind us of the source of our salvation," replied Arthur. "But say not that we have won a victory this day; rather, say that God in his mercy has cut short the tribulation and spared our lives."

The Wise Emrys motioned to Gereint, who, bearing the Most Holy Grail, entered the chapel. We followed, silently, each wrapped in his separate thoughts, to join the young warrior at the altar. He had replaced the cup and it sat on the stone, glimmering softly in the light of its own gentle radiance. The king gazed long upon the cup, then bowed his head and wept for his lost Cymbrogi. In this he was not alone; I, too, gave myself over to my grief for the dead, as did we all.

After a time, Myrddin stirred and, in his clear, strong voice, began singing a lament for the dead. He sang The Last Returning, a fine and fitting song for a warrior who has fallen in the fight and will not be going home with his king. Then the Wise Emrys led us in prayers of thanksgiving for our deliverance.

Our voices filled the chapel and our hearts lifted under the benison of Myrddin's comforting words. Holding fear at bay for so long is a wearisome labor, and I felt my spirit ease as the prayers did their work. I cannot say how long we stayed in the chapel, but when I rose at last, a massive weight had fallen from my shoulders.

Myrddin was attracted to the carvings on the walls; while the others talked in low voices at the altar, I joined him to ask what he made of the strange markings. "Do they speak to you?" I asked.

"They do." The Bard of Britain ran his strong hands across the etched designs as a mother might trace her fingers over the sleeping face of her much-loved child. Entranced, he walked the walls and embraced the messages in silent wonder.

"Make no mistake, Gwalchavad," he said, turning to me at last. "Llyonesse was not always the wasteland it is now, and it will be redeemed. One day Llyonesse will prove a boon of great blessing to all Britain."

The others joined us then, and the king, awed by the chapel, remarked on the mystery of the place. "To think," he mused, "this chapel has been here—here in this blighted realm—from the beginning."

"The beginning?" said Myrddin. "Know you, the beginning was long, long ago."

"And yet the chapel remains," Bors pointed out. "It was not destroyed."

"Yes, the chapel remains," agreed the Wise Emrys.

"Let all who love the truth think on that and engrave it on their hearts."

Turning abruptly, he stepped before the altar and, while we all stood watching, took the edge of his cloak between his hands and tore off a portion. Then, bowing in reverence to the cup, he carefully covered the Grail with the cloth. This done, he took up the cup and addressed us. "The Holy Cup of Christ has been reclaimed. It is time to make our way back to Ynys Avallach." Cradling the cup, Myrddin stepped from the altar.

We emerged from the chapel into a cold, gray dawn. The vile yellow had washed from the clouds and the rain pattered steadily around us. We stood for a moment, looking into the sky as the healing rain streamed down our faces. Water dripped from the branches of the trees all around, filling the air with the woodland scent of wet bark and leaf mold. Even in the pale dawnlight, I could see further into the wood than before. Darkness had loosed its hold on the land and shadows no longer reigned in this place.

Morgaws' body lay where she had fallen, eyes wide in the shock of her undoing. Llenlleawg sat a little apart, his back to her, his head low, rain beating down on him. Arthur, calm and resolute, strode to where Llenlleawg sat, and stood for a moment looking down at his fallen champion. "Get up," he commanded after a moment.

Llenlleawg did not so much as raise his head.

Summoning Peredur and Gereint, the king indicated that they should raise the Irishman between them. The two pulled Llenlleawg to his feet and remained beside him— more to support him than to prevent him from escaping.

Llenlleawg stood before the king as if he no longer possessed the use of his limbs, or perhaps lacked the will to stand and did so only by happenchance. Head bowed, shoulders slumped, abject in every line and ligament, he swayed slightly on his feet. Remorse dripped from him like the rain which spattered upon his head and trickled from his sodden hair in rivulets, dribbling off his downcast face. Guilt pressed full on him and he bent under the terrible weight.

Arthur gazed upon his former champion and friend. I could see the conflict warring in the king's features: his mouth frowned with repugnance and distaste even while his eyes, soft with sorrow, searched for some redeeming sign. "Do you know what your betrayal has wrought?" asked the king at last, his voice tight, almost breaking.

Llenlleawg gave not the slightest indication that he had heard, so Arthur repeated the question. Still Llenlleawg made no answer.

"I take your silence to mean that you own the consequence of your deeds," said the king. "Do you have anything to say in your defense?"

Unable to bring himself to look upon the lord he had betrayed, Llenlleawg did not raise his eyes, but muttered something in a voice so low, I could not hear it.

Gwenhwyvar, stepping close, said something to him, and the Irishman, glancing quickly from under his brow, breathed a quiet reply before lowering his head once more. Gwenhwyvar, grave and sorrowful, relayed his words to the king; her eyes never left her kinsman as she said, "He offers no defense, but begs his lord for the judgment due his crimes. He wishes to be killed now and his body left to the birds and beasts."

"So be it," Arthur concluded. "By reason of your treachery, I condemn you to the death you ordained for your swordbrothers." With that he took Caledvwlch in both hands and raised the blade.

"Arthur, no!" called Gwenhwyvar. She stepped boldly between her kinsman and the king's upraised sword. "Do not kill him."

"Step aside, woman," the king said. "Justice will be served."

Gwenhwyvar flared at this. Drawing herself up full height, green eyes ablaze with righteous anger, she glared at her husband. Turning to Myrddin, she demanded, "Am I not a queen? Am I not both daughter to and wife of a king?"

"You are," Myrddin replied.

Facing Arthur once more, she said, "As Queen of Britain, I claim my right to intercede for this man's life."

"He has betrayed his lord, slain men who were under his command, and aided an enemy who schemed to destroy us all," Arthur replied firmly. "Do you deny that he has done these things?"

"I do not," replied Gwenhwyvar smoothly. "Neither do I deny that any one of these crimes is worthy of death."

"Then step aside," said Arthur.

"I will not, my lord. I speak on behalf of my champion—your champion. He saved our lives. When awakened to the knowledge of his error and Morgaws' wickedness, he roused himself to our defense and killed the true traitor."

"If not for him," the Pendragon countered, returning his queen's defiant stare, "such defense would not have been necessary. He knows his crime and accepts his punishment."

"Then punish him, by all means," Gwenhwyvar replied scornfully, "but know you this—hear me, all of you." She turned and included the rest of us in her appeal. "Llenlleawg was bewitched and he was beguiled. His will was weak and he chose to follow that temptress, yes. But we were all of us deceived by Morgaws, and we all took part in her schemes."

Arthur lowered his arms and rested the sword. "All men are responsible for their actions," he maintained stolidly. "Some gave in to evil and allowed it to overtake them; others did not. I do not make him answerable for the evil, but only for his failure to resist it. For this failure, I do condemn him."

Queen Gwenhwyvar folded her arms upon her breast and gazed imperiously at the men around her. "It seems to me you condemn him not for his failure, but for his weakness. What is more, it is a weakness all men share.

"Tell me now," she demanded, exquisite in her wrath, "who among you has never experienced a moment's weakness at the sight of a beautiful woman?" When no one answered, she searched the circle of faces and called us by name: "Gwalchavad? Bors? Peredur? If Morgaws had fastened on you, could you have resisted? Rhys?

Myrddin? How long before you would have given in? Look into your hearts, all of you, and tell me that you would not have weakened if you were in Llenlleawg's place. If you had been the prey the huntress stalked, would you have escaped unscathed?''

I cannot speak for the others, but I was only too painfully aware how very close I had come to giving in to Morgaws' seduction. I knew full well how weak I was, and I had not experienced even the smallest part of what she had directed at Llenlleawg.

"He succumbed, and others did not," Arthur maintained. "Do you think I take pleasure in this judgment? Lady, I do not. But justice must be done."

"Is there no place for mercy in your justice, Great King?" Gwenhwyvar stepped close and put her hands over the king's hands as they rested on the sword. "Please, Arthur," she said softly, pleading for her kinsman's life, "we have all been bewitched in one way or another. Let us not presume to judge Llenlleawg more harshly than we judge ourselves."

The Pendragon looked to his Wise Counselor for advice, and we all turned to see what Myrddin would say. The Emrys joined Gwenhwyvar, taking his place between Arthur and Llenlleawg. "God knows death is justified nine times over for his crimes," he said. "Punishment is your right, and justice demands it. But there is much we do not yet know of Morgian's insidious designs. Therefore, I beg you to withhold judgment until we have penetrated the dark heart of this lamentable affair."

The Pendragon regarded his wife and his counselor for a long time, contemplating what he should do. We all waited on his decision. At last, he said, "Very well, let it be as you say. I will make no judgment until our understanding is complete." He made a motion with his hand. "Now step aside."

Gwenhwyvar and Myrddin moved aside and took their places with the rest of us looking on. The king gazed upon his friend sadly and said, "Hear me, Llenlleawg: from this day you are no longer my champion, and your name will never again be spoken in my presence. Further, you

will go with us to Caer Melyn, where you will be put on
a ship and exiled to Ierna, where your crime will be
known to your people. There you will stay until I make
my final judgment." Having delivered his decree, Arthur
considered the abject warrior. "Do you understand?"

A warrior myself, I understood only too well. It occurred to me that Llenlleawg might rather have parted
with his head than with his lord and swordbrothers. In
Ireland he would be an outcast among his own people—
a disgrace to them and to himself. Llenlleawg's honor,
whatever might be left of it, could not long endure . . .
and then what would become of him?

The Irish champion nodded slowly. "How long must I
wait your decision?" he asked, and oh, the defeat in his
voice cut me to the heart.

But Arthur was not moved. "God alone knows," he
replied, then added, "Seek Him—perhaps He will show
you the way to your salvation."

So saying, the king turned on his heel, leaving his former champion standing lonely and forlorn—bereft of dignity and friendship, yes, but not, I think, without hope of
redemption, however remote.

We followed the king from the chapel yard. Gwenhwyvar waited until Arthur had reached the perimeter of
the clearing, then offered a hasty word of farewell to her
kinsman. She pressed his hand and, after a last sorrowful
look, hurried after the king. Peredur, at Arthur's nod, resumed the duty of guarding the prisoner and led him
away.

With few weapons and no provisions to carry, we could
travel lightly, if hungrily, until we reached the nearest
habitation where we could get food; and, as we did not
know when we might get good water again, we all took
a long drink from the holy well before setting off. I was
the last to drink, and after a final lingering look at the
Grail Chapel, I turned away and hurried to join my
friends.

Chapter Forty-one

𝒯hus we began our journey, walking in silent file behind Myrddin along the rain-wet trail. We had not traveled far, however, when the sun burst through the clouds and sent dazzling bright spears of light striking through the trees.

It had been so long since I had seen the sun, I stopped in my tracks and turned my face to the glorious light as if to drink it deep into my soul. A winter sun, but no less welcome for that, I felt its warmth bathe my features and thanked the Lord who made me that I yet roamed the world of the living.

We continued on and it was not long before I noticed a very strange thing. All around me, the woodland was steaming as the sunlight penetrated the wet trees and ground. Now, that in itself is not remarkable, but as the misty vapors rose and curled in the sun-struck air, the forest itself seemed to be dissipating, fading away with the mist—as if the very trees themselves were nothing more than a night fog which vanishes when touched by the light of day. The forest was thinning and receding before my eyes.

We all stopped and gaped at this wondrous sight. And when we turned once more to the path, the woodland had grown thin and the way stretched wide before us. We moved on, and quickly paired with one another—Arthur and Gwenhwyvar walked together, heads bent near in close discussion; Bors began questioning Rhys about what

376

had happened after the Cymbrogi became separated in the forest. Peredur dutifully followed a half step behind his prisoner, who lumbered forward with head and shoulders bent. I found myself walking beside Gereint, amiable enough in his silence, but I had questions that needed answers he could not supply.

I saw that Myrddin walked alone at the head of the party, and decided to join him. "Here, now," I told Gereint, "let us hear what Myrddin has to say about all that has taken place." Adjusting our pace, we soon fell into step beside the Wise Emrys.

"How long must Llenlleawg remain in exile?" I said, asking the first question that came to mind.

"Until the penance for his crimes has been fulfilled," the Wise Emrys declared, then added in a gentler tone: "God alone knows how long that may be, but I believe that either he will die there, or Arthur will one day welcome his champion back into his service."

"To think it could happen to the likes of Llenlleawg," I mused. "I wonder why Morgaws chose him to aid her treachery."

Myrddin gave me a sideways glance. "She deceived us all! Gwenhwyvar spoke the truth: Morgaws bewitched and beguiled every last one of us."

"We were all deceived, of course, but only Llenlleawg sided with her and carried out her purposes."

"Why wonder at that? Great Light! Only by God's good grace do any of us stand or fall. I think it praiseworthy so many resisted." He was silent for a moment, meditating on this; when he spoke again, he said, "But you see how it is. Even though she could deceive us, she could not overwhelm us; her powers were not of that kind. She could seduce but she could not subdue, and that is the way of it."

Again I confessed I did not understand, so Myrddin explained. "The Enemy's powers are far less than we imagine. The Evil One cannot overwhelm us by force. Indeed, he can use against us only the weapons we give him."

I allowed that this might be so, but it did seem that

Morgaws had no trouble getting whatever she wanted.

"Did she not?" demanded Myrddin. "See here: Morgaws wanted the Grail and she wanted Arthur's sword. For all her vaunted powers, she could not get these simple things for herself. No, she required someone else—and even then, she could not keep them. Despite her skills and schemes, she could not meet us face-to-face, but required one of our own who could be turned to her purposes." Myrddin sighed. "Alas, it was Llenlleawg who succumbed."

"I still do not understand why he did it," Gereint put in. "Betraying the king . . ." He subsided, shaking his head as if it were a thing that would remain forever beyond his comprehension.

"Evil ever chooses the weak and willing," Myrddin replied. "But I think it was really Gwalchavad she wanted."

"Me!" He startled me with this unexpected announcement.

"You were the first to find Morgaws," he stated simply. "You are Lot's son, after all, and Morgian knows you. It would have served her purposes well to bend you to her will."

The thought made me uneasy. "Then Morgian was behind it after all?" I asked.

Myrddin pondered this before he answered. "I believe Morgaws was Morgian's creature from the beginning, and acted on Morgian's command," he said, then, in a voice heavy with regret, added, "Would that discernment had come to me sooner—how much suffering might have been saved . . . the waste . . . the sad, sad, waste."

"What will she do now?"

"We have removed yet another weapon from the fight," he answered. "I have no idea what she will do now. But I think it prudent to assume we have not seen the last of Dread Morgian."

The threat implicit in this statement hung over me for a long time. I fell silent, thinking about the things Myrddin had said, and was roused some while later when Gereint suddenly cried out, "Riders approaching!"

The shout startled me like a slap in the face. Deeply immersed in my reverie, I had not been attending to what was happening around me. I looked up to see that the forest had completely disappeared: every tree—root, branch, and twig—had vanished with the mist. There was nothing of the forest to be seen anywhere, and we were once more in the low-hilled barrens of the blighted land.

I had no time to marvel at this, for Myrddin and Gereint stood a few paces ahead of me, and beyond them, some small distance away, a mounted warhost was advancing swiftly.

Arthur, with Gwenhwyvar beside him, joined us quickly, and Bors and Rhys pushed in as well. We stood there in a tight knot as nearer and nearer they came. Soon I heard the dull rumble of the horses' hooves on the ground, and I scanned the onrushing ranks quickly and determined that there must be close to fifty riders—too many to fight, if it came to that.

"Maybe they are some of Cador's kinsmen," speculated Rhys, shading his eyes with his hand.

Before anyone could reply to this, Arthur loosed a wild whoop and started running to meet the riders.

"Arthur!" shouted Gwenhwyvar; she darted forward a few paces, halted, and called back to us over her shoulder. "They are not Cador's men. It is Cador himself!"

"And Cai, and Bedwyr, and all the rest," proclaimed Myrddin, a great, exuberant grin spreading across his face. "They are alive!"

It was true.

By some miracle known only to God himself, they lived. Within moments we were surrounded by the very kinsmen and swordbrothers we had committed to a fiery grave in the forest. Alive again! They were all alive! Words alone cannot tell how startling and rapturous was that miraculous reunion. My heart soared like an eagle as I ran to greet them.

"Cai! Bedwyr!" I cried, rushing to embrace them as they slid from their saddles. "Cador! You are alive, praise God. You are . . ." That was all I managed to get out before the tears came. I am not ashamed to say that I stood before my friends and wept; I cried the happy tears of one who has had his fondest wish answered before he could even articulate the longing.

For their part, the lost Cymbrogi regarded us with bewildered amusement. They stood shifting awkwardly from one foot to the other while we tried to express our immense relief at their unanticipated resurrection. We all talked at once, and tangled over one another, and succeeded only in making the thing more obscure for all our explanation.

"What do you imagine happened to us?" asked Bedwyr, eyeing us with bemused curiosity.

"Brother," announced Bors, "we thought you dead!"

"Why should you think that?" wondered Cai, squinting in amazement.

"We saw your bodies!" Rhys exclaimed, exasperation making him blunt. "Back there in the forest." He gestured vaguely behind him to the low, barren hills.

"Truly," said Arthur, his handsome face alight with the all-surpassing pleasure of seeing his friends once more, "we saw your corpses hung up in a tree like the carcasses of deer after a hunt. Indeed, we burned the tree so that you should not be dishonored in death."

Bedwyr shook his head and looked to his companions, who merely shrugged and allowed that some dark mystery had clouded events—which was only to be expected, after all.

"After you entered the forest," Bedwyr told us, "we lost sight of you. The fog came down and—"

"The fog," echoed Arthur softly. "I had forgotten about the fog."

"When we could no longer find the path, we made camp and waited until the daylight to resume the search."

"You have been searching all this time?" asked Rhys.

"Aye," affirmed Cai, "since first light this morning."

"How can that be?" Bors blurted. "It is at least seven days since we last saw you."

"Seven if one," agreed Gereint, then added uncertainly, "Though we had no sun to go by. Still, it seemed a long time."

"You make it more than it is," replied Arthur confidently. "Indeed, it could be no more than three days by my reckoning. Though it is true the sun did not show itself the while."

"Three days and nights together at least," Gwenhwyvar confirmed.

Cador, shaking his head solemnly, said, "However that may be, I assure you all, only one night has passed, and that quickly. We rode out to find you as soon as we had light enough to see the trail."

"It is but one night since we left you," Cai maintained doggedly. "But can you imagine our surprise when we could not find the wood we left just the night before?"

Well, it could not be denied that the wood had disappeared. Cai suggested that perhaps the same enchantment which had shown us the corpses of our friends had somehow stretched one night to seven for those who had entered that bewitched domain. We then speculated on how this could be accomplished. Myrddin, growing impatient with our ignorant babble, put a stop to it.

Drawing himself up, he said, "You speak where you should be silent. Heaven is not the only eternity; Hell is eternal, too. If more explanation is required, let us simply say all that passed in the forest was, like the forest itself, wrought of sorcery. Yet, by the Great Light's grace, we have endured the worst the Enemy could devise and we have prevailed: the Summer Realm is saved, and the Most Holy Grail is restored."

He straightened himself, and turned his face once more towards the trail, saying, "Look your last on the Wasteland, my friends; Llyonesse is no more." He paused and, as if gazing beyond the veil of years, added, "Ah, but what was once will be again. Hear me: when the Thamesis reverses its flow and the sea gives up that which has been given to its keeping, the world will marvel at the glory that is Llyonesse."

So saying, he put his feet once more to the path and, without a backward glance, began striding toward Ynys Avallach. Arthur and Gwenhwyvar walked beside him, refusing the mounts offered them by Bedwyr and the others. However, I did as I was bade and stood for a moment to look upon the Wasteland one last time,

Then I turned and followed the Pendragon and his Wise Emrys back to the land of the living, where the Summer Realm was waiting for its king.

See, now: more seasons have passed than I care to count. I see the land blossoming with peace and plenty under Arthur Pendragon's reign, as under the warmth of a bright summer sun.

To be sure, the drought and plague persisted into the following year, giving way only slowly and grudgingly. They continue to bring painful memories to all who survived them, and we will be a long time restoring the damage. As always, there is so much to do.

And in the doing, there is blessed forgetting. Most of those who followed Arthur into Llyonesse do not willingly talk about what happened, and very few outside the Dragon Flight have heard what took place during that long snowless winter. Britain will never know how close she came to destruction. Yet it seems that not a day passes but I find some reminder of the terrors we endured. It is often that I have sat alone at day's end, gazing into the dying light and contemplating all that took place during those strange, confusing days.

It still seems a dream to me in many ways. I see her face before me, and I feel her breath hot on my neck. My passion stirs within me and I wonder: would I have given in? If it happened again, would I be able to hold out? I would like to say that it could never happen, that I would remain steadfast and strong. In truth, I cannot say I would not fall. Therefore, I pray God I will never be tested beyond my endurance.

The Queen of Air and Darkness was the power behind Morgaws' actions, of that I am certain. Some have said, and some believe, that Morgaws was simply Morgian in a different guise. The Wise Emrys never believed this, however, and after long contemplation, I fear he is right. Morgaws was not Morgian—much as I might wish otherwise. Who, then, was she?

The power of evil is another mystery to me. How was
it we believed those endless deceptions? Why did it assume such mastery over us?

Bishop Elfodd, whose advice I have sought on this matter more than once, believes that the power of any evil—
great or small, it makes no difference—derives not from
its own strength, much as some profess and many believe.
"No, in order for it to succeed," the bishop explained
one day in the spring following our return, "evil must
first remove the preserving goodness of the thing it would
destroy. For the truth is that even the smallest good is
more powerful than the greatest evil."

"All appearances to the contrary," I added wryly.

"Oh, yes!" he exclaimed, growing excited. "Appearances are always to the contrary—always. Much of Morgaws' power lay in her ability to make herself appear
something very different from what she was. It is the Evil
One's oldest deception, and we are no less vulnerable to
it than we ever were." He shook his head sadly. "Yes,
and it is also the one deception that must be preserved at
all costs, for once mortals truly understand what a weak
and contemptible thing evil really is, the Ancient Enemy's
destruction is assured."

I did not fully believe Elfodd when he said that, but as
I have puzzled over the thing, I am persuaded he may be
right. It would explain why Morgaws stole the Grail and
desecrated the chapel—that is to say, she made Llenlleawg do it, because I think she could neither possess nor
command the objects she so desired. Llenlleawg also
threw Caledvwlch into the well—perhaps because even at
his most depraved and hopeless, he could not bring himself to wield that weapon against his king. So it was that
by cleansing the altar, Bors, Gereint, and I, however un-
wittingly, prepared the way for the Grail Maiden to re-
consecrate them. Though we did not know it at the time,
we helped return a mighty weapon to the battle.

What to say of Llenlleawg? Myrddin and Arthur remain
adamant that all men must answer for their actions.
Bishop Elfodd, too, is of the opinion that the former
champion must be punished for his sins. "Remember,"

the good bishop has said, "we are not required to defeat evil, but only to stand against it. That is enough—the outcome remains with God; it is His battle, after all. However, we are required to refrain from actively helping the Enemy, and Llenlleawg helped the Enemy greatly."

That he did. No one denies it. Llenlleawg, exiled and outcast, is paying the price for his treason now. But I know how easy it is to slip, to fall, to be overtaken by a will greater than your own. Perhaps alone of all the rest, I understand Llenlleawg best—because I, too, stood near the flame and was very nearly singed. "We were all deceived," as Gwenhwyvar said, and it is true.

Moreover, I believe that deception began long before we knew it. I long considered I was the first to set eyes on Morgaws; however, now I am persuaded that Rhys met her before I did—that day he went out to look for water. He has no recollection of it at all; he remembers neither leaving nor returning to camp, nor the bite on his arm. But I remember, and I think he met Morgaws by that pool, surprised her, perhaps. Or maybe she tried her seductions on him and failed. She tried me next, but found an easier victim in Llenlleawg. Who can say? So much of Morgaws—like the deaths of the Cymbrogi—was illusion, after all.

"Be that as it may," the Pendragon is quick to point out when asked, "the fact that their deaths were an illusion does not lessen Llenlleawg's treachery. Let us never forget eight brave warriors died defending the Grail Shrine that night, and fifteen pilgrims were slain."

He is right to remember, of course. Those deaths are lamentable. Still, the fact that the Cymbrogi were not slaughtered has gone a long way towards softening Arthur's heart where his former champion is concerned. At least the king no longer speaks of taking Llenlleawg's life in expiation of his crimes. Therefore, I will continue to hold out the hope that one day soon a way will be found to redeem the Irishman and allow him to take his place in the king's service once more. Who knows? After that night in the forest, I never again expected to see Bedwyr, Cai, and Cador drawing breath in this world, but here I drink ale with them every night as if nothing had ever happened. So who is to say what miracles may occur?

In the meantime, life goes on. There is Caer Lial to rebuild, and that work takes up most of our time. The old City of the Legions in the north is home once again to Britain's defenders. Upon our return to Ynys Avallach, Arthur understood that the Grail Shrine was a mistake, and that the Grail, most precious and holy treasure, must be guarded with more subtlety and greater vigilance.

Therefore, the High King returned it to its first and foremost Guardian: Avallach now keeps it, and that is only right. But the Grail is known now, and will continue to draw the attention of anyone who hears about it. Thus, the Pendragon has determined that the Grail should be removed to a place of greater safety. Together, Arthur and Avallach are making plans for a new stronghold—somewhere in the north, far away from Llyonesse. Arthur never held a great love for the south, in any event—a northerner myself, I know he finds the southern hills too close and the wooded valleys too cramped; it makes him uneasy when he cannot look out across the wide and empty hilltops and see the distant horizon—and Caer Lial, though long abandoned, yet possesses strong walls, and enough rubble stone for restoring many of the buildings.

Thus we have come north—where my tale began, and where it now ends. I have set the thing down in the best way I know. Make of it what you will. See now: I lay down my sharpened reed and I will not take it up again. Tomorrow, when I arise, I will be a scribe no more. I mean to take my place beside the Pendragon and, God willing, there shall I remain until the end of my days.

STEPHEN R. LAWHEAD's writing has firmly entrenched him in the front ranks of contemporary fantasists. In addition to his bestselling PENDRAGON CYCLE, Lawhead is the author of two other critically acclaimed fantasy series: THE SONG OF ALBION and THE DRAGON KING TRILOGY. Born and raised in America, his research into Celtic legend and lore brought him to Oxford, England—where he now resides with his wife, writer Alice Slaikeu Lawhead, and their two sons, Ross and Drake.